Abiding Echoes

Kay Springsteen

δ

Dingbat Publishing

ABIDING ECHOES
Echoes of Orson's Folly, Book 3
Copyright © 2013 KAY SPRINGSTEEN
ISBN 978-1-940520-24-7

First edition 2013 Astraea Press LLC
Second edition 2014 Dingbat Publishing

Published by Dingbat Publishing
Humble, Texas

Also by Kay Springsteen

Lifeline Echoes
Elusive Echoes

Heartsight
Heartsent
Camp Wedding
Operation: Christmas Hearts
Heartfelt
The 13 of Hearts

Regency Romance
The Toymaker
Teach Me Under the Mistletoe

With Kim Bowman
A Lot Like A Lady
Something Like A Lady

Anthology
"Inner Flame" in Kick Ass Chicks

Dedication

For my Heavenly Father, who made me who I am, to fulfill a Destiny only He knows. May my life and heart reflect You always.

For Mom and Dad, who I know are together forever, as that was surely their Destiny.

For all the Christian guides and leaders who have touched me over the years. Yes, Rev, I was listening when you talked about spark plugs and lawn mowers! And yes, Pastor Jeff, you were right – I did find my spiritual voice. Thank you to all who inspired me, pushed me, and otherwise lit a fire of faith in my heart.

Thank you, Cindi, for your insights into herbal healing and spirituality, and for teaching me about the beauty of raptors.

And thanks to an old friend, who taught me when all else fails to go fly a kite!

Chapter One

Current day

Justin chased the last of his piece of lemon meringue pie around the plate, snagging every tiny crumb before popping the fork into his mouth. Lemon and sugar exploded against his palate and he closed his eyes, savoring the bite. As breakfasts went, it was pretty satisfying.

Of course, everything Charlotte Haines created in that kitchen of hers at Valentine's Bar and Grill was tasty. A grin tugged his mouth upward, and he sent a longing glance to the other half of the pie, still in the tin.

Naw, better put it off.

Likely his health-conscious daughter-in-law, Sandy, wouldn't approve of the piece he'd just had, let alone a second one. She'd warned him the night before, when Charlie had dropped the pie off, not to eat the whole thing at once. But since she and the baby were out for the day with his other daughter-in-law, she wasn't there to stop him.

He'd just have to make sure he got some with his lunch. That way, Sandy couldn't accuse him of eating it all in one sitting. With a workable plan, he gave a satisfied pat to his stomach and set his dish in the sink. Then he grabbed his battered Stetson from the hook next to the door and stepped outside.

The sapphire blue of the sky reached to the heavens, unmarred by clouds. The nip of winter still lingered, but the promise of spring held fast. The first calves were already born with many more on the way. Lots of work and long days ahead, but the Cross MC was consistently hitting the black for the second year in a row, something that hadn't happened for two decades.

And Justin was late getting to the day. He settled his hat on his head and stepped off the back porch of the main house. Just as he'd figured, Ryan was nowhere to be seen, apparently already out making the rounds. The fool boy'd gone and gotten it in his mind that the old man needed to take things easy. Problem was, he'd convinced the rest of the family to tiptoe around, too.

"Sean and I have things covered outside," Ryan had said the night before. "We need the books done so we can hit the bank for a loan next week."

Justin knew an excuse when he heard one. Sean had the head for accounting and he kept meticulous books, always up to date. No, they were enforcing his supposed need to rest. Still, Justin had never expected one of his sons would sabotage the morning routine by unplugging his alarm clock and pulling the shades in his bedroom. Oh, he'd recognized Ryan's handiwork. No one else but Sandy saw through his gruffness and she worked in more subtle ways. If the boy had been a few years younger, Justin would consider taking a switch to his backside. He chuckled as he crossed behind the house.

Right. As if he'd *ever* been able to carry out such a punishment.

He picked his way across the rough cement slab they laughingly called *the patio*. Cracks crisscrossed the concrete and the once-crisp edges had long ago worn into rounded smoothness, except for one long gouge that radiated from a good-sized chip. A bit of dark green twined up through the grill on the barbecue and trailed along the red brick to the ground, dotted along the way with tiny star-shaped white flowers. Sandy kept talking about fixing the patio up, but it wasn't a priority since it had nothing to do with the ranch itself. Still, it might be nice to have family gatherings out there again.

Upon rounding the corner of the house on his way to the barns, he was greeted by a carpet of bright yellow that hadn't been there only the day before. Hundreds of daffodils spread over the ground like liquid gold, their faces turned in his direction as though waiting for him.

Beth had planted a small patch of them soon after their wedding. She'd always kept the bulbs confined to her garden along the side of the house, but after her death, Justin hadn't had the heart to yank the spreading plants as his wife had done. Of course, they'd quickly taken over the side yard from the house to the old cottonwood, fifty feet away.

The spring breeze carried the acrid-sweet scent of the trumpet-shaped blossoms to his nostrils, and Beth's face floated into his memory. Curly blond hair like summer sunshine, green eyes that held laughter through the worst of times. A burst of wind blew the daffodils nearly sideways. Just as suddenly it stopped, and the happy yellow faces bobbed upright again.

"Hello, Beth," murmured Justin, smiling. If he stood very still, he could almost feel her arms encircling his waist in a hard hug. "Come by to check how your garden's growing, did you? We haven't put in the vegetables yet. You know how hectic calving season gets."

A gust of air tickled at the hairs on his arms. Logic told him it was just the wind. Beth had been gone for years, her life cut short one branding season by an incident up at Little Green River. Of all the places on the ranch, though, her presence lingered in the garden she'd loved. And sometimes he talked to her as though she were still kneeling on the ground there, chatting to her flowers and tugging weeds.

He smiled and rubbed an errant twinge in his shoulder. "Our boy thinks I'm getting old, Dilly. He thinks I need to sleep in these days instead of getting at the day."

Odd how he wanted to linger in the midst of the sunny flowers longer than usual. Justin inhaled the scent of Beth's garden again and began walking toward the barn with a sense of reluctance. A black-and-white border collie lifted his head and thumped his tail on the ground in greeting as Justin passed.

"Hello, Patch. Everything looking good today?"

Heaving a sigh, the dog merely dropped his head to his paws again, and Justin chuckled.

The clatter of hooves on wood and the bellow of a cow in distress drew his attention. His heart thumped hard as he altered his direction from the main barn to the birthing barn. If Ryan had brought one of the girls in, she was probably having some trouble.

"Come on, sweetheart, let's get this baby out of you." Shirtless, with his right arm pushed inside the cow up to his shoulder, Ryan's face contorted in pain as the mother bore down, trying with everything in her to expel her calf. "I can touch the foot, but I'm not getting a grip."

"Do we need the chains?" At the sound of a second male voice, Justin's heart gave a hopeful little leap.

When he looked past Ryan, though, Justin soon recognized the speaker as his younger son, Sean. Of course it couldn't have been Gus Hanson, the old Cross MC foreman. He sighed and acknowledged the fresh wound on his heart. The mind did play tricks sometimes.

A frown marred Sean's brow as he hovered behind Ryan. Justin's heart poked him with another twinge of sadness. Gus had worked his last calving the prior spring. The man had been older than dirt and spryer than anyone Justin knew, including his youngest son, Ricky. Emotion crowded his throat.

No one lives forever. And now Gus rested next to Jenny, his wife, in the McGee family plot.

Ryan shook his head. "Calf isn't far enough down to get a grip."

"You need to walk her some," offered Justin, stepping into the stall.

Ryan jerked backward and slid his arm out of the cow. "Dad. You're up."

Justin grunted. "You didn't think I'd sleep the day away,

did you?"

"No, it's just… I didn't hear you come in." Looking a mite guilty, Ryan peeled off the disposable arm-length glove and pitched it in the trash. He glanced down at his arm and grimaced. Shaking his head, he grabbed a scrap of towel that had been draped over the edge of the birthing stall and wiped downward from his shoulder.

"You had your hands full," said Justin, snickering at the unintentional pun. He advanced toward the cow. "How long's she been laboring?"

"I noticed she was restless last night so I went looking for her this morning." Unclipping her lead, Sean backed the brown-and-white cow from the birthing stall and walked her toward the center passageway of the barn. "Okay, Mama, come on."

The cow balked, spreading her forefeet and locking her knees. Then she swayed her head back and forth and emitted a low moan as she strained to push out her calf. Justin frowned and rubbed his jaw. Something was off. What were they missing?

When the cow stopped straining, her knees buckled and she tried to roll to her side.

"Watch it!" barked Justin, knowing once she went down they'd never move her until she gave birth or died where she fell.

Sean's face reddened and his biceps bulged, but he managed to keep her upright as he led her in a circle around the wide middle aisle then back to the birthing stall. Her sides looked like they would split if they didn't get the calf out.

"She's too big," muttered Justin. He glanced at Ryan. "You said you can feel a foot but it's too high? Like not engaging in the birth canal?"

Ryan nodded. "You think the calf's too big?"

Justin studied the cow as Sean led her past. Could the calf be turned sideways? It seemed to be awfully tight in there. He sure as hell hoped they didn't have to deliver the calf surgically.

"Got time to get the vet out here?" he asked.

"Already called Doc Pickeril," answered Sean.

One side bulged and Justin could have sworn he saw the calf's head. Or its hind end. But the bulge on the other side at the same time had almost the same shape. If the calf was that big, it was already half grown. The cow's shape was off, too. Way lopsided, even for a sideways-turned calf. He'd seen this kind of shape before. It didn't happen a lot, but when it did, it was almost always a dangerous delivery.

"Get her in the stall," he ordered, already shrugging out of his shirt. "I know what's wrong."

Sean and Ryan panted with the effort of moving a cow that didn't want to be moved, but amid their grunts and her groans, they got her in the stall again.

"She's got twins," Justin explained, directing Sean to one side of the cow and Ryan to the other. He washed his hands and shook his head when Ryan offered him a glove. He needed to be able to feel what he was doing.

Gingerly he slid his left arm inside the cow and felt around. An angry bellow from the cow told them what she thought of the whole thing as she pushed against his invasion with brutal force that stole his breath. Pain shot up his arm and into his jaw but he waited it out, and when the cow relaxed again, he found what he was looking for. "Two noses," he announced. "Sean, the one on your side is closest to engaging, but I think they're holding each other up. Maybe we can move them from the outside. Ryan, see if you can push the one on your side back toward Mama's head while Sean pushes his side my way."

With agonizing slowness, the calves moved by half-inches at a time. Finally, Justin was able to grasp a foot, and then a second foot. *Please... let these belong to the same calf,* he prayed silently.

When the cow's contraction hit, he gave a steady pull, gripping the slippery feet as tightly as the confined space would allow, afraid if he let go they'd lose all the ground they'd gained. Sucking and smacking sounds mingled with the groans of the cow and the grunts of all three men. Finally Justin got his arm halfway out of the cow, and then all the way, and then two tiny hooves showed.

Sean moved to Justin's side and added his hands to help

ease out the calf's legs and then its face. At last the tiny baby lay in the straw.

"Good call, Dad!" Ryan tossed a grin in Justin's direction as he grabbed a bit of straw and teased the calf's nostrils to stimulate breathing. He picked up a towel and began the process of wiping down the calf as it took its first breaths. "Huh. Not a bad size for a twin."

Ryan's voice carried the same hoarse gruffness Gus's had when he'd been emotional. Justin shook his head against the wooziness that assaulted him. The cow's nervous bellow drew him back to the task of birthing the second calf.

Sean took over, reaching in with a wince on his face. "It's still fairly high, Dad, but I think I'm feeling back feet first."

Justin cursed under his breath. They were running out of time to get the baby out. The mother was already too tired to give much help. He edged alongside the cow and palpated. It was impossible to tell how the calf was positioned, but it was definitely too high.

"Let me in there," he ordered brusquely, moving back to the business end of the cow. "My arms are longer."

He slid his left arm in again, struggling against the pain in his shoulder. He must have strained it pitching feed the day before without realizing. After pulling a couple of calves, he was going to be interested in some aspirin and a hot shower. The cow tried to roll onto her side again, but Sean kept her upright while Justin eased the calf outward. It was definitely breech, but they had no time to try turning it. He only hoped they got it out in time and it didn't get stuck. Once he'd seen his daddy slaughter a stuck calf to get it out and save the mother, and he'd just as soon avoid that experience.

With a wet plop, the second baby was deposited in the bed of straw. Ryan's joyful cry of relief joined Sean's as he stepped back to help with the calf. Justin barely heard them. Both voices seemed to come from a distance. The light in the barn dimmed. Had they been at it long enough to run out of daylight or were they in for a storm?

An odd assortment of disconnected thoughts scrolled through Justin's mind, disorienting him. He'd left his bedroom window open... a storm could soak the hardwood floor and ruin it... when was Sandy expected back? He wanted to talk to her about setting up a little playground for Bethany and for Sean and Melanie's boy when he got bigger... why was it so dark? He hoped the rain didn't pummel Beth's daffodils to the ground...

Something was wrong, but he couldn't put his finger on it.

Guess I won't get any of Charlie's lemon meringue pie for lunch after all.

Searing agony clutched Justin's jaw like a fist of molten iron, then radiated to his chest and back to his neck, where it strangled him with pulsing torture. It sucked the breath out of his lungs and he struggled to pull air back in, but something squeezed his chest in a tight grip. He couldn't move. As his surroundings blurred around him, he stumbled, unable to remain standing, and slammed against the side of the stall. Had the dang-fool cow kicked him in the chest?

Sean cried out, but he sounded as though he was under water. Then Justin hit the limestone screening floor of the barn, face down in the straw and unable to move as scorching pain consumed his body.

* * *

The muffled *beep...beep...beep* didn't sound like Justin's morning alarm, but it nudged him into wakefulness nonetheless. A steady *whoosh-hiss* lashed at his consciousness, the sound reminding him a bit of Walt's air compressor filling car tires. Justin tried to lift his hand to his face, but nothing moved. He concentrated his effort and gave it another try. This time one finger lifted. The endeavor wore him out. For whatever reason, he couldn't move. Perhaps what surprised him more, though, was the fact that he didn't want to. He enjoyed the sensation of floating but it felt wrong somehow. He was supposed to be somewhere else, not reclining on some bed of soft fluff.

His eyelids felt like they'd been taped shut, but his arm remained too heavy to raise a hand and check. With a lot of concentration, he forced his eyelids to cooperate. Colors bled together and swirled around him like a psychedelic kaleidoscope, then finally settled into separate blurry shapes against a pale green wall.

Part of his mind recognized a hospital room, though it had been a while since he'd seen one from flat on his back. The ceiling seemed farther above him than it should have been, and the walls surrounding him felt tight, as though he were looking upward from the bottom of a long shaft. A movement to his right caught his eye, and Justin became aware that he wasn't alone.

When he rolled his head slightly, his gaze locked on the most beautiful woman he'd ever seen in his life. A riot of blond curls reminded him of a lion's mane as they cascaded to her shoulders. Her lips curved gently upward and her emerald green eyes crinkled at the corners.

"Hey, there, cowboy. I see you're awake."

"Dilly?" Justin tried to smile through the fog of confusion.

She laughed, a full-bodied sound that he remembered well. He closed his eyes again and let it wash over him, like a babbling brook through a dry desert.

"And who else were you expecting?"

Justin frowned, trying to understand what was going on, but his mind felt as leaky as a rusty old bucket with holes in the bottom.

"Where am I?" he whispered. "What happened?"

"You're in the hospital," she said, scooting her chair closer. "You had another heart attack... a bad one this time."

Beth touched him on the arm and he jerked. Her hand was warm and firm.

"You're real?" he murmured, trying to recall why he thought she wouldn't be.

Her lips tilted upward again and she nodded.

Memory filtered in. Something had happened... The river. They'd had a funeral. He frowned. *Hadn't* they? Or had he lost his grasp on what memories reflected reality? "Why are you with me?"

She shrugged. The wide lacy collar of her yellow dress slipped off one delicate shoulder with the movement. "I'm just keeping you company while you're here."

Justin was afraid to ask but he supposed he had to know sometime. "Am I dead, then?"

Beth shook her head slowly and this time her eyes were filled with pride. "No. Our sons saved your life. They've both grown into quite some men, haven't they?"

Emotional pain threatened to swamp him again, and Justin closed his eyes. "Yeah, they've grown up good."

Beth curled her fingers around the back of Justin's hand and squeezed three times. "You did a fantastic job with them *both*, cowboy."

Justin opened his eyes again and settled his gaze on the woman sitting next to his bed. Slowly he shook his head. "It don't always feel like that, Dilly Gal. I tried to raise 'em like you would... but I didn't even see Ryan for far too many years."

She shook her head right back at him and pinned him with a green stare. "He came home, Justin. When he was ready."

A sigh slipped out. "He's got a lot of you in him."

"And I came back, didn't I? He's always known where he belongs. Just like I did." Beth smiled at him and all at once, Justin felt her confidence bolstering his mood.

He returned her smile. "You could have gone anywhere, girl, had anything, done anything you wanted."

"But I told you... everything I ever wanted was right here in Orson's Folly," she whispered. "And I knew that from the moment I heard your voice." She stroked his arm. "Do you remember when we met? What you said to me?"

"I remember it all." Justin swallowed back the emotion that rose and squeezed at his throat. "I always will. You're a hard one to forget, Daffodil Gal."

And in the grand scheme, thirty-five years didn't seem so long ago...

Chapter Two

Spring 1978

"Okay, Zeke, let's take the scenic route home." Justin gave the big chestnut gelding underneath him his head as they meandered along the trail back to the house. The sun still hung fairly high in the sky, and with his parents in Jackson, no one waited for him. He was in no hurry to get back to the ranch and prepare his own supper.

It was a lonely life at the end of the day, and sometimes he missed the crowd of school friends he'd made up at University of Wyoming. He took a deep breath, inhaling the sweet fragrance blowing off the mountains. The cloudless sky was big today, a crisp blue he'd never seen matched anywhere. A smile pulled his lips upward. He liked his friends, missed them, missed the fun they'd had and the hell they'd occasionally raised together. But days like this, out on the ranch with the sky so big and the boundaries so wide he couldn't tell where one ranch ended and another began... he wouldn't trade that for anything. The Cross MC was his home, his life.

A cluster of vibrant color, out of place near the road,

drew his attention and he squinted at it, trying to make sense of what he was seeing. A vehicle of some sort was pulled over to the side. Only one reason for anyone to be pulled over out this way. Someone must be having car trouble. Justin altered Zeke's course and stepped up the pace.

It only took a few moments for them to close in on the vehicle, a German-made microbus painted with swirls of rainbow color that formed patterns of flowers and peace signs. He shook his head. Some damn fool city person... out to see the country and probably out of gas thirty miles from nowhere.

"Good thing we were taking the scenic route, eh, Zeke?" Justin chuckled. Whoever it was might have spent one long night out in the cold.

The tiny rectangular door on the rear engine compartment was propped open. A pair of long legs encased in wide bell-bottomed blue jeans emerged from beneath the rear of the van. Justin's lips tugged into a smile when he noted the bare feet with the hot pink toenails. He'd never considered himself a foot man, having developed an appreciation for the more curvy aspects of the female form. But he shifted in his saddle anyway for a better look at those painted toes. Yep, he just might need to make an adjustment on his preferences.

A soft curse floated from beneath the van and one foot began to jiggle in an agitated fashion.

Justin cleared his throat. "As nice a view as this is, and I could pretty near watch it all day, I can't help but wonder if your fingernails match your toenails."

The jiggling foot froze. An instant later, the legs slid out from under the van to reveal they were indeed attached to some shapely curves. But it was the mass of dark golden curls tumbling about the woman's shoulders that captured and held Justin's attention.

She was young, probably a couple of years his junior. Smears of oil and road dust decorated the gauzy white blouse with long belled sleeves that fell to the tops of the legs Justin had admired. The garment was loose, but somehow managed to reveal the very fine assets beneath as it fluttered in the afternoon breeze. His gaze slid down to her fingertips and he grinned at the flash of hot pink nail polish.

"Find what you're looking for?" she drawled in a voice drenched in Midwestern twang. She placed a hand on her hip and cocked her head to the side, an obvious challenge that Justin wanted to take her up on.

Instantly in tune with her saucy attitude, he met her gaze and winked. "Yes, ma'am." Touching a finger to the brim of his hat, he introduced himself. "Justin McGee."

Then he angled his head and squinted to get a better look at her. Patches and welts of angry pink skin ran from beneath the collar on her blouse, up along her neck, and onto her jaw and cheek. The back of her right hand had red wheals as well as a couple of nasty looking yellowish blisters about the size of dimes. He winced. That had to be painful. It sure as the devil made *his* neck hurt just looking at it.

She followed his gaze and wrinkled her nose. "Don't worry, I won't offer to shake your hand. It's poison ivy and poison oak. My name's Bethany — Beth. Rushton." She swiped her hair off her face with her left hand.

"Poison ivy *and* poison oak?" Justin narrowed his gaze, noting the tops of her feet had traces of rash as well. "If you don't mind my asking, how'd you manage to run afoul of so many poisonous plants?"

Beth scratched her arm through the sleeve of her shirt and wiggled her shoulders, as though shifting to get away from the touch of her clothing. "I'm studying environmental science at University of Michigan. I came out here to document an area where the two plants are cross-pollinating and creating hybrids — for my thesis on plant genetics."

Why anyone would want to study those nuisances, Justin had no idea. But at the moment, with a more pressing question on his mind, he pushed his hat higher on his head and regarded her with raised eyebrows. "And how exactly does a person study poisonous plants? By rolling in them?"

Beth giggled, and the sound homed in on the sensual part of Justin's brain, heightening his awareness of this intriguing damsel in distress. As if that was possible.

"Only if that person happens to be clumsy enough to trip and land in the stuff. I just want to get to the nearest town and buy some calamine lotion." She scratched her neck, winced, and dropped her hand with a sheepish look.

Justin rubbed at a phantom sensation on his own neck, but forced himself to stop and clenched his hand into a fist. "Well, you got a couple of problems as far as getting to the nearest town."

"Yeah, Clara's engine started overheating. I think it's just a loose wire on the cooling fan, but I can't reach it from the top and I can't find it from the bottom." Beth looked at Justin with hope in her eyes. "I don't suppose you know anything about..." She gestured to the psychedelic van behind her.

Rather unexpectedly, Justin found himself hoping he'd be able to play knight to her damsel. "I can take a look at it. But you got a potentially bigger problem if that's the direction you're traveling."

"It... was," she answered, wariness entering her eyes.

"Well, then, the nearest town to here is thirty miles that way." Justin nodded up the road in the opposite direction.

Beth's eyes widened. *That* was a *town?*"

Justin smiled. "'Fraid so, ma'am. Orson's Folly."

"And the nearest town in that direction?" She pointed the other way, roughly northwest.

Justin shrugged. "About ninety miles or so. But it's a fair sight larger than Orson's Folly."

"All it needs is a gas station to be bigger than Orson's Folly," muttered Beth. She scraped her nails along her jaw.

"Oh, we have a gas station," supplied Justin, frowning when he realized he was scratching his neck again.

"I must have blinked," muttered Beth, but her smile took away any sting. "I don't suppose there's a motel back in Orson's Folly."

Justin stared, unable to take his gaze from all that golden hair, enjoying the way it glinted in the late afternoon sun when she moved her head.

A sigh escaped her lips. "Of... course there isn't." She chewed her lip, a frown spoiling her pretty oval-shaped face. "I have family in the area, but they don't know I'm here and I — um, don't want them to freak out or anything if I just... you know, show up on their doorstep." She scratched at her neck and winced. Then she seemed to come to a decision and stood up a little straighter. Her voice became stronger and more resolute. "Look, Clara's set up for camping so I was wondering if I could maybe park somewhere around here?"

She was the most enthralling woman he'd ever met. He blinked as it registered that she'd stopped talking. "Clara?"

She ran a hand along one rainbow-hued fender in an affectionate gesture. "Yes, Clara." A smile spread across Beth's face and just like that, the sun seemed a lot brighter. "I can camp in her — there's a little mattress on the floor in back and I have a sleeping bag."

Justin looked around at the whole lot of nothing surrounding them. Would she feel the same when night coated the land in inky blackness, and the coyotes started howling? Probably not, he decided, taking her measure. For all her casual dress, she screamed city girl.

"You can stay at the ranch."

Beth flicked her eyes over him and let out a soft chuckle. "And I suppose you have a big ranch house with lots of spare rooms and you'd be happy to set me up in one? Like, maybe the master bedroom?"

"Well, ma'am, it's like this." Justin resettled his hat over his eyes. "If you want my folks' bedroom, that's fine with me, but I'm thinking you'd be a fair sight more comfortable in the guest room."

The strain in Beth's features eased some. "You have parents?" She cut herself off, eyes wide and pink edging into her face. "I mean, of course you have parents — everybody has parents. I meant you still live with them?" Tension returned tenfold as her obvious embarrassment increased, and finally she stopped talking and just cast him a helpless stare.

Justin squinted back at her. For the space of a few hard-thumping heartbeats, their eyes met, hers the purest pale emerald he'd ever seen. He could look into those eyes every day for the rest of his life and not get enough of them. When she broke the gaze between them by turning and glancing at her van, Justin eased out a breath. Until that very minute, he hadn't believed his parents' claim of instant attraction. Such connections simply didn't exist, Justin had always scoffed.

Now... Oh, man! He'd definitely have to reevaluate if the nervous knots in his stomach were anything to go by.

Doors to intriguing possibilities opened before him and he smiled. "My parents are in Jackson until the end of the week. You can take any room you want. I'll bunk down with Gus."

Beth stood stock still for a moment, her eyes still looking in the direction of the van. Then she swung around to face Justin again, her mouth forming a giant O. "That's very generous." Her gazed flickered to Zeke. "Um, that's not — ah, *Gus,* is it?" She stooped to rub the top of her right foot.

Justin chuckled, desperately fighting a losing battle to rein in his heart. "Would it win me points with the lady if I said yes?"

"I think I should just... maybe stop talking." Her lips twitched, and she clamped them shut and mimed zipping them.

Laughter refused to be contained. "This here's Zeke." He patted the reddish horse's neck. "Gus is our foreman and lives in a cabin he likes to call the bunkhouse."

Beth's smile became a grin and a single giggle slipped out. "That's a generous offer. But if I could just maybe park in the yard or something, I'd be happy enough to sleep in my van."

Justin shrugged. "Suit yourself." He looped the reins around the pommel and slid to the ground. "Wait here, Zeke."

Beth's eyes went wide, and she gave a nervous chuckle then backed up a couple of steps. "Did you just talk to your horse?"

"Yep." Justin strode over to the open hood of the microvan.

"Does he listen?" A note of wariness had crept into her voice.

Justin smiled as he peered into the engine compartment. "Sometimes."

"Aren't you a-afraid he'll, um, run away?"

A glance over his shoulder assured Justin that Zeke stood in place, a hopeful gaze turned on Beth. Dang horse was likely wondering if she had an apple. "Nope. The only place he's likely to run is home."

He leaned into the tiny compartment. Crap, it was like looking at a go-cart engine. Where did the squirrels live? And what the hell did a cooling fan motor look like? He pushed at a couple of brittle wires that had seen better days. In fact, the whole engine appeared to have a lot of wear. A sticky film of dirt-coated inkiness covered the oil cap. The fan belt was beginning to fray. How far had she driven the thing in such bad repair?

Next to him, Beth whimpered softly, clutching at her neck as though holding her head in place. Probably trying not to scratch. She had to be in all kinds of misery. After a moment, she gave up the battle and gouged at the spot that was already sporting broken skin.

"Might be I can come up with some calamine lotion for you back at the house."

She stilled her hand but kept it in place. "*That* would be fab."

Justin returned his attention to the engine with a smile tugging at his lips. *City gal.*

It took him a few long moments and some eyestrain before he spotted the loose wire hanging by the end of a rusty connector. He slid his hand into the pocket of his jeans and found his penknife. Using the tip, he attempted to snag the wire. After three tries, he was ready to give up, but stubbornness kept him going, and on the fourth try, he caught the wire on the edge of the knife and drew it upward. With a grin, he anchored the wire to what he prayed was the cooling fan and stepped back.

"I think that'll get you to my place. You're going to need a better repair than this, though. I can help you get it to Walt's in town and he can do a proper job of it." He closed the engine compartment and tapped the cover to be sure it was secure.

"Thank you, thank you, thank you!" Beth danced around him, the bell bottoms swishing over the tops of her feet, the diaphanous white blouse fluid against her curvy form. "I'd hug you but, ah... I'm covered in urushiol."

As tempted as he was to risk contact with the toxin from her poisonous adventure for the chance to hold her in his arms, Justin grinned and sauntered over to Zeke. "I'll tell you what would be reward enough." He stepped into the stirrup and threw his leg over the saddle. When he was seated, he smiled down at her. "Share a meal with me at my table this evening."

"Oh, but I've already put you out."

Justin rubbed his jaw while he formed his reply. "Well, now, fact is, I eat alone most nights. You'd be doing me a favor — keeping me company." He cocked his head to the side and studied her, taking in her slender figure, her pallor beneath the rash. "You eat steak?"

"What?"

"Steak? You know, beef?" He shrugged. "You aren't a vegetarian?"

Beth looked genuinely baffled by his question. Finally understanding seemed to dawn and she shook her head. "Oh, no! No, I'm not a vegetarian." She glanced over her shoulder as she headed for the driver's side of the van. "Should I just follow you?"

Justin glanced up the road and considered the tedious ride back to the ranch with her van following at Zeke's pace. He shifted to gaze out over the prairie. By separating, she could drive at a normal speed and he'd still probably make it there before she did. Or she could decide not to show up.

He really hoped she didn't opt for the latter, but he couldn't take Zeke over the longer route at any pace resembling reasonable, and they'd end up getting back to the house long after dark.

"Take this road to the first drive you come to — it'll be on your left about ten winding miles the way you're heading." He gestured toward the prairie. "I'll take Zeke through the pasture and meet you up at the house. Probably get there about the same time."

Beth peered along the road then swung her gaze back to Justin with a big grin. "Far out!"

She climbed into her van and started it, then gave Justin a thumb's up, put the vehicle in gear and inched forward.

Justin wheeled Zeke around and set off at a decent clip across the field.

Chapter Three

As she drove along the deserted two-lane highway, Beth considered her options. Find Alice and Brody's ranch, drive another couple of hours to a larger city and find a motor lodge, or take Mr. Justin McGee up on his offer. She must be crazy to consider going to the home of an interesting man she'd only just met — especially when no one would know where she was, and the man had openly admitted the two of them would be alone for the evening.

Justin had seemed kind of cool, though... sort of laid back and mellow. He certainly had a chivalrous streak. And, oh, good grief, he was handsome to go with his good manners, with those muscles that had rippled beneath his pale checked shirt when he'd moved, and the easy way he'd covered the ground on those long legs. Although his chiseled jaw and square chin gave his face a serious, intimidating façade, when he'd cracked a smile, he'd outshone the sun, and charisma had rolled off him like waves rushing a beach.

Not to mention all that strawberry blond hair that swept across his forehead from the left in disheveled waves and just kissed the tops of his eyebrows... and those eyes... *Oh, man!*

Eyes like his really drew a person in. As blue as the sky on a crisp, early spring morning — well, those just ought to come with a warning label. Beth bit her lip while she worked at stemming the lava flow of excitement Justin had ignited in her.

Oh, he hadn't overtly appraised her — she suspected he was far too polite for that. But his gaze had lingered in the right places for just the right amount of time to warm her in those places. And Beth's mind was more than happy to speculate that perhaps he might have liked the overall presentation.

She turned the wheel to avoid a piece of blown truck retread in the road, and scratched an itch just above her wrist. Alice would insist she stay with her and her husband on *their* ranch. But the truth was, Beth had never been close to Alice, and it was likely they'd only take her in out of obligation — or to look good for their daddy, who still thought Alice was a lot nicer than she actually was. Besides, Alice's husband just plain gave Beth the creeps. Why couldn't Alice have married someone as neat as Justin?

At the intrusive thought and the accompanying mind-picture of her sister with the cowboy who'd fixed Clara, Beth scrunched up her face. It would be nice — just once — to enjoy the company of a good-looking guy without her sister hanging around, showing off her assets, making her interest clear as she hovered like some kind of man-eating harpy.

The driveway loomed on the left, just as Justin had described.

Don't think, don't analyze. For once in your life, dive into the deep end and see where you end up.

Beth giggled at her self-admonishment, especially since she'd been doing that for the past month or so. Starting with the day she'd purchased the used hippie bus and decided to spend her summer researching rather than vacationing at the lake house on Higgins Lake, or staying home in Bloomfield Hills.

The van reached the edge of the driveway.

Just go for it!

Holding her breath, Beth yanked hard on the steering

wheel. The tires spun into the dusty path as the van rolled under a wooden sign. "The Cross MC," she said, testing the name on her tongue. "Catchy."

The drive forked off, with the leg on the right circling up to the house. She turned there rather than continuing toward the rear of the property where she could see two barns and some stock pens. The Cross MC was a fair-sized operation. But Justin had said it was just him and the foreman. So did he have day help that didn't live on the ranch?

She braked to a stop and peered through her open side window at the quiet yard. The house was fair-sized, as well, if a bit old. It looked like it had gone through some additions in its lifetime. Fieldstone and board paneling, the house was two stories with a covered plank porch that ran across the entire front of the building. A couple of cottonwood trees stood nearby, not yet big enough to shade the building from the heat of the afternoon sun but perhaps planted with that in mind. The place needed a paint job, but it was clean. As she slid out of the van, Beth caught sight of Justin striding up from the stockyards.

"I see you made it." He took off his hat as he directed her onto the porch and through the door. The hollow clomp of his boots became muffled as they left the weathered wood planking for the solidity of a glossy hardwood floor.

He led her into a sitting room to the left of the door and gestured at one of two leather chairs parked on either side of a stone fireplace that was set on an angle in the corner. The home was sparsely appointed with serviceable furniture. It looked comfortable but not altogether homey. Apparently the McGee family didn't clutter up their house. Three silver picture frames stood on the fireplace mantel, but before Beth could lean in to study them, Justin spoke.

"Have a seat. Can I get you something to drink?"

She stared at the pristine chair and considered how grubby she felt. "Um, I — if I touch anything, I might spread this rash to other people."

Justin grinned and held up a large white jar. "I got this from our foreman. Our neighbor, Kendra Ford, gave it to him when he got into some poison ivy last season." He made a face at the jar. "It's made from some plants and smells wicked awful, but Gus swears he started healing in less than a day."

"Made from plants?" Despite the itching, which was now becoming quite painful, Beth found her interest piqued.

"Kendra's mother was Shoshone, and Kendra uses a lot of natural medicines." Justin shrugged, scuffing one foot on the floor as if scraping some unseen smudge of dirt. "We, um… also have calamine lotion in the medicine cabinet upstairs."

"I'll try the plant remedy." Beth crossed the distance between them. "Do you know what's in it?"

"Probably some jewelweed, maybe tea tree oil and aloe vera." Justin shrugged. "Don't know what else."

"That's right, jewelweed is supposed to counteract poison ivy." Somewhere in the back of her mind, she'd known about the natural remedy. Too bad she hadn't remembered that jewelweed usually grew near poison ivy. She could have squished up some leaves and made a paste early on, and prevented the worst of the rash.

Justin handed over the jar. It was surprisingly light. Beth unscrewed the top and took a tentative sniff of the greenish-yellow salve inside. Vegetation with a strong vinegar base, for sure. Her eyes watered and her throat threatened to close. She looked up and caught Justin watching her.

"There are some alternatives in the medicine cabinet upstairs. My mother usually takes an oatmeal bath and lathers on calamine lotion."

"A bath…" Beth sighed at the thought of such a luxury.

Justin's grin told her she'd been transparent. "Follow me." He crossed the foyer to a set of steps, and they climbed to the second level of the house. Beth sucked on her bottom lip and chided herself for being so reckless. But the thought of cleaning up, maybe soothing some of the itch… it was too much to resist, and she padded after the handsome cowboy.

The claw-footed tub ruled the bathroom. Its pristine whiteness invited her to fill it and soak away her troubles. Justin bent to the tub, inserted the plug, and turned on the hot water.

"Do you have any rubbing alcohol?" she asked.

Justin stood, opened the cabinet above the sink, and

pulled out a bottle of rubbing alcohol and a roll of gauze. Then he picked up a quart-sized Mason jar filled with ivory-colored powder. He handed her the alcohol and gauze with a shake of his head. "This'll burn like heck."

"Yeah... I know." She sighed. "But the oil's been on my skin for a while now, and I should get off what I can before I get into a bath."

"This here's my mom's blend for itchy rashes." Justin set the canning jar on the countertop. "Just add a few capfuls and stir it well, climb in, and soak away." He nodded at the tub. "I'll let you adjust your own water temperature."

The water gurgled into the tub like a mountain creek as steam rose into the air between them. Beth found her breaths coming ragged and short as the intimacy of their circumstances struck her. She was afraid to meet Justin's eyes, afraid he'd see the awareness of him that threatened to take over her good sense. She busied herself with fiddling at the faucet instead and then added the whitish powder to the water. Instantly, the water took on a creamy appearance.

Justin leaned over her shoulder and swirled his hand through the water. "You want to mix it up real good, look for any clumps and break them up." He stood and opened a cabinet behind the door, then pulled out towels and a washcloth and set them on the counter.

"I'll leave you to it," he murmured. "You can find the calamine lotion and some antihistamines in the medicine cabinet. Use anything you need."

When Beth tossed him a smile over her shoulder, his blue eyes glittered down at her and he winked. Her stomach fluttered and her face burned. She hadn't hidden one silly X-rated thought!

After he left, closing the door with a soft click behind him, Beth scrambled to tear off her clothing. As she fumbled at the fastenings on her jeans with shaking hands, she cursed the clothing designer who had come up with the concept of a button-fly. Finally the jeans were open and she slid them down and stepped free. She peeled her blouse over her head and dumped it on top of the jeans. Next she stripped off her bra and panties, sinfully small scraps of hot pink lace and nylon that she'd purchased from a mail order lingerie company based in Hollywood. She'd never worn anything so decadent before, and she knew no one could see what she wore beneath her clothing, but it made her feel more adult and... well, pretty, for want of a better word, when she wore them. She dropped them into her pile of dirty clothing.

The label on the rubbing alcohol read ninety percent — so the good stuff. She twisted off the bottle cap and dumped a liberal amount onto the gauze Justin had left. Starting with her face and neck, Beth dabbed the soaked gauze over her skin, wrinkling her nose at the burn in her nostrils from the pungent smell. As Justin had predicted, the welts and wheals felt like they had been lit on fire. Gritting her teeth against the searing pain, she picked up fresh gauze and saturated it with more alcohol, repeating the cleansing process until she'd blotted each patch of rash. Then she took a final swipe over the rest of her body for good measure. Tears from the sting in her eyes streamed down her face by the time she finished. She struggled for each breath, and her stomach performed a slow flip-flop.

The tub was nearly full and Beth stepped into the water then sank into the bubbling bliss. Reaching forward, she turned off the flow and then leaned back again and rested her head on the edge of the tub. The burning itch on her hands and feet eased. Then, finally, the welts along her neck stopped bothering her. She splashed some of the bath water up over her face.

She could remain in the warm bath for the rest of the evening and be content. Too bad she hadn't brought a book in from the van.

"Oh, shit!" She sat straight up. She hadn't brought in anything to wear, either. She gazed at her pile of discarded clothing and considered how much urushiol must be coating the garments. Amid the sheer bliss of the bath, the thought of donning her contaminated clothing brought on a shudder.

A gentle knock interrupted Beth's deliberation and her heart started a ragged gallop against her ribs. Surely Justin wouldn't just barge in!

"Um-um, just a minute." How quickly could she exit the

tub and wrap herself in one of the plush towels he'd laid out?

Justin's low chuckle rumbled through the door, and a tingling sensation shot through Beth that had nothing to do with her urushiol rash.

"I'm not coming in, Bethany. But I noticed you didn't bring in a change of clothes. I didn't want to go prowling through your van, so I picked out some of my mother's things you can borrow. I'll leave them right outside the door and then I'm gonna see to dinner, so I won't be back upstairs."

Beth blew out a breath. She'd been right about his sense of chivalry and decency, after all. Though she had to admit wearing his mother's clothing would feel odd, it had been a sweet thing to do. "Thank you," she called out as she eased back under the water and relaxed into the mellow sensation.

Chapter Four

The charcoal smoldered white in the brick pit Justin's father had built at the rear of the house. James McGee was a thorough man, and he'd designed and constructed the barbecue pit to exacting standards. Had Justin been eating alone, he'd have simply broiled a steak in the drawer beneath his mom's new range. Steak was one of his dad's favorite meals, second only to Mary McGee's Sunday pot roast.

Justin swallowed over the emotion clogging his throat. His dad hadn't enjoyed steak or roast in a very long time. Not since a routine chest X-ray had shown some spots in the base of his left lung.

After Justin stirred the coals, he set the grill in place. Then he laid a fat T-bone steak across the wire, followed quickly by a second. He'd used his mom's special sauce recipe and could only hope Beth would like it and not consider it too spicy.

"That smells amazing." Beth's voice startled him from behind. He hadn't heard her approach.

Concentrating on keeping his cool, he turned and slowly ran his gaze upward. His mother's peg-leg jeans were too long.

The cotton shirt in red plaid fit nicely, though, bulging just a bit across the chest and, *oh, sweet mercy,* she wore nothing underneath. He hadn't known what to do about undergarments, and had assumed she'd use his mom's clothing just to get to her van for her own things. With a herculean effort, Justin forced his eyes to move on. She'd pulled some of her hair back, taming it away from her face and securing it somehow behind her head, but the majority still caressed her shoulders.

Sudden longing to experience that spun gold brushing over his bare skin ripped through Justin like a harvester chewing up hay, and he battled just to breathe.

"I didn't know what to do with my clothes." Beth laughed nervously. "Burn them, maybe."

His sensual thoughts waned with her words, and Justin chuckled. "We may live out in the country, but we stopped using the creek to do laundry a few years back. You're welcome to use our washing machine." His eyes drifted toward those gaping buttons on her blouse, and he forced them back to the pit and flipped the steaks, even though he'd just put them on.

"That bath worked wonders," murmured Beth, stepping next to him. She leaned over and inhaled deeply. "Mmm. What's in that sauce?"

She'd used his mother's shampoo and her hair smelled of lemons. The riot of curls floated within his reach...

Justin clenched his hands against the resurgence of desire. Would it flow like liquid silk through his fingers?

She angled a look up at him, her eyes questioning. Right. She'd asked him about the sauce.

"It's my mom's special recipe," he answered, forcing himself to concentrate. She was still warm from her bath, and the heat reached out to him with enticing, invisible fingers.

He retreated a half step — needing the space but not wanting it — and groped along the cement side-shelf for the barbecue tongs. The wooden handle was solid in his hand, something to hold onto. The stainless steel ends flashed as he stirred the embers, located the potatoes wrapped in aluminum foil, and turned them over.

Beth placed a hand on his shoulder and leaned close again. "What are those?"

Good question. Justin stared at the lumps of tin foil in the coals, but all he could think about was how warm her hand felt through the thin material of his shirt. "Potatoes — baked potatoes," he choked out. He stood up too quickly, sending Beth into a backward step.

Her feet caught on the bottom hems of the pant legs and she stumbled toward the barbecue pit.

"Watch it!" Justin snapped out a hand and clamped it over Beth's forearm, jerking her back away from the fire.

And up against him.

His body knew instantly what *it* wanted to do, and he sucked in a gulp of air as he fought for emotional and physical control.

With another one of her nervous laughs, Beth recovered her feet underneath her. She clutched Justin's upper arm while she pulled the hems of the jeans out from under first one foot and then the other. Stepping back, she raised her face to his, laughter still sparking in her green eyes. Her gaze collided with his and she stilled. Her lips parted and her body seemed to melt into him.

Justin bent and placed his lips gently to Beth's forehead, allowing himself the briefest brush, before he stepped back and dropped his hand, ignoring his body's immediate protest. "Okay now?"

Beth stared with wide eyes for a heartbeat and then blinked. "Yeah, sorry. I guess I'm showing how clumsy I can be."

A chuckle escaped Justin's lips. "Naw, you're just showing that my mom's legs are longer than yours. Come over here a second." He picked up her hand again and led her to a metal lawn chair, its bright yellow paint muted in the dim light of dusk.

When Beth was seated, Justin crouched in front of her and eased her left foot into his lap, gently rolling the bottom of the pant leg into a wide cuff. Then he set her foot back on the ground and lifted her right leg, repeating the process. Her slender ankle trembled in his grasp. He finished rolling the second cuff, allowing his fingers to linger against her calf. She'd smeared the wicked-smelling goo over the top of her foot, but the slop appeared to be working its magic. The wheals were less raised and more of a dull pink now than the flaming red they had been. He ran his thumb in a line next to the worst one.

With a tiny giggle, Beth jumped. He couldn't help but consider where else she might be ticklish.

"Careful you don't catch poison ivy from me." Her face screwed into an expression that might have been concentration. "Or that spot might be from the poison oak." She lifted her shoulders and cast a carefree grin in Justin's direction. "Whichever, I guess. You don't want it, either way."

Justin released Beth's foot and stood. She pulled both legs into her chair and crossed them at the ankles. The movement pulled the blue jeans tight across her hips, but she didn't seem to mind. Rather than embarrass both of them with physical reactions that were giving him a devil of a time, Justin turned to tend the steaks and found them just nearing medium-rare status.

"How, ah..." He cleared his throat. "How well done do you like your meat?"

"I'm not that picky. Anywhere from not quite mooing to burned black." She bounced to her feet and picked her way over the grass toward the pit again. "What can I do to help?"

Reflexes kicked in and Justin threw out an arm to bar her from getting too close — to the barbecue pit or to him.

She stopped short and giggled again. "Right, sorry."

"Tell you what, you can go on inside and set the table. Plates in the cupboard to the right of the sink, glasses to the left. Silverware in the top drawer."

Some of the perkiness on her face changed into a regretful pout. "Oh, okay. I thought we were going to eat out here."

Justin glanced around. The cement patio Jim McGee had laid but never finished would have been a nice touch on their evening meal. Hating to disappoint her but not really having much choice, Justin gestured at the grass they stood on. "Sorry. My mom always wanted to fix up a nice patio with fancy furniture, but they never got around to getting it done."

Beth pulled her bottom lip into her mouth. "That's too bad. It's so nice out here. Peaceful." She brightened. "But there's still time, right? For them to finish the patio?"

Justin's heart slammed into his throat as pure emotion of a different sort rose to squeeze his lungs. He didn't want to get into the numerous reasons why they really didn't have so much time. "Yeah. Yeah, there's time."

Some of her animated energy returned. "I know what we can do! Do you have an old blanket we can sit on?"

She really had her heart set on eating outside, didn't she? At that precise second, Justin couldn't deny her anything. If Beth had asked him for the chenille spread off his parents' bed, he'd have run upstairs and grabbed it. "In the utility room — the doors just through the kitchen. Plenty of blankets in a cedar closet in there."

Warmth spread across Beth's face with her cheerful smile. "I'll be right back," she called over her shoulder as she raced across the lawn toward the house.

Justin watched her until she disappeared through the back door, wishing he had a glass of lemonade or iced tea to alleviate his suddenly parched throat. He turned the meat one more time and brushed the last of the sauce over the top. By the time he had pulled the second T-bone from the grill, Beth was back, a blue plaid blanket folded under one arm and her other hooked through the handles of the family picnic basket.

"I found this in the utility room, too." She set the basket on the ground. Then, after studying the area for a few moments, she finally selected a spot and spread out the wool blanket. "So I put our plates in it and some silverware." She knelt and plucked items from the basket, placing them out with a fairly precise order. "Oh, and I found a pitcher of lemonade in the fridge, so I brought that and some glasses."

Justin's mouth fell open and he stared.

As if becoming aware of his gaze, Beth stopped moving and glanced up. "I'm sorry, did I do something wrong?"

"Wrong?" echoed Justin, wondering where the kick-start was to fire up his brain. "Ah, no. I just seldom see someone as organized as you are." At least, not outside of his immediate family.

Beth giggled once more. She seemed to do that a lot when she was nervous. "I guess it's all the science labs at school. Neatness counts, you know?"

"Makes sense." Justin considered telling her that he was familiar with the routine in a science lab but decided it could wait. Just one more complicated explanation about something that no longer held any meaning for him. He carried the platter of T-bones and foil-wrapped potatoes over to the blanket and placed it amid the things Beth had set out.

"Come on, sit." Beth patted a spot next to her. She'd laid out the spread on one side of the blanket so they'd sit together without anything between them. He dropped to the ground. The blanket was situated in the perfect spot, with level ground and no rocks underneath to poke at them.

Beth didn't wait for him to dish up the food. She picked up a plate and loaded it with a steak, then peeled open one of the foil-wrapped potatoes and plopped it next to the meat. She glanced sideways and caught him watching her. "I found butter and sour cream. Didn't know which you put on your potatoes." She held the plate out in his direction, her bottom lip pulled deeply into her mouth.

"You fixed me a plate," he murmured softly as he accepted the dish. Great, he'd said that out loud. Heat crept up from his neck.

Beth stopped biting her lip and gave him a smile. "It's only fair since you did all the cooking."

They finished prepping their dinner in silence. Justin didn't know what to say to carry on the conversation. He'd never been prone to shyness, but Miss Bethany Rushton left him a bit tongue-tied. Odd, though, how the silence between them didn't feel particularly awkward.

They could barely see anything by the time they'd finished dinner and cleaned up. Justin carried the picnic basket with the condiments and the dirty plates into the house. When he stepped back outside, Beth was lying on the blanket, gazing upward. She propped herself up on one elbow as he approached and once again patted the blanket next to her.

"Come look at the sky!"

He strolled over and sat, taking care to keep to the edge of the blanket without being obvious. The stars had hung over him at night when he'd been out on the trail during roundups; they weren't an unfamiliar sight. But as he eased onto his back and allowed his eyes to adjust to the darkness, he took on a new appreciation for the vastness of the Wyoming sky.

Beth rolled onto her back again with a sigh and began to speak in a soft voice. "Back home, we have too many city lights, so we only see a few of the brightest stars. I can't imagine being able to walk outside any night to look up and see this view. It's like holes in a curtain... or maybe a comfortable old blanket with little pieces of heaven shining through."

Justin's heart did a little flip-flop and he concentrated on slowing his breathing. "Do you reckon someone's out there looking back on us while we're looking at them?"

Beth shifted onto her side and supported herself on her elbow again. Her hair shone pale in the diffuse moonlight. "As big as the universe is, I can't believe we're the only ones here. But if they are looking at us?" She chuckled softly. "I wonder whether they think Earth is really all that interesting."

Justin rolled over and propped his head on one arm so they faced each other. He knew something on Earth that interested *him*. Or rather someone.

Beth moved closer and Justin stopped breathing while she arranged herself on her back against his side. "See the Big Dipper?"

She pointed into the sky and he tried to follow her gesture. Finally, with a helpless shake of the head, he gave up, wishing he'd at least learned how to find a couple of constellations while he'd been out on cattle drives.

Beth picked up his hand, holding it with the back against her palm. She nudged his forefinger apart from the rest and used it to draw an imaginary line in the sky. "See that bright star there?"

Following the line of his finger as Beth held it made it surprisingly easy to pick up a star that was definitely brighter than others around it. "Yeah." He nodded, excitement taking over. "Yeah, I do!"

Beth gave Justin's hand a quick squeeze. "That's Dubhe. It's part of the cup on the Big Dipper. So if you follow a line down, the next bright star almost underneath it? That's Merak. And then move across... this way..." She drew the line with his hand. "You'll see Phecda. Then up a little to Megrez, over to Alioth, to Mizar, and a little bit down to Alkaid. See it?"

He did. Quite clearly. Lightness eased into his heart for the first time in months and a chuckle slipped out. "It's like playing connect the dots!"

She laughed with him, and then began pointing to other constellations, naming some, making up outrageous names for others. "I think we'll call that one... hmm, Justin's Cowboy Hat." She laughed. "See? It even has a bent brim, just like yours does."

Giddiness rushed his system and a grin stretched his lips. She'd noticed his favorite battered Stetson — with the brim he'd bowed over the years by constantly pulling it down to fight the sun's angle.

Chapter Five

The smell of brewing coffee teased Beth's nostrils until her eyelids fluttered open. Where on earth was she? Little by little, blurry shapes sharpened and colors brightened. Early morning sunlight filtered in through lacy white curtains and splashed shadowy patterns on dark wood-paneled walls. A shiver of awareness raced through her.

Justin McGee's home!

He had carried her battered brown suitcases up the stairs and settled her in the spare room, and then he'd excused himself to go bed down in the bunkhouse occupied by the ranch foreman. Nothing Beth said had swayed him from his chosen course.

"No, ma'am, my mother'd be concerned if we shared the house without a chaperone," he'd told her with a firm shake of his head. Apparently he'd been serious, because as soon as he'd determined she didn't need anything, he had left, closing the bedroom door behind him with a soft click.

Beth rolled onto her back and laced her fingers behind her head. Drawing a deep breath, she picked up the tangy scent of bacon mingling with the coffee and her stomach growled. If he was cooking for her again, Justin was going to spoil her. And she could get very used to being spoiled.

Anxious to get at the food she smelled, Beth jumped up, pulled her nightgown over her head, and grabbed a clean pair of jeans. After wriggling into those, she slipped on a fresh blouse. Her reflection pouted at her from the dresser mirror. Such a plain and uninspiring face. She'd never figured out makeup, though it somehow didn't seem all that appropriate on a ranch anyway. And her hair... She looked closer and groaned.

"What a rat's nest!" Oh, why couldn't she have nice hair, straight and smooth, and easily tamed?

She tugged a brush through it, impatient with each stupid knot she had to stop and work loose with her fingers. There! The last of the tangles came free. Quickly she gathered it into a loose ponytail, securing it with an elastic band at the nape of her neck.

The stairs she took two at a time at a gallop. At least until she got close to the bottom of the staircase. For the last several steps, she forced herself to slow to a more sedate — and ladylike — pace. By the time she followed her nose to the kitchen doorway, she was managing a composed stroll.

Diffuse morning light filtered through the open window. A cool breeze blew in and toyed with the sheer white curtains edged in sunflowers, lifting them until they ballooned outward then allowing them to fall, and then repeating the process.

But it was the man who dominated the room.

Justin stood in front of a large white range, tending to bacon sizzling in one pan and eggs frying in another. He wielded an expert spatula as he flipped the eggs. Then he picked up a fork and pulled the bacon from the pan, one perfectly crisp strip at a time, and laid it on a plate sitting on the counter.

This was a man as at home in the kitchen as he'd been on the back of a horse. His quiet presence filled the room; he owned his space without saying a word.

"Mornin', Miss Bethany," he said without turning around. "How did you sleep last night?"

Her jaw dropping open, Beth stared. How had he known

she was there? It wasn't like she'd stomped into the room. "Good morning," she mumbled. "I slept very well, thank you. But I still feel badly about chasing you from your own house."

He glanced over his shoulder and smiled. "It wasn't a hardship at all. How's that rash this morning?"

She lifted a hand to her neck to find the welts had gone down some. Her skin had stopped burning and now barely even itched. Funny, she'd been in such a hurry to get downstairs she hadn't even noticed. "It's better."

"Good." He returned his attention to the range and pulled out two more strips of bacon. "You'll probably have some traces for a couple of weeks yet. But maybe you got to it in time so you won't break out any more. Any of your blisters burst?"

Beth shook her head. "No, but a couple on my feet look close. Why... why doesn't this itch? Is it the ointment you gave me?"

"Probably." He looked back and met her gaze again, his twinkling blue eyes reminding her of the stars the evening before. "Gus said some of his blisters went away without even bursting when he used it."

With economical movements, Justin shut off the burners and scooped the eggs out of the pan, then slid them onto a plate. As he turned from the range, his lips curved into one of the most devastatingly heart-stopping smiles Beth had ever seen.

One more item to add to the list of things about him that should come with a warning label. Butterflies waltzed in her stomach, and after a few seconds, she remembered to breathe.

Justin set the plate of bacon and two eggs-over-easy on the table, and then indicated Beth should take the seat. After she did, he placed a second plate across from her and sat down.

Assorted jars of jam and jelly rested between them, next to a sugar bowl and a creamer. A glass carafe of coffee sat on a hot pad made of colorful ceramic tile. Justin poured himself a cup of dark brown liquid and raised the pot in Beth's direction. She slid her cup closer to him so he could fill it. Then he added so many spoonfuls of sugar to his cup she lost count.

Would you like some coffee with your sugar? Stifling a giggle, Beth picked up a perfectly crisp piece of bacon and nibbled on it, savoring the saltiness. "Have you been up long?"

"Hmm, couple hours." Justin chose a piece of toast and slathered it with strawberry preserves. "I threw your jeans in with one of my loads, and your blouse and... ah, underthings in with some of my mother's laundry. I double-rinsed everything and it's all hung on the line outside." He bit into the toast and chewed, then picked up his coffee mug and sipped.

Realizing her mouth had fallen open again, Beth closed it and tried to stop staring at the man across the table. "So my, um, my — stuff — is — on the clothesline... *outside?*"

"Yep." Justin scooped a forkful of fried egg into his mouth and chewed.

Beth followed suit, trying not to think about her decadent underwear blowing in the breeze... or about how it had gotten there. But she glanced up to find Justin studying her and knew without a doubt that he was aware of her discomfort.

Oh, mother of invention, just shoot me now. She inclined her head and gave him her best smile before smearing grape jelly across her toast.

"What are you planning to do today?" He poured a second cup of coffee, spooned half the sugar bowl into the aromatic liquid, and sat back in his chair.

She blew some of the heat from the surface of her own coffee then sipped. Buttery-nutty sweetness exploded across her tongue. Why would anyone need to smother such flavor with a hundred spoonfuls of sugar?

"Well, I should find someplace to stay." She took another drink, bigger this time. "I'd like to find a motel or something, but it sounds like the closest one is kind of far away from the area I've been studying." Unable to resist, she finished off her coffee and actually considered a second cup, but she didn't want to bounce off the walls of her van. "And I should get that wire looked at on Clara, I guess."

"What about your family?" Justin stood and began gathering dishes. "You said you had family in the area?"

Beth scrunched up her nose and stared down at the table. The prospect of dropping in on Alice and her husband was even more dismal in the light of a new day than it had been when her van had broken down.

Justin laughed softly. "Now, that's about as sour a face as I've ever seen."

Was there a diplomatic way to answer that? She ran her finger along the edge of the wooden table. "Alice and I — we don't — really get on that well. She'd take me in... but neither of us would be... happy. And her husband is..." What could she say about Brody MacKay? That he was weird and creepy? That didn't sound particularly charitable.

"Alice?" Justin's face became a mask of wariness and he frowned, apparently working on some problem in his head. "Alice and Brody MacKay are your kin?"

Judging by the aversion that flashed ever so briefly in Justin's eyes before he lowered them to study his plate, she'd be lucky if he didn't send her packing before they finished breakfast. "Alice is my sister," she admitted, unable to stop from twisting her mouth slightly. "Well, half sister, actually. We have the same father." She scratched at a persistent patch of poison ivy rash on her hand. "We don't really get along very well."

"That's not surprising," murmured Justin, crunching his last piece of bacon.

Beth jerked her head up, surprised by his tone, but he'd gone all poker-faced. She wondered who he objected to, Alice or Brody, but she didn't ask.

Justin stood, stacked Beth's plate on top of his, and carried them to the sink. Heat flooded her face. She should have been the one to do that. He set the dishes down and abruptly turned from the counter.

"You could stay here," he blurted, as though the words were torn from his throat. Then he flushed deep red and lowered his gaze toward the floor. "If you'd like to."

Beth considered the previous evening under the stars with Justin, the comfortable bed she'd slept in, the delicious meals. The sense of peace and security. She was sorely tempted. But she lifted one hand in a helpless gesture. "I don't know... I can't keep kicking you out of your house and since you won't sleep in it while I'm here—"

"A few more nights."

"I'm sorry?"

"I'll only have to bunk with Gus for a few more nights. My parents'll be home by Friday." He closed the distance between them. "If you don't want to stay with your sister, you can stay here. I have to check fences out near where I found you yesterday. If you're of a mind to go with me, I can get you up on a horse. Then we can get your van—" He smiled and Beth's heart gave her a little electric shock. "Clara, was it?"

Blinking, she struggled to keep up. She'd stopped hearing much after the word *horse*. But he'd asked her a question... oh, about Clara's name. Without speaking, she gave him a jerky nod.

"We can get Clara looked at tomorrow when I run a couple of errands in town."

"A... *horse?*" Her entire body gave an involuntary shudder at the thought and she shook her head. "I don't think—"

A huge grin spread across Justin's face and he guffawed. "You can point to the stars in the sky, but you can't get your mind around riding a horse?"

"It's not the how — well, it's partly the how. As in, I don't *know* how."

"Relax, we'll get you up on Abe. He's so mellow, you couldn't make him throw you off if you steered him through a bee colony." Justin began running water into the kitchen sink. He poured a measure of soap and wiggled his fingers in the water stream. One by one, he began scrubbing breakfast dishes.

Beth stood and crossed to the sink. A yellow checked dishtowel hung over the door of the bottom cabinet, so she grabbed it and dried the plates Justin had already set in the white plastic drainer. These, she stacked on the countertop so Justin could put them away.

To ride a horse or not to ride. That had become the question of the moment. Zeke had towered over her the day before. What would it be like to sit on his back? More to the point, what did it feel like to fall off?

Still, the idea of spending the day with Justin appealed. She wrinkled her nose. So did the idea of avoiding her sister.

Beth reached for the coffee cup in the drainer, but Justin snatched it back. When she raised her gaze, his eyes were crinkled at the corners, his lips turned gently upward. "All that thinking just to decide if you want to go riding?"

Heat flooded her face. She *had* taken a long time to mull over her answer. "Okay. If you promise your mom won't mind."

Justin's grin sent her heart into a funny little skipping rhythm.

* * *

"He has blue eyes." Beth stared into the giant pool of swirling sapphire set into the snowy white hair of the horse's face. The light coloring disconcerted her. "I didn't know horses could have blue eyes."

"Well, as it turns out, Abe's only got one blue eye." Justin scratched him on his nose and the horse turned his head to reveal a pecan-colored eye set against pale brown. The color circled his eye and ran upward to cover his ear on that side.

She'd never seen a more mixed-up animal. Splotches and blotches of color made him look like a tan horse someone had dropped a bucket of white paint on.

Or a white horse that has some kind of rash.

Beth chuckled and scratched her neck. "We match."

The brown eye circled, the horse assessing her as she studied him.

Justin rubbed the back of his neck. "Yeah, I wasn't going to mention that, but you more or less do."

She looked up... and up. The horse was a giant. "I've never ridden, you know."

"Really, now. I wouldn't have guessed." Justin's lips pulled up into a half-smirk. "Time you learned, don't you think?"

"But he's *really* big."

Justin glanced over Beth's shoulder and squinted at Abe.

"Well, he's on the large side for a quarter horse, 'bout fourteen and a half hands or so. But Zeke here's closer to sixteen hands."

Beth had no idea what a hand was, but Zeke looked a good six or eight inches taller at the shoulder than Abe. Not that it mattered. Both horses loomed over her five-foot four-inch head. "Maybe I should just drive, or... walk or... something." She scuffed her toe in the dust. She had on a fairly new pair of Western boots borrowed from Justin's mother. Beth sure hoped the woman didn't mind that she was apparently making herself at home and using all her things. But Justin had said her tennies were dangerous for riding because her foot could slip through the stirrup. Luckily Mrs. McGee's boots had been a good fit.

"You'll do fine. Abe's a sweetheart, nice and gentle. Come on, I'll help you get up on him." Justin held out his hand. Beth's glance flickered between the man and the horse.

Finally she placed her hand in Justin's and allowed him to lead her to Abe's left side.

"You only want to approach him from the left," he explained, patting the horse on the shoulder. "That's how he was trained." He surveyed Beth's legs with a shake of his head. "It'll be easier if we get you over to the fence so you can get your foot in the stirrup. Come on, Abe."

Justin snagged the reins and led the horse over to the fence. Then he pointed to the rails, indicating Beth should climb up.

She did so, feeling like a kid again, and giggled. That giddy schoolgirl sensation had been happening a lot since she'd met Justin.

"Okay, put your left foot in the stirrup and hold onto the pommel there, then swing your right leg over his back and slide on into the saddle." Justin demonstrated with his hands as he gave the instructions.

Beth got so caught up watching his hands, she almost missed half his instructions. With just a little awkwardness, she managed to get herself into the saddle.

Justin put the reins in her hands. "Now hold still and I'll show you how to guide your horse. It'll be easier if I do that when I'm up on Zeke."

She froze in place.

Moving with self-assuredness Beth could only long for, Justin swung himself onto Zeke's back. Then he edged the chestnut horse close to hers and showed her how to lay the reins alongside the horse's neck. "Don't pull on his bit or you can hurt him," he explained. "If you want him to turn left, touch the right side of the neck with the rein and squeeze in with your left leg." He laid the rein on the right side of Abe's neck to demonstrate and the horse turned his head to the left. "Think of it like pushing the horse where you want to go instead of pulling him."

Justin held out the reins with a confident smile.

Beth eyed the offering without moving. The reins might have been snakes for all she wanted to touch the strips of worn brown leather. After a long moment of tangled gazes, during which Beth was certain all her secret insecurities had been laid bare, she accepted the reins with a wobbly smile.

Abe shifted his stance, the movement giving the impression the saddle was sliding sideways. Then Beth realized *she* was sliding — right out of the slippery saddle. She grabbed onto the part of the saddle that stuck up like a handle.

"Are you sure you can't just, like, pull me along behind you or something? Then I can just hold onto this handle thingy and I won't fall off."

He turned away quickly, but Beth caught his smile and knew he was fighting to hold back laughter.

She made a face at his back and set the pale straw hat — also borrowed from Mrs. McGee — on her head. "Sure, go ahead. Laugh at the city girl who's never ridden a horse before. I'm sure this is all just a huge funny story you'll tell around the campfire someday."

After Justin set his own hat on his head, he swung around and regarded Beth again. He didn't say a word, but his eyes squinted at the corners. "No, ma'am. Not laughing at all. It wouldn't be right to laugh at someone for being equine-challenged." But one side of his mouth twitched upward. He clucked his tongue and did something with the reins and Zeke took his first steps.

Abe stood still, so Beth jiggled the reins and gave a little forward bounce in the saddle. The horse turned his head to regard her over his shoulder. His funky blue eye mesmerized her with its slow misty swirl.

"Hey, how do I get him to go?" she called out.

As if he understood, and for no other apparent reason that Beth could discern, Abe started forward, nearly unseating her.

"Oh!" She grabbed at the handle again and missed her grip, flailing her hands until she found it.

Unaffected by her balancing act, Abe kept plodding forward.

"Okay, ah, never mind, I think I've got it."

Abe drew abreast of Zeke, and the horses walked side by side.

"You know, until you get your balance, you might want to hang onto that handle thingy with one hand." Justin tilted his head and sent her a sidelong glance. "Oh, and it's called a pommel, but you might know it as a saddle horn."

Right. He'd told her that earlier, hadn't he? She didn't know what it was about the man, but he had the power to fluster her just with his nearness.

Chapter Six

The tall grass whispered as they cut a path through the northwest pasture. Neither of them spoke. Justin didn't know if Beth felt the same appreciation for the peace that embraced the land as he did, but she began to loosen up into a more natural seat as they rode.

"So much space," she said, shielding her eyes as she scanned the plain around them. "Back home, you can't see past the next house. If you're lucky that might be fifty feet."

Justin nudged Zeke into a slightly faster pace, taking care that Abe followed suit. "Just where is home, anyway?"

"Umm... Michigan." She concentrated on balancing herself as Abe shifted to avoid a rock on the trail. "A suburb just outside Detroit — Bloomfield Hills."

Sounded pretentious, Justin decided, but he kept the thought to himself.

As they passed a stand of scrub trees, song sparrows began to chorus, their trilling song perfectly synchronized. Beth angled her head and a dreamy expression settled over her face.

She sighed as they left the birdsong behind. "You don't

get this kind of entertainment in the city."

"So what *is* a city gal doing studying weeds in Wyoming?"

"We studied natural selection last term. I love gardening — all those flowers? I guess bright colors attract me." She tilted her head and cast him a questioning glance.

He couldn't hold back a smile as he thought about her van. "I kinda picked up on that."

The smile she shot back dazzled. "Well, there's this flower company in Pennsylvania that's been trying the principles of natural selection to cross new roses with old ones for better hybrids."

Justin shifted in the saddle to get a better look while she spoke. Her voice was filled with the sort of vibrancy that told of her passion for the subject. Then she launched into a detailed description of plant genetics that went right over his head, but her excitement was contagious, and he found himself listening to everything she said about making engineered roses hardier by encouraging crosses between grafted roses and wild roses.

She stopped for a second while she drew in a breath. When she glanced up and found him watching her, pink worked its way into her cheeks. She glanced over her shoulder in the direction they'd come then back at him and offered a rueful smile. "I've been going on for a long time, haven't I? You're probably bored out of your mind."

Odd, but he hadn't been, not really, even if he hadn't understood everything she'd said. So he shook his head. "It's not much different from how we breed a better cow. Keep a fair share of the hardier and stronger ones for breeding, cull out the less desirable ones, pick the best bulls each season, and take care of the rest."

She paled a bit and swallowed hard, and Justin gave himself an imaginary slap to the forehead. He'd gotten so comfortable in her company, he'd forgotten Beth was a city gal and probably never gave a thought about where her weekly roast beef came from.

Her lips curled into a weak little smile. "I don't believe I've ever considered the similarities of plant and animal breeding."

Justin nodded, his lips tugging into a grin of admiration. *Nice recovery.* But he wanted to see more of her former animation. "What I'm wondering here, though, is why, if you're interested in roses, you're out here studying poison ivy and poison oak."

"I'm *not* interested in roses. Not really." Beth's face brightened. "But I'm interested in how two different species of plant came to a state of hybridization on their own, and if this hybrid is the beginning of a true new species or if the new plants are sterile."

Understanding took root and he grinned. "You want to know if the new plants can breed or if they're mules."

"Exactly!" She threw her head back and let out a delighted chortle. Her hat slipped off, caught by the string around her neck, and settled against the middle of her back.

Completely caught up in her laughter, Justin almost didn't notice they'd arrived at the fences he needed to check. He pulled Zeke to a stop and Abe followed suit. Beth looked at him with a query in her eyes and he nodded to the trail on the left. "Might be we'll find what you're looking for over that rise. I have to check that grove over there for strays before we go back. We moved the bulk of the herd up to the high pasture a couple weeks back, but odds are we missed a few."

And odds were he'd never find the several head more than "a few" that he knew for a fact had gone missing under suspicious circumstances, but that was why he needed to check the fence. He was also more or less sure he'd find signs they hadn't left of their own accord.

Beth eyed the wooden fence posts strung with barbed wire. "What's on the other side of the fence?"

"That'd be your brother-in-law's place," said Justin, trying to keep an even tone so they wouldn't have to go through awkward explanations of exactly what he was looking for on the property line. He nudged Zeke down the trail, sparing a glace over his shoulder to make certain Abe followed. "You know what you're looking for?" he called back.

"Oh, yeah." Making a face, she rubbed the worst patch on her neck. "And I'll be a lot more careful about how I examine it, too. I need to collect some samples and some bits of roots if I can. I brought some plastic bags and a pair of gloves."

They entered the copse of blackjack pines and the footfalls of the horses became muffled on the soft bed of brown pine needles. The trail sloped gently downward and they followed it, allowing the horses to pick their own way on the soft footing. At the far edge of the grove, Justin pulled Zeke up again and nodded at some brush. "Poison ivy in there. Don't see any poison oak."

Beth scanned the area and shook her head. "I don't see any either, but sometimes one species is more dominant and the other can be hard to sp— there! We have both here. Now I just have to see if there's any hybridized." She glanced up at Justin, a look of entreaty in her eyes. "I don't know how to get down."

Smiling along with her, Justin slid off Zeke's back and walked around to Abe. "Tuck the reins in your left hand."

She did so with care and, smiling, held up her hand, ready for the next step.

"Okay, you can hold onto the horn." He waited while she got a grip, then he nodded. "Good. Okay, make sure your left leg is in place." He adjusted her foot so it was solid in the stirrup. "Now, stand up in the stirrups and slip your right foot out, then swing your right leg up and over old Abe's rump. As you move your leg, move your right hand to the back of the saddle."

"Ummm..." She drew and released a quick breath and followed his directions well, if a little haltingly. As her leg moved over Abe's back, she started to slide downward. "Ah! Ah!"

Justin caught her by the hips. "You're okay. Kick out of the other stirrup."

Still a little tentative, she managed to release her foot, and he allowed her body to slide down until she stood in the circle of his arms.

"See, as soon as you get your leg over the horse's back, gravity takes over." He stepped back, taking her with him. "When you do this for yourself, you need to balance with your hands and then kick your left foot free of the stirrup and just drop down. You'll want to push with your hands a little bit so you come down a little ways from the horse instead of right next to him."

Beth leaned against him and sighed. Sunshine and outdoors and the faint scent of soap teased his nose. Her softness fit so perfectly against him, he could stay like that for the rest of the day and ranch business be hanged.

She whirled in his embrace and threw her arms around his neck, pressing her face against his chest.

Scratch that previous thought. She'd found a much nicer alternative.

"I rode a horse!" she said with a little squeak in her voice. Then she pressed a light, fast kiss to his jaw. "Thank you!"

He stopped breathing for a few heartbeats as her obvious happiness slammed into him full force. Then she stepped back. Her sudden absence left him not knowing quite what to do with his hands. So he tipped his hat and grinned. "Pleased I could be of assistance."

Something he couldn't define flashed in her eyes, and the moment stretched to several as their gazes locked. She broke the spell with a shaky laugh and a gesture toward the horse. "I should get out my gear."

The saddlebag was just out of her reach even standing on her tiptoes, so Justin pointed to a nearby boulder that was solid enough to use as a step stool. Apparently without a second thought, she clambered onto it and started rooting through the leather bag. As she pulled out the items she'd need to collect her samples, Justin scouted the area, staying well away from those shiny leaves of three. He itched just looking at Beth's various patches of rash, and held no desire to join her in the experience. Other experiences, though... there were a few he could think of he'd like to join her in.

"Whatcha thinkin'?" She bounced into him from behind and to the left, clutching his arm when her foot slipped on the soft ground littered with old pine needles. "Whoops!" she exclaimed with a hearty laugh.

"Dirt's dry," Justin mumbled, placing a steadying hand under her elbow. "Haven't had rain in a while and it goes to dust when it's dry." He glanced down at the assortment of plastic bags, a notebook with two pens clipped to the front, a shovel, and a pair of gloves. *The tools of a scientist.* "You'll want to watch your footing. Stick to the trail as much as possible."

Beth set her burden down on top of a big rock to the side of the trail. "Gotcha." She pulled a brown corduroy strap attached to a 35-mm camera over her head and set the expensive-looking camera with her other things.

"I'm going to ride along this fence for a bit." He squinted into the distance and considered how far he'd go before turning around. "Should be back in an hour or so. Will you be all right on your own here?"

Beth looked around. "An hour?" A bit of something that might have been uncertainly flickered in her eyes, but she nodded her head. "Sure."

He'd half expected her to offer a protest. For a city girl, she did have some grit to her.

*   *   *

Beth leaned forward, staring after Justin and Zeke as they rode back up the trail. He sure presented a nice view from the rear. Something scampered past her feet. With her heart pounding hard in her throat, she executed a hasty sidestep. Probably a mouse. Just a mouse. Snakes didn't scurry.

Justin hadn't mentioned wild animals. Hopefully that meant none were around that should cause concern. Surely he'd have told her about bears or wolves or mountain lions nearby, wouldn't he? He'd tucked a lethal appearing rifle into the holster on his saddle, though. A shudder tickled her spine. What if he'd simply forgotten to say something?

The little stand of brush and trees had seemed so idyllic when Justin had been with her. A rustling in the brush on the far side of the copse drew her attention — okay, *that* sounded much bigger than a mouse. Leaning forward for a better look, she saw nothing. Abe's snort cut through the hush and she jumped, her breath caught in her throat. Slowly she relaxed.

Birdsong filtered in, and then the relentless buzz of insects. The little glade wasn't as silent as she'd first thought. She just wasn't acclimated to the local sounds was all. Until she was, she'd hear mountain lions and bears everywhere.

She closed her eyes and just listened. Except for the occasional snuffle of one very indifferent horse and the whispering song of the breeze in the treetops above her, all was peaceful.

She twisted and glanced again in the direction Justin had taken, smiling when she saw him turn around just in time to spot her looking at him. He tossed her a casual wave and she lifted a hand in response, feeling suddenly weak in the knees.

"Time to get to work," she told Abe, who snorted again. She had an hour and she planned to have all her samples pinched and cut and dug and bagged and tagged before Justin's return. This time, preferably, without the tumble into the oily weeds.

She started with a quick examination of the cluster of plants, snapping a few pictures of the general layout. When she'd used up her roll of film, she swapped it for a fresh one. Then she added a description of their locations in relation to each other in her notebook. Edging along the outside of the cluster of bushes, Beth found a spot where they grew in a thinner pattern and carefully stepped between the plants, doing her best not to brush against any of them.

Grouped around the stump from an old downed tree, some short plants with cone-shaped orange flowers were just starting to take hold. Mother Nature offering up her remedy for poison ivy. Beth snickered. If only she'd remembered that the day before, she might not still be fighting the itching and burning effects of her close encounter with urushiol oil. As an afterthought, she snapped pictures of the jewelweed and recorded in her notebook the placement of those plants, as well as a rough idea of their age.

"You're not going to go rolling in that now, are you?" Justin's voice sounded loud against the stillness in the little stand of trees.

Beth gasped and dropped her notebook, but managed to

hang onto her camera. She spun around, a smart-ass comment ready on her lips, and then lost her command of speech. Dappled patches of sunlight danced over Justin, sitting astride Zeke on the trail about ten feet away. His eyes gleamed with merriment, and he grinned at her while she blinked, wondering where her language skills had disappeared to. Quickly, before the moment was lost, too, she raised her camera and snapped his picture.

Had it been an hour already? Beth checked her watch and noted it had actually been closer to an hour and a half since Justin had ridden off.

"I... I'm almost finished here," was all she could think to say as she turned and made her way back up the slight hill. Her feet slid on the dirt and for one horrible moment, she was certain she was, indeed, going to end up on her back in the middle of a poison ivy patch for the second time in as many days.

But Justin made it to the top of the embankment and reached out, closing his hand around hers before she even realized he'd climbed off his horse. He gave an easy little tug, and Beth found herself back on the trail — and for the second time in as many hours standing dangerously close to one ruggedly handsome cowboy. She tried to swallow but her mouth had gone dry.

Perfectly shaped lips pulled into a half-smile and Justin shook his head, but he didn't say anything as he led her back to the horses.

"Did you get the fences checked?" she asked, more for something to say than any other reason.

"Yep, most of 'em, anyway." He held her saddlebag open while she filled it with her notebook and the samples.

She checked her camera and noted she still had nearly a full roll of film left, so she pulled the strap over her head and settled it around her neck. Then she was ready to mount. She made a face at the stirrup, knowing there was no way she'd ever be able to reach it with her foot. She assessed the rock she'd been standing on. Would the horse hold still long enough for her to get into the saddle? The only thing worse than being helped on and off the horse would be to fall on her butt.

"Problem?" asked Justin, his patient voice reminding Beth of the way an adult talked to a small child.

"No," she answered quickly. Then she offered him a rueful smile. "Well, kind of... I'm not sure about this part yet."

Justin's chronic smile became a grin. He advanced on Beth, startling her when he placed his hands on her shoulders and turned her to face the horse. Then he cupped his hand. "Come on, I'll boost ya."

Feeling a little foolish, Beth grabbed hold of the front and back of the saddle and then stepped into Justin's hand. He gave a quick heave and she found herself at the right level to throw her leg over the saddle. From there, it was simple to settle her feet in the stirrups. Even so, by the time she was settled and ready to move, Justin was already on Zeke. He made everything seem so effortless.

"So what are you looking for when you check fences?" she asked as he started them back up the trail.

A muscle tensed in Justin's jaw. A hint of trouble glittered in his eyes, but it just as quickly winked out when he flashed a grin her way. "Broken posts, loosened wire. Anything that needs repairing so the cattle stay where we put 'em."

"What if they don't stay where you put them?" she couldn't help asking. "What happens if they break through the fences?"

Justin smiled and offered an indulgent shrug. "Then we have to go get 'em." But his blue eyes took on the look of flint just before he sped up to take the lead where the trail narrowed. An instant later, they broke out of the copse and Justin slowed until they rode side by side again.

"It's so open," murmured Beth, looking across the meadow. "Where's the other pasture? What did you call it? The high pasture?"

Justin nodded to the mountains in the distance. "Foothills. The grazing's better, grass is lusher from all the winter runoff. We generally run the herd up there right after calving season, as soon as the majority of the calves can make the journey. Then we brand the calves, take care of the bull calves, and turn the whole herd loose up there for the summer."

"Branding..." Beth shuddered. She didn't think she'd enjoy that. "Wait. Take care of the bull calves? You said that before. What does that mean?"

Justin swung his gaze in Beth's direction again and he looked at her with a hint of a laugh hovering on his lips. "Turn most of them into steers."

"You mean... you mean you cut off..."

"Yep, that's what I mean." Thankfully he didn't say the rest out loud.

Beth's stomach flip-flopped. Now she knew she didn't want to ever see that side of ranching. She swallowed. "I know it's all necessary, but it's ever so much nicer to see cows in the pasture and think of that as their permanent home."

Justin's cough sounded a bit too much like a laugh.

After passing the trail they'd traveled out on, he led them along a path that intersected with a small stream. When she saw the fence on the other side of the water, Beth understood. They were still following the fence while Justin checked it for breaks.

The verdant grass along the bubbling creek grew tall, hiding the banks for the most part, though occasional gray boulders poked through the green. Gradually the grass thinned and the creek became lazier, the rocks smaller, more spread out, until they rode along gravel with a stand of trees opposite the creek.

"The creek floods here," Justin explained, gesturing at the land surrounding them. "If it rains enough, it covers this gravel bed all the way to those trees.

"It's beautiful," Beth breathed, her eyes lighting on the scattered splotches of lavender and white covering the ground in front of them.

The cabin seemed to rise out of nowhere. One minute Beth was looking at the shallow creek and the next a run-down cabin stood in her way. Windows without glass stared sightlessly. The roof was more than half caved in, but the fieldstone foundation looked solid. Along the front of the cabin, a bright patch of yellow trumpeted flowers captured her attention.

"Daffodils!" she cried out in delight.

Justin pulled his horse up and dismounted. Beth started to move, but then paused, frowning as she tried to recall the steps, performing each movement as it came to her. *Hold onto the horn, stand in the stirrups, swing my right leg over the horse's rump, and kick my left foot free of the stirrup. And don't forget that jolt when you land.*

Beth's feet hit the ground next to Abe and she gave a triumphant little cry. When she turned around, Justin stood in front of her, so close his body warmed hers. He settled his hands at her waist and steadied her, but he didn't step back right away. Instead, he kept an intense gaze on her face, as though seeking the answers to some unasked question. Without giving it any thought, Beth found herself drawn to him, leaning in his direction until they touched.

Abruptly, Justin broke the loose embrace, stepping away and averting his gaze. "Sorry, I... thought you'd need help getting down."

Never before had Beth felt such strong awareness, such a mix of powerful need and emotional mayhem. She regretted instantly the distance he placed between them, but then considered it was likely for the best. After all, she'd only just met him, and they'd been playing cat and mouse ever since.

Chapter Seven

"We'll stop to eat here," Justin said after he recovered some control over his racing heart. What a mistake it had been to stand so close again, knowing her scent would entice, that his brain would again entertain all sorts of sensual thoughts. He nodded toward his saddlebags. "I packed sandwiches."

Beth's eyes lit up at the mention of food, and Justin stepped to his horse to unload their midday meal. The blue blanket he'd brought along was the same one they'd used the night before, and he smiled at the memory of stargazing with the fascinating Miss Bethany Rushton. He allowed his gaze to wander until it caught up with her.

Heart have mercy! She had dropped to her knees and buried her face in the bright yellow flowers. He closed his eyes for a second while he blew out a slow breath through pursed lips.

The square root of pi is one point seven seven two four five... Crap! Not doing it. Math problems weren't going to keep his mind off the one-plus-one equation he really wanted to perform.

If you can't beat it... join in.

Justin sauntered over to the flowers. Beth glanced up at his approach, offering a blissful grin as she settled her behind onto her calves. "Daffodils always look insanely happy."

And thinking of the flowers that way apparently brought Beth her own sense of happiness. Returning her smile, he dropped the bag with their sandwiches into the grass then lifted the blanket to catch the air and spread it across the ground. As he lowered himself, Beth scooted over to join him.

"I never thought about lunch," she murmured, and nearly did in what little resolve Justin had achieved by running her tongue over her upper lip. "Most days I forget all about eating."

Justin cleared his throat. "It's not much. A couple of cold roast beef sandwiches is all." He dug one out and handed it to her, still wrapped in the butcher's paper he'd used when he'd put their lunch together.

Beth unwrapped the offering and sniffed, laughing when her stomach growled its appreciation. But she waited for Justin to unwrap his own sandwich before she took her first bite. She closed her eyes and moaned out loud as she chewed.

"Oh, wow! This is *good.*" She bit again.

The urge to tease the city gal was too great. "Yeah, Old Bessy turned out to be a good roast, after all."

Beth froze in mid-chew. She swallowed her mouthful with obvious effort. "Old Bessy was a cow?"

Justin only grinned. After all, someone somewhere must have named a cow Bessy.

"You named your food and then *ate* it?" Her eyes blinked a frenzied beat. Was she trying to adjust to the thought or trying to get it out of her mind? "You can't eat something you've *named*. It's against the rules!" She dropped her sandwich onto the wrapping paper and looked at it in horror.

Unable to contain himself any longer, Justin tossed back his head and allowed the laughter to break free. "Relax," he said after a moment, still trying to rein in his chuckles. "There was no Old Bessy — not at the Cross MC, anyway. This is my mom's cooking, and she generally gets her meat from the butcher, same as most folks around here. And it was more likely a Bob than a Bessy."

"Oh, you're bad!" Beth cried.

"You have no idea." And probably best if she never found out.

Her lips turned upward and her soft laugh signaled her mirth. After one more suspicious glance, she picked up the sandwich again. "Bob, huh?" She eyed Justin up and down, stopping her perusal in the vicinity of his lap, and then, with a narrow-eyed glare, she opened her mouth and took a huge chomp out of the sandwich.

Twin sensations raced through him, one pain, the other pleasure. Justin could only stare as she ate, no longer taking delicate nibbles, instead indulging in large bites and chewing with renewed relish, keeping her gaze locked on his until she'd finished the last crumb and licked her fingers to boot.

Ouch.

He shoved the rest of his sandwich into his mouth. He'd need the energy to keep up with this tiny bit of dynamite.

"Too bad we don't have dessert," Beth murmured, neatly smoothing the butcher's paper and folding it over two times before setting it aside.

"Actually..." Justin opened the lunch sack and removed two apples. "We do." He polished one on his shirt and offered it to Beth, who glanced at it and then lifted her eyes to his.

"Isn't it Eve who's supposed to carry the apples around to seduce Adam?" Her green eyes glinted with glee.

Then she lifted one arm and flicked her hair over her shoulder with the back of her hand.

The world froze save for the two of them. The sun shone a little brighter. He tried to draw air, but his lungs were full.

Breathe! Smiling through the pain, he exhaled slowly and then pulled in his next breath. When Beth reached out to take the apple, her fingertips brushed across his palm, and chills ricocheted up and down his spine.

Get it together. Prime numbers... yeah... two, three, five, seven, nine — no, not nine, eleven, thirteen... spider monkeys. Aw, hell!

He was having some kind of attack, right? No matter what his dad always said, nobody went this over-the-moon in less than twenty-four hours.

She bit into the apple, back to the dainty bites again. Then she licked the juice from her lips after each one. He couldn't stop watching her eat. She took another nibble and swiped her tongue around her lips, but missed the spot just at the right corner of her mouth. Justin leaned forward slowly, intent on catching that sweet dewy drop.

Angus, Hereford, Texas longhorn, Brahman... Oh, boy! That sun's getting hot.

Beth snaked her tongue out and beat him to the prize. Giving his head a vicious shake to clear the thoughts, Justin eased backward and forced his gaze to the tree line, mentally tracing the jagged tops of the dark pines until his heart stopped echoing in his ears.

When he returned his attention to Beth, her eyes locked on his and she smiled then took another dainty nip. Oh, man, was it possible he had entered the Garden of Eden with a temptress after all?

"What is this cabin?" Her question popped him out of his reverie.

He glanced at the dilapidated house. "It's the original McGee homestead. Built in the mid-eighteen hundreds by my great grandfather Keagan McGee for my great grandmother, Greta Orson McGee."

Instant recognition of the name flared in Beth's eyes. "Orson? As in *Orson's Folly* Orson?"

With a grin, Justin nodded once. "Yes, ma'am."

"So... do you, like, own the town or something?"

Justin's laugh echoed off the front of the house. "Nope. It's just named for my great-great grandfather, since he was one of the founding fathers."

"So someone named Orson was your great-great grandfather, and the town was named after him." Beth shook her head, and the rays of the sun painted her curls with hundreds of tiny golden glints. A smile pulled her lips upward in slow motion. "Far out."

Actually, since he'd grown up with the stories, it had always been just a bit of family history as far as Justin was concerned. But seeing it through Beth's eyes, he decided it was, indeed... *far out.*

"So what was Orson's *folly?*" she asked, mirth still dancing in her eyes.

"Some say it was coming out here from Chicago in the first place." Justin shrugged. "Some say it was mining for gold."

A frown settled over Beth's features. "I didn't think much gold was ever found in this part of Wyoming."

Justin stared at the old cabin. His grandfather had shared some wild stories around the campfire when the whole family had ridden roundups together. Some of them had been so fantastical, even as a young boy Justin had known they were tall tales. But others of them... He wasn't so sure they weren't based in truth, however obscure that truth might be. Rather than go into any of the tales, tall or otherwise, he simply shrugged. "I guess that would make mining here a folly then, wouldn't it?"

"So how did — Keagan, was it? How did *he* come to be here?"

"Keagan McGee was a drifter. The youngest son of seven, out of Chicago. Some accounts tell of a falling out with his father. Some say he just knew, as the youngest, he'd have to make his own fortune." Justin settled back on his elbows and watched as Beth looked around. She listened to him, asked intelligent questions. But her mind was also busy assessing their surroundings.

"So, he fell in love with a gold miner's daughter," she mused, pulling her knees up and bending them until she sat cross-legged.

"What makes you think they were in love?" Justin asked, laughing.

Beth gestured toward the flowers. "She planted daffodils. Like I said, happy flowers. They always make me think of spring — when they bloom. But you plant them in the fall. That takes patience and it means you have hope. That you know the winter might cover the ground with ice and snow, but when it's gone, there'll be flowers."

"All that deduction from what was planted in a garden?" Justin glanced over at the sea of yellow heads bobbing in the light breeze. Darned if they didn't look happy doing it.

"I think daffodils are my favorite flower ever." Beth reached out and cupped one of the yellow flower faces between her fingers. "Especially these old-fashioned yellow ones. Yellow's my favorite color."

It was his, too. Now.

No longer caring if she caught him, Justin openly watched as Beth went on to explain with a great deal of animated hand gestures about planting and naturalizing, how some people planted for patterns or to be in fashion, but she planted flowers that made her feel good, wherever she thought they'd be happiest. How one day she'd have a place of her own with a flower garden, a vegetable garden, and an herb garden.

On impulse, he snatched up her camera when she directed her attention to the flowers. By the time she turned back, he'd figured out the workings and focused it. When she laughed and struck a pose, he snapped her picture against the backdrop of happy yellow flowers.

* * *

"It's so gorgeous here, I could stay all day." Beth pulled her gaze from the old garden that had somehow withstood time itself, and her words caught in her throat along with her breath. Justin stared at her, an intense, almost hungry expression filling his eyes.

"What?" she managed to croak.

"Nothing..." he murmured, shaking his head slowly. "Everything. You keep talking like that, and I think I'm going to have to kiss you."

A wave of warmth rushed over her, swamping sanity and reason in its wake. "Oh, I wish you would," she whispered, swaying toward him.

Justin rolled to a sit and shifted closer. With a forefinger, he reached out and brushed a strand of hair from her face, allowing his fingers to linger on her neck just below her ear. He kept his gaze locked on her as he moved closer, slowly but smoothly, without any sense of hesitation. As he glided his lips over hers, he slipped the hand behind her head and cupped her neck.

Her eyelids grew heavy as desire shot through her on tiny darts of awareness. The kiss was soft and feathery, just a tease. He drew back slightly, but he only adjusted his angle, and then his lips were on hers again, still gentle but allowing no doubt who was in command.

His tender embrace was... fresh air and wide open spaces... apples and sunshine. Beth sighed, Entanglements of the kind he offered smacked of everything a girl like her should avoid.

The concept of avoidance was something she'd never quite grasped.

Her palm landed on Justin's chest as she leaned in, already knowing the truth. One kiss, one embrace, one lifetime... it was never going to be enough. When he moved closer, she slid her hand upward and hooked it on his shoulder, holding on while he spun her along on the ride of her life. His tongue swept her bottom lip, and she opened up for him with a little whimper.

Justin changed position again, pulling back and dragging Beth with him until she was sitting half in his lap. He moved the hand at her neck upward, weaving it through her hair, and then he closed his other arm around her waist and arched her closer, pushing aside the hem of her shirt and running his fingers along the base of her spine like he was playing a flute. He left her mouth to trail kisses along her jaw, upward to her temple, then back to her mouth, where his tongue once more sought hers, as though he couldn't quite get enough either.

Sensations swamped her and she lost herself to them. Tentatively, she touched her tongue to his, exploring, tasting, giving, taking. His palm rested flat on her back, warm against her bare skin as his embrace drew her deeper, and a tide of emotion pulled her under. She threw her head back with a groan of surrender.

A low answering moan issued from Justin's throat as he eased back with obvious regret, slipping his hand from her hair but leaving it on her shoulder just at the base of her neck. There, he traced a line that Beth couldn't see, but she knew from memory he was touching the edge of her poison ivy rash.

"It's going away," he murmured.

"I think my bath last night got most of the oil off, but I hope I don't spread it to you," she whispered.

"I'm okay with taking my chances." He traced another line, a crooked smile teasing his lips.

The sudden change of direction from passionate kissing to tender teasing threw her off balance. She should do something, pull out of his grasp to show him... what? That it hadn't affected her? It *had*. That she didn't care if he did it again? She *did* want him to do it again. So she didn't move.

He did, though. With incredible gentleness, he righted her and untangled their limbs. Then he looked at her long and hard. "We'd best be getting back."

* * *

Justin stuffed the remains of their lunch in the paper sack and shoved that into his saddlebag. As he shook out the blanket, Beth picked up the other end and walked toward him, meeting him in the middle. Their fingertips brushed and a static shock arced.

"Oh!" cried out Beth, and then she laughed. "I guess you have a shocking personality."

"Me?" Justin cracked a smile. He couldn't help it. Everything about her beguiled him, and her lighthearted spirit was infectious. "Maybe it's you who's electric."

She slid her hands along the edge of the blanket to one end while Justin reached the other, and they folded the ends together again. Then they repeated the same process one more time. By that stage, Justin could easily have folded the blanket without her help, but he was having too much fun meeting her across the blanket and grazing fingertips. Finally, it was too small to fold again and Justin pushed it into the saddlebag.

He moved closer to Abe so he could give Beth a boost into the saddle, but she stood, unmoving, near the daffodil garden, her camera resting in the palm of her hand. He smiled as he watched her cock her head to one side, looking like one of the sunny yellow blooms bobbing in the wind.

"Hey, Daffodil Gal, you ever gonna come over here so I can help you get on your horse?"

Instead of answering, she kept her back to him and held up a hand, one finger extended in a *wait-a-minute* gesture. She leaned toward the cabin, her head still angled.

"Do you hear that?" she asked softly.

Justin closed the distance between them in two strides and listened, but all he heard was the wind kissing the flowers. He shook his head, but before he could form words, he did hear something, a faint squeak from the direction of the dilapidated cabin.

"Something loose inside maybe," he acknowledged, ready to turn away.

Shaking her head, she laid a hand on his arm. "No, it's something alive. It's crying." Without waiting for him, she headed for the cabin.

Moving quickly, he caught up with her and grabbed her arm, stopping her just before she stepped on the ruined porch. "Beth, no! It's not safe inside." He backed away from the building, hauling her with him.

"But we have to help whatever's crying in there."

Justin frowned at the house. Odds were, if Beth was hearing the cries of an animal, it was a raccoon or a rabbit. If it was injured, it would be best to leave it, let nature take its course, or at most put the animal out of its misery. He cast a sidelong glance in Beth's direction. She was a city gal and a tenderheart. She wouldn't react well to either option.

"You *do* hear it, don't you?"

Reluctantly he nodded. "I *might* have heard something. But it's not safe for us to go inside." When she opened her mouth, no doubt to protest, he held up a hand. "Oh, I'll go in, but *you* need to wait out here."

Fresh alarm widened her eyes. "But if it's not safe... what if something happens to you?"

Emotions began to pluck at his heartstrings like a harpist's fingers. She'd driven halfway across the country in a van that should have seen its last roundup years before, probably without a second thought, but she balked at the thought of letting him enter a rundown shack because he'd said it was dangerous. The gal was an enigma.

And the puzzle of Bethany Rushton was one Justin planned to decipher.

The high-pitched squeaking came from the cabin again and dang it all if the sound *didn't* carry the eerie hint of something crying.

Justin scratched his jaw and gave a shrug. "Well, if anything happens, then you get on old Abe there as best you can, and head him up that trail right over there." He waved his hand at the trailhead to the right of the cabin. "Give him his head and he'll take you back to the ranch, and you look for Gus and tell him where I am."

Beth stared, first at him, then at the cabin, then back at him again. Finally she let out a long breath and gave a quick nod. "Okay."

Justin took off his hat and handed it to her. "I'll be right back."

Beth offered a wobbly smile. The breeze teased a wisp of golden hair into her eyes but she didn't seem to notice.

So Justin skimmed it back from her face for her. "Don't look so nervous, Daffodil Gal. I'm a cat on his first life."

Her smile faltered, then widened and some of the tension left the set of her shoulders.

With a half-grin, Justin grabbed his gloves from where he'd left them hooked on the saddle. His gaze fell on the Winchester in the holster, but he decided against taking it with him. Beth was freaked out enough without adding to her angst. Besides, more than likely it was a catbird nest, which meant the most *he* was likely to run into was an irate mother bird.

Making an exaggerated show of confidence, he strutted like a rooster toward the cabin, followed by Beth's giggles. He shot her a grin and a wink over his shoulder before turning to concentrate on the task ahead.

The entrance was covered by nothing more than a slab of decayed wood, barely hanging by one rusty hinge, which groaned when it moved. With one push forward the aged iron gave up its hold, and the door twisted away from him. Justin could only jerk backward as wood splintered and crashed into a pile of kindling on the floor. Dust rose from the heap of broken lumber and played in the sunbeams slanting through the collapsed roof.

He poked his head back through the opening. "I meant to do that."

Beth was already halfway to the cabin, and he motioned her back. She stopped but held her ground, sucking on her bottom lip as she continued to watch him, her face scrunched into a frown.

Returning his attention to the interior, Justin frowned. When he'd played in the cabin as a kid, it hadn't been near as close to collapse. He took a step along the outer edge of the room, wincing as the floor gave a little and moaned beneath his feet. As the dust settled, the putrid scent of cadaverine hit him full in the face. It was only by the blessing of a favorable wind they hadn't been assaulted by it as they ate.

Something in the homestead's ruins was dead.

He took another cautious step, then another, and elicited a rattling sound that ended with a creak. Each footfall into the room brought him closer to the sickening smell. Keeping his mouth closed and his breaths as shallow as possible, Justin managed to cross the room to the fireplace without falling through the floor. As he lifted part of the fallen roof, the odor punched him in the gut, threatening his lunch. At the same time, the squeaking he'd heard earlier returned with urgency, only this time he could discern the plaintive cries of a desperate baby animal. A flash of white caught his eye and he crouched, easing the brittle plywood aside.

The dog was dead. No doubt about that. Just as there could be no doubt that what had killed her was a small caliber bullet wound to her right hindquarter, which had festered. From the smell she hadn't been dead long. Plenty of flies, but no maggots. She was a skinny girl, hadn't been too old, a black-and-white border collie, and she looked vaguely familiar. Beneath her, three — no, four pups, little miniature copies of their mother, squirmed and cried. He picked one up, crooning to it as he settled it in the crook of his arm. By some miracle, the pups were all fat and healthy, although their fur was matted and they carried the stench of death. Their cries grew louder as he picked them up to carry them out. He did a quick check to make sure none had been left behind and then began the perilous journey to the door with his arms full of squirming pups.

Beth met him at the porch, a soft cry on her lips, a look of distress in her eyes. She reached to take two of them, but he shook his head. "I got this covered. These guys really stink." He walked toward the horses and stopped where they'd eaten their lunch. There, he laid the puppies on the ground and crouched down to examine them.

The pups all huddled together as they had in the nest. In the light of day, he could see they were about four weeks old. Their eyes were open and they looked fairly healthy, considering their beginning. The littlest one, a male, was missing part of his right rear leg. Justin ran his thumb over the stump. The leg simply ended at the knee, but he found no sign of trauma. It appeared the pup been born with the deformity. That sucked. No one would want a dog that couldn't work. Not in a ranching community.

"What happened to him?"

Justin grunted. "Birth defect. It happens sometimes." What in the name of Christmas was he going to do with the little guy? Or with the whole litter, come to that?

"Where's their mother?" asked Beth, a guarded look settling across her features.

Never had Justin hated delivering bad news more. Best not to pull any punches, though. "Dead. Probably going on twenty-four hours. Not sure what I'll do with these guys."

"Do with them?" Wariness turned to horror on Beth's features.

"They're still suckling. They'll need to be fostered or bottle fed."

"How on earth did they survive?"

Justin looked down at the little clubfoot pup nestled in the palm of his hand. "Only God knows," he admitted softly.

The mechanical *click-whirr* combination of camera shutter and auto-advance broke the silence, and Justin glanced up in time for Beth to snap another picture. He shook his head; he could only guess at his expression. Pictures of him tended to turn out showing an intimidating scowl on his face.

"What happened to the mother? Could you tell?" Beth glanced at the cabin.

Justin studied the woman in front of him as he considered how much to share with her. She leveled a steady look back, squinting against the glare of the bright afternoon sun. Each time the breeze ruffled her hair, tiny threads of gold glinted. *Tenderheart.* "Probably a fight with another animal," he hedged. Considering humans as animals, that wasn't a *bald-faced* lie.

"What will you do with her?"

Do with her? He'd planned on leaving her there for nature to clean up, but one look at Beth's stricken face put an end to that. The sun still hung high. Mid-afternoon. That meant plenty of daylight to dig a grave and still get back home.

So much for protecting her from the stink. She'd have to watch the pups while he took care of their mother. Sighing, Justin handed Beth the crippled pup and then pushed to his feet.

This time she didn't follow him to the ruined house.

Just inside the door, he picked up a broken two-by-four with a sharp end and took it to the side of the cabin, keeping well out of Beth's line of sight. Digging a grave without the benefit of a shovel would be awkward and slow going in the hard, dry dirt. He should have borrowed Beth's little garden trowel. He wouldn't go back to retrieve it, though. *Just get it over with.* He jammed the end of the board into the rocky earth and scraped back a pitiful layer of dust.

Justin worked up a sweat as the sun beat down on him, but at last the hole was large enough, and he slipped back into the cabin through a break in the wall to collect the remains of the mother dog. She sure was a sorry sight as he laid her in the grave. He made short work of pushing and pulling the dirt over her body, adding a few rocks from around the cabin's foundation for good measure. Scavengers would probably have her dug up before suppertime. Beth didn't need to know that, either. He returned to find her seated on the ground near the daffodil garden, smiling and laughing as she let the smelly pups crawl all over her.

"You know, they're looking for you to feed them now that their mama's out of the picture."

Beth looked up with her typical sunny expression. "How *will* we feed them?"

Justin's lips twitched. *We.* So she'd joined them together to care for the puppies, obviously ready and willing to take on the responsibility. He lifted a shoulder. "Gus'll be able to come up with some kind of formula we can feed 'em for the night. We'll get 'em to the vet tomorrow, and he'll probably be able to look after 'em until he finds homes."

He frowned, distracted by the thought that he'd seen the mother dog before — or one like her, at any rate. If he could figure out who she belonged to, he might find the answer as to why she'd been shot.

Beth's voice brought him back from his dark thoughts. "You mean you won't keep them?" she asked, her face falling.

In the space of time it took his heart to beat once, Justin knew he'd never willingly deny Bethany Rushton anything *her* heart desired. He found himself nodding. "Sure, we can keep 'em. Just have to get the vet to check 'em out."

Her eyes glistened. "Even the one who's missing a foot?"

Oh, man, she wasn't going to cry, was she? Any second his heart would punch its way out of his chest. "Sure, we can keep the one without the foot. What're you planning to call him?"

She nibbled on one corner of her bottom lip while she considered the pup. "Lucky seems kind of obvious, doesn't it?" Beth glanced up as if seeking approval.

A smile tugged at Justin's lips and he gave over to it. "A three-legged dog named Lucky? Kind of sounds like the beginning of a sad song to me."

Beth set the pup down a few inches from the rest of the litter. Immediately he pushed himself along the ground until he was pressed against his siblings. "Wow, look at you go. That leg certainly isn't holding you back, is it, little guy?"

Justin chuckled. "I'd say he thinks he's off to the races."

"That's it!" Beth picked the puppy up again and nuzzled him. "Derby! Like Kentucky Derby. Only he'll be Wyoming Derby."

When she tossed her head back with a happy laugh, Justin's heart squeezed against his lungs. She could have named the pup Cow Pie for all he cared. Whatever made Beth happy made Justin *insanely* happy.

"Well, now that he's named, that only leaves the problem of how we're getting them all back home," said Justin when he found the breath to speak.

"I could maybe carry a couple of them," suggested Beth.

"Not a good idea. If one squirms and you lose your grip, he could fall. Or you could." Justin rummaged through his saddlebag, pulling out the remains of their picnic and the blanket. "I think they'll fit in here. Might be a bit snug, so we'll take a break partway home to check on 'em."

He split the lunch sack at the seam and used it to line the leather saddlebag. Then he picked up the puppies one at a time and laid them carefully into the bag, resting for a second to let them adjust themselves. When they stopped wriggling, he folded the saddlebag closed.

After he boosted Beth into the saddle, Justin hoisted himself across the worn leather. He folded their picnic blanket across the saddle in front of him and started Zeke on the trail for home, casting a quick glance over his shoulder to be certain Abe followed with Beth.

Chapter Eight

It only took about an hour to get back to the ranch, and they went in a completely different direction than Beth would have chosen. The whole time she'd thought they were traveling away from the house, they'd been heading home! So much for exploring the extensive McGee spread on her own. Who knew where she'd end up?

They pulled their horses up in the stable yard, and Beth actually managed to do a decent job of dismounting. At least she didn't lose her balance, and this time Justin wasn't standing right behind her to surprise her heart into high gear. Of course, whether her racing heart then had been the result of being startled or if it was from being close to Justin was debatable, since her pulse leaped with awareness at every little glance the man gave her.

She scratched an itch on her neck. At least it hadn't bothered her for most of the day.

Justin looked her way and raised an eyebrow. "You okay?"

"I'm peachy," she said, rubbing her arm. "Just starting to itch again. No big deal."

He inclined his head in an *if-you-say-so* movement then unbuckled his saddlebag and began unloading puppies. Beth made it to his side in time to be handed two of the squirming babies. She smiled to herself when she noticed he held onto Derby. Had that been by design?

"What do you have there?"

The voice came from the shadows beyond the stable door. A man of medium height stepped into the sunlight and sauntered across the yard toward them. Stocky of build, with a shock of dark hair sticking out at crazy angles from beneath his gray Stetson, he was maybe fifteen or sixteen years older than Justin by Beth's best guess, but he appeared to carry the weight of more than his years.

"Beth, this is Gus Hanson, the Cross MC foreman," introduced Justin.

Gus tipped his hat. "Ma'am. Nice to meet you." He shifted his focus to the squirming mass of fur in Justin's hands. "Got yourself some pups, eh? What happened to their ma?"

"Dead," said Justin, flipping the saddlebag closed again.

Gus ran a finger over Derby's body, frowning when he got to the back leg. "Huh, I guess this guy needs seeing to. Want me to take care of him?"

Take care of him? Beth's heart leaped with alarm at Gus's matter-of-fact tone. He meant take care of him as in *feed* him, right?

Beth's gaze flashed between the two men, noting the guy signals they sent with their eyes. She clenched her hands into fists against the urge to snatch Derby out of Justin's hands until both men promised they wouldn't hurt him.

With a fleeting glance in her direction, Justin shook his head. "Naw, he's made it against the odds this far. Let's see how far he goes."

One bushy eyebrow raised, but Gus said nothing.

Just to be on the safe side, Beth took possession of Derby, ignoring the baffled expression that crossed Justin's face. "I can help take care of them. They just need to be cleaned up and fed, right?" The little puppy stretched his neck toward her. Beth brought him closer to her face, but he still smelled terrible and she stopped short, thinking better of kissing his matted fur until he'd had a bath.

"Gotta find a way to feed 'em," said Gus, taking one of the other puppies from Justin and examining it closely. A few deep wrinkles sliced across his forehead with his frown. "Didn't MacKay have a pair of black-and-white herding dogs? Might be their ma was one of his."

Startled, Beth looked up. "MacKay? These might be Alice and Brody's puppies?" Her heart thumped upward into her throat, making it hard to breathe, impossible to swallow. Alice would surely make sure Derby got put to sleep, especially if she knew Beth had taken a liking to him.

Justin looked at the ground and scuffed the toe of his boot in the dust. "No..." He shook his head as he handed off the rest of the puppies to Gus. "No, the pups' mother was brown-and-white." Abruptly he turned and strode toward the stable, calling over his shoulder as he did. "We have to find something to feed these guys with. Then maybe we can get Beth started and you and I can take care of the horses."

"I got plenty of calf bottles, but those'll be too big." Gus took his hat off and scratched his head as he followed Justin, walking more slowly and with a bit of a limp.

Beth stared after them, frowning. "Oh, hey, don't worry about me. I'll just — stand here," she muttered, scratching at the sensation of crawling irritation on her neck. The itch became the sting of a thousand bees, and longing rose for another oatmeal bath.

With a sigh, she dropped to the ground and crossed her legs. Within seconds, the puppies crawled over to her and nuzzled her knees. She stroked one tiny black nose with her forefinger. "You're all going to need names, aren't you?"

The puppy latched onto her thumb and tried to suckle. *Poor hungry baby.* Beth craned her neck, trying to see into the stable, but Justin and Gus seemed to have been swallowed by the dark interior.

* * *

The workbench seemed as good as anything for taking

out his frustration, so Justin slammed the flat of his hand against the wooden surface.

"Easy there," said Gus as he set a latex orphaned-calf nipple on the bench. "That bench do something to offend you?"

Justin blew out a long frustrated breath. "No, more like *I* did something to offend me. I lied."

"Lied about what?"

"The mother dog."

"What about the mother dog?"

Justin turned to face his friend. "Beth didn't see the mother dog, but I got the full view, since I buried her. She was a black-and-white border collie, and I *thought* she looked familiar." He shrugged away his revulsion and anger at the memory of the lifeless animal and her senseless death. "It wasn't until you mentioned MacKay that I realized it was probably his dog."

Gus squinted at Justin, clearly having trouble following the conversation. "Then why did you say the dog was *brown-and-white*?"

Justin removed his hat and set it on the bench then picked up the calf nipple. He squeezed the supple latex between thumb and fingers and watched it spring back into shape. "We might be able to make a smaller nipple by cutting this down some."

Gus cleared his throat. "Answer my question, kid. Why'd you lie about the dog?"

Justin kept his eyes on the nipple while he spoke. "Beth is Alice MacKay's sister from back east." He watched his lifelong friend, his mood every bit as defiant as it had been at sixteen, when Gus had caught him with a bottle of whiskey he'd liberated from his father's liquor cabinet.

"What?" Gus rubbed his jaw. "She's *their* kin? What the devil is she still doin' *here*?" He waved his hand, clearly specifying the ranch.

"She's not—" Justin began forcefully, then lowered his voice. "She's not like them. She's sweet. Kind." *And pretty, and funny, and I just might be falling for her.*

"Yeah, and we all thought Alice was going to set Brody on the straight and narrow. But *that* woman turned out to be a damn rattler." Gus snorted. "Only thing worse than having one rattlesnake crawl out from under a rock is having two of 'em."

As though they had minds of their own, Justin found his hands curling back into fists. He clenched his jaw and concentrated on forcing his anger down.

Gus Hanson had lived on the Cross MC since Jack, his single father, had signed on as foreman before Justin was born. About fifteen years separated them, and as a kid Justin had followed Gus everywhere, probably harangued the good-natured older boy more than an actual baby brother would have.

When Gus and his father had been involved in a tractor accident that had claimed not only Jack Hanson's life, but the life of Justin's grandfather, Ryan McGee, as well, Justin's father had taken over as head of the household and had offered Gus the job his father had held.

They had a history together, Justin reminded himself, slowly unfurling his fingers. Gus was every bit as much family as if they had the same blood. Justin had idolized the man who had barely left boyhood behind when he'd filled his father's shoes. But if Justin's idol didn't quit comparing Beth to her rattlesnake sister, he would find himself flat on his back and possibly missing a few teeth.

Gus cocked his head to the side and took a good, long look at Justin. Sighing heavily, he shook his head. "Oh, kid. You go fallin' for kin of Brody MacKay and you're asking for a world o' hurt."

Funny, Gus had said something similar about the whiskey. He'd been right about that, since Jim McGee had noticed the missing liquor and come looking for it before Justin had even managed to crack the top on the bottle. Without getting a taste of the whiskey he'd pilfered, Justin had ended up with a month of lost privileges and two months of extra chores.

But Gus *wasn't* right about Beth.

"She's not *Brody's* kin," Justin muttered under his breath.

Making a rude noise, Gus turned and stared into the

stable yard. "Now, you know kin by marriage is still kin. And she *is* kin to Alice."

Justin picked up his hat and jammed it on his head. Then he snatched the latex nipple and strode past Gus toward the doorway. "I'll rig up something with this at the house and be out in a few minutes to see to the horses."

Gus stopped Justin with a hand on his shoulder. "Just take your girl and take care of the pups. I'll see to the horses." He gave a quick squeeze and then let go. "This time."

Justin swallowed over a sudden lump of emotion in his throat. It was all the peacemaking gesture his friend was likely to make. But it was enough.

He was nearly through the door when Gus called him. Stopping short, Justin drew in a deep breath, knowing exactly what was coming next.

"Did you find any sign of those missing cows?"

"No." He swung around and met Gus's steady gaze. "No, but someone's strung some shiny new wire along the northwest pasture."

"Is that a fact." The words weren't spoken as a question. Gus glanced in Justin's direction, but Justin knew he was looking through the stable door toward Beth. "You know whose land *that* joins."

Yeah, Justin did know. He also trusted the gut feeling that told him Beth had no knowledge of missing cattle beyond what he'd told her himself.

"Whole nest of rattlers, you ask me," Gus muttered, grabbing a feed bucket and heading toward the back of the stable.

* * *

The pups had cleaned up well, and the meal was working its magic. The one in Justin's hands greedily sucked the milk from one of the makeshift bottles he'd fashioned with scraps of the latex calf nipple, rubber bands, and his mother's glass salt and pepper shakers.

Seated on the floor next to him, Beth pushed her legs out and straightened her back against the front of the dryer. Her gentle laugh teased little chills along his spine. She lifted the empty bottle from the floor next to her and studied it. "Are you sure your mom won't be mad that we used these?"

"Naw, she won't give a hoot." *She'll just threaten to kill me.* But Mary McGee wasn't going to know anything about it if Justin had his way. And as long as he remembered to pick up a new salt and pepper set when he took Beth to town the next day so Walt could look at her van, his mother would remain blissfully unaware.

Justin set down the empty bottle and laid the pup in the wicker laundry basket — he'd need to pick up one of those, too. The tiny black-and-white fuzzball immediately sought contact with the other pups, one of her two sisters and Derby. Beth laid the last puppy in the basket and stroked her fur with one finger until her head drooped and her eyes closed.

"Ick... I'm kind of dusty and — grimy." Beth scratched at the back of her left hand. "Itchy, too. I was wondering if I could maybe clean up?"

Justin's lips tugged, but he forced the smile back. "Well, that could be a problem. See, we're only allowed one bath a week out here."

Beth's face fell, but she recovered nicely and smiled. "Oh, I see. Okay."

"But you know, I don't want to see you in misery all grimy and... itchy. So I'll give up my weekly bath for you." He allowed the smile to form.

"Oh, no!" She was quick to protest, shaking her head as she spoke. "I don't want to do that. I mean, you need to get cleaned up, too."

"Now, that's no trouble at all. I'll just use the water hole out back."

Her eyes widened, but Justin wasn't sure if it was astonishment or hope he saw in them.

"Really?" she whispered.

His smile widened into a grin and he shook his head, unable to contain the chuckle. "No. We don't limit our baths to Saturday nights here. Go on up and get the trail off ya."

One hand flew to her mouth, and Justin wasn't entirely convinced she wasn't about to punch his lights out with the other. But she only stood and planted her hands on her hips.

"Justin McGee!" She glared down at him through narrowed eyes. "And here I was thinking you were one of the nicest men I'd ever met." Turning on her heel, she trounced from the laundry room without sparing him another glance.

He stared at the empty doorway for several minutes, then he leaned back against the washing machine until his head banged gently on the shiny white appliance as he considered Gus's words about the MacKays. Justin had no doubt Alice was every bit the rattlesnake Gus considered her. And he sure as the devil knew Brody wasn't to be trusted.

So what in heck are you doing with one of their family, Justin?

As he pulled a hand over his face, ending at his jaw, the day's whiskers scratched his palm, and he paused. He could do with a good cleaning up himself. Pushing to his feet, he took a last glance at the sleeping pups then padded through the kitchen. The shower in the bunkhouse beckoned like a siren's call.

* * *

The water eased aches in muscles Beth had been unaware she possessed before the long ride on horseback. The actors in movies and on TV made riding look so easy. *Justin* made riding look effortless. But, damn, her muscles screamed at her that riding a horse took *effort*. Lots and lots of it.

She closed her eyes and sank into the warm embrace of the bath. Instantly, Justin's voice whispered through her memory. *I'm going to have to kiss you.*

And then he had… he'd kissed her until she could barely remember her name. The rush of heat that spread through her as her thoughts drifted back to those kisses had little to do with the bath water.

Umm-umm, the man can kiss.

Did he regret it? He'd ended the kiss just as she'd given herself over to it. It had been just the two of them out there. Had she done something wrong? Doubt crept in like an early morning fog. Maybe he wasn't free to indulge in a few kisses.

He lived with his parents and she'd seen no sign of a wife — not that she'd asked. But even if he had no wife, he might have a girlfriend... or a fiancée. He didn't really act like he was attached to anyone, but still...

It didn't really matter anyway, did it? After all, she wouldn't be sticking around much longer. She'd taken the spring term off, but summer semester would start in just over a month. She'd waited a whole year for the opening in independent study of plant genetics with Professor Everett.

So why was the idea of getting home to take the class suddenly not as appealing as it had been just a couple of days earlier?

Beth swished her toe through the water and watched it ripple off the edges of the white porcelain. "Justin," she whispered into the empty room. In less than twenty-four hours, he'd gotten under her skin — *far* less time than that, if she was being honest. Specifically, when they'd lain on their backs looking up at the stars the evening before, and he'd not only listened to her talk about them without laughing, he'd asked questions. He'd shown a level of interest in what she'd said that couldn't be feigned. As they'd watched the stars winking at them, she'd experienced the kind of connection with Justin McGee most people never felt in a lifetime of searching.

That was why it was going to kill a part of her deep inside when she left.

Then why leave? whispered the tiny voice in her heart.

"Because I have to," she murmured. She'd worked so hard for the grades to be accepted at U of M, and not just into one of the women's professions of teaching or nursing, but into a science program. She'd always dreamed of being so much more than a career housewife married to a young upwardly mobile executive working in her daddy's automotive firm.

Riding the range with Justin had been so real, though. The wide open space had her reconsidering every life choice she'd ever made. Being a rancher's wife was a far cry from being an executive's wife. *What if...*

Beth shivered. The water had gone cold while she'd been daydreaming. Quickly, she pulled the plug, then stood and stepped onto the plush blue mat to dry off. After she pulled on more of that oh-so-decadent underwear she'd indulged in, she glanced at her clean clothes and suddenly didn't want to put on jeans and a plain shirt.

With the towel wrapped around her and secured in the middle, she pulled the door open and poked her head into the hallway. The house had a decidedly deserted feel about it. She tiptoed along the hallway to the guest room where Justin had set her up and closed the door behind her. Then she stopped dead. The clothing she'd worn the day before, which Justin had laundered, lay neatly folded on the bed, the tiny bits of lace and satin underwear sitting right on top. Embarrassment warmed her face; that was quickly becoming a chronic condition.

Suddenly everything she'd packed seemed wrong. She'd gone for a mix of sensible and trendy and had ended up with an impractical collection of clothing that made her look like a lost hippie or a gypsy. She'd have to get fairly creative to look feminine and alluring. A laugh popped out.

"What do you think he's going to do, Beth? Declare his undying love after a day and a kiss?"

She stood with her hand hovering over one of the dresses she'd packed. Made of soft cotton in denim blue, it was stamped with the outlines of white hearts in various sizes. The dress fit snugly at her bust and waist, but flared out at her hips. An intentionally uneven hemline just kissed her knee on the right and then draped to her calf on the left. The rounded neckline scooped fairly low, with quarter-sized eyelet cutouts in the shape of hearts lining the edges and revealing more skin than she was used to showing. Too casual for the parties she'd attended with her parents back in Bloomfield Hills, it had been an impulse buy that Beth had thought she might wear on her trip. She smiled. Wear it she would! It seemed like a prom dress in comparison to the jeans and shirts she'd been dressing in.

What would Justin think if she appeared for dinner in such impractical attire? He'd probably think she'd read too much into his kiss — or that she was coming on to him. She squared her shoulders. Well, so what? Maybe she *was* thinking of coming on to him. He could always say no.

And rip her heart out with it.

Beth moaned and moved the dress aside in favor of an ivory-colored peasant blouse. She had that partway over her head when she changed her mind and pulled it off again. Snatching the dress from her suitcase, she shook it out. If it was wrinkled, she wouldn't wear it.

It wasn't wrinkled.

Holding the dress up in front of her, Beth checked her reflection in the full-length mirror mounted on the back of the door. Darn it all. She liked the dress, and she wanted to look like a girl for once. If Justin even noticed the outfit... well, that could only be a plus. She pulled the garment over her head and zipped it before she could change her mind. Then she slipped on a pair of low-heeled hemp sandals and twirled in front of the mirror, enjoying the cool feel of the fabric as it swished against her legs. On impulse, she grabbed the bottle of cologne she hadn't really expected to use on her trip and spritzed just a bit at the base of her throat, glad her rash hadn't spread that far.

She left the bedroom, no longer quite so worried she was making a mistake, but terrified she'd chicken out. But at the soft click when she shut the door, a sense of calm settled over her like a favorite blanket.

The stairway banister was cool beneath her touch. Its smooth, dark oak attested to the glide of many hands over the decades. What would it be like to know the kind of rich family history Justin had described as they'd sat by the original homestead? What had it been like for him... growing up in a house that had also seen prior generations grow up?

Chapter Nine

Justin entered the foyer, shuffling through the letters he'd retrieved from the mailbox, and huffed out a sigh. "Bills, bills, and bills," he muttered under his breath.

Time enough for those tomorrow.

He stepped into the office and dropped the lot of them on top of the pile his father had left in the middle of the desk. With a last glance at the growing stack, he shook his head. Best allow some extra time to go through the bulk of those, too. His dad wouldn't be in shape to do much of anything when he got home. But no point in ruining the end of a good day.

He stepped out of the office, pulling the door shut behind him. Beth stood poised on the bottom step, one hand on the banister, and his heart stumbled. She'd left her hair loose and it floated about her shoulders like a golden veil. Her dress was the color of faded blue jeans, but the material looked soft as combed cotton. He brushed his thumbs across his fingertips, just itching to find out, but at the same time afraid he'd rumple her. The uneven hemline sparked a vision of hands sneaking under and lifting the bottom of that dress higher and... higher. He flicked his eyes upward, continuing their appraising journey lest that particular scenario became too tempting.

A long silver chain dipped beneath the low neckline of her dress. Oh, how intriguing it would be to follow that chain with his lips, taking the time to taste that expanse of fair skin until he discovered what was hidden in the valley between her breasts.

Breathe! It seemed he'd forgotten how to pull air into his lungs. And he sure wished someone would jump-start his heart.

With perfect timing, she took the last step into the foyer, angling her head and sending him a timid smile. "I've been living in nothing but jeans for the past three weeks. I kind of felt like dressing up a little."

"Good," he managed to squeeze out over a too-tight throat. He refrained — barely — from tugging at his shirt collar.

When she widened her smile, Justin's heart kicked into gear with an electrical jolt that started in his chest and arced outward. Returning her smile, he stepped closer. The sweet scent of a light perfume floated up to tantalize. He skimmed his fingertips upward along her bare arms, pausing in his exploration at her shoulders where her skin met the fabric of her dress.

If Beth had looked uncomfortable, he'd have stepped back. She didn't appear in the least ill at ease. Her emerald eyes glistened in the soft lamplight from the side table. The same radiance was reflected by her wild curls, and every movement of her head reminded Justin of sparks rising off a campfire. Beth parted her lips and swayed in his direction. With a soft moan, he gave up the fight, slipping one hand around to her back and lifting the other to cup her cheek.

He took her lips slowly, savoring their softness, intrigued by the fruity taste of her lip gloss. Small fires kindled every place their bodies touched. Turning his head for a better angle, he deepened the kiss. When she sucked on his bottom lip, want and need collided in a storm of explosive bolts that left him helpless to his rampaging desire. Their tongues dueled briefly, and then he slid his into the welcoming sweetness of her mouth.

One of them groaned. Or maybe it was both of them. Her softness seemed to melt over him, around him as he surged against her, pressing her back against the wall. Then she settled her hands at his waist and held on as she sagged into his embrace. Her palms seared through his shirt, igniting a firestorm.

It was almost too much.

Restraining a groan of frustration, Justin gentled the kiss, drawing back slowly. But he couldn't resist trailing butterfly kisses along her jaw. Couldn't resist dragging his mouth down her neck to settle at the base of her throat where her pulse beat like a hummingbird's wings. There, he closed his eyes and inhaled the subtle scent of her perfume. He'd remember it forever. "What's that fragrance?"

She tensed. "Wha-what?"

"Your perfume." The words came out in a hoarse croak, but he didn't clear his throat. "I love it." That was an understatement. Combined with her natural scent, it was intoxicating, addictive.

Beth laughed softly. "It's called White Lace."

"You should always wear it," he murmured, burying his face in her neck and breathing deeply once more, knowing he was lost. Impossible as it seemed, after meeting Beth Rushton just a day earlier, he needed her with everything in him; needed her far beyond simple desire that had been fueled by the proximity of a beautiful woman. And he'd want her forever with everything in him.

He retreated a step, knowing he was at the edge, not ready to push boundaries, his own included.

"Justin?" Beth gazed up at him, the glow on her face an indication that she'd been moved as well. She leaned into him again, but he slipped an arm around her waist and held her back.

Reluctant to lose the contact, he rested his forehead against hers. "I... think maybe we'd better come up for air here."

She sighed and squared her shoulders, but a tender smile still curved her lips.

Settling a hand in the small of her back had seemed like a good idea until he did it and just in touching her nearly lost his hard-won control. "What do you say we find some dinner?" He eased them in the direction of the kitchen over the protests from his body that he was leading Beth in the wrong direction.

From her shy sidelong glance and the red staining her cheeks, he suspected she was experiencing similar feelings.

* * *

Chills worked along Beth's spine, starting where Justin rested his hand as he guided her to the kitchen. She knew the way by now, but suspected if he hadn't helped her along, she might have walked in a tight circle in the foyer until she dropped of exhaustion.

He talked as they went, his voice deeper than normal and a little husky. "I pulled some chicken from the freezer this morning so it should be defrosted. Want to help me fry it up?"

"Fry it up?" Panic fluttered up from her stomach. "You mean, like— cook it? In a pan?"

Justin flashed a grin. "That's usually what 'fry it up' means."

And... that was her cue to tell him she didn't know how to cook, and then he could have a good laugh at her expense.

Then they were in the kitchen and Justin dropped his hand from her back as he crossed the room. A sizzling smile in her direction when he pulled out a frying pan sent tingles from her fingertips to her middle and back. Justin set the pan on the range with a clatter and then walked to the refrigerator and pulled out a white serving plate on which rested a whole raw chicken minus feathers and head.

Beth took one look at the pale whitish pink meat and shuddered. Oh, she'd really rather go back to kissing Justin. She didn't... *really* need to eat to survive, did she?

He set the platter on the counter next to the range and pulled a knife from a butcher block holder. Then he looked over at Beth, obviously expecting her to join him by the dead bird.

Bile rose in her throat. "Ahh, was that — ummm...

walking around here at some point?"

Glancing at the chicken and then back at Beth, Justin broke out in laughter. It was a few minutes before his chortles subsided enough so he could speak. "No, with chicken, you're safe. My mom refuses to keep chickens on the ranch."

"I like your mom already," Beth muttered under her breath, sending a stern glare in Justin's direction.

"She's going to like you, too," murmured Justin, turning back to the chicken on the counter. The overhead light flashed on the stainless steel as he deftly sliced through the meat.

Beth's breath caught. She hadn't expected him to hear her. Fairly quickly Justin had separated legs and wings from the body, and then worked on the thighs. She didn't want to watch, but his movements were so self-assured and easy, she found herself mesmerized. She should contribute to dinner, but she had no idea what she *could* contribute. So she hovered in the middle of the kitchen. What did Justin expect her to do? Before she could put voice to the question, he answered as though reading her thoughts.

"There's a potato bin in the corner." He pointed with the knife.

Beth hastily shifted her gaze to the direction of his gesture and away from the gross piece of chicken skin that clung to the tip of the knife. There was the bin all right...

"Can you grab us a few and peel them for mashed potatoes?"

Peel them? Beth worried at her lower lip as she shuffled across the kitchen to the bin and lifted the top. An earthy smell wafted up, not unpleasant but certainly a scent she'd never have expected to discover in a kitchen. She stared at the pile of brown tubers. *They're just plants, or parts of plants, anyway.* The problem was, she hadn't a clue how to remove the peels. Casting a surreptitious glance over her shoulder, Beth noted Justin had finished cutting up the chicken and was systematically rinsing the individual pieces at the sink and setting them into a bowl. She refocused her attention on the potatoes. How many should she peel? How many potatoes would two people eat? Surely not more than one each.

That decision made, she reached in and plucked two

large brown potatoes from the bin and shut the lid. The next problem hit her as she turned around, unsure of where she should carry her prizes. Where exactly did one peel potatoes?

Justin finished rinsing the chicken, set the bowl aside, and looked up, smiling when he caught Beth's eye. He motioned for her to join him at the sink. His glance fell to the potatoes she carried and he raised a brow. "Not very hungry?"

Actually, she was starving, and her stomach grumbled softly as if to prove it. Justin's words seemed to indicate she hadn't chosen enough potatoes, so she shrugged and played the *helpless female* card. "I couldn't carry them all."

"Gotcha." Justin winked as he crossed the room to the bin, returning in short order with two more fat potatoes. "Do you use a vegetable peeler or a paring knife?"

Beth stared, unable to form an answer simply because she had no earthly idea what a vegetable peeler was. While she could guess what a paring knife was, she had no idea how she would use a knife to take off only the peels. Scrape the surface maybe?

She opened her mouth to explain, preparing herself for his ridicule, when he simply pulled out the second drawer next to the sink and rummaged through the utensils until he found what he wanted. After he pushed the drawer shut, he held up an instrument that looked like a knife with a split in the middle that formed an inverted blade.

She eyed the tool with suspicion. That had to be the peeler, though it looked more like a knife that someone had turned inside-out. It didn't look all that complicated to use. But it did look sharp. She accepted it with two fingers, not having a clue what she was going to do with it.

Beth cleared her throat. "Justin, um... I don't — *cook*."

He stared, his face showing no expression at all. Then he tilted his head and his forehead knit into a confused frown. "Oh. You don't cook." He sounded like she'd just confessed to having arrived from Mars.

She let out an impatient sigh. "I— Actually, I don't know *how* to cook. I never learned." She averted her gaze, waiting for his laughter. When none came, she chanced a peek in his direction.

Justin's eyes twinkled and he wore a bemused smile. He rubbed two fingers back and forth along his jaw as he studied her. No doubt contemplating how utterly useless one female could possibly be.

She offered him a weak smile and a tiny shrug. "Sorry."

He stared a second longer before he moved, and she scarcely had time to register the intent in his eyes before his lips claimed hers. He moved closer, crowding her against the cabinet. This was no gentle lead-up to a soft kiss. It was straight-out passion — fervent, unleashed, and wild.

Raw need surged through her. Of their own accord, her hands crept upward along his taut chest, where she fisted them in his shirt and clung as he took her on another heated foray into the land of longing.

Justin stroked his tongue along her lips and she shivered, parting them beneath his touch, granting him access. Pressing herself shamelessly against him, Beth was convinced the flames of pleasure licking at them would soon ignite. And she didn't care. She understood, without knowing how, that on some level she'd always belonged with Justin. She'd only been waiting to find him.

With his left hand, he tunneled into her hair and cupped the back of her head, holding her steady when she felt anything but. He slid his right hand from her waist, grazing her hip, stopping at her outer thigh. She felt him twist the fabric of her dress into a knot where his hand rested, and for a moment Beth thought he intended to yank the garment from her body.

But he seemed to merely be using it as a tether to hold her in place. He needn't have worried. She wasn't going anywhere. *Not yet, anyway.* The sudden thought intruded with a clamor of warning bells.

The alarm bells sounded again, their strident trill cutting through the desire-induced haze in Beth's brain like the foghorn on the Lake St. Clair lighthouse.

Justin withdrew with a groan, but the clanging peal continued to drill its way through Beth's awareness. With a lingering look in her direction, he inched his way along the kitchen counter. As another shrill ring exploded in the relative silence, he muttered a curse under his breath and picked up the receiver of the avocado-green telephone on the wall next to the door. "Hello," he almost snarled.

Beth turned away to give him some privacy.

"Oh, hello, *Alice*." Justin spoke a bit forcefully and when Beth glanced at him, his gaze bored into her.

Stark fear opened her eyes so wide they hurt, and she was certain they'd explode from their sockets. Shaking her head, she made frantic negative hand gestures. Finally, crossing the space between them, she laid a hand on his forearm and squeezed. Hard. How had her sister found her?

"Who? Your *sister?* I... didn't know you had a sister." He winced as he spoke the lie and Beth loosened her grip on his arm. "Is she as pretty as you?" He listened and then he chuckled at something Alice said. "You'll have to be sure to introduce me when she shows up at your place then." He chuckled again. "No, you know how it is. If a stranger blows through Orson's Folly, everyone in town knows inside of ten minutes." He pinned Beth with a stare while he listened some more. "Nope, haven't heard a bit of gossip." His lip curled in distaste and he forced a laugh. "I sure will. If I see a young lady who looks lost, I'll steer her where she needs to go."

He isn't giving me up!

Biting her lip to hold back tears of relief, Beth turned away. Her body trembled inside and out. She heard Justin speaking as though from a distance, knew he was forming words, but hadn't a clue what he was saying. The clatter of the phone being hung up registered. Afraid of what she might read on his face, in his eyes, Beth couldn't look at him.

Several moments passed in silence. Then he startled her by stepping close and sliding his arms around her waist from the back. He dropped his head onto her shoulder and turned his face inward, his warm breath tickling her neck. "Let's get this dinner started. I'll show you how to peel potatoes." He aimed for the kitchen sink and walked them there without turning her loose.

Standing behind her, Justin guided Beth in the process of removing the peels from the pile of potatoes. As the brown peels collected in the white enamel sink, Beth knew an insane sense of accomplishment. With the last potato peeled, she ran her forefinger over a two-inch chip on the edge of the sink. The blackish mark stood out against the enamel like a scar.

"My mom made that with her iron skillet during the only argument I remember between her and my dad." His voice was quiet, almost reverent. "Just about a year ago now."

She opened her mouth to tell him she hadn't meant to be nosy. When she looked in his eyes, the intense sadness there seeped into her soul and she touched him on the arm instead.

Slowly he set one of the peeled potatoes on the cutting board and sighed, and the moment was over. "This is a paring knife." He held up a short but lethal-looking blade with a wooden handle. "And you just cut these into chunks like this." He drew the knife through the potato's middle with a quick stroke. He continued to slice through the pieces until he had a handful of one-inch cubes. Using the edge of the knife, he swiped them into the pan of water.

Next, he placed the knife into Beth's hand and she gulped, fumbling the implement before finally managing an awkward grasp. It was ridiculous that she was so clumsy; she'd used knives to collect samples from plants and make grafts. But when she set the blade against the slippery potato, it slipped off. What the heck was wrong with her? All she needed to make the evening complete would be to cut off a finger. She jumped when Justin placed his hand over hers and guided it back to the potato.

"Think of it as one of your specimens you're cutting up," he whispered, his breath stirring the hair at her neck.

How did he know?

A giggle escaped, stealing the last bit of air in her lungs. Beth concentrated on drawing her next breath but it wasn't easy as the sharp edge of desire scissored through her. He gave her no time to think about any of that, though. Using gentle pressure, Justin took her through the motions he'd demonstrated moments earlier, though she barely felt the potato or the knife.

Why didn't he ask her about Alice? The knife handle rolled, and she sliced off a tiny sliver of potato.

"Oops!" He reset the knife. "There ya go."

"Justin..."

"Shh, just cut," he murmured.

Was he somehow in her head? He seemed to be on some kind of mission to keep her mind off her family. But she knew the subject wouldn't be off limits forever. His interest in the topic was definitely the third party in the room with them. He stepped away, obviously leaving the last potato for her to chunk while he busied himself at the stove.

Beth shivered at the sudden chill left by his absence.

* * *

Justin slid the pan of breaded and browned chicken into the oven to finish cooking, just as Beth awkwardly cut her last potato chunk and plopped it into the waiting pot of water. She smiled up at him, her sense of accomplishment rolling off her in waves he could feel. She was an enigma, a riddle of contradictions that he found intriguing on so many levels, he didn't know where to begin the discovery process. He knew she wanted to finish college and work in science. But when he'd found out Beth couldn't cook because she'd never learned, it had blown his mind.

In the moment she'd confessed her secret, her demeanor half-defiance and half-apology, she hadn't been the self-assured scientific mind she normally presented. She'd been vulnerable, expecting... something, some reaction from him. And that incongruity with the personality he'd come to know had been just enough to chase good sense and accountability to the back of his mind. In that moment, he'd known he was hers and always would be.

Then the phone call from Alice had added another variable to the equation of Bethany Rushton. It had been easy to guess from Beth's reluctance to stay with Alice and Brody, not to mention the rather broad statement she'd made about not getting along with her sister, that they weren't exactly candidates for the All-American Happy Family Award. And the way Alice had gushed over her sister and gone on about how worried she was didn't jibe with Beth's words and actions.

So he'd lied, or at least hedged the truth, which,

according to his mother, was still a lie. But one look at Beth's pale face and he'd figured he might as well be hung for a cow as a calf. Or maybe in this case a herd of cows, since he'd compounded his lie of omission by making a promise he'd never intended to keep. He'd chew his arm off before he'd willingly give up Beth's whereabouts to Brody or Alice MacKay — at least not before she had a chance to explain her aversion.

Sure, his actions might bounce up to bite him in the seat meat like Gus thought, but it just felt like the right thing to do. Justin glanced up in time to see Beth set the knife on the sideboard. Casting him one of her hundred-watt smiles, she rinsed her hands. Yep, the right thing...

Unexpectedly, Justin wasn't sure he wanted to know her reasons for hiding out from her family.

Plaintive puppy cries sounded from the laundry room.

"I guess it's feeding time again," murmured Beth.

Justin shrugged. "Looks like. Happens a lot at this stage." He eyed her fancy dress. Somehow he didn't think she'd had sitting on the floor and bottle feeding a litter of pups in mind when she'd put it on. "Wait here." He pointed at the kitchen table and then stepped into the laundry room.

The pups tumbled over one another, their cries growing louder when they spotted Justin. He grabbed one of his mom's aprons from the hook behind the door before he picked up the basket and returned to the kitchen.

Beth hadn't left, but neither had she sat at the table to wait for him. As he entered, she was just turning from the sink, holding the two makeshift puppy bottles, already filled with the formula Justin had concocted earlier. She set these on the table and accepted the blue floral print apron with murmured thanks as she pulled it over her head.

As soon as he set the basket on the floor near the kitchen table, she picked up Derby — no surprise there — and took a seat. Justin picked up one of the other pups and sat across the table. Beth laughed as Derby latched onto the nipple and began tugging.

"Alice was almost seven when I was born," she began, resettling herself in her seat. "I didn't know she wasn't my full sister until I was about eleven. My mother was always Mom, and it never occurred to me that Daddy had been married before or that Alice hadn't been my mother's child the way I was."

She used the tip of her forefinger to scratch between Derby's ears. Gut instinct told Justin to wait her out. Beth didn't need questions or prodding to tell the story. So he remained silent and concentrated on feeding the puppy in his hand.

"I walked in after school one day and found Mom and Alice in the middle of an argument. A huge one." She shuddered. "They disagreed on a lot of things. It wasn't unusual to walk in on a fight, but this one was worse. Alice had punched holes in the wall with her fist, and she'd broken the glass in the picture frame with our family portrait."

Derby finished his meal and Beth placed him back in the basket, then stood and refilled the bottle. After she sat down again, she picked up one of the other little girls and coaxed her into taking the latex nipple.

"Alice was almost eighteen, and she wanted to go to a concert and then a party and stay out all night. Mom said she wasn't comfortable with her doing that. Alice was a bit wild and always seemed to be getting into trouble."

No surprise there, either. Again Justin held his tongue.

"Alice screamed that Mom wasn't even her real mother and she couldn't order her around. She was going to take her car and go to the party." Beth smiled sadly. "Mom said the car belonged to Daddy and he'd decide if Alice drove it or not. But my head was still stuck on Alice saying Mom wasn't *her* mother."

Justin's puppy finished her meal, and he set her back in the basket so he could refill his bottle for the next one.

"That's when they noticed I was standing in the hallway. Alice cursed Mom out and ran off."

There was more to it. Justin would bet on it. The back of his neck prickled, but he didn't have a hand free to rub the sensation away.

"I asked Mom about what Alice said and she put me off. So I asked Daddy when he got home. He told me he was sorry

I'd found out like that, but it didn't make any difference to me. He loved Mom and me, and he loved Alice." Beth shrugged. "I found out later that Alice's mom had killed herself. She'd overdosed on some pills or something, and Alice had found her."

Her second puppy finished the bottle and Beth set it aside. Then she looked the puppy in the face. "The thing is," she continued in a voice that was much quieter, "when Alice's mom died, Alice was eight and I was one."

Justin sat forward. "So your dad and her mom were, what — divorced?"

Beth nodded. "They'd been divorced for a while — since before Alice was born. Alice was three when Daddy married Mom. Alice said her mom used to tell her if my mom hadn't been there, and hadn't had me, she would have gotten him back. After I was born, Alice's mom knew he'd never get back with her. She used to tell Alice he didn't want either of them because he had a new family. Then she died, and Alice came to live with us. But I was so little I don't remember any of that. As far as I knew, she was always with us."

Justin stared, unable to imagine living in such a complicated family situation. He cleared his throat, wanting — needing to say something. "So, from the time you were eleven, you knew Alice essentially blamed her mother's choice to overdose on your existence."

Beth nodded, followed by a weak smile. "That's about it."

Justin shook his head. No wonder she didn't want to stay with her sister. "Alice seemed to think your parents were worried about you."

"Daddy." Beth's face took on a troubled expression. "It's just my dad now. Mom passed away. She tripped and fell down the stairs... fractured her skull on the foyer floor when I was eighteen. Right after that, Alice came out here with a couple of girlfriends who'd taken up with some cowboys in a rodeo."

Justin locked his mouth shut. There was a name for that sort but it wasn't polite.

Beth curled her hands into fists, glanced at them with a startled expression, and visibly relaxed. "Her friends drifted away, but Alice started following the rodeo circuit. Every time she sent a letter home, she was standing next to a different cowboy. Drove Daddy nuts. She met Brody there." Beth scrunched her face into a frown. "But I think there was someone else she liked more at first."

Yeah, Justin remembered that year. "Braden?" he asked, unable to stop himself.

A bright smile spread over Beth's face. "That's it! I liked the way he looked at Alice in the pictures. I wished she would have married him. Do you know what happened to him?"

Justin rubbed his palm across his jaw and blew out a long breath, wishing he'd left that particular sleeping dog alone. "Braden was Brody's cousin. They followed the circuit together. Brody was the one with the money for the original stake, but it was Braden who had the talent. He's the one who brought in the winnings."

Beth narrowed her eyes and pinned Justin in a bright green gaze. "You're leaving something out."

"Alice dated them both, followed them home when the season was finished. She spent the next few months playing Braden and Brody against each other. It was... obvious." Justin stopped speaking, but at the raised eyebrow from Beth, he decided to finish. "Alice said she was pregnant and the baby was Braden's. So he agreed to marry her. After Braden and Alice announced their engagement, Braden also announced that he was quitting the circuit. Braden and Brody had a falling out and stopped speaking."

"But Alice married Brody," insisted Beth, the pitch of her voice high with emotion. "And... she doesn't have a baby."

Justin shrugged and sought to look anywhere but into Beth's eyes as he talked about her sister. "Braden had an accident not long after they got engaged. Got thrown from a horse and fell over a cliff near his place on Diamond Peak. Alice claimed she had a miscarriage with the shock of it. Next thing anyone knew, she'd moved in on Brody. They settled on the MacKay ranch. You pretty much know the rest."

And that was all Justin planned to say on the matter. No need to tell Beth that Brody had inherited his cousin's entire estate, or that most people didn't believe the miscarriage story. In fact, Orson's Folly gossip was more or less split down the middle on whether Alice had ever *been* pregnant or whether she'd done something to eliminate the baby. *Rattlesnake.* The name suited.

Beth reached across the table and startled Justin with a touch on the back of his hand. "Where did you go?"

He shook his head. "Sorry. I was thinking about that summer your sister got here. I guess I can see why you wouldn't want to stay with her. But she sounded worried. Maybe you should call her and let her know you're okay."

Beth shook her head. "She's acting. Alice only worries about..." She wrinkled her nose. "...Alice. If I call her, she'll pressure me to stay with her. And she'll call Daddy to put pressure on me. He thinks I can't take care of myself. The only reason he agreed to me coming on this trip was if I looked up Alice. He expected I'd stay with her. So he'll want me to go there. He still thinks we get along. And it's not just—" Her eyes widened for just a moment and then she pressed her lips together.

What had she been going to say? The last puppy finished the bottle and Justin placed her back in the basket. He'd take them back to the laundry room later. For now, though, Beth had gone pale and her hands had developed a fine tremor.

"It's not just... what? Is something else wrong, Beth?"

Idly she slid the rigged-up puppy bottle back and forth on the table in front of her. "It's probably nothing. I was probably just imagining things."

"Imagining what?" Justin's gut tied itself into a knot as he waited for her to answer. He couldn't picture this story taking any more weird turns, but somehow he knew it was about to.

Beth kept her eyes locked on the table in front of her. "I've met Brody just a couple of times. I don't — I don't like him. He scares me. It was the way he looked at me, and when Alice wasn't there... how he'd lay his hand on my shoulder or stand too close."

Justin stopped breathing. Pain shot from his hands up his arms and into his shoulders. When he lowered his glance, he realized he was white-knuckling the edge of the table and his hands had cramped. Using intense concentration, he forced each finger to peel away from the surface. Beth had stopped talking, but she never looked up.

"You probably weren't imagining things," he said in a low voice, still fighting for control. He stood and rounded the table, touching her on the hand, then lacing their fingers together and pulling her to her feet until she stood directly in front of him. "And I think you know that."

Beth flashed her eyes upward. Trouble stirred in their depths, mixed with resolution, and she blew out a long breath through pursed lips. "Yeah. I know that." She stepped against him and wrapped her arms around his waist. "Thank you for not ratting me out."

Chapter Ten

Beth stared at the kitchen tool Justin held out toward her. The thick wooden handle surrounded a large-gauge wire that fanned out at the end then bent back upward to form a loop. The rounded zig-zag shape at the bottom reminded her of a winding river.

"Potato masher," he explained as she took it between thumb and forefinger and turned it around to study it. He added a splash of milk and about a quarter of a stick of butter to the cooking pot. "You use it to smash all the lumps out of the cooked potatoes."

"Hence the name." Smiling, she squished the wire into the softened potatoes, surprised that it was more like playing in anemic mud than snow. She stirred and smashed, finally achieving a bit of rhythm with the task. As the potatoes gradually took on a whipped appearance, she swung her arm around and around, beating the muddy mix against the edge of the pan.

Every once in a while she stole a glance at Justin. His mouth was drawn into a grim line as he used a spatula to remove the oven fried chicken from the pan.

Stupid! Talking like that about her family, about *Alice.* He was probably working out how to ask her to leave.

There was something he wasn't saying — maybe a lot of somethings. His mind had definitely wandered while she'd been telling him about Alice, but he hadn't elaborated when she'd asked.

She pounded the masher into the mixture with a clatter of the wire against the metal pot.

"If you're finished pulverizing the spuds, the rest of supper's about ready."

Beth forced her hand to a standstill. She lowered her gaze to take in her handiwork. The lumpy potatoes had indeed been smashed into pale paste. She gave the masher a final sweep and then sheepishly parked it, leaving the handle sticking upright in the middle of the pot.

"Sorry," she mumbled, stepping back out of his way.

Justin raised an eyebrow but said nothing as he scraped the creamy-white potatoes into a brown stoneware bowl, then swiped a finger through some of fluffy mix that clung to the side of the cooking pot and brought it to his mouth. He sucked his finger thoughtfully and then shot a grin at her.

"Perfect."

Beth couldn't have said why it mattered, but there it was; that little quickening of her heartbeat, followed by the hitch in her breathing that she couldn't quite control.

"My mom canned these last year." He picked up a bowl of snap green beans and carried them, along with the potatoes, to the table. "She said these were the best she'd ever grown." He glanced up as he set the dishes down, his blue eyes fairly dancing with laughter. "Of course, she's said that every year as long as I can recollect, so I figure one of these years she'll be announcing she grew perfect green beans."

Beth smiled, more from his tone than the story. "And what happens if she grows the perfect green bean?"

On his way for the chicken platter, Justin paused and grinned over his shoulder. "Well, then I reckon she'll have to work on growing perfect peas."

With the table set and the food arranged in the middle, Justin held out a chair for Beth. Then he gave her the second surprise of the evening when he dimmed the overhead light and turned on an old brown radio that sat on the countertop. The mellow voice of John Denver filled the kitchen and Justin dialed the volume down a bit.

"Not quite like going out to dinner," he apologized with a smile.

If he had taken her to the most exclusive restaurant in the world, Beth couldn't have felt more pampered and cared for. "I love it," she murmured, unable to take her eyes off her dining companion.

Conversation lagged as they dished up their food, but the atmosphere remained comfortable. The clink of silverware against the heavy brown dishes seemed to keep time with the soft country music. Beth's mouth watered as the chicken beckoned from her plate.

"So, did you find the samples you needed today?" Justin poured iced tea from a pitcher into his glass and took a sip.

"Mostly, yes." Beth stared at her chicken leg, trying to figure out if she should just eat it with her fingers. Her mother would have been appalled at eating anything without the proper fork. "I can't tell if the hybrid plants are actually breeding or if the proximity of the poison ivy and oak to each other is just making a lot of hybrids. I think I'll almost need to grow some hybrids in a lab with controls to test that." With a little shrug, she picked up a chicken leg and began to nibble. Immediately her mouth watered and she took a bigger bite. "Oh, man! This chicken is far out!"

Justin almost choked on his bite of potatoes. "Far out, huh? Looks to me like it's right there in your hand."

"No!" she was quick to correct. "I meant..." Catching his smothered smile, she stopped talking. Then she smiled back at him. "And... you're teasing me."

"Not at all," he said, shaking his head, but then he grinned. "Actually, I am, yeah."

A feeling of warmth settled over Beth's heart. Without a doubt she was physically attracted to Justin, and he seemed to be attracted to her. Never before had she felt so comfortable around another person — not even her father, and she'd always considered their relationship to be a close one.

"What's it like?" she asked softly. "Living here? Is it lonely?"

A bemused expression crossed Justin's face. Then his mouth widened into a pleasing smile. "No, not so much. Not lately, anyway." The glance he sent her sizzled along her exposed skin, little electrical charges of awareness.

Beth's heart stuttered, and heat crept into her cheeks. She lowered her gaze, her brain a jumbled mass of confused thoughts writhing against each other like a nest of snakes. *Was* Justin hinting at something between them? The notion was insane. They'd known each other just a little over twenty-four hours. Besides, even if she did often think about how much Justin had managed to turn her world upside down in that time... that didn't mean he felt the same way. No, he had to have meant something else.

She forced her breathing to slow and feigned a relaxed attitude as she scooped up a forkful of mashed potatoes drowning in butter. Once the bite was in her mouth, she risked a glance across the table while she chewed. Justin watched her with a flare of intense heat in his eyes, and all of Beth's newfound bravado fled. Warmth suffused her cheeks, and she was grateful for the dim lights. With effort, she tore her gaze from his and shifted her concentration to her plate.

The plate that had maybe two bites of potatoes left on it.

When she had scooped the last of those into her mouth and swallowed, she took a sip of iced tea, hoping the cold liquid would provide some relief from the conflagration that had begun in her veins. But the icy drink seemed to have the opposite effect. Beth dabbed at her mouth with her napkin and slid her chair backward.

"Dinner was delicious." She stood and gathered her dishes. "I'll get these washed."

Justin picked up the remains of his own meal, and they ended up bumping into each other at the sink. A nervous giggle escaped, and Beth was quick to press her fingertips against her mouth as if she could push the childish sound back in. The last thing she wanted was for Justin to regard her as a child.

One of his mysterious smiles tugged on his lips and his

eyes crinkled at the corners. "Why don't we clean up together?" His arm brushed hers as he reached beyond her and twisted the hot water tap.

Her heart gave a little leap at the brief contact. She'd spent the bulk of her teenaged years like a mouse in the corner, nose buried in a book. Boys had been a mystery. But it didn't matter — no amount of experience would have prepared her for the force of nature that was Justin McGee.

Water spurted and then gushed forth over the white enamel. Justin shoved the stopper into the drain and the sink began to fill. Steam rose to blanket the window above.

When Justin squeezed a measure of green dishwashing liquid into the water, white suds built like puffy clouds on a summer day. After a moment, he turned the tap and the water stopped.

Beth sighed with the sheer bliss of spending an evening doing something so completely normal and homey as making a meal, sharing it, and cleaning up afterward. Soft piano and guitar blended on the radio behind her, and soon Elvis began crooning about falling in love.

"Mmm. Oh, yeah." Justin slid the dishes into the bubbly water, and then picked up a dish towel. Mesmerized, she followed his actions with her gaze. The towel was old and thinning; the giant sunflower splashed across one end had faded. After he dried his hands, he set the cloth on the counter. Then he turned from the sink and held out his hand, a tender smile curving his lips upward.

Slightly mystified and off balance with it, Beth slipped her hand in his and found herself drawn into a loose embrace. He began swaying in time to the music, and it seemed the most natural thing in the world to move across the kitchen floor with the dance partner she'd waited her entire life for.

She laid her face against his chest and inhaled. He smelled so good, a mix of soap, fresh piney woods, and worn leather. The strong pulse of his heart beneath her ear seemed to complement the tender strains of the song. Beth lost herself in the moment, enjoying the heat of his hand as it wandered up and down her spine in leisurely time to the music. Their steps matched perfectly, and he rested his cheek on top of her head as Elvis's smooth tones flowed over them like the river he sang about.

* * *

As Beth melted in his arms, Justin's heart stammered briefly then settled into a steady pounding that seemed to echo the gentle rhythm of the song. He wished to heaven he knew what he thought he was doing. No one had ever felt so right in his arms, even though he knew from the things they'd talked about that any feelings he developed could go nowhere. She had a life to return to. She was going to go places. She had dreams. Plans.

And he was already in the life he'd been destined for since his birth.

A sigh whisked past his lips. None of that was going to prevent him from enjoying their time together. The cloud of golden curls beneath his cheek was soft as a kitten's fur. Justin inhaled her light perfume. He'd remember that scent, White Lace, for the rest of his life. Then he exhaled slowly and — *just for tonight,* he warned himself — allowed his heart to lead the dance. As Elvis offered up his whole life, Justin experienced the odd realization that the sensations rocking his body were less heated and more affectionate. He filed the unusual recognition away to take out and ponder later, intent only on enjoying the dance, the moment.

All too soon, the music came to an end and the mood dissipated in the jingle of a soft drink commercial, advising America to look up and *"find the real thing."* Beth seemed reluctant to leave their embrace. As she drew back, one hand lingered on his waist, the other eased slowly out of his grasp with a long brush of fingertips to fingertips that sent a tingle up to his brain and then down to his toes.

At the same time, she angled a glance at him and smiled almost shyly. "Thank you for the dance."

There was only one logical course of action. Justin steadied Beth's chin with his fingertips and he bent, skimming his lips over hers. For just an instant, some indefinable emotion flashed, but then she closed her eyes and exhaled softly, leaning into the kiss.

Justin was ready for the flare of passion. He was ready to tamp back his body's expected reaction to holding and kissing a beautiful woman.

The feeling of tenderness that rooted in his heart blindsided him. He drew back after one sweet moment of clinging lips and wrapped his arms around her, tucking her against his chest, where he wanted her to spend the rest of their days. He swallowed, dialed back the overwhelming feelings a notch, and then gave her a gentle squeeze and let her go.

The breath he pulled in shook his entire body. He took a step back and planted himself against the sink, locking his knees against the wobbly feeling of a newborn foal. When he finally dug deep enough to find the courage to meet Beth's gaze, her eyes were huge and maybe reflected as much unsettled feeling as he had racing through his system.

She cleared her throat. "The dishes won't do themselves, will they? Do you want to wash or dry?" Without waiting for his answer, she stepped in front of the sink, picked up the sponge next to the faucet, and began washing.

Which, Justin supposed, was a good thing, since his brain was still processing the mushy sensation in his heart.

* * *

With a lingering look over her shoulder, Beth moved in the general direction of the staircase. She bumped her shoulder into the doorjamb, giggled, then righted herself and gave him one more smile before she disappeared up the stairs. Justin couldn't have wiped the grin off his face if it had meant his life. A shudder of pure delight gripped him briefly, and then he settled his hat on his head and stepped through the back door, making certain he locked it behind him.

Not that doors needed locking on the Cross MC, but it might give Beth some peace of mind being as she was from the city. If he was honest, since she was staying alone in the house, it eased his own mind, too. A tuneless whistle on his lips, he slipped the fat cigar he'd snagged from the humidor in the office out of his shirt pocket and took off the end with his cigar nipper. Then he stopped whistling as he stuck the blunt stogy between his teeth and fished in his jeans pocket for his lighter.

The cloudless sky overhead drew his eye and he slowed his steps. Some of the larger constellations Beth had shown him seemed to leap out at him as he mentally connected the dots. He'd think of her every time he looked into the night sky.

Shifting his eyes back along the dark path to the bunkhouse, he replayed the evening. He sure hadn't expected his heart would dive in the way it had. They'd just met and yet it felt like they were old friends. That dance earlier had been a more intimate connection than any he'd ever felt. He'd been no saint in his lifetime, but everyone before Beth had been physical. Even his feelings for a woman he'd once thought he could fall in love with hadn't come close.

He pulled open the bunkhouse door, but before he crossed the threshold, he looked back up at the house. The silhouette in the guest room window was unmistakable. She stood watching him leave, not in the darkness, which would allow her to see him better, but with the light on. When he tipped his hat, she raised her hand and laid it against the glass.

Then she snapped off the lamp.

Justin smiled to himself as he stepped into the bunkhouse.

Gus sat in an ancient leather chair reading a ranching magazine. He glanced up as Justin entered, and after raising one bushy eyebrow, he laid the magazine on the table next to him. "You sure you know what the hell you're doing, kid?"

The shudder wracked Justin again and he shook his head. "Nope. Not at all. Isn't that a rub?"

Chapter Eleven

Once again, Justin was in the kitchen already when the aroma of brewing coffee led Beth downstairs. If she hadn't seen him cross the yard the night before, she'd have sworn he'd never left the main house. She lingered in the arched doorway, watching him flip pancakes on an electric griddle he'd set up on the range top.

"Good morning," he said without turning around.

Beth jumped. "What did you — I mean — I thought I was — h-how did you know...?"

Justin glanced over his shoulder and grinned at her. "Maybe it's ESP," he said with a grin.

Beth opened her mouth, but nothing came out.

"But the truth is a lot simpler. I caught your reflection in the toaster." He nodded toward the counter.

Easy laughter escaped Beth's lips when she saw herself in the chrome toaster sitting next to the sink. Its rounded contour gave a funhouse mirror effect, and she looked like a squat troll in a red shirt.

He returned his attention to the griddle and flipped another pancake. "Help yourself," he said, gesturing to the stack of pancakes on a platter next to him. "We have maple syrup in the pantry."

Her mouth watered as she padded across the spotless off-white linoleum and into the pantry. The brown bottle was at eye level, right at the front of the shelf next to chocolate syrup and a box containing several packets of flavored drink mix. Someone in the house had a sweet tooth. She reached for the syrup but then paused and glanced over her shoulder when she realized how quiet the kitchen was. "Why don't I hear the puppies? Where are they?"

"I took them out to the bunkhouse earlier." Justin unplugged the griddle. "The vet's coming out to see a couple of our pregnant cows that're late delivering, so he can check out the pups, too. Gus'll look after them while we get your van to Walt so he can repair your cooling system."

"Do you really think he'll be able to fix it?"

"Well, now, that I don't know. I've never known him to be stumped by a car, even a foreign one." Justin set the platter of pancakes in the center of the table. "But I'll tell you this. He's the best around. If he can't fix it, I'm not sure anyone can."

Beth got two plates out of the cupboard next to the sink and took them to the table while Justin gathered silverware. She set the plates on the table, her hand lingering there. Was she going to need a contingency plan for getting home?

Justin set two red and white checked mugs on the table and filled them with coffee from the pot. He set the decanter down on top of a trivet in the center of the table and stepped over to hold Beth's chair while she sat.

"I promise you won't be stranded," he murmured. "Leastways not unless you decide you wanna be." He helped her scoot the chair forward then rounded the table and sat across from her.

Beth stared, trying to think of a witty comeback. When no words formed, she uncapped the bottle of syrup and dumped some on her pancakes.

* * *

Beth's colorful van coughed and smoked, but the ugly thing kept running for the forty or so miles from the ranch into Orson's Folly. Following along behind her in the Cross MC's dark blue pickup, Justin breathed a relieved sigh once they hit the outskirts of town. At the green and white cinder block building marked by the familiar faded sign that read *Blackstone's Tire and Auto*, she made the turn into the gravel parking lot and stopped.

Walter Blackstone, Jr. was a wiry man who'd attended school with Justin from the time they'd hit kindergarten. The business belonged to his father, and in keeping with most businesses in Orson's Folly, it was in the process of being passed from father to son. Justin was convinced his old pal had a truck engine for a heart. From the time he could walk, he'd worked on cars and trucks with his old man. Walt exited the work bay wiping his greasy hands on an orange rag. He jammed the rag in the back pocket of his blue-gray coveralls and offered his hand to Justin, just as Beth joined them from the other side of her psychedelic van.

"Walt." Justin nodded as they shook hands.

"What the hell have you brought me this time?" Walt squinted around Justin at the van, all but ignoring Beth, likely not for any other reason than the man knew more about interacting with engines than with people.

"Hi, I'm Beth Rushton." She stepped in front of him and held out her hand.

He hesitated for a bare second before he gripped her hand as though it would break. "Walt Blackstone, ma'am."

Without a flinch for the grime that clung to the mechanic, Beth firmed up the grip and pumped his arm. "Very nice to meet you."

Poor Walt glanced a little uncertainly at Justin, but didn't jerk free. "Is there something I can do for you?"

"I sure hope you can help me." Beth gestured toward the van. "My cooling system is acting up."

The mechanic looked again at Justin, but he smiled and nodded in Beth's direction. After a moment, Walt shrugged and stepped to the rear of the van. "This has one of them air-cooled engines, don't it?"

"The belt keeps slipping on the cooling motor, and then the engine overheats. You can work on a foreign engine, can't you?" Beth worried at her bottom lip with her teeth.

Justin held his breath, waiting for the scathing response about little women leaving the inner workings of cars to their men.

Instead, Walt only nodded as he propped open the access panel and squinted inside. "Yep, the belts stretch out when they get too old." Frowning, he leaned in and pushed on the gray-black strap. Then he tapped on the engine and grunted. "Belt's not only loose, it's starting to fray. Might be I have one in stock that I could rig to fit, but it'd be better if I send a runner up to Jackson to get one from the dealer there. That'll take the best part of a day." He closed the access panel and stepped back, rubbing his jaw with the back of his hand. "I expect I can get one by late tomorrow if Raym' ever gets over his flu and comes to work."

"Raym'?" whispered Beth, angling a glance at Justin.

"Raymond. Younger brother, long story," he murmured. "He's probably fishing."

"I'm thinking I can have the repair completed by no later than day after tomorrow," said Walt, meeting Beth's gaze.

"That sounds workable to me." She gave him one of her sunny smiles, sending a knife of pure jealousy to Justin's heart. "Should I just leave it here?"

Walt scratched his dark head. "Yeah, yeah. You shouldn't drive it any until I get the new belt on. Come on inside and we'll get you wrote up." He started toward the office, talking as he walked. "Are you staying nearby?"

Beth froze in her tracks and she glanced at Justin with wide eyes.

"She's staying at my parents' place," supplied Justin quickly, taking Beth by the hand and giving a little squeeze before they followed Walt into the building. "So you can just give me a call when it's ready, and someone'll bring her in."

Walt made a note on his clipboard, tore off a small manila key tag and attached it to her key, then extended the receipt in Justin's direction.

Beth intercepted the handoff with another smile. "Thank

you, Mr. Blackstone."

Twin spots of color invaded Walt's cheeks. "Pleasure meeting you, Miss Rushton."

Justin held out until he'd seated Beth in the cab of the pickup and then climbed behind the wheel. But the minute the truck was on the road and headed for the center of town, he couldn't contain his mirth any longer and the laughter bubbled forth.

"Okay, *what* is so funny?" Beth shifted to sit sideways on the bench seat, obviously mystified.

Afraid he might laugh them right off the road if he didn't get some control, Justin steered the truck into the first parking lot he came to, which happened to be the town's only church. The white van, its side emblazoned with *New Life Christian Church* in crudely painted red block letters, was tucked up in the back corner of the parking lot, but Brother Johnny's pickup wasn't in evidence.

"Walt is a great guy," Justin said, still struggling against the laughter. "But he don't much like women telling him anything. He's kind of got the opinion that only men know the mysteries of engines and cars, and women belong in the home, preferably in the kitchen."

Beth stiffened. "*That's* not very funny. He sounds like a chauvinist."

Tears from not-quite-suppressed laughter sprang to his eyes. "Honey, when they put the word in the dictionary they stuck his picture next to it."

"Why are you laughing?" she asked with exasperation.

"Because you knew what you were talking about — probably know more about your van than he does, but he can't admit *that*."

The ground rumbled and a red cab-over roared past, pulling a silver trailer, probably avoiding the scales on the interstate and needing to make up time. Still chuckling, Justin hoped the driver felt the sizeable ticket he'd likely receive from the deputy posted up the road with a brand new radar gun would be a good trade-off.

A gently clearing throat brought his thoughts back to the pickup.

With effort, he managed to put a cap on his laughter so he could explain. "It doesn't take a day to get to Jackson and back. He needs the time to study up on the workings of your engine."

She shot him a hard glare. "*You* are easily amused."

Justin grinned and gestured to the two-lane highway they sat next to. "Sweetheart, that's Main Street and the semi that just passed by is heading for a major speed trap about two miles up ahead. And *that* is about as much excitement as we generally get around these parts. We gotta do *something* for fun."

"Really..." She narrowed her eyes at him for a moment but then pointed across the street. "So what's happening there?"

Justin swiveled in his seat and studied the parking lot, filled with a half dozen pickups bearing the names of various local subcontractors. "Now *that*... used to be the local watering hole, but the owner went out of business five or six years ago. Looks like Tom Valentine got the funding and the licenses to go ahead and renovate the old place."

And that just might keep Orson's Folly from dying a not-so-slow death.

He depressed the clutch and shifted the truck into first. "AJ's General Store's the best place to pick up the few things I need. Do you need anything while we're in town?"

Beth giggled and Justin glanced in her direction, raising an eyebrow in silent question. But she only gave him a secret smile while she lifted one shoulder. "You have things that tickle your funny bone, and I have things that tickle mine."

Instant and completely irrational desire raced through Justin like a rifle shot. He clung to the steering wheel, almost afraid he'd have to pull off the road again. Not to mention that making out in his truck near the center of town wasn't exactly conducive to maintaining a low enough profile to keep Beth off Alice MacKay's radar. He frowned at the sour taste the thought of her raised in his throat.

"You know, it'd be almost as easy to run up to Jackson... to the five and dime up there."

Beth caught her breath and she hesitated for almost a

minute, as though trying to come to a decision. "You're trying to avoid Alice, aren't you? Can she make life hard for you and your family if she finds out you helped me hide out?"

Once again she surprised him with her perceptiveness. Justin ran his hand over his jaw as he took a second to weigh his answer. "Make life hard?" He stopped at the only red light in town and angled a glance in Beth's direction. "You aren't jail bait or anything, are you?"

Beth snickered. "Is that your not-so-subtle way of asking my age?"

Justin's lips pulled up of their own accord. "Is it working?" He knew she'd taken college classes, so he wasn't particularly concerned that she was underage. But he'd been wondering for the best part of the past couple of days just how old she was. Sometimes her attitude made her seem almost as old as his mom. Other times, she exuded childlike qualities that fascinated him.

"I'm twenty-one," she said, crossing her arms over her chest. "How old are *you?*"

"Old enough to know better and young enough to want to anyway," said Justin, hitting the accelerator a little hard when the light turned green. "And no, your sister can't do a danged thing to me or my family. She'll likely make a lot of noise, probably tell anyone who'll listen I can't be trusted." *And she might call you a few unflattering names in the process if the relationship's as bad as you say.*

"And will anyone be listening?" asked Beth quietly, just as they entered the small blacktopped lot in front of AJ's.

Justin found an open space in the tiny lot and swung into it. He turned the ignition off then pulled the key, holding it in his palm as he studied the worn, goldish edges that outlined the silver-colored octagon behind the shank. "There'll always be *someone* listening." A fact he knew altogether too well. But he wasn't going to let that ruin the day. He glanced sideways at Beth and grinned. "Ready for your first trip to a real country store?"

She grinned back. "Is it going to look like something from a Laura Ingalls Wilder book?"

"Geez, I hope not, since the way you just said that makes

it sound awful." Justin popped open his door and jumped down. "But it *is* a whole different world in there, darlin'. Just so you know."

Beth met him at the front of the truck, surprising and pleasing him when she slipped her hand into his. Arms swinging between them, they crossed the short distance into the town's main gossip hole.

Chapter Twelve

"Try our ten flavors of homemade ice cream," Beth read from the white and brown sign planted at the edge of the parking lot. She wrinkled her nose as she considered the possibilities. "All at once?" But her mouth watered. She was a sucker for ice cream.

"I'm usually a two-scoop man." Justin chuckled. "But we could each get five scoops and trade off."

"Aw, you'd do that for me?" Beth smiled into Justin's twinkling blue eyes and giggled. She did that a lot these days but everything about being with him gave her a giddy feeling that just made the giggles slip out. "Thank you! But I'm a two-scoop gal, myself. So the other flavors will just have to wait until next time."

Justin raised an eyebrow and opened his mouth but closed it again without saying a word. Good. She liked the thought that she occasionally left him tongue-tied.

Quaint didn't begin to describe the hub of Orson's Folly commerce. Parts of the freestanding building had probably existed since the Wyoming gold rush in the 1880s. *AJ's General Store* was scrawled in bright white across the top of the freshly painted, dark brown façade. The smell of oil paint lingered on the air, stinging Beth's eyes. It was impossible to tell how many layers coated the structure, but the texture of the wood was no longer visible, and the spaces between the vertical boards were just shallow indentations with all the built-up paint. The stark appearance of the storefront was softened by orange clay pots of red geraniums placed in front the dark posts.

Beth stepped onto the raised porch of weathered and foot-worn gray boards that ran the length of the building. Her eyes took a second to adjust to the shade created by the overhang covering the porch, but when they did, the enchantment of simpler times beckoned. Forest green benches beneath each of the four display windows offered rest for weary shoppers, while a silver chest labeled *ICE* in red block letters stood at the end of the long porch.

"Hey, there, Justin McGee," greeted a skinny gentleman with snow-white hair and more wrinkles than face. He sat in a rickety ladderback chair, staring at a game of checkers resting atop a wooden barrel. Across from him, a younger man made a move with a red checker before looking up with a friendly smile.

Justin nodded in reply. "Mr. Wayne." Then he turned to the younger man. "Tom."

Both men stared at Beth with open interest and next to her, Justin tensed a fraction. She squeezed his hand, hoping to convey the message that she was fine with whatever introduction he chose to make.

"This is a friend of the family," said Justin. "Her van broke down so I helped her get it to Walt's."

Mr. Wayne grunted but nodded with apparent approval. "No better man than Walt for fixing a truck. Even one of them foreign ones."

Beth jerked backward. How did he know *that?* She slid a glance at Justin, who only shrugged, not a speck of surprise in his expression. Gossip was apparently another favorite pastime in Orson's Folly. And apparently it traveled faster than a pickup could drive a half mile up the street.

Justin nodded to the men and guided Beth toward the

wooden screen door. With an odd challenge in his glance, he held it open for her. She smiled at the two men playing checkers and then crossed the threshold into the nineteenth century. The plank floor inside wasn't as weathered as the porch, but the floor was worn smooth in places and had gone gray from years of foot traffic in the same patterns around display shelves.

A shelf laden with candy caught Beth's eye. The round wooden unit gave the effect of a sugar carousel, but instead of horses, canisters of hard candy, chewy candy, chocolate, and penny sticks graced the platform. "Oh my, I'm gonna get cavities just walking past that," she murmured, allowing her eyes to linger on the bin of colorful sourballs. Then a bin filled with orange confections caught her attention and she groaned. "Mmm, peach rings! What is all this sugar doing right at the front of the store?"

"Well, this shelf used to hold staples." Justin tapped a finger on the silver lid of a canister of lemon drops. "Flour, sugar, corn meal, salt. All set out convenient-like so customers could come in and get what they needed real easy." He shrugged. "But AJ took a correspondence course in marketing last summer. According to him, putting the staples in the back means customers have to walk past displays of possible impulse purchases. And candy counts as his biggest impulse purchase, so he sets it front and center. If people don't buy it on the way in, they'll think about it while they shop, which should make them hungry so they'll buy more in the store and then pick up what they're really hankering after — the candy — on the way out." Justin angled a glance in Beth's direction. "Is it working? Are you hungry?"

Yet another giggle slipped out. "More than I was five minutes ago? Ah — no. Sorry." Beth giggled again — she simply couldn't help herself. "But we can tell AJ it made me ravenous if it'll make him feel better."

The door burst open, and a boy of about three or four barrelled across the threshold with the energy of a spring tornado. Showing no hesitation, he raced straight for the candy carousel. His scuffed cowboy boots made each clomping step echo like an explosion against the battered floor. The fringy ends of walnut brown hair peeked from beneath his straw cowboy hat. One side of his overalls drooped where it hung unclasped over a blue and white checked shirt.

An ache began in Beth's heart and then moved lower, coming to rest in her belly. She adored kids. Maybe one day she'd have a rambunctious little one. Her wishing center formed an image... a little boy with blond curls and laughing blue eyes beneath a cowboy hat.

A slender woman entered the store. Her waist-length black hair flowed freely over a denim jacket that topped a mid-calf length pink floral skirt. She didn't look old enough to be anyone's mother, but her focus immediately settled on the child at the candy. "Colton Ford, you are not allowed to run away from me like that."

"Mama, can I have lemon drops?" Colton shifted from foot to foot, looking up so hard his hat fell off his head and caught on the strap that ran under his chin.

"Then there's the kid variable to the impulse purchase." Justin nodded to the woman. "Mornin', Kendra."

The dark-haired woman whirled, a smile lighting her distinctly Native American features. "Hello, Justin. Nice to see you." She flicked an interested glance in Beth's direction.

"Kendra, this is Beth Rushton. She's been staying at my parents' place while she's studying poisonous plants."

"Very nice to meet you." Her dark-eyed gaze zeroed in on Beth's neck, and she winced.

With a sigh, Beth raised a hand to her rash, which obviously wasn't disappearing as quickly as she'd hoped. "I tangled with some. It's nice to meet you."

"I gave her some of your salve and my mom's oatmeal bath mix."

"Good!" Kendra's lips lifted into a gentle smile and her eyes softened. "You keep using that and you'll feel better in no time. Make sure to call me if you need more."

"Thank you," murmured Beth, grateful and somehow not the least surprised by Kendra's kindness.

"Mama! Lemon drops!" demanded her little boy.

"The tyrant calls," said Kendra with a rueful shrug. "It was nice meeting you." She turned and joined her son at the candy counter. "Only a small bag, Colton."

With a grin stretching his lips, Justin laid an arm over Beth's shoulders and steered her deeper into the store. "He's a good kid."

"He's adorable," she whispered. Unable to resist, she twisted so she could see Justin's face and asked, "Do you ever think about having kids?"

His expression never wavered. "Sure, I think about it. I'd like two or three." He shrugged and something flickered in his eyes. "Probably ought to get a wife first, though."

No more than a handful of people wandered the merchandise-packed aisles, but that was enough to clog the traffic pattern with all the stock that took up every inch of shelf space and even some of the floor. Justin grabbed a wicker basket like the one he'd put the puppies in, but it was oversized and bulky. After the second mishap involving a stack of towels, he chuckled and loaded his other purchases into it, and then propped the basket on his shoulder with one hand.

"You look like a merchant on the streets of Cairo," Beth said, laughing.

Justin barked out a laugh. "And when were you in Cairo?"

"Well, I haven't *been*... yet." Beth scrunched up her nose. "But I might go there to study plants or something one day. You never know."

"Think they have poison ivy over there?" He touched the tip of her nose and chuckled when she swatted his hand away. But then he grew serious. "You know, Beth... the Middle East is..." A pained expression settled over his features. "It's not real safe... especially for an American woman."

If her father had said those words, Beth would have bristled instantly. Coming from Justin, they made her heart trip along with happiness. Another easy laugh bubbled out. "Why, Justin, I believe you care." She turned into the housewares aisle, but he grabbed her arm.

"Hey." He tugged gently until she turned and glanced into his suddenly all-too-serious face. "I do care, Beth. I hope that's okay because it's not apt to change."

Her heart crowded into her throat and she had to swallow a couple of times before she could speak. "I... it's — I like that."

"Good." His smile returned and he nodded toward the end of the aisle, breaking the seriousness of the mood. "I need a set of those salt and pepper shakers."

Beth wandered toward a rack of simple cotton blouses. The one she'd borrowed from Justin's mother had been practical and incredibly comfortable. She didn't think she'd looked half bad in it either, if her recollection of Justin's expression the other night could be trusted. She pulled out one in pale blue and examined it.

"The green one'll look better," Justin whispered in her ear. "It matches your eyes."

Beth's skin tingled, but whether it was because Justin was so near or because he'd noticed her eyes, she couldn't have said. She shoved the blue blouse back on the rack and pulled out the green one instead, tilting her head back to meet his gaze over her shoulder. His smile set the butterflies in her stomach to fluttering.

"It's unbelievable how much is packed into this tiny store." Beth slid a pair of dark blue jeans from the rack and blinked at the tag. "Is this price for real?"

Justin leaned over her shoulder and glanced down. "Yeah, why? Too much?"

"Hardly. I'd pay at least twice as much as this back — home."

Odd how it was suddenly hard to squeeze that little word past the emotion in her throat. Justin touched her on the arm. She should have known he would notice.

"Hey, there... feeling homesick?"

How could she explain that she wasn't missing her home but realizing how much she would miss Wyoming — and Justin — when she left? It seemed a silly notion. She knew he'd understand, but she wasn't quite ready to share the thought. He continued to watch her, so she just nodded and shrugged. She hung the jeans over her arm along with the blouse.

"Come on." He led her back toward the front of the store.

"I think we've made enough impulse purchases."

"Justin, what if—" A chill settled over the air, interrupting Beth's train of thought. The center of her back developed a stabbing sensation that raced into the nape of her neck.

"Bethany Rushton!" Alice's brittle voice rang across the store.

Maybe the other patrons *didn't* all turn to look in her direction, but in Beth's imagination they sure did. Forcing herself to stand up straight, when what she wanted to do was shrink into a ball of nothing, she aimed herself in the direction of her sister's voice.

Alice wound her way around the precariously balanced aisle displays like a viper on a mission. Justin lowered his laundry basket to the floor and stepped next to Beth.

"Where have you been?" Alice's green eyes flashed with fury. "Daddy's out of his head with worry."

"Why would he be worried, Alice? I've called him right on schedule the last two Fridays." Anger curled Beth's fingers into her palms, and her nails bit into soft flesh. "Did you call him and complain because I didn't race to your house?"

"I *called* him to see if he'd heard from you when you didn't show up. He hadn't." She settled her malevolent glare on Justin. "I thought you said you hadn't seen my sister."

Justin drew in a sharp breath, but Beth touched him on the arm to let him know she had it covered.

"Knock off the inquisition, Alice. Justin found me when my van broke down and helped me get it to a service station. You have a problem with that? Think maybe he should have just left me there?"

Some of the bluster left Alice's sails, and she addressed Justin a little more calmly. "Oh, I... didn't know you just found her. Thank you."

He stared at her for a long time before he gave one curt nod. Then he bent and picked up the laundry basket he'd filled with his "impulse purchases."

Alice leaned closer to Beth. "What's the matter with your face?"

The urge to scratch at the sting and itch renewed itself.

Beth flexed the fingers of her free hand. No way was she going to embarrass herself in front of her sister by gouging at the rash. She held Alice's gaze and smiled. "Hazard of the job. I tangled with some poison oak and poison ivy when I was collecting samples."

Alice's eyes widened and she backed off a step. Justin snickered softly and turned his head to look across the store, seemingly content to let Beth handle things.

"Well, it seems you've had quite an... adventure already, haven't you?" Alice eyed the jeans and blouse draped over Beth's arm and made a face that indicated her distaste. "If you're finished *shopping*, I'll take you home. Or you can follow me if your car's fixed. Where is it?"

"I left my van at Walt's." It was costing Beth's back teeth some enamel, grinding them as she did in an effort to keep her tone civil. "But I'm not going back to Brody's ranch with you."

"What do you mean, you aren't coming home with me?" Alice's face pinched into a frown. Had she been near a mirror, she probably would have flipped out at the massive valley that created across the center of her forehead. With any luck, Alice's face really would freeze like that one day, the way their dad had always threatened.

"Well?" snapped Alice. "Are you going to explain yourself?"

Beth suppressed a sneer. Much as she'd love to torment her sister, it wouldn't do to start something. "I *mean*... that I made other arrangements."

Alice's gaze cut back to Justin and a nasty smile crossed her face. "I see. And is Daddy aware of your *other arrangements*, or did you keep *him* in the dark, too?"

"Grow up, Alice. I'm twenty-one. It hardly matters what Daddy thinks." Beth rolled her eyes, but under cover of the blouse she held, she crossed her fingers against the lie. "He won't care as long as I'm safe."

"Won't care that you're shacking up with a cowboy?"

Beth's temper flared past her ability to contain it. "Oh, like you didn't sleep your way out here and back and then out here again!"

"That's not—" Alice glanced around and stared hard at

Kendra, who stood across the store watching, her head cocked to the side.

Giving a curt shake of her head, Kendra rushed her son past the little group.

"Might I suggest we pay for our purchases and take this outside?" Justin asked, speaking slowly and exaggerating his Western drawl.

"There's nothing to take outside," snapped Alice, grasping Beth's forearm with one hand. "Come on." She started for the register, hauling a stunned Beth with her.

"No!" Beth balked, planting her feet, but Alice's steady forward motion only caused Beth to slide along the worn plank floor. "Stop! Damn it, let go of me, Alice."

Justin stepped in front of Alice, halting their progress toward the exit. "It doesn't look to me like the lady wants to go with you, Miz MacKay."

"Well, she doesn't have a choice. The only way our father agreed to allow her to come out here was if she stayed with me." Alice curled her lip and narrowed her eyes. "She's not staying with you, Justin. If you want a woman to warm your bed, go on up to Jackson and find one of the lucky ladies who walk the streets."

"That's a filthy thing to say!" Beth yanked her hand from her sister's grasp and gave Alice a little push away from her.

"She's *not* staying with me," Justin answered through gritted teeth, putting himself between Beth and Alice. "She'll be staying at the house with my parents. I'm in the bunkhouse with Gus."

"Well, isn't that convenient?" Alice looked from Beth to Justin and then settled her gaze back on Beth. "If you don't come with me right now, I'll go home and call Daddy. He'll make sure you toe the line."

"Go stuff yourself in a closet, Alice!" shouted Beth, glaring at her sister. Man, she hated that Justin was witnessing the petty fight.

Alice stared hard, but after a moment, she backed up a step. "Fine. But this isn't finished. We'll see what Daddy has to say about you being a cowboy's whore." Turning on her heel, she stalked toward the door.

Beth launched herself toward her sister, but Justin caught her around the waist with one arm and pulled her back. "Hold on there, Dilly Gal. She sure as hell ain't worth it."

Beth strained against Justin's hold, intent on doing her sister bodily harm. Or at least pulling out clumps of her dirty blond hair.

"C'mon, darlin', stay here with me," he murmured in her ear. "You won that round. If you didn't, she'd never have walked out."

"But she'll cause all kinds of trouble," said Beth, as the tension eased from her shoulders and the red haze from her vision.

"And I told you she can't do a blessed thing to me or mine." He pulled her back against him into a quick one-armed hug, and then released her so abruptly she had to brace her feet to keep from falling forward. "Now, if it's yourself you're worried about..."

"No, it's not me." Beth allowed herself another long look through the glass door, but Alice had moved out of sight. And anyway, the intense urge to strangle her sister had dissipated. A little afraid of what she'd see reflected on Justin's face, Beth turned around slowly. But he only regarded her with mild concern.

"I'm sorry," she whispered. "You shouldn't have had to see that." With a heavy sigh, she trudged to the register, conscious of Justin following right behind her.

The man on the other side of the counter was a surprise that ordinarily Beth would have enjoyed. Closer to Justin's age than the old man she'd pictured, he chatted about the weather while he rang up her purchases. But it was clear from the nervous glances he continued to cast at the door that he was worried Alice would return.

Justin stepped up to the register and Beth pushed a hand in her pocket, groaning when she encountered the two canisters of 35-mm film she'd shoved in there just before they'd left the ranch. She pulled them out and held up the yellow and black rolls. "I forgot I was going to see where I can get these developed."

"I can take care of that, miss," said AJ with a smile. "I send developing up to Jackson. Takes two days."

Two days. She could stay around for two days — *wanted* to stay around for much longer. Plus she was anxious to see the pictures from her outing with Justin. She nodded and set the canisters on the worn wooden counter.

AJ opened a drawer and pulled out two bright yellow envelopes. "What name should I use?"

"Use mine," said Justin before Beth had a chance to answer. "You already have my particulars."

After the rectangular developing envelopes were filled out, Justin finished paying for his purchases. He picked up the two paper bags, and Beth began to walk toward the door.

"Hold up a sec," he called out before she could push it open.

When she glanced over her shoulder, she found he'd stopped at the ice cream counter. The last thing Beth wanted after her run-in with Alice was a sugary dairy confection, and she opened her mouth to tell Justin as much.

Then he grinned at her.

Oh. Wow. Forget Alice. Forget the rest of the world.

When he gave her that look, she'd just about do anything he wanted. She shuffled over to join him. The menu was handwritten on a chalkboard behind the display freezer filled with five-gallon barrels of frozen goodness.

Justin glanced from Beth to the freezer and back to Beth, one eyebrow raised in silent question.

She browsed the sizes and prices listed on the menu board and shifted her gaze to his with an answering grin. "Make mine a triple."

Eyes alight and dancing, he inclined his head. "Name your poison."

Beth's mouth watered up. Any second now she'd embarrass herself by drooling. She leaned over the freezer and peered inside, reading over the labels. *Vanilla, French vanilla, chocolate, strawberry* — all rather unimaginative names, as far as she was concerned. She shifted her eyes to the second row. "Oh! Butter pecan, chocolate mint, and maple walnut!"

When Justin said nothing, Beth looked up to find him

staring at her, eyebrows struggling to reach his hairline and jaw slack. "You sure about that?" he asked slowly.

Beth peeked at the ice cream then returned her gaze to Justin and smiled with as much confidence as she could muster in the face of his blatant disbelief. "Yeah," she said with a shrug.

"Well, okay, then." He grinned at the clerk who'd rung up their purchases earlier. "Did you get that, AJ?"

"Yep!" The other man grinned as he slid a pointed brown sugar cone from a stack of them behind the counter. "How about you, Justin?"

"Well, now, let's see." Justin leaned over the display case, his brow furrowed in concentration. "I'll go with the French vanilla, a scoop of double chocolate chip, and top it off with banana walnut."

Leave it to Alice to ruin what had been a good day. As Beth waited for her ice cream, she glanced around. Would AJ find it intrusive if she shot a few pictures of the store? The blend of old-fashioned and modern all crammed together in a tiny space wasn't exactly something out of a Little House book, but she found its charm endearing. A rack of colorful postcards stood on the counter near the register, and next to that an old glass milk jug, more than half filled with silver coins and a few dollar bills. The scrap of paper affixed to the front was yellowed and curled on the edges, and the words that had been printed across the front in block letters — *TIPS FOR A NEW BALL FIELD* — had probably started out black but had since faded to a brownish color. How long had the town been saving for that project?

Chapter Thirteen

AJ handed Justin the first cone, his gaze roaming between the two of them, a hint of speculation in his eyes. Beth accepted the cone from Justin and went back to focusing on a rack of postcards that couldn't possibly have been all that interesting. Not that Justin could blame his old friend for being curious, but he mentally cursed Alice for being such a mean-spirited bitch and drawing so much attention. He slipped a five out of his wallet and passed it over the counter. When AJ handed him the change, Justin dropped it into the tips jug.

"See ya later," he said to AJ, and then caught Beth's eye and nodded toward the exit.

She'd recovered her composure, but neither spoke as he fell into step next to her and they crossed the tiny parking lot to his truck.

Justin held out his ice cream cone, and she accepted it with a raised eyebrow. "If you'll hold this a second, I'll get these things squared away." He weighted the purchases down with one edge of his battered green toolbox. Then he pulled open the door and seated Beth in the cab of the truck and hurried to the driver's side.

She handed him back his cone and smiled, her green eyes glinting. He might have only known her a few days, but it had been an intense few days, and he recognized that look. She was up to something.

"What?"

The expression on her face was one of studied innocence. "Nothing."

"Uh-huh. Sure." Justin started the truck and put it in gear.

"You just surprised me," she admitted. Then she indulged in a long, lazy lick of ice cream from the bottom scoop to the top.

Justin could only imagine the blend of flavors and he wasn't certain he'd consider it the least appealing. "Oh, yeah? How'd I do that?"

Her tongue snaked out, and she drew it upward along the scoops with agonizing leisure. His body began to stir in a predictable manner. Justin turned his attention to the road ahead as he licked at his top scoop.

"Well, your flavors are kind of... plain."

Justin pulled the cone away from his mouth in mid-lick. "Plain? It's ice cream. Sugar and dairy."

"I suppose." She swirled her tongue around her bottom scoop near the edge of the cone.

He caught the tongue-on-ice-cream action in his peripheral vision and held his breath. They'd be lucky if he didn't drive them off the road.

"Only... well, it's kind of unadventurous."

Justin couldn't hold back the loud bark of laughter. "I suppose that makes the combo you picked... *adventurous*, then?"

"A little bit, yeah. I like all the flavors, but I've never had them at the same time." She turned so she sat sideways in the seat, and he made the mistake of glancing in her direction just as she gave another lengthy swipe of tongue along her ice cream.

He sucked in a sharp breath. The drive was getting painful. He might even go insane if he didn't somehow get his hands on the girl in the seat next to him. He swung the pickup into the unfinished parking lot of the new athletic field. The place was deserted. And perfect.

He killed the engine and pulled the parking brake. Then he turned to face Beth just as she closed her lips over her top scoop and pulled it into her mouth. Maple walnut, his mind reminded him, and fierce need began to coil inside him. She closed her eyes as she swallowed the creamy confection. Then she swept her lips with the tip of her tongue. "Ummm." She popped opened her eyes again and regarded Justin with a steady gaze. "What's this place? Why are we stopping here?"

Words eluded him as he glanced through the windshield, barely registering the dirt parking lot lined by newly planted cottonwood trees running the length. "The town started developing an athletic field... for... athletics... baseball, and... stuff."

She slid her tongue around her ice cream, down to two flavors now... make that one and a half.

She swallowed her mouthful. "You... want to play baseball or something?"

The game he wanted to play definitely included bases and... He squeezed his eyes shut. Too late. The image of Beth pulling the rest of her second scoop into her mouth and clamping her lips around it would remain with him forever.

"Your ice cream's melting," she observed, pointing at it with her chin. Her tongue dipped out and scooped a bit of butter pecan then disappeared behind her lips.

Justin glanced at the cone in his hand. His flavors had started to run together, little streams of sticky melted cream flowing over the cone to coat his fingertips.

Beth popped the last of her cone into her mouth, chewed and swallowed. "Wow, you must be... hot... to melt your ice cream so fast." She smiled and settled her hands around his and pulled the cone toward her mouth. "Let me just get this for you," she murmured, and proceeded to slurp the dripping ice cream. She started with a tentative lick at the edge of the brown wafer, but quickly drew her tongue around the not-so-frozen treat and swallowed every melted drip while his hand still held the cone. Then she turned her attention to the errant flow that ran over his fingers.

Fundamental awareness of her increased tenfold, and Justin's body exploded to life. Her mouth was cool as she wrapped her lips around his pinky, but it became warmer as she drew each of his fingers into her mouth in turn. Then she released his hand and sent him a sweet smile that tilted his world.

"You ate my ice cream," he murmured in disbelief. Where had she found room in that tiny body for roughly five scoops of ice cream?

Laughing softly, she guided the cone to his lips and he slurped the last of the French vanilla. The sugar cone tumbled from Beth's fingers as she leaned forward and pressed her warm lips against his. When she parted those lips and invited him in, the sweetness lingered, tantalizing his palate.

Justin hovered at the edge for just a moment, parried with her teasing tongue while he tunneled his hand through her silky curls to gently cup the back of her neck. Holding her still, he gave himself over to the moment and tasted every bit of her mouth. He would have urged her closer, pulled her into his lap, but she was already there, leaning into his kisses, giving more of the sweetness he'd just plundered.

Like a cat, she crawled up his body and clung to him. Mindful of the steering wheel that had to be pressing into the small of her back, he swiveled in his seat to avoid crushing her... not that she appeared to notice. He kept one hand buried in her hair while he allowed the other one to travel beneath the hem of her blouse and tickle her spine.

Never in his life had Justin experienced such a frenzy of passion surging through his blood. Never had he been as aware of another person as he was of Beth. His whole body strained against the boundaries of decency as he explored her softness with his hands and mouth.

He pulled back, gasping for breath as consciousness of where they were filtered into his overheated brain. Beth flopped back into her seat, her green eyes nearly glowing with stirring emotion.

"I'm sorry," began Justin, feeling the *need* to apologize more than the sentiment behind the apology itself.

"I'm sorry, too," murmured Beth, curving her lips gently upward.

Her words turned his heart to lead, and it sank to somewhere near the vicinity of his stomach.

Shaking her head, she snatched up his fingers like a frog snapping a fly. Then she gently tugged his hand closer and flattened it over her heart. "Feel that?" Her voice was as unsteady as he knew his would be if he could speak. Her heart leapt so violently against his touch, he wondered if he wouldn't soon be holding it in his palm. She drew in deep gasps of air as if oxygen-starved, and her chest heaved up and down with the effort.

Because he couldn't speak, he nodded slowly.

"So..." she whispered. "Maybe we should establish what it is we're sorry about." She touched the fingers of her free hand to his lips. "Because I'm only sorry that we have to stop."

Justin stared. *No other woman.*

She eased her hold on his hand and laced their fingers together. "So... did you bring me here so we could play baseball?" Her hair spilled to her shoulders and shrouded her face like a veil. She shook it back, but it only fell forward again.

"No," he answered quietly, reaching out to push the hair from her face so he could see her brilliant green eyes. "But I didn't stop here to make out like teenagers at a drive-in, either."

Interest flickered in her gaze and her lips twitched into a smile. "You still have drive-in theaters here?"

"Not in Orson's Folly, no. But up in Oslow there's one still operating." He grinned. "Why? Got a sudden hankering to see a movie?"

Beth twisted in her seat and shifted her gaze to stare out the window for a few heartbeats. Justin held his breath. She was definitely up to something now.

The gaze she finally leveled on him was filled with heat and a suggestion of wildness. "I'm sure we wouldn't see much of the actual movie. I'd much rather save the money and make out under the stars tonight."

Justin stopped breathing. *Oh, man. From zero to engines*

revved and waiting on the green flag in six words or less. He had to get away from the enclosed space with her, or they'd quite likely get picked up for public indecency. Wouldn't Sheriff Tenbaum just love that?

He popped open the door and hopped out, striding to the back of the truck on shaky legs. He took his time searching through the brown paper sacks for his own impulse purchase, hoping to recover his self-control before Beth climbed from the pickup to join him.

"What's that?" she asked as she approached, eying the roll of red tissue paper wrapped around two balsawood sticks. Squinting at the label, she read, "*Sky Master?*"

Grinning, Justin grabbed the spool of string from the bag and headed for the center of the ball field.

"Wait a minute!" she cried out from where he'd left her. "Wait... you brought me here to fly a kite?"

Justin glanced over his shoulder but didn't stop walking when he noted her trotting to catch up. "You ever flown a kite?"

"Ah..." Beth chuckled nervously. "Not since I was about eight. And *it* landed in a tree."

Suddenly he was on top of the proverbial world. "Then it's time you try again." He gestured to the open field. "See? No trees. Nothing to get snagged on."

Beth stood stock still except for two slow blinks of her eyes. She swallowed once, and then launched herself at him. Justin dropped the kite kit and braced himself with one foot behind him to avoid falling over as he opened his arms. She was warm and squirmy and laughing... happy. And when she drew back and gazed into his eyes, she'd lost the little line that had been pinching the bridge of her nose since they'd run into Alice at AJ's.

Leaning forward again, she laid her lips on his for a quick, hard kiss that was somehow more intimate than the hot and heavy kisses they'd just shared in the cab of his pickup. Then she pulled out of his arms, bent to retrieve the kite, and grabbed his hand as she took off for the center of the field. "Come on," she said, laughing. "I wanna fly this kite."

As Justin joined her in a flat-out run, he noticed the

little things. The glint of gold in her hair as it bounced against
her shoulder... the warmth of her hand in his... the delighted
peal of her giggles when she turned and caught his eye.

No. Other. Woman.

* * *

"I can't believe you sacrificed part of your shirt so the
kite would fly." Beth rocked back onto her palms and squinted
at the red dot floating amid fluffy white clouds on a clear blue
backdrop. With her eye, she followed the string from the kite
back to the man next to her, lying on his back with his boots
off, legs crossed at the ankles and occasionally giving the
string a languid tug.

He glanced at his now ragged shirttail and shot her a
cheeky grin. "Something I hope my mom never finds out, since
she gave me the shirt for my birthday."

The breath hung up in Beth's throat, and she could only
stare speechless for several seconds. Then she chortled.
"You're crazy."

He winked and nodded. "A point on which I have no
doubt my mother will agree."

Beth shielded her eyes to better regard the speck in the
sky. "How far up is that, do you think?"

Justin lifted the ball of string he held in his hand and
studied it, then glanced up at the kite. Rolling his head
sideways, he shifted his gaze to meet hers. "About three
hundred feet, maybe a little less."

"It looks so far away."

"It... *is* far away," he said slowly. His tone might have
been lazy, but his sharp blue eyes sparked with amusement.
"It's three hundred feet up in the air."

The stiff breeze toyed with the shock of blond hair falling
across his forehead. Beth reached out and wound a strand
around her finger. "I never would have pegged you for the *let's
fly a kite* type."

Justin chuckled and tipped his head back to assess her
through half-closed eyes. "You wouldn't, huh? What type *did* I
strike you as?"

She gave the strand of hair a little tug and found herself grinning as she remembered how they'd met. "Gallant rescuer, maybe? White knight?" She paused to enjoy the pink staining his cheeks. "I kind of see you as someone who takes things in stride, but... more all-businessy."

"All-*businessy*? Is that even a word?" Justin uncrossed his legs and rolled to a sitting position.

The lock of hair Beth had been playing with slipped through her fingers like fine silk and she dropped her hand to her lap. "It's a word if I say it is."

Justin shrugged. "Well, you're the one who's gonna have a string of letters following your name one day."

He yanked twice on the string. The bit of red in the sky dipped and rose sharply. Grinning, he pulled the string tight and then jerked it a couple of times in quick succession. The kite plummeted toward the earth, but then caught the wind again and began to soar left, then right, then left again.

Laughter bubbled up from Beth's throat. "It's dancing!"

Justin flicked a glance in her direction and grinned. Then he turned his attention back to the kite and let out some more string. "You know what's cool about kite flying?" he asked softly.

"What?"

"There's this sense of being connected to it. Here I am, holding onto this thing that's flying, just sailing on the wind." He tugged the line again. "And I have some control over it, but it's also up there at the whim of the wind."

"The best of man and nature coming together," murmured Beth. She glanced at the half-completed bleachers. The peace surrounding them warmed her. "It's flying so free up there, like it has no cares... and yet it's tied to the earth."

Justin's smile came from someplace deep inside... a place Beth suspected few people were ever invited into. "We all spend so much time looking at our feet and the junk on our path. When you fly a kite, you look up, to the sky, the freedom. And you can be the anchor or you can be the wind. But me... I'm the kite! Tethered to reality yet floating on a dream."

"Or trapped." Beth gasped and pressed her fingertips to her lips. "I'm sorry. That just came out."

His smile turned outward again, and he directed it at her. "Is that what you feel, Beth? Trapped?"

She started to deny it with a shake of her head, but he raised one eyebrow, silently challenging her response, and she swallowed back the words. The wind blew her hair into her face and she brushed it back. "My dad loves me. He's been strict my whole life, but it's not a mean kind of strict. I don't think he knows how to be mean. Sometimes, though—" She stopped as her dad's face shifted in her memory. The next words tightened in her throat and she pulled in a deep breath and blew it out before she could continue. "He can be suffocating with his love. And I'm sure Alice felt smothered, too, before she left, but — from my point of view, she always had more freedom than I did."

Justin's eyes swept over her, an acute awareness in them that rocked Beth to her core. "So this trip to study poison ivy is your way of rebelling?"

Beth shrugged, unwilling to admit outright how close to hitting the nail on the head he'd actually come. "Kinda. I could have studied poison ivy and poison oak in Michigan. We have some state parks with good trails." She sighed. "But I always wanted to see the world."

A muscle worked in Justin's jaw just before he lifted his gaze back to the kite. "What made you choose Wyoming? Alice?"

Beth groaned. "Wyoming was my dad's choice because Alice is here. I was so happy to be allowed some freedom, I didn't complain."

Justin began winding the string back onto the ball, reeling in the kite. He angled his head to meet her eyes. "And when your adventure is over? What then?"

Beth smiled and shrugged. "Who says my adventure ever has to end? The world is big. Too big to see if I'm sitting in one place."

He didn't answer, just focused on rolling up the ball of string as he relentlessly reined in the kite. She watched with a pang of sadness as the kite lost its altitude, slowly but surely... its descent inevitable. When it was about twenty feet away, the red kite took a sudden dive and landed nose first in the center of the pitcher's mound. Startled, Beth stole a glance at Justin, wondering if he'd aimed to do that, but his face was blank of all expression.

Chapter Fourteen

As they pulled into the yard, Justin caught the glance Beth slid in his direction and tried to ignore the little stab in his chest at the wariness in her eyes. She had every right to be cautious. He hadn't been the epitome of friendliness on the way back to the ranch. His heart had crowded a sackload of emotion up into his throat at her announcement that she planned to see the world. Not only had actual speech been difficult but finding the words — any words — to hold a conversation just hadn't been possible.

Things like that happened when a guy went and let his heart get in front of his brain.

Beth opened the door and slid to the ground before Justin could get there to help her, which was just as well.

"I want to check on the puppies." She sent him a wavering smile over her shoulder as she pretty much skipped to the barn.

"Go ahead. I'll catch up." Justin rested a hand on the open door of his pickup and watched her taking bouncy steps away from him. She'd be doing that for good soon.

At the barn, Gus met her in the doorway. Justin was too

far away to hear what he said, but the tinkle of Beth's delighted laughter echoed across the stable yard. Jealousy flared, instant and hot. He should have walked with her, should have been privy to whatever was going on. *He* should have been the one to make her laugh.

Beth caught his eye and gestured for him to come over. "Hurry up, pokey!" she called with another laugh. "Gus has a surprise!"

He could give Gus a surprise of another sort. Justin slammed the pickup's door with a little more force than it required and stomped across the yard, taking care to ease the glower he knew was etched across his face before he reached the barn.

"So... a surprise, huh?" Justin glanced between the pair as he approached. Excitement lit Beth's face, but Gus wore an edgy frown.

"After Doc Douglas looked at 'em, we left the pups in one of the stalls here and checked on the girls." The foreman shifted from foot to foot. "After Doc left, I came back and the one with the bum leg was the only one in the stall."

Alarm sprinted through Justin, leaving little footprints of dread in its wake. But from the grin splitting Beth's face, she already knew what had happened to the pups... and it wasn't anything bad. He concentrated on drawing his next breath, knowing Gus would get to the rest of the story in his own time.

"I didn't see no blood or anything, so I didn't think a wild critter'd gotten in." Gus took off his hat and scratched his head. "As I stood there trying to figure out what'd happened to 'em, one-a the old barn cats came slinking into the stall from the tack room. Then the durndest thing happened. The old biddy grabbed the lil' pup before I could stop her and dragged it off."

Justin shook his head, somewhat mystified and growing irritated. It could take Gus half a Sunday to announce he'd been to church. Most of the time it didn't bother Justin. This was not one of those times. He bit back a curse and asked, "So what did she do with them?"

Replying with a smirk, Gus sauntered into the barn with

a wave for them to follow. It took a second for Justin's eyes to adjust to the dim light, but he could walk the barn in the dead of night if he had to. He captured Beth's hand as Gus led them to the tack room at the back of the building.

Squealing and mewling emanated from a dinner plate-sized hole in the wall behind the workbench. Gus held out a flashlight and Justin accepted it then crouched to have a look.

"Well, dang," he murmured at the sight of the four pups curled up next to a litter of three brown tabby kittens, all suckling on a matching mother cat. He motioned for Beth to join him and shone the light through the crack.

She caught her breath and then made a crooning sound in the back of her throat that instantly gave Justin a few inappropriate thoughts. "Well, aren't you just a natural mom?" she asked the cat.

The mostly feral barn cat mewed in response instead of hissing or growling, and Justin's jaw dropped. When Beth reached through the hole, though, the new mama covered all the babies with her scrawny body and edged back from the opening.

Beth turned her head and caught Justin's gaze. "What are we going to do with them?"

He jerked, startled by the question. "Do with *who?*"

Beth tilted her head and threw him one of her killer smiles. He didn't even know what she was about to ask of him, but he knew he'd do it.

"What will we do with the new family?" she asked.

"Uh, leave 'em where they are?" He sighed and glanced around the tack room for a box to carry the babies in.

Next to him, Gus chortled and Justin sent him a glare. Really? All the scrapes the man had helped him through and this time he was leaving him hang?

Beth's face clouded. "But what if Mama takes them away somewhere? Or puts them in a nest that's too high and they fall? What if they get kicked by a cow?"

Justin opened his mouth, but no words came out. How could he tell her that crap like that sometimes happened on a ranch — that it was just one of the things ranchers got used to?

She regarded him with an unblinking green stare while she worried at her bottom lip with her perfect white teeth. Oh, man, if his mom and dad came home to find their home had been turned upside down and a barn cat welcomed inside, they'd flip out.

Gus cleared his throat. "You know, that mother cat's raised probably six... seven litters. Half the cats out here are hers." He shrugged. "She's a good mama. But she won't take well to losin' her freedom, not bein' able to do her job."

Beth tilted her head sideways and knit her brow. "Her job?"

"Yes, ma'am." Gus nodded. "She's in charge of rodent control. She won't know what to do with herself in the house."

"But if she raises the puppies... will they... will they hunt barn mice, too?"

Bending his head, Justin scratched his jaw to hide a smile. Only his Daffodil Gal would worry about a litter of pups identifying with the wrong species.

Whoa! My *gal?* His heart thumped hard against his chest as though to answer in the affirmative.

Beth returned her attention to the mother cat. "You take care of those babies and I'll visit every day." She bent closer and whispered, "I'll bring you all kinds of treats."

She could have offered to give the damn cat the run of the pantry for all Justin cared. His brain stopped processing anything past "visit every day." Which meant she maybe planned to stick around for a little while.

When Beth stood, she locked gazes with Justin and stole his breath. Her eyes, so big and round, held a mix of fear and pain that he wanted to wipe away forever. Whatever she needed from him, he wanted to give it. He stepped forward and settled an arm around her shoulders. This was a woman who wanted to take on the world, yet she was terrified for the safety of a litter of puppies.

"This kind of thing happens all the time. They'll be fine." *I hope.*

Gus developed a coughing fit and Justin shot a warning glance at his friend.

"Okay..." Her mouth worked silently as she cast a last

glance at the hole in the wall and then allowed Justin to lead her from the stable.

When they arrived at the truck to retrieve their purchases, Beth flashed another of those smiles that made him want to lasso the moon for her. "What are we cooking for dinner tonight?"

Already reaching into the back of the pickup, Justin halted, a chill rolling over him in a slow, delicious wave. His heart slammed against the inside of his chest and he spun around. Dinner? Who cared about food when everything he would ever need stood barely a foot away?

Ravenous for the type of nourishment only Beth could provide, he stepped forward and nudged her into the side of the truck. He slid his hands upward along her arms until he reached her shoulders. Her eyes widened, twin pools that had deepened to a mossy green when her pupils dilated. Her lips parted and the tip of her tongue peeked out.

That was all the invitation Justin needed. Angling his head, he swooped in and devoured her mouth. Tongues met, played, then hers eased back and he followed with his, not asking for admittance, demanding it.

With a low cry, Beth molded herself to him, the fit so perfect she surely had been made for him. His body stirred to life, warmth spreading inward to pool low in his belly. She tasted of sunshine and sweetness. She was clover and he was the bee. When she rolled her head back, Justin changed the angle of the kiss, taking them both deeper. Using a light touch, he traced a hand over her slender hips, pausing at her waist before skimming the back of his hand up along her ribcage. Beth's soft moans became whimpers. He splayed the fingers of his other hand along her cheek and rubbed his thumb lightly back and forth. Tremors rippled through her as heated awareness flared in her eyes.

Blood roared through Justin's ears, mimicked by a persistent distant thrumming that swelled and rumbled until it pervaded his whole being then faded into a low growl at his feet. He was drowning and he didn't care. Beth hooked one leg around his and caressed his calf. Wild notions took flight with the many creative ways they could sate the hunger.

Icy wetness splashed across Justin's forehead and flowed down his cheek, jerking him back to reality. Blue-white lightning coiled and writhed across the sky, followed quickly by the slow heavy roll of thunder.

"Come on!" Justin grabbed the bags containing their purchases from the back of the truck and snagged Beth's hand.

Laughing, they raced across the yard to the ranch house, aiming for the front door. Once they reached the shelter of the overhang, Justin turned around and regarded the torrents of water pouring straight down from the darkened sky. More shrieks of laughter gurgled from Beth's mouth, harmonizing with the pinging drum of rain as it splashed into the brown puddles already dotting the yard. A curtain of water cascaded off the eaves overhead, bubbling and foaming in little eddies at the base of the porch.

She stepped away from him and shook her head, spraying droplets from her saturated hair. "Where did that come from?"

Justin pulled a hand down his face, squeezing the rainwater from his skin. "It's been building all day. I thought we'd have a bit of time before it hit."

"But it was sunny when we went into the barn."

"Welcome to Wyoming." Justin pushed open the front door and held it for Beth, his body still tingling with the residual effects of their intimate embrace.

Chapter Fifteen

The rain gave every indication of hanging around for a while. In fact, the wind had picked up. Standing in the window of the guest room, Beth peered out at the gloom. Occasionally she was able to glimpse the barn through the veil of water that at times seemed to be driven sideways. In contrast to the gentle flutter of the curtain caught in the breeze of the fan on her dresser, the tree outside her window waved its branches like an old man shaking his fist in anger.

The force of the storm sent a shudder up her spine. Yet Justin hadn't seemed particularly concerned when he'd suggested she get changed out of her drenched clothing. She glanced over her shoulder at the closed door and considered the man who was most likely in the kitchen cooking dinner. She should join him... and she would. Just as soon as her palms stopped sweating and her heart slowed to a less frantic rhythm whenever she thought of him.

That kiss...

She sighed as thrills zapped her body all over again. She'd grown used to Justin's kisses... maybe a bit too used to them. His little pecks, his tender grazes. His heated embraces.

But *that* kiss had been the back-bending, life-changing stuff of romance novels... or a movie. He'd swept her away like Rhett had done with Scarlet. It had been... electric.

Lightning sizzled across the sky in sheets of blue. For a moment, the yard outside was lit in brilliant fluorescent white. Thunder crashed and the house shook. Startled, even though she'd expected it, Beth clutched at the windowsill. The next flash lingered and the thundering response rolled in with a slow grumble. The wind's low howl became a whistle. The clatter of pebbles hitting glass panes echoed through the room, sending Beth jumping away from the window, her heart racing now for an entirely different reason.

Didn't hail mean tornadoes? It did in Michigan!

The furious wind grew louder, more insistent. The sturdy limbs of the tree on the other side of the window bent — would they snap?

Darkness, immediate and complete, blanketed the room. The steady whir of the fan on the dresser ceased. Beth found herself taking in sharp, quick breaths and concentrated on calming herself before she hyperventilated. Using illumination from the quick bursts of lightning, she found her way to the door just as it was pushed open from the hallway, admitting the thin thread of a flashlight beam.

"Beth? You all right?"

Relief coursed through her as she tumbled into his arms. "Justin! I've never seen a storm like this. Are we—" She was almost afraid to ask, but she had to know. "Are we okay?"

He rubbed a hand briskly up and down Beth's spine. "We'll probably be in the dark for the rest of the night. If it slows down a bit, I'll go fire up the generator."

"Generator?" Beth pulled back with a frown. "You mean go outside?"

He nodded. In the dim light it was impossible to see whether he was smiling, but she heard the warmth in his response. "When things settle some. You'll be okay in the house. I promise."

Impatience punched the breath from Beth's lungs and she pushed against Justin's chest. "You doofus! It's not *me* I'm worried about."

* * *

A pleasurable silly feeling swelled through Justin. Beth... worried about *him*! He couldn't stop the grin from spreading across his face. Maybe the darkness was a good thing, after all. He shone the flashlight toward the stairway.

"Come on, let's get downstairs. We're having a picnic in the living room."

"Really?" A delighted giggle rippled forth and she slid her hand through the crook of his arm. "Lead me to it. I'm at your mercy, here in the dark."

Silly flashed into sizzle in the space of a lightning flash. Beth's warm grasp on his arm crackled over his skin and raised goose bumps — along with an acute awareness of the hallway lined with too-convenient bedroom doors. Heat pooled in a southern direction. Justin pulled in a sharp breath and held it as he hurriedly guided her to the steps.

Each soft laugh as they negotiated their way ratcheted his need a notch tighter. By the time they reached the bottom of the staircase, he trembled with the effort of reining in his instinctive responses.

"Go on through here," he murmured at the archway into the living room. "I've got it all set up."

"O-o-oh," she breathed when she stepped into the golden glow of the candles he'd lit. She let go of his hand and spun into the room and farther into the light. Justin blinked. She was barefoot. Her yellow cotton dress swirled with her movements. Tiered layers were connected with loosely crocheted lace in the same shade, and Justin caught glimpses of fair skin and pale silk. He struggled to swallow, but his mouth couldn't be drier if he'd chewed down a cupful of sand.

With effort, he dragged his gaze upward only to stop breathing when he took in her bare shoulder at the edge of a wide neckline edged in the same crocheted lace. Her hair, only a shade or two darker than her dress, cascaded like spun gold. She skipped the couple of steps over to the blanket on the floor in front of the hearth, where he'd lit more candles.

"It's too windy to start a fire," said Justin when his

tongue unstuck itself from the roof of his mouth. "Once it calms some, we can try." He joined her at the blanket and gestured for her to sit.

Beth seemed to float to the floor. Her dress settled about her like golden waves at sunset, and she tucked her knees to the side. Pink-painted toenails peeked out from beneath the softly flowing fabric.

Yum! He stared, his mouth watering, and not for food. He'd love to start at her pretty toes and kiss his way along one leg until—

"Aren't you going to sit down and eat with me?"

Beth's lilting voice brought him back to the living room. *Right. Eat.* He'd forgotten. He lowered himself to the floor and lifted the lid off the covered dish between them. "We got us a real cowboy supper here."

"Beans and franks." She leaned forward and laughed. "And you cut the franks into bite-size pieces!"

"Only way to eat 'em out on the trail."

"You still do that? Go out on the trail?" She picked up the top plate and dipped the serving spoon into the orange-brown mixture.

"Yes, ma'am." Justin waited while she loaded the plate and then accepted it with a nod of thanks when she passed it to him. "Takes a couple of days to drive them to the high pasture and take care of business."

A shiver rippled through her, and she held up a hand in a stop gesture, evidently recalling what he'd said about that side of things.

"I guess I thought of it as going fast — like I might read in a book or see in a movie." She finished loading her plate and replaced the lid on the casserole dish.

Justin's lips twitched, but he held his chuckle inside and said nothing.

"So you really sleep outside... Is it fun?"

The lip twitching became a smile and his aching muscles relaxed as he warmed to the topic. "I love being outside. I can't think of anything more peaceful than sleeping in the fresh air." And after the other night, he'd add stargazing to the mix.

"I think I'd like sleeping outside."

Three strobe-like flashes of lightning bounced into the room, followed by a lazy roll of thunder.

"Obviously not tonight," said Justin with a wink.

Beth chuckled and scooped up a mouthful of beans. "Umm... I love these. They're sweet!"

"Secret recipe." Justin chuckled. *Thanks, Mom.*

She took another bite and chewed. "This is so much better than I'd have expected."

"And..." Justin lifted the lid of the cooler beside him. "Since we're not on the trail, we have our choice of beverage." He held up two bottles. "Beer or cola?"

"Umm, ah..." She pointed at the longneck brown bottle. "Beer, if you're up for splitting one with me. Love the taste, but the second I drink more than a few sips I get crazy loose."

Justin coughed and set aside the green-toned bottle with the hourglass shape. "Beer it is." He twisted off the cap and dropped it next to the soda bottle. "So no wild college parties? Or just none you can remember?"

"You know, not all college students are about going to Saturday night keggers and sparking doobies." Beth lifted the bottle from his hand with a chuckle. "Most maybe, but not all. Definitely not me. All it took was one beer and an evening with my best friend holding my hair to motivate me in the other direction."

Adding his chuckle to hers, Justin sat back against the base of the couch and crossed his ankles. Candlelight glinted off the brown bottle as she tilted her head back and took a long swig.

He remembered to breathe. Just.

When she handed the beer back, he raised it to his mouth. Beth's lips pulled gently upward into a hint of a smile. Justin stopped in mid-drink and their eyes connected over the bottle. Awareness rippled through him and he finished his swallow, then set the bottle safely out of the way on the stone hearth. Still she stared, that secret smile curving the lips he wanted to taste again.

"What?" he asked when he couldn't keep silent any longer.

"Not a lot. Only..." She lifted one shoulder. "It's never

been this easy to be around someone before, you know?" She nodded at the beer. "Sharing that just made me realize it."

Justin knew exactly what she meant, because he felt the same way. For whatever inexplicable reason, they "fit." But as much as he wanted to, the notion of agreeing with her out loud terrified him — as though to speak the words would somehow put the concept even further from his grasp.

"How about some dessert?" he asked instead, reaching for the plate beside the cooler and pulling back the aluminum foil to reveal cellophane-wrapped golden cakes.

Beth squealed in delight. "Twinkies! I love these things!"

As the easy grin spread over his face, his tension drained. Apparently he'd gotten it right when he'd raided the pantry for snack food. He picked up the package and tore open the end, then slid one of the cream-filled sponge cakes into his hand and offered it to her.

She held his gaze captive as she leaned forward and closed her lips around the cake, biting into it with a soft moan. As her eyelids fluttered downward, instant desire swamped him. He eased his arm back, but she clamped a hand around his wrist and stopped his motion while she took another bite.

All the air rushed from his lungs, probably killing a few brain cells in the process.

She took the last mouthful and licked a bit of cream from his fingers. His nerve endings seared hopeful little thoughts into his bloodless brain. Rolling to her knees, Beth picked up the package and slid out the second Twinkie. Then she aimed it in his direction, and obediently Justin opened his mouth. When he sank his teeth into the soft treat, sugary cream gushed from the inside of the cake and spread over his tongue.

Beth crawled closer. With the candlelight glinting off her golden hair and reflecting in her green eyes, she reminded him of a cat. A wildcat intent on her prey... which would be him. She teased him with the other half of the golden cake, bringing it close then pulling it back. On her third pass, he grabbed her hand and pulled it to him, taking another bite before releasing her. The sweetness filled his mouth again.

But a cream-filled sponge cake wasn't what he craved by a long shot. So when Beth popped the last bite into her mouth and shot him a wicked grin, Justin locked his hand around her wrist and tugged, bringing her up against him for just a moment before he intentionally toppled over backward, pulling her with him. Her surprised little squeal sent liquid heat to delicious places.

* * *

Sprawled over Justin, her body molded to his by gravity, Beth sought purchase with her elbows to steady herself, but he pulled her arms over his head and kept her off-balance and resting her weight on him.

The flickering candlelight played shadows over his face, and his blue eyes gleamed with quiet intensity as he gazed up at her. He was not unaffected by their intimate embrace, yet he made no move to deepen it. And he wouldn't — Beth understood that.

But it was costing him.

Her hair rained down around her face as she bent and touched her lips to his, softly at first. At his sharp intake of breath, she took advantage of his parted lips to settle her mouth more firmly on his. He brought his hand down to cradle her neck. Beth angled her head and opened her mouth, and with a groan he took her up on the invitation. Their tongues met, dallied, and then he pushed in deeper. The hand at her neck fisted in her hair. The one at her waist knotted the fabric of her dress.

Lightning burst several times like the flash of a camera, bathing the room in momentary brilliance. Then they were alone with the candles again. Thunder rolled in the distance. The storm was leaving them.

On the other hand, the tempest brewing in Beth was only just beginning. She shifted, easing back to graze soft kisses across the corner of his mouth. Then she glided her lips along his cheek and jaw until she reached the sensitive spot just below his left ear.

Justin moaned and rolled them over, bracing his weight on his elbows as he trailed wet kisses along her neck to her throat. He inched lower toward the elastic neck of her dress, and she melted into a quivering puddle of boneless surrender beneath him.

"Beth," he murmured, and her name on his lips sent fiery chills running through her veins. With his mouth and chin, he nudged the material off her shoulder. His warm breath fanned her already overheated skin, and she arched into his touch.

He rained kisses back along her throat and claimed her lips in another deep kiss before he slowly pulled back. Beth cried out in frustration as she tried to make him stay.

"We gotta stop, Beth," he murmured gently, easing back another inch.

She might not have yet been a woman of the world, but she was well aware that she'd turned him on. Thrilling electrical charges raised the hairs on her arms, which were already pebbled with goose bumps. "It's okay," she murmured, locking her arms around his neck. "It's okay, I want this... want you..."

But when he only smiled and rose up on his hands, she allowed her fingers to slip away. He rolled over and sprang to his feet, then quickly gathered up their plates and carried the remains of their dinner from the room without saying a word. Beth lay as though glued to the floor, bereft with his abrupt exit and washed in a sudden chill.

Shivers wracked her body as she pushed herself into a sit. What had just happened? Why had he stopped? Had she done something wrong? For the first time, she wished she was more experienced in such things. Shivers gripped her and her teeth chattered. She shifted to her knees and snatched the colorful crocheted afghan from the back of the leather sofa. But wrapping it around her did nothing to alleviate the cold that radiated from inside.

Her hands trembled and she clasped them together to still the violent shaking. When she spotted the half empty bottle of beer on the hearth, she seized it and downed it in two big gulps. Lightning splashed the room with blue-white light. The thunder took so long to rumble its answer, she almost didn't catch it.

"Beth." Justin's murmur came from the doorway.

Her heart leapt into her throat, and her whole body jerked as though operated by invisible strings. She set the empty beer bottle back on the hearth and turned. Long fingers of light cast by the candles reached across the floor toward him. In the shadows, his face appeared haggard and a little drawn. He leaned against the doorjamb without making a move to enter the room. When he spoke, his voice was low and coarse, difficult to hear. "If we make love, I'll never be able to let you go."

Let her go? Beth blinked in surprise. Didn't he realize her heart was already begging him to hold it forever?

"But I said... I mean — I meant it..." Awkwardness stole her voice.

"Would you marry me, Beth?"

Her pulse leaped and her breath caught in her throat. Was that some kind of cowboy proposal? Stand across the room in the doorway and pop the question?

His tone took on soft desperation. "Would you give up your dreams of traveling, of seeing the world, to settle down with a rancher?"

She stared, not quite understanding what he was getting at. "I don't — don't... What are you asking?"

Justin pushed away from the doorjamb and gestured around the room. "This? This is my..." He ran his fingertips over his jaw. "I don't know what to call it... my heritage? My destiny, maybe? This is who I am. A rancher, all set up to follow in my father's footsteps."

Her mouth worked, but none of the words her brain tried to form would come out.

"You want to see the world," he reminded her.

She concentrated on the fat candle directly in front of her but could find no words with which to answer him.

"Thing is... when I make love... it's all or nothing. Once we took that step, I'd be unable to back away." He drew a deep breath. "So you'd have to stay... or I'd have to leave with you."

Her heart lightened. Of course, the perfect solution. He could come with her and then they'd return home to Wyoming together. "That would—"

Beth blinked in surprise. Justin no longer stood in the

doorway. She could only stare at the empty space where he'd been. Suddenly everything seemed more complicated, not at all simple. She sank onto the leather sofa and stared at the flickering candles lined up along the hearth like soldiers.

His words spiraled through her mind like miniature corkscrews, drilling holes, offering hope. *"Once we made love... all or nothing... unable to back away..."* And just as quickly dashing it. *"...set up to follow in my father's footsteps..."*

No, he hadn't been proposing. What had she been thinking? Who did that after knowing someone only a few days? What was wrong with her? Was she so star-struck by the first cute cowboy who came along that she'd begun thinking in terms of tulle and satin? He'd been right about it all. Right to remind her of her dreams... right to put on the brakes.

And yet... her heart whispered... *what if?*

She yawned and considered moving. The day was catching up with her. She should sneak on up to the guest room. She could use one of the candles to light her way.

In a moment...

* * *

Justin blew out the last of the candles just as the blaze he'd started in the fireplace took hold. He set the screen in place and turned, allowing his gaze to roam over the sleeping woman curled up in one corner of the couch. Wrapped in the afghan his mother had made the previous winter, Beth still shivered occasionally. Without power, the bedrooms would take on a chill in the wake of the storm, so it was better to sleep by the fire. He stepped closer to her and picked up the soft brown blanket he'd brought down from his mom's cedar chest. After he draped it over her, he sighed. She looked a little lost, not at all comfortable.

Lifting the blanket again, Justin sat down and eased Beth into his arms, drawing the blanket back over both of then. She stirred and whimpered but didn't open her eyes.

"Shh..." He smoothed a hand over her soft hair and gently pushed her head onto his shoulder.

What am I going to do with you? And how could he have fallen so hard so fast?

Chapter Sixteen

Beth stirred. Something thumped from across the room. She was a little stiff and cramped, but warm... so delightfully warm. A heart beat beneath her cheek, steady and measured. She inhaled deeply and the comforting woodsy scent she'd come to associate with Justin teased her to wakefulness. Cocooned in his cozy embrace, with her head tucked beneath his chin, she sighed. Could she wake up in his arms for the rest of her life and always be so content? His arm lay heavily over one bare shoulder where her dress had been pulled off while they slept. He breathed deeply and evenly... still asleep? How had she gotten into his arms?

The electricity had been out... but the turned wooden lamp on the end table was lit now, so power must have been restored. *Think. What happened?* She'd rested on the sofa and then... What?

He moaned softly and squeezed his arms a shade tighter, then sighed and relaxed again.

"Justin James McGee! Just *what* is going on here?" The controlled feminine voice breaking into the peace carried an undertone of disbelief and anger.

Justin jerked beneath Beth and sat straight up, wrapping her more tightly against him. She chanced a look at his face. Crimson crept up his neck into his cheeks, but his eyes were wide open and alert.

"Mom," he said in a soft, level voice.

Beth's eyes widened. "Mom?" she mouthed silently, her heart stampeding in her chest. Rolling inside of Justin's hold, she directed her gaze at the doorway.

The woman in the doorway didn't look like anyone's mom. Dressed in tight jeans, her slight frame nearly swam in the brown sweatshirt with WYOMING stenciled in a yellow half-circle across the chest. She raised an eyebrow, not in question, but in a subtle demand for an explanation.

When silence prevailed, she blew out an exasperated breath and shifted her stance to tap one booted foot. Her light brown hair fell to her chin and held streaks of gray, but her crisp blue eyes glittered, and Beth knew instantly where Justin's beautiful eyes had come from.

Awkwardly, Beth struggled to leave the shelter of Justin's arms, but he held her still.

"Where's Dad?" he asked, squinting into the hallway.

"He's—" Mrs. McGee blew out a fast breath. "He'll be along later."

Confusion crinkled Justin's brow. "Didn't he come with you?"

"No. He didn't."

Justin sucked in a deep breath and then turned his face toward the window, where sunshine streaked in through the glass. "What time is it? I expected you both this afternoon."

Mrs. McGee stiffened. "Obviously."

Easing into a stretch, Justin released Beth from his grasp, and she scrambled across the sofa, out of his reach.

"Beth, this is my mom, Mary McGee. Mom, this is Beth." He stood and stretched some more, rubbing the back of his neck as though he had a crick. "She's been staying here for the past few nights."

Mary crossed her arms over her chest. "Oh, she has."

"Her van broke down," Justin offered, holding his hand out to Beth.

Quaking inside and out, she grasped his firm hand and stood. "It's nice to meet you, Mrs. McGee."

Sharp blue eyes narrowed and pinned Beth in a stare. "Broke down, huh? I didn't see a strange vehicle outside."

He heaved a sigh and muttered something coarse under his breath. "Because it's at Walt's, Mom. He's fixing it. Beth didn't have any place to stay, so I put her up in the guest room."

"No place to stay..." Mary inclined her head. "So this isn't Alice MacKay's younger sister? The one she saw fit to call Tilly Mitchell about, complaining over the two of you out here shacking up together?"

"That's a crass way to put it," he said quietly.

"Well, the choice of words originated with our dear neighbor, Alice." She angled her head. "Have something you want to tell me?"

Justin subjected his mother to a hard stare that had Beth squirming on the inside. "I never said she didn't have kin in the area, Mom. Only that she didn't have anywhere to stay. And for the record, I've been bunking with Gus."

Mary McGee returned his stare with pursed lips. "And yet here you are."

"It's not — it's not — nothing happened... like..." Heat flooded Beth's face and she lowered her gaze to the floor, unable to meet Mrs. McGee's eyes, because if she'd had her way the night before, something most certainly *would* have happened.

"Mmm." After another head-to-toe raking glance, Mary dropped her arms. "I expect you'll want to freshen up now that you're... awake."

Under Mary McGee's scrutiny, Beth suddenly became aware of the stretchy neckline of her peasant dress still falling off one shoulder. She tried to swallow, but her mouth was too dry. She settled for straightening the neckline of her dress. "Yes, Mrs. McGee, I'd dearly love to get cleaned up and get dressed and..." *Oh, just great!* Because *that* didn't sound like she and Justin had just shared an innocent night.

Mary McGee stepped aside and inclined her head. Beth didn't need any more invitation.

"Excuse me," she mumbled as she scooted past and raced up the steps to the guest room.

"I need coffee," Justin grumbled as Beth's foot touched down on the upper landing.

* * *

"What are you doing here, Justin?"

No one could make people squirm in their seats quite like Mary McGee. Justin rubbed his eyes and yawned, feigning the need to wake up rather than answer the question. He shouldn't have followed her into the kitchen. Should have taken a moment. Or six.

They'd done nothing unseemly... he and Beth. Mostly. And he suspected his mother already knew that. Just as he suspected she was well aware of the potential for what she would consider "doing wrong." Black and white. That was how his mother saw everything. If something wasn't white then it had to be black.

Mary filled the glass coffeepot with water and set it on the heating element. Then she set the glass bulb of the vacuum drip system on top with the tube in the water and added precisely four scoops of coffee. After she sprinkled a pinch of salt over the top, she set the lid in place and flipped the switch on the base.

This was her element. She ruled the kitchen with an iron fist when she was home. Which was all the time.

Until recently.

She swung around and leveled her gaze on him. "Well? Are you planning to answer me? What's Alice MacKay's younger sister doing in my house... sleeping with my son?"

"We're not—" Justin bit off a curse and concentrated on relaxing his clenched fist. "It stormed last night and the power went out."

"Yes, I saw the power company working on the lines running alongside the highway." She tapped her fingertips on the countertop. "That doesn't explain why you two were together when I came in."

"The storm was bad — you know how they get. She'd

been spooked. So I lit a fire and we fell asleep talking." *More or less.* At least that was the story he was sticking with. What his mother didn't know couldn't hurt him… or Beth.

Mary opened the refrigerator and pulled out a package of bacon and a carton of eggs. After setting those on the counter, she bent and retrieved her iron skillet from the pots and pans cupboard. This she dropped onto the range with a clatter. Whirling, she captured Justin's eyes before he had a chance to look away.

"I know you're lonely out here, and you didn't want to come home from UW. I know one day you'll have to think about settling down." She sighed. "And I know you might want to sow some of those wild oats before…" She put her hands on her hips and glared at him. "But with Alice MacKay's *sister…* of all people?"

"You don't even know her, Mom," murmured Justin, picking up a paper napkin and folding it into smaller sections, unhappy with the direction of the conversation. Lots of potential for embarrassment going on, but he'd no clue how to redirect. "Besides, it's not like that."

Mary's eyes flashed. "It's not? I saw the way you were holding her while you slept."

Irritation flared and he rolled his eyes. "It was cold, and that old couch isn't all that comfortable."

His mother heaved an exasperated sigh. "Nothing happened?"

He did his best to inject his voice with innocence. "Nothing happened."

"Nothing's been happening?"

"No!"

"And do you plan to keep nothing happening?"

Definitely a lot of potential for embarrassment, but as a rule he didn't outright lie to his mother. Stretched the truth a time or two, maybe, but never told her an outright lie. He sucked in a deep breath. "I can't say."

Mary winced. "And there it is."

"There what is? She's smart and funny and… and I like her." Loved her, really. "Is it a far stretch that I enjoy spending time with her?"

"Alice MacKay's *sister*, Justin!" Mary grabbed a knife from the butcher block and ruthlessly sliced into the package of bacon.

"She's not like Alice, Ma." Justin slumped in his seat and softened his tone. "And from what I saw yesterday, they don't even get along."

The bacon spat and sputtered when Mary laid the strips in the pan. "So she's not likely to seduce you and then pretend to be pregnant so you'll marry her?"

At the gasp in the doorway, Justin spun around in his seat. Beth had changed into faded jeans and another of her gauzy blouses, this one white with red embroidery around the edges. The red ribbon designed to tie the neck closed dangled to the middle of her chest and the fabric of her filmy shirt was thin enough he could see the lacy bra beneath. Any other day he'd have stopped to admire the sight, but she clutched the doorjamb, her green eyes wide, obviously distressed.

How much had she heard? Obviously enough to steal the color from her cheeks.

Sending his mother a glare, Justin pushed away from the table and strode to Beth's side. When he tried to lay an arm across her shoulders, though, she flinched away from him.

Searing knives stabbed his heart, but he clenched his teeth against the emotions. It wasn't the time to think about himself. Beth had obviously overheard the harsh words about her sister. He stepped in front of her and laid his hands on her shoulders. She didn't pull away. *Good*. But she directed her gaze somewhere in the vicinity of his right shoulder. *Not so good.*

"Beth, look at me," he begged quietly.

Behind him, Mary McGee drew a sharp breath. Good. He'd shocked her, but just maybe she'd realize how she'd gone too far with her veiled accusations. He planted his knuckles beneath Beth's chin and lifted gently. Her eyes swirled with a mix of tumultuous emotions. Against his touch, her chin quivered.

"Listen to me, Beth. Mom's only talking about what I told you the other night — about Alice playing Braden and

Brody." He sighed. Desperation dictated his decisions now, and everything he'd hoped to spare her was about to hit her between the eyes. "There were some people who thought maybe — *maybe* Alice hadn't ever been pregnant, that she'd just said that to force Braden into getting married."

She swallowed and then wet her lips with the tip of her tongue. "I wouldn't — I couldn't—"

"I know that, sweetheart." For just a second, Justin flashed back to the evening before, when in the heat of the moment she'd begged him to make love with her. "I know you wouldn't," he said simply, realizing they both spoke the truth. He used the pad of his thumb to wipe away the single tear that rolled down her cheek.

"I'm... sorry." Mary's knuckles were white around the fork she held.

Justin slid his arm over Beth's shoulders and turned to face his mother with a heavy sigh. "I know, Mom. It's just—" He struggled to find the right words, hoping like anything he wasn't about to embarrass the woman in his arms. "You don't know Beth like I do."

"I can see that," she admitted quietly. With a flicker of a smile, she turned back to the range and pulled the bacon from the pan. He watched her for a moment, a sense of sadness enveloping him. He didn't want to fight with his mother, not when she was already going through so much.

"I... think I should see if Walt got the part for my van and if it can be repaired today," Beth said, the words stilted and forced, her voice holding the barest hint of quaver. "I should leave."

Justin's heart raced into a full-panic sprint as hurt folded itself over him and squeezed. *No... not yet.*

"Please don't leave because of me," Mary said, retrieving a bowl of eggs from the refrigerator. "Justin's right. I spoke out of turn. I'd like to get to know you." She gestured toward the kitchen table. "C'mon, you two. Sit down and have some breakfast. How do you like your eggs? Over easy? Sunny side up? Scrambled?"

"Over easy," Beth answered softly at the same time he did, and Justin smiled.

Mary McGee's mouth gaped briefly before she snapped it shut and turned to the range, where she cracked eggs into the pan.

Justin eased out the breath he'd been holding as Beth shuffled hesitantly to the table and allowed him to hold her chair. Their gazes engaged and the chill of reality swamped him. He'd been dreading her looming departure, still clinging to hope she would change her mind.

Dazed by the direction of his thoughts, he frowned as he slid into his seat. Holding onto such hope wasn't fair to either of them.

At the clink of china, Justin shook his head and forced his attention back to the kitchen. Instead of the red and white mugs with the assortment of chips they usually used, his mother had laid out the bone white china with the pink flowers around the edges. A smile pulled at his lips. She was trying.

Mary tipped the glass pot and poured steaming brown liquid into Beth's cup. The acrid aroma of strong coffee burst forth and clung on the air. He could barely wait for her to finish pouring his cup before he attacked it with the sugar.

Beth giggled.

Justin faltered with his hand over the sugar bowl. "What?"

"Have some coffee with your sugar?" Her blue eyes glinted with merriment.

Mary chuckled as she set a plate of bacon, eggs, and toast in front of Beth. "She's got your number." She set a similar plate in front of him then returned to the range and picked up her own plate.

Justin glanced between his mom and Beth, noting the apprehension had drained from Beth's eyes. His mother took her seat and raised an eyebrow. In defiance, Justin plunged the spoon into the sugar bowl one more time and loaded it to heaping before dumping it into his coffee. Both women smiled and for the first time since waking up to his mother's voice, the knots in Justin's stomach eased.

"So what brings you out to Wyoming?" Mary sprinkled pepper across her eggs, paused and squinted at the pepper shaker with a tiny frown pinching her brow. Then she shrugged and set the shaker on the table.

Justin jerked his head up, prepared to answer for Beth, but she smiled. "I came to study poison ivy and poison oak."

"Really?" His mom wrinkled her nose and tilted her head. "Why?"

Beth swept a butter knife laden with strawberry jam across a piece of toast. "They're cross-pollinating, and I'm trying to determine if they're producing a new subspecies, or if the plants that result are sterile." She took a bite of her toast.

Mary leaned forward and studied Beth, and Justin winced. The look on her face usually crushed full-grown men, himself included.

But Beth straightened in her chair and met his mother's gaze head-on, eyes wide, a gentle smile gracing her lips.

Things could get interesting. Justin sipped his coffee, watching over the rim of the cup as the two women he loved most in the world sized each other up. His heart did a slow flip as the thought registered, and he took a deep breath, releasing it slowly. That was something he'd be considering later.

Mary sat back and picked up a piece of bacon. "Did you roll in a patch?"

Hot coffee met the back of Justin's throat just as a chuckle forced itself out. The full-bodied liquid rolled a relentless path downward to sear and tickle his windpipe, and he sputtered, unable to breathe. At last the sip went down and with a final wheezing cough, he pulled in a huge gulp of air, blinking back tears.

Both women sat frozen, staring at him.

Mary cleared her throat. "Something strike you as funny, Justin?"

Another giggle escaped Beth, and she slid a glance in Mary's direction then her eyes drifted back to Justin. "He asked me the same thing you just did."

"He did, did he?" His mother bit a piece of bacon and turned to look at him while she chewed.

No way would he wager to guess what was going on behind those all-seeing blue eyes. So he offered a smile and a shrug.

Mary turned back to Beth. "Well, the rash seems to be healing nicely, at least."

Beth touched her fingertips to the rash on her neck. "Justin took wonderful care of me. He gave me an oatmeal bath and—" A bright crimson stain crept into her cheeks and she raised a hand to her mouth and stared at Mary, horror reflected in her eyes. "I mean, he gave me the oatmeal mix he said you use for rashes, and he also gave me some ointment, and he even washed my clothes for... me..."

Oh, damn. His mom would move in for the kill any time now.

Mary raised an eyebrow and sent a speculative look in Justin's direction that promised him she'd have an explanation out of him or know why not.

The color in Beth's cheeks darkened to that of fresh-pickled beets.

Justin risked another gulp of coffee, this time relishing the burn as it went down.

"Well, I'm glad to see my son took good care of you." Mary sipped her coffee. "You can hardly see the rash now. How long ago did you get it?"

Justin narrowed his eyes and glared at Mary. *Oh, you've still got it, don't you, Mom? You still know how to ask one question and get the answer to another.* Like the time she'd caught him making out with Sylvia Sanders in the stables. Instead of asking how long they'd been going at each other, she'd casually mentioned that she hadn't known he had a visitor and asked Sylvia if she'd been there long. Yep, she was still good. Except he was no longer a kid of sixteen.

"Only about—"

Justin held up his right hand. "Beth's been here for three nights, Mom. Last night was the first night we slept under the same roof, and that happened only because the storm was so bad."

Mary's eyebrows shot up. Then the lines in her face smoothed, and she sent him a stunning smile that stripped the years of worry away.

No wonder Dad fell in love with you...

"So what is going on with Dad, anyway?"

When his mom blinked and stared in confusion, Justin chuckled and offered a shrug. "Guess you'd have had to be in my head to make the logical leap to the question."

Returning his chuckle, Mary shook her head. "I don't know if I *want* to wander around in *that* mess."

Beth picked up her coffee cup, her big green eyes darting back and forth between Justin and Mary. But she kept silent. What was going on inside *that* head was the question *he* was most interested in. Likely he'd never be quite sure.

Mary stood and began gathering dishes. Beth shot out of her seat and snatched up Justin's plate, sliding it on top of hers with a gentle clatter. She gathered the silverware and set it on top of the plates, then carried it all over to the sink.

"You cooked breakfast. Let me at least wash up." She laid on her own particular brand of smile.

Justin laughed softly as he crossed to the back door and grabbed his Stetson. "I'm heading out to see what damage the storm did." He chuckled again as he pulled the door closed. Mary McGee might never know what hit her.

Small branches from the cottonwood tree lay scattered along the back of the house, but the shingles on the roof appeared intact. He whistled as he crossed the yard toward the stables. The cottonwood over the south paddock had dropped a limb and cracked the top rail of the fence. Something else he'd need to repair. The ranch usually took mild casualties during storms. One year his dad—

"Huh." He slowed his steps. Strange... he'd asked his mom twice about his father, and she'd redirected the conversation both times. He stopped and spun around, squinting at the house, as though the log and stone would spell out the answers. But the structure maintained its indifferent silence.

Chapter Seventeen

Beth folded the dishtowel and laid it on the edge of the countertop. Leaning over the sink, she peered through the window and worried at her lower lip with her teeth. It was a delaying tactic, nothing more. With the dishes washed, she had no clear reason to avoid turning around and conversing with Mary McGee. Still, rather than facing Justin's mom, she stared out the window.

Coward.

A few leafy twigs lay scattered on the ground outside, bits of green fluttering in the gentle breeze. Other than that, no evidence of the storm remained. The thirsty earth had soaked up the deluge from the night before without even leaving a muddy puddle to stomp in. Where had Justin gone? Of course he probably had daily chores. Had she kept him from work while she'd stayed at the ranch?

"Thank you." Mary's voice broke the hush, startling Beth.

She'd almost convinced herself Justin's mom wasn't there. But she was. Of course she was. Where would she go?

"It's not often I get to relax after a meal," continued

Mary.

Beth pulled in a deep breath and squared her shoulders. Smiling, she turned. "It was my pleasure. Thank you for the marvelous breakfast."

Justin's mother sat with her feet up on an adjacent chair, sipping the last of her third cup of coffee. "You know your way around the kitchen."

Heat flooded Beth's face. The last thing she'd wanted to admit to Mrs. McGee was that she couldn't cook. "No, not really. I hardly know how to boil water…"

Mary smiled, the gesture reflecting in her eyes. "Let me rephrase that. You seem to know your way around *my* kitchen." She nodded toward the cupboards. "You didn't need to ask where to store the dishes."

Beth's heart crowded her throat and prevented her from swallowing. She stared at Justin's mom, but Mary's smile remained. "I… um, I… it seemed the l-least I could do… to help with the dishes… and… stuff. And — and I'm a fast learner…"

Mary's smile widened and a chuckle slipped past her lips. "It's very nice to have a houseguest who helps out and doesn't need directions." She gestured to the seat opposite the table. "Care to sit for a while?"

It might have been phrased as an invitation, but Beth instinctively knew it was more of a command. She sank into the chair. "Thank you."

Mary dropped her feet to the floor and swiveled to face Beth. "Coffee? There's a bit left."

"Thank you, but I'm kind of coffeed out."

"And I drink far too much of it." Mary pushed her cup aside and leaned on the table. "So… studying plant cross-pollination. Are you an avid gardener? Or is this for school?"

"It's kind of both. I love gardening, but it's for a horticulture class. I'm studying environmental science at U of M – ah, the University of Michigan."

"College? That's a lot of work, I imagine… studying and all." She rounded up a few grains of sugar that had spilled on the table and drew her fingertip through them.

Rats! I should have wiped down the table. Why didn't I

remember to do that? Should I get up and do it now? No, that would be too obvious. Beth squirmed in the seat. Where *was* Justin? Had he abandoned her to his mother's inquisition?

"Do you work?"

Beth jerked her attention back to the kitchen. "I'm sorry?"

"I wondered if you work, too." Mary's smile never wavered, yet her eyes seemed to have sharpened.

Splip. The tiny drip from the faucet splashed into the sink, the sound thunderous in the silence between them.

"I was working in the science department as a teaching assistant." Beth swallowed back the waver in her voice and tried again. "I took the spring term off to come out here."

"Where you apparently find poisonous plants fascinating." Mary wiped the sugar into her palm and stood. "Or is it the cross-pollination you find fascinating?"

"Definitely the pollination," Beth said with a chuckle, relaxing against the back of her seat.

Mary tossed the sugar into the sink and washed it down, and then turned off the faucet with a bit of extra push. She certainly was the mistress of her kitchen.

"Justin was at the University of Wyoming. Did he tell you?"

Beth frowned. Justin had gone to college? "No... he never mentioned it. What's he studying?"

"He was running a double major in agriculture and business management." Mary sighed, the slow whisper of breath an echo of sadness. "He only had a year left, but we needed him here." She opened the refrigerator and pulled out a package wrapped in brown butcher paper, weighing it in her hands before setting it on the counter. "That's how it happens sometimes." She pinned Beth with a direct stare. "On a ranch."

"I'm sorry," murmured Beth. She tried to picture Justin in school, walking to classes, sitting in lecture halls. The only image that sprang to her mind was of him on the back of his horse.

"You and Justin have gotten close in the past few days."

Close? Beth didn't know how it had happened, but she

knew she wanted to spend the rest of her life with him. "I guess we do seem to... click."

Mary raised an eyebrow. "He likes you, you know."

Why did she suddenly feel like she'd gone back to junior high? "I like him, too. He's... special, I think."

Mary angled her head and raised both eyebrows. "Special enough to alter your life plans for?"

Beth's stomach fell to the level of her toes. While it was down there, she should just give it a good kick so her breakfast could make a reappearance. "We've, ah... actually we've ha-had this conversation." *Or near enough to it.*

"Have you, now..." Mary grabbed a knife from the butcher block and slid it under the string holding the brown paper closed. "I love my son, Beth, and I can see you care for him a great deal." She pulled the knife upward and the string fell away from the paper. "I just don't like the idea of seeing him hurt."

A chill spread over Beth like a snowy blanket. She'd been thinking in terms of how hard it would be for her to leave the ranch. The thought of hurting Justin stole her breath. She hadn't considered it — he seemed so self-reliant, so strong. She couldn't imagine him needing someone to make his life complete. Not the way Mary was hinting at. She looked up to find Justin's mother watching her. All she could do was shake her head — no words would form.

Mary spread the paper to reveal a hunk of red meat. "I'm making pot roast." She opened a lower cabinet, stooped, and rooted inside. When she stood, she held a blue enamel roasting pan speckled with white. "Jim and Justin hate when I heat the house up with cooking, but pot roast is Jim's favorite..."

The tone of her voice had changed, no longer sounding like an interrogator. In fact, she seemed almost... vulnerable. She didn't say anything as she rubbed the meat with spices and laid it in the roasting pan, and Beth didn't know how to break the silence. She cast a glance through the arch into the hallway beyond, and wondered if she dared slip out and back up the stairs. Or better yet, through the front door. She'd run and run, race all the way to town if she had to. Anything to get away from the awkwardness that had fallen over them.

Mary slid the pan into the oven and closed the door, then adjusted one of the dials on top of the range. With a heavy sigh, she turned.

"Beth, I know you'll think I'm a terribly overbearing mother. I love my son and I'm well aware he's a grown man." She rinsed off her hands and wiped them on the dishtowel before turning around. Her face was pinched and her eyes heavy. For the first time, Beth noticed how dark the circles beneath them were.

"Is something wrong?" she asked when she found her voice.

"See, this would be the part where I beg you not to make my boy fall in love with you, not to tempt him to leave... not to offer him anything you can't give." She leaned against the counter. "Not to offer to stay when your feet are itching to take you around the world."

Beth opened her mouth but what could she say? She *had* thought of begging Justin to come with her... and if he refused, she *had* considered staying.

"But I'm not saying that here, Beth." Mary slashed at her eyes and she drew in a deep breath. "I can see my son's attached to you. And I see you have at least some feelings for him. The next few—" She blinked and inhaled deeply again. "The next few weeks are likely to kill him."

Beth's head jerked up of its own accord.

"Emotionally, I mean." Mary shook her head sadly. "I haven't even told him yet, so I can't go into details, but something makes me think I can trust you... that you care enough about him to be there for him." She lifted her face. Tears glinted in her blue eyes. "Or am I wrong?"

Beth shivered against the cold that began at her core and radiated outward. "You're not wrong. Whatever it is... I'll be here for him as long as he needs me to be." She took a step toward Mary. "I promise," she whispered, pulling Justin's mother into her embrace.

A sob escaped, then another. Suddenly, like a punctured balloon, Mary seemed to deflate and great wracking shudders rippled through her body. "I don't know what I'm going to do," she said through the tears.

* * *

It took several good whacks with the flat of the hammer to loosen the cracked fence rail. Justin gave a last mighty swing, catching the white-painted wood with a hearty *thwap* that reverberated into his shoulder. The board split in the middle and one end went flying over his head.

A shriek split the air behind him. *Beth!* Fists clenched, Justin spun around. If her sister or MacKay had come for her—

She stared open-mouthed at the board, on the ground about two feet in front of her. Then she looked up and caught his eye, and her laughter bubbled up and washed over him in odd little chilling waves that left heat in their wake. Shaking her head, she kicked the board to the side, spurring him forward with the movement.

"Dang, Beth, I'm sorry. I had no idea you were there." He stretched out his arms and took her by the shoulders, studying her face for signs of the smallest scratch.

What he found were bright green eyes beckoning to him, drawing him deep into her soul. She stood on her toes and leaned into his touch, and he did what he always wanted to do when he was around her. He folded her against him, splaying his hands along her spine, one up and the other down.

Her shoulders rose and fell with her deep sigh, and she pushed her arms around his waist until she was snuggled tight. Closing his eyes, he buried his face in her hair and breathed in her breezy floral scent.

Too easy... too easy. He couldn't get used to this. She wasn't his to hold. Beth belonged to the world that she wanted to see. No matter how he tried to work it out, when it was time for her to leave, she'd have to go.

And he'd have to stay behind.

Beth tilted her head back and Justin forced his eyes open.

"You can throw wood at me any time you want, if it'll get me a greeting like this." She stepped away, gesturing toward the damaged fence and the heavy limb on the ground next to it that he'd yet to haul away. "From the storm?"

"Yep. The way it was blowing, we were lucky. This looks to be the extent of the damage." He pulled his hat off and settled it on her head. "Sun's strong today."

Her lips curved gently upward and she lifted one hand to touch the brim. "Thank you."

"So are you gonna ask about the pups?" He grinned when her eyes widened and she stared in obvious astonishment. "You know you want to."

Beth crinkled her nose and gave a little shrug. "I was afraid to."

Laying an arm across her shoulders, he walked with her toward the stables. But she hesitated. He hated the troubled expression that came over her face. Whatever it was, it was going to be bad.

"Justin... I was actually coming to get you." She stopped walking and turned slightly so she faced him. "Your mom asked me if I'd let you know she wants to speak to you." Perfect white teeth sank brutally into one side of her lower lip. "I think it's important."

Bile rose in direct proportion to the frisson of fear that rocketed through him. He'd known. He'd been too busy thinking of himself and hoping his mom and Beth would get along. But deep inside... yeah, he'd known. His mom had dodged his questions about his father because it was something bad.

"She up at the house?" he barely choked out.

Beth pulled in a breath and held it. Finally, she released it and gave him a single quick nod. "She had a bad moment or two while I was up there, but she was better when I left her. She said to tell you not to hurry."

Not to...

The blood drained from his head, leaving him as shaky as a tree in the wind. "Go on in there and visit the pups." He pointed through the stable door. "I'll come find you."

Without looking back, he took off for the house at a flat-out run. As he sprinted across the side yard, he was startled by a small blue and white truck parked in front of the house. The side bore a logo that consisted of a pair of interlocked hands with the name *Jackson Medical Supply* stenciled beneath.

His pounding heart eased its grip. Okay, maybe his mom just needed to tell him that his father was coming home with more medical equipment. At least he must be coming home, since a pair of men were obviously in the process of unloading boxes of supplies. Justin nodded a greeting as he slipped past them into the foyer.

His mother stood just inside the door, a clipboard in her left hand, a pen in her right. She ran down the list, periodically pausing to make a notation. When she finished, she glanced up and smiled.

"I'm sorry. I should have spoken to you earlier — planned to, but..." She shrugged and turned away, but he'd already seen the tears shimmering on her lashes.

"Mom," he said softly, reaching out to touch her on the arm. "What is it?"

"Well, it's your dad. He... I— Oh, this is so hard."

Justin led his mom to the staircase and sat her on the bottom step. The two men maneuvered a folded hospital bed into the hallway. He motioned for them to push it against the wall.

The taller man accepted the clipboard from Mary, pulled off the yellow copy, and handed it to her. With a polite brush of fingertips across the brims of their blue caps, the delivery men left, closing the door behind them. Justin crouched in front of his mother.

"Is—" He choked on the words and cleared his throat before he tried again. "Did they find more cancer in his lungs?"

How would they go through more rounds of debilitating chemotherapy and radiation treatments? The cure had almost killed Big Jim McGee before.

Mary shook her head. "No, actually, his lungs are healthy... what's left of them."

Justin eased out a breath of relief.

"But the cancer metastasized before they removed his left lower lobe. It's spread to his spine and his right hip. It's aggressive, and it's not operable. He's..." She pressed her palm against her mouth and closed her eyes.

A spasm of fresh pain cut a path upward from Justin's belly to his chest in an emotional gutting that threatened to still the beat of his heart. "Is there no treatment? Maybe more radiation?" He forced the words past lips that didn't want to form them, even through his pain recognizing that his mother was incapable of telling him anything without help.

She shook her head, "It's gone too far for anything to work. It didn't hurt so much at first. He thought he was just stiff from sitting around. And now... he's too weak. The treatments themselves would kill him."

Justin worked his mouth and tongue, desperate to push out words he was afraid to speak aloud. When he got his voice to work, it was little more than a croak. "What does — what happens now?"

"He comes home. An ambulance will bring him this afternoon." She glanced at the hospital bed that all but blocked the foyer. "The hospital taught me to—" She pulled in a trembling breath and released it. "—to give him his pain meds... shots..."

"So he comes home to... die?" The last word barely squeezed past his constricted throat. He wouldn't — *couldn't* make himself ask how long they had.

Mary nodded. Tears cascaded freely down her cheeks.

It's not supposed to be like this. His mom had always dried *his* tears, had always guided *him*, kept *him* in line. It wasn't right that she was no longer the strong and able woman he'd depended on while growing up. And it wasn't right that he was powerless to change any of it.

Justin pushed to his feet and stood, locking his knees against the unfamiliar weakness consuming his body. With a muttered curse, he punched the wall. The plaster caved in slightly under the force of the blow. Instant shame heated his neck and face. "Sorry," he mumbled.

Mary's jaw dropped as she stared at the dent in the wall.

"I'll get some spackle and—"

He barely had time to jump out of the way as his mom plowed her fist into the space next to the damage he'd done. She pulled her hand back and landed another blow, following that with a strike from her left hand. The helpless wails of a wounded animal burst from her lips as she slugged the wall; first her left then her right… her right again and then her left. Justin grabbed for her arms, but she pushed him away and continued pummeling the wall.

Beth emerged from the kitchen and rushed to his mother's side. Without a word, she stepped in front of Mary and slid her arms around her waist, pushing her back away from the wall and into Justin's arms. They stood in the hallway, arms around each other with his mother between them, waiting for Mary's sobs to subside.

Thank God for Beth's loving touch… and that his mom responded to it. The hollow ache in the center of his chest eased its grip just a bit.

As Mary calmed, she sniffed and wiped at her eyes with her fingertips. When she spoke, her voice was hoarse, but she seemed to have regained some control. "He won't be able to climb stairs, so I thought we should set him up in the living room." She sniffed, but the tears didn't start up again.

"Let me help you get his room set up," murmured Beth.

Sighing, Mary nodded. "Thank you."

Startled into action, Justin stepped to the archway that led into the sitting room. Had it been only that morning his mother had found him and Beth curled up on the couch? Late morning sunlight painted the windowpanes golden. Warmth cloaked the room, but ice sprinted through Justin's veins.

They were about to set up Jim McGee's death bed.

* * *

Beth stood in the doorway, studying their work. With the three of them pulling together, the transformation from living room to home hospital room had taken less than an hour. It was hard to believe only the night before she and Justin had shared a picnic in there by candlelight. The sofa they'd spent the night on had been straightened and now, instead of lining up with the angled fireplace in the corner, it faced the silver and brown hospital bed they had placed against the opposite wall. They'd carried the leather chairs that had graced either side of the fireplace into the office across the hall.

Justin stepped close behind her and slid his arms around her waist. "Thank you for helping," he murmured, nuzzling her neck. "With this and with Mom."

Inhaling deeply, Beth leaned back into his touch. His musky woodsy scent filled her nostrils, heady and intoxicating. She twisted around until she stared into his bright blue eyes. Over the last handful of days, she'd grown used to the fun-loving spark in their depths.

The merriment wasn't gone, but his gentle teasing seemed tempered, his natural happiness overshadowed by deep hurt swirling in the pools of blue, along with... fear. Beth lifted a hand and cupped his cheek, moving her thumb back and forth. He closed his eyes and a shudder rippled through him. His hands at her waist clutched and released, then clutched again.

She wanted to hold tight to him forever, to ease his ache and send it packing. Of course she couldn't take away his pain — no one could. And what scant comfort she could offer wouldn't come close to making things better, she knew from experience. She pushed tighter into his embrace, laying her cheek against his chest with a deep sigh.

"Beth, I—"

Sunlight flashed through the window, and the growl of a powerful engine filtered in from outside.

"He's home!" said Mary in a breathy voice.

From the corner of her vision, Beth caught a blur of motion in the foyer as Justin's mother hurried to the door. How long had she stood in the hallway, waiting for her man to come home?

Justin loosened his arms by inches, seeming reluctant to let go. Beth offered him a smile. It wasn't enough, it wasn't nearly enough. She gave his hands a squeeze and then the connection was broken. He pulled himself up and squared his shoulders as he strode across the maroon and white patterned carpet.

Emotion worried at Beth's heart until her chest hurt like a throbbing toothache.

She slipped into the foyer and lingered near the stairs. Frowning, she ran her hand over the deep indentations Mary's blows had made in the plaster. Fine cracks crisscrossed the dents, and wheat-colored chips dangled by thread-sized strips of paint, exposing white plaster beneath. Could the damage be repaired? A chunk of plaster popped out under her finger and fell to join the dust on the hardwood floor.

Justin stepped back from the open door and joined her in the out-of-the-way space while the ambulance attendants maneuvered the wheeled stretcher over the threshold. Covered to his chin with a white sheet and blanket, and belted to the gurney with thick black straps, Justin's father was almost lost beneath the covers. Beside her, Justin tensed and Beth slipped her hand into his, squeezing three times. He shot her a quick glance and relief washed over his features.

Jim McGee appeared to be sleeping, but just before he was pushed into the living room, he opened his eyes and looked around. His gaze connected with Beth's and sharpened with interest. He shot her a dazzling, though somewhat wan smile.

Beth offered a tentative smile in return.

He was tall enough that his feet hung off the end of the stretcher. She could easily picture him broad-shouldered and as vital as his son. But the skin behind the clear plastic oxygen mask had gone gray and hung wrinkled and loose on his skeletal cheeks. His eyelids fluttered closed again as the stretcher passed into the living room, as though he'd fought to keep them open and lost the battle.

Justin started to follow, but Beth hung back. He gave her hand a little tug, and she pulled free with a shake of her head.

"I'll just wait out here. I don't want to get in the way."

His face fell and he gave a little nod. "Okay."

"Justin, wait." Before he moved off, Beth caught his hand again. "He doesn't know me. He's probably been poked and prodded by strangers for like — ever. Help him keep some dignity — get set up without some houseguest he's never met looking on." She squeezed his hand three times again and angled a glance up at him. "When he's settled and ready... I'd love to meet him." She released him and held up her hand with her small finger extended. "Pinky promise."

He jerked back in surprise. "Pinky what?"

Giggling, Beth snatched his hand again and wrapped her little finger around his. "Pinky promise. It's the second most important promise in the world between two people."

He gaped at her for several heartbeats. Then he gave a little shake of the head. "What's the first?"

Beth's heart raced and heat blossomed from her neck into her face. Why had she opened her big mouth? Now he'd think she was *asking* for a marriage proposal.

"Um, it's nothing... just a kid thing."

A grin spread across Justin's mouth and for the first time in hours, true amusement flickered in his eyes. He leaned forward and planted a quick, hard kiss across her lips. When he drew back, he winked and then turned and entered the living room.

Beth sank down to sit on the second step. *Wha-a-at just happened?*

Chapter Eighteen

Jim McGee didn't look anything like Beth had expected. He reclined in the hospital bed, but on top of the covers and fully clothed in faded blue jeans and a blue checked Western shirt, with a pair of worn brown moccasins on his feet. "It's a real pleasure to meet you, Miss Bethany," he said, his voice a coarser version of Justin's, heavy with years and possibly the ravages of his illness.

Beth shifted her perch on the edge of the leather sofa. "It's nice to meet you, too. And I sure do appreciate the hospitality."

On the other end of the sofa, Justin lifted one foot and dropped it onto the coffee table, then flopped back into the cushions and locked his hands behind his head. It was a comfortable move, habitual. Beth could easily picture family night in that room, with a lot of lounging and laughing and conversation.

"From the sounds of it, you had quite a trip cross-country." Jim leaned his head back with a sigh as though the very act of holding it up tired him. "What brought you out here?"

Tempted to play with her cuticles, which were rapidly growing fairly ragged, she instead laced her fingers together to keep her hands still. She met Jim's clear gray eyes and smiled. "I'm studying the cross-pollination of poison ivy and poison oak."

Jim raked her from top to bottom and back with a critical, narrow-eyed stare.

Self-conscious, Beth fluttered a hand at the healing rash on her face and neck. "And no, I didn't roll in the stuff."

Jim's eyebrows shot toward the ceiling. "I didn't figure you did. Only a damn fool'd think that. Don't think I've lost my mind yet."

Justin dropped his feet from the coffee table and sat forward with a mild cough. "Actually, Dad, Mom asked Beth that question this morning."

"What am I being blamed for now?" Mary bustled into the room with a tray of tall glasses and a pitcher of lemonade. She set it on the coffee table in front of the couch.

Justin lifted the pitcher and poured a glass, handing it off to Beth and then poured another, offering it to his mom. She shook her head, and Justin shrugged then took a long sip from the glass.

Jim's tired eyes twinkled. "Our son called you a fool."

"Guess it takes one to know one," murmured Beth softly.

Justin coughed again, louder this time. His mother swept her gaze over him, one eyebrow raised. "Drink go down wrong?"

Watching Justin and his mom over the rim of her glass, Beth drank to hide her smirk. Somehow Mary McGee was well aware of the direction the conversation had taken. From the moment Jim McGee had arrived home, the three had fallen into a relaxed rhythm. Would she and her parents have had this degree of spirited camaraderie without Alice and her troublesome scheming? Beth tempered the pang of sadness with a swallow of tart-sweet liquid.

"Did I smell pot roast when I came through the door?" asked Jim.

Mary beamed. "You did. I thought we could set up the card table in here and—"

Jim shook his head. "Nope. We're eating in our kitchen, the way we always do."

Justin's mom opened her mouth and took a breath, but almost immediately clamped her lips shut and nodded. Then she stood. "Okay, then. I'll finish up and set the table for an early supper."

"Can I help?" asked Beth, feeling a bit like the fourth wheel on a three-wheeled cart, not needed and maybe a bit in the way. "I'm not much of a cook, but I can set the table, at least."

"Not much of a cook, huh?" Mary sent her son a *what-were-you-thinking* look and then returned her gaze to Beth. "We'll see about that. Come on." Bending, she gave her husband a quick kiss and a pat on the shoulder. Then she stood and sauntered toward the kitchen.

Swallowing hard, Beth followed. Even the air seemed to get out of Mary McGee's way when she wanted to get someplace. If she didn't already wish her son had left Beth on the side of the road, she likely would as soon as she learned just how little help she was going to be in the kitchen.

"Did you find any of our missing cattle?" asked Jim.

"Wish I had, Dad. It's not much of a mystery where they went but..."

A smile tugged at Beth's mouth. Except for the hospital paraphernalia and his gaunt frame, Jim was every bit a vital part of the ranch. As she passed the staircase, the battered wall caught her eye. She didn't know what his diagnosis was, but obviously it didn't come with a positive prognosis.

* * *

Chills washed over and through Justin as he sank into the green leather chair behind the desk. He didn't quite fit the seat that had always been his dad's. For as long as Justin could remember, Jim McGee had spent long evenings poring over the books and working his particular brand of magic on the finances.

Then he'd developed a cough that wouldn't go away, and the nights hadn't been as long. Later, an X-ray had found "just a small spot."

Justin picked up the clear plastic pen and twirled it like a baton between his fingers. The conversation he'd just had with his father replayed in his mind like it was on some kind of insane repeating loop...

"I'm leaving you and your mom with a hell of a mess, boy."

"Dad, don't—"

He held his hand up in a stop gesture. "No, you don't. I know exactly what kind of crap hand I got dealt, and you know I hate sugarcoating anything. I'm out of chips and because I am, so are you and your mom. I'm sorrier about that than anything else. A man likes to know he took care of his family."

The air left Justin's lungs in a whoosh. His dad had never pulled punches in his life. Surely he deserved the respect of Justin's honesty now. Swallowing past a dry throat, he glanced at the lemonade, but his stomach rebelled. So he nodded, unable to form the words he desperately needed to give his father — the assurance that everything would be all right, that he and his mom would be okay.

Because the truth was, nothing was going to be all right. How could it be when the foundation they relied on would no longer be there to hold them up?

"The bank note on the land is a month behind," his dad continued, not noticing or, more likely, ignoring Justin's troubled silence. "If that can be brought back into date, you won't be paying the late fees." He frowned. "I was thinking selling off a third of the herd might buy you some time, but prices keep going down and this ain't the right time of year to be heading to market."

"I'll take care of it, Dad," Justin finally managed to say. "And I'll look after Mom."

A full gamut of raw emotion bathed Jim's face, but he quickly schooled his features. Jim was a practical man and he'd figure breaking down was a useless gesture. He surprised Justin with his next words. "I wish you coulda finished up at U of W."

Justin chuckled. "It's okay. I got what I needed there. Most of the ranch is run by common sense — that's what you *always told me, anyway."*

Jim's face contorted into an expression of physical pain, and he shifted in the bed with a little grunt. It took him a moment to recover, pulling in a few deep breaths then blowing them out through pursed lips. After a moment, he pinned Justin with his tired stare. "Times are changing. Some things'll probably be the same for a while but…" He sighed and gave a head-shake. "You have to keep up with the changes, son."

"We're going to keep the ranch, Dad, and keep it going. I promise."

But Jim shook his head again. "This… this is just geography, boy. People… that's the important consideration. You, your mom, Gus." He leaned toward the edge of the bed as though to get a better look at Justin. "That gal you've got your eye on."

Justin smiled as the memory faded and the study filtered back into his awareness. So his sharp-eyed old man had noticed his affection for Beth. That wasn't much of a surprise. His dad had always been too astute for Justin to pull anything over on him. He hadn't bothered telling his dad the two of them could have no future. What was the point of crying in his beer about things that could never be?

A sudden wind whipped through the window and lifted the wispy white curtains. The papers on the desk fluttered, and Justin eyed the pile with a frown. He'd put it off long enough. Time to figure out what was what and who needed paying first.

After an hour, he slumped back in the chair. Strange how sixty minutes of reading and decision-making didn't make him feel any more like the rancher his father was. He pressed his body deeper into the chair, the responsibility for the ranch a nearly unbearable weight.

The three piles in front of him represented three stages of need: pressing, more pressing, and pray to strike gold. He rubbed his eyes with the heels of his hands. They wouldn't starve, but his dad was right. The late charge on the mortgage was eating up their resources. He reached for the yellow pad with the list of bills and amounts and flipped to a clean sheet, scribbling a quick calculation to figure how many head of cattle would have to go at current market rates to bring the loan current.

His heart landed like lead shot in his stomach. He pulled a hand down his face, stopping at his mouth, then sat there, cupping his chin, as he studied the figure that represented just under a third of their herd. The numerals blurred, the blue lines running together on the yellow paper and rearranging themselves into a pixie-faced woman with a mass of golden curls.

A soft knock on the door interrupted his daydream and the vision popped; the page became columns of numbers again.

"Come in," he called out. He picked up the pressing bills and grabbed a paperclip from the tray, then glanced up with a smile as he clipped the papers together.

His automatic smile became real and his heart instantly lightened at the sight of Beth lounging in the doorway. She'd braided her hair but the curls in front were already pulling free.

"I'm supposed to tell you supper's about ready and remind you to wash up." She pushed off the woodwork and entered the room, gesturing to the frilly pink and white flowered bib apron covering her jeans and T-shirt. "Like it?" She did a pirouette. "I think your mom feels if I look the part, one day I might not burn water."

Abandoning the bills, Justin rounded the desk and met Beth halfway, snagging her around the waist as she twirled again, and hauling her back against him. When she squealed, he found himself laughing. She squirmed in his arms as he nuzzled her braid until it began to work apart.

"Burned water, eh?" he murmured against her neck. Dang, she smelled good. Like her normal sweet flowery scent, but mixed with fresh-baked bread. He nibbled with his lips where her neck joined her shoulder until she trembled.

"Well, boiled the pan dry, at least." She turned in his arms and teased the corner of his mouth with her tongue. "So are you gonna come out and see what your mom and I cooked up?"

"Ye-ea-ah…" He allowed himself to wander in her eyes. "Beth?"

"Hmmm?"

"Do you think you can wear the apron later when we make out?"

Giggling, she snuggled herself tighter into his embrace. With her lips on his cheek she asked, "Should I tell your mom why I need to borrow it?" Then she pulled free except for her hold on his hand and tugged him in the direction of the door.

How was it that just sharing space for a few minutes with Beth always made his whole world right again?

His father's voice in his mind whispered the answer. *"People… that's the important consideration."*

* * *

Beth dried the last glass from dinner and slid it into the cupboard. As she shut the door, she grinned.

"I see that." Justin pulled the dishtowel from her hands and tossed it into the laundry room. "What's that grin about?"

Heat bloomed in her face. "Nothing."

He shook his head. "Not buying it."

Well, no way was she going to tell him that for the first time in her life she felt like she was part of something special. Especially since she wasn't *really* part of anything. She was just a guest because they'd taken pity on her.

"I never knew doing dishes could be fun," she said instead. "I never did them before I came here."

He paused in the doorway that led to the living room, his blue eyes glittering in the overhead kitchen light. Wavy blond hair fell across his forehead, but he didn't bother to brush it back. He just kept staring at her, one side of his mouth lifted in a half smile, as though he was trying to fathom something about her. Did he have any idea how handsome he was? Didn't seem like it.

"The lady is an enigma. Never cooked, never did dishes. But she travels across the country in a broken-down old hippie van and crawls under it to try and fix it when it stops running."

"Well, someone had to fix it. I didn't see any coyotes offering assistance." She grinned, happy to be steering away from dangerous territory. "Besides, I wanted the full experience."

Justin snickered. "The full experience of what? Breaking down?"

"Maybe..." She flicked down the light switch and brushed past him. The skin along her arms tingled where it touched his. She inhaled deeply of his woodsy scent, and her whole body broke out in goose bumps. "And maybe... I was timing how long it would take for a handsome cowboy to show up and rescue me."

With a chuckle, he fell into step beside her and slid an arm around her shoulder. Beth sighed.

Something special.

* * *

"Will you stop fussing, woman?" Jim's voice contained more laughter than frustration. "If I wanted to go to bed, I'd've climbed into the contraption."

Beth's glance connected with Justin's as they reached the archway into the living room, and his eyes crinkled at the corners as he smiled. An insistent pounding on the front door startled Beth, and Justin arrested his turn into the living room, releasing her as he spun on his heel and headed for the door instead.

"I'll get this. You go on in and save me a seat."

"Did I hear the door?" asked Mary as Beth padded across the soft carpeting.

"Justin went to ans—"

"I don't care if the President of the United States is paying you a visit. My sister's here and I intend to see her."

Alice's discordant tone raised the hairs on Beth's neck and she froze in mid-step. Tremors assaulted her body, making it impossible to turn. As the edges of her vision faded to purple, she realized she'd stopped breathing and sucked in a gulp of air.

Then Mary was at her side, though Beth hadn't been

aware of her moving. "Are you okay? Breathe, honey. Justin'll take care of it."

She wanted to let him. It would be so easy to just let him send Alice away. Beth sighed. It wouldn't work anyway. Alice was like a dog with a bone when she took on a self-righteous attitude. Even if Justin did manage to push her out the door, she'd only be back.

"No, I need to," she murmured, turning around. "And after I do... would it be too much to borrow your phone to call my dad? I can make it a collect call," she added in a rush.

Mary studied Beth for a long moment and then nodded. "Okay."

Praying the quivering on her insides wouldn't bring her dinner up, Beth strode into the foyer.

Justin blocked the doorway, making it fairly apparent he hadn't done the neighborly thing and invited Alice inside. Beth loved that protective streak. Hated that he felt it necessary. She straightened her back and squared her shoulders, and then stepped next to him.

"Hello, Alice. Nice of you to call." Beth slipped her hand into Justin's, not feeling quite as strong as she'd thought after all. "But nothing's changed since I saw you yesterday."

Alice narrowed her eyes and appraised Beth with a cool green gaze. The man standing next to her lifted a hand and brushed a shock of ginger hair off his forehead. Beth blinked. Had he been there all along? His flinty gray-blue eyes pierced her with a hot stare. A thin bead of sweat arose along his upper lip and he rubbed his mouth with the back of his hand. A chill raced up Beth's spine, but she forced air into her lungs.

"Hello, Brody." At least his name didn't stick in her throat, though her stomach began churning again.

Brody MacKay acknowledged her with a curt nod, but he held his silence.

"Actually, a lot has changed," said Alice in a clipped tone. "I've spoken to Dad and you're to come with me. He said going off on your own wasn't part of the bargain he made with you." She tapped one red fingernail against the door frame. "So get your things and we'll be out of the McGees' way."

Justin squeezed her hand, calming the frantic pounding

of Beth's heart, and she quit chewing the inside of her cheek. "No. I'm fine where I am and I don't plan to leave."

Alice opened her mouth, but Justin beat her to the punch.

"The lady's made her decision, Alice. And as I explained, we really aren't in a position to be receiving visitors this evening. So if you'll excuse us…"

He crowded the door, but Brody crowded back, pushing Alice aside as he went chest-to-chest with Justin. "Now, hold on here, McGee. My wife's just interested in following her father's wishes to look after her little sister."

Justin met Brody's hard stare without moving. Beth's breath stalled in her throat while the two men squared off in silence. After an eternity of drawn-out heartbeats that exploded through Beth's ears, Brody coughed and stepped back.

"Invitation's open for Bethany to stay at our place," he mumbled gruffly, raking her with a glance that made her want to rush upstairs and shower. "My wife was hoping to spend some time with her sister is all. She promised their daddy she'd look out for her."

Alice pressed her lips into a tight line.

"Thanks, MacKay." Justin remained rigidly in place and blocking the door. "Beth's got it covered. She hasn't broken any agreement with her father."

Brody gave a curt nod. "Evening, then." He stepped back and turned around.

After sending Beth a hard glare, Alice pivoted on one foot and stomped off the wooden porch. She pointedly stared away from the house as she opened the door of the pickup and climbed inside.

Prickles of uneasiness crawled along Beth's arms as Alice slammed the door and the porch light flashed off shiny black paint. Then trepidation became perplexity, bringing on a frown. If times were so bad for ranchers, how was her brother-in-law able to afford a brand new truck?

Justin laid his arm over her shoulders as the taillights dwindled into the night. When they rounded the bend in the drive and disappeared from sight, he turned her and caressed her with his gaze.

"You okay?"

Nodding, Beth drew in a deep breath and blew it out again.

"Good." He slid his grasp from her shoulders and captured her hands, rubbing them until she relaxed and opened her fists. "Because she's not worth this." He brushed his thumbs over her palms.

She gaped at the half-moon indentations her fingernails had made. "I... I, um..." She hadn't even been aware of clenching her hands into fists. "I need..."

Mary met them in the foyer. "Justin, show her to the phone in the study." She gave him a gentle shove toward the door and swung her gaze to Beth. "And no more nonsense about collect calls. Just call direct." She moved off toward the kitchen. "I'm getting Dad some ice cream."

Justin pushed open the study door and motioned Beth through. "I'll give you some privacy."

"No!" Heat rose to her cheeks. "I mean, he'll... want to talk to you."

* * *

"Hi, Daddy." Beth's eyes brightened and she brushed at them before leaning forward across the desk and reaching for a tissue. Balancing the black phone receiver on her shoulder, she dabbed at her eyes. Then she dropped the tissue in the trash and sat back, looking more at home in Jim McGee's chair than Justin had ever felt.

"I know it's not Friday, Daddy." She giggled and began winding a strand of golden hair around one finger. "Yes, I saw Alice. Yes. Did she call you?" She dropped the strand of hair she'd been playing with and heaved a sigh. "Yes, Daddy, you told me not to drive that broken down piece of— It *is* being fixed. It's in the shop right now."

She glanced up at Justin and rolled her eyes.

"I don't need a new car, Daddy. The van's going to be fine." She picked up the strand of hair again and began twirling.

Her face took on a crimson hue and Beth jerked forward in the chair, slamming her palm against the top of the desk. "She told you what? That's vulgar, and—" Slowly, she curled her fingers inward. "No. That's certainly not true, and I—" Her breaths came fast and short.

Oh, man, don't let her pass out from hyperventilating. How could he explain *that* to her father?

The door to the study opened and his mom peeked around the corner.

"I can't believe you're listening to her crap!" exploded Beth. "You know what she's like." Tears formed in her eyes and her voice tightened. "And you know *me*, Daddy."

Justin caught his mother's concerned gaze and shrugged. He could only guess what Alice had told their father, but he knew without doubt she'd played on his protective fatherly instincts.

"No, I won't go stay with her. Brody's there and he's creepy." She pushed out of the chair and paced, her movements hampered by the relatively short phone cord.

Mary's shoulders rose and fell again with her soft sigh as she strode to the desk. "May I?" she asked, pointing to the receiver and holding out her hand.

Beth blinked in surprise but handed the phone over without a word. Then she ducked under the cord and crossed the room to Justin. Her chest rose and fell rapidly with her agitated breathing.

"I don't believe—"

Mary snapped her fingers and, when she had their attention, pressed a forefinger to her lips. "Hello, Mr. Rushton, this is Mary McGee. Your daughter has been staying on the ranch with us."

The lilt of her laughter echoed through the room, and Beth's tension eased. They stood together watching as his mom worked her brand of magic.

"Well, it's very kind of you to say that, but I assure you I have a grown son." She nodded. "Yes, I know. Yes, she's a very lovely young woman." Smiling, she caught Justin's eye and winked. "I'd say my son's a very handsome young man, yes."

Geez. Warmth began in Justin's neck and rolled upward

until the tips of his ears felt like they were on fire.

"No, Mr. Rushton, I understand completely. But I trust my son. May I ask why you aren't accepting Beth's answers as the final word on this?" Mary hooked a finger in the coils of the phone cord and twisted.

Beside him, Beth tensed.

"Oh, I see." She chuckled and eased a hip up onto the desk. "Yes, I certainly understand overprotectiveness. Especially when it comes to a young lady as beautiful as your daughter."

She raised her eyes to meet Justin's again and gave him a thumbs-up.

"That would be wonderful. Yes, she's been a terrific help." Laughter rippled forth. "No, I promise to send her back to you— Ah, I don't know, but I can ask Justin." She moved the receiver away from her mouth. "Does Beth need her father to buy her a car to drive home?"

Justin stared for a long moment until Mary raised one expectant eyebrow. Spreading his hands, he shrugged and shook his head, completely unsure of how to answer. Of course, he'd feel better knowing she was driving something reliable. For the first time, a prickle of apprehension rode along the back of his neck, and he realized just how little he knew of Beth and her family. Other than his opinion of Alice, at least. And that particular opinion was rapidly heading down from zero into negative numbers.

But buy her a new car? He frowned. That sounded casual, like paying for an ice cream cone with pocket change.

"Well, my son shook his head, but he's frowning." Mary's words startled him from his musings. "I'll tell you what. Our local repair shop is the best. If Walt Blackstone doesn't give it a clean bill of health, how about I give you a call?" She giggled again. "It was nice talking to you, too. Call any time you want." She rattled off the phone number and then dropped the receiver back into the cradle.

Beth stared at the phone. "He... didn't want to talk to me again?"

"Nope. Said he wanted you to take some time to cool down." Mary smiled. "Okay, I don't know how much influence your dad has on your sister, but at least now you know anything she says to *you* didn't necessarily come from your father."

Beth's face screwed up in concentration. "What did he say?"

"Parent stuff." Mary laid an arm along Beth's shoulders and inclined her head to Justin. "Let's see what we can salvage of the evening, huh?"

Chapter Nineteen

Beth took a seat on the opposite end of the sofa from Jim, wondering just what Mary meant by salvaging the evening. She had a feeling it wouldn't take long to find out.

Casting his wife a sidelong glance, Jim leaned back and stretched his legs out, parking his feet on the coffee table. "I feel like music."

Mary froze in the center of the room and stared at the table with one eyebrow raised. "Funny, you don't look like music. You look like my husband." She turned and started for the door. "I'll just be a moment. Consider finding a place for those big feet that doesn't involve the coffee table before I get back," she called out without looking over her shoulder.

Beth giggled. Their rhythm was so comfortable and easy; it was obviously a well-established routine, and surprisingly she didn't feel like an intruder. Even though the situation was grim, Beth caught only rare sad glances between them, as though they were determined to thumb their noses at Jim's illness. He was tired, the shadows beneath his eyes deep, but he never stopped smiling.

Did it hurt? Justin had told her it was lung cancer that

had gone to his bones. She'd heard bone cancer caused merciless pain. But Jim didn't show any sign except for moving stiffly sometimes.

"Hey... you're a long ways off," murmured Justin in her ear as he dropped onto the couch between her and Jim. "Still thinking about your dad?"

She shifted to face him. *No, I'm thinking about your dad... and about what'll happen to you when...*

She smiled and nodded. "Silly, huh?"

"Nah," he said softly with a shake of his head. "I expect you miss him."

"A little." Oddly, not as much as she'd thought she would. She wrinkled her nose. "Some."

Justin opened his mouth to speak, but the soft twang of guitar chord interrupted. Beth blinked. When had Mary returned? She sat on the floor at Jim's feet, looking like she'd been there for a while. Justin's dad cradled a guitar in his lap. He strummed it again, made an adjustment at the top, and ran his fingers over the strings once more. Then he grinned and the weariness slid from his face.

He plucked out a rhythm in three-quarter time, his eyes dancing to the music as he began to sing about a strawberry roan bucking bronco. Beth fell into the beat of the song and began tapping her foot. Jim seemed to pull more strength from the music, or perhaps from the people in the room. His voice came out in a clear baritone with just a hint of gravel and a measure of breathlessness when the song picked up speed.

When he finished with a flourish, Beth giggled and clapped her hands. She slid a glance at Justin. His grin widened when their gazes locked, and he caught her hand, lacing his fingers through hers. With his touch so warm and firm, Beth felt the strength that had been sapped from her encounter with Alice returning.

Jim began to pick out a complicated tune with his fingers. Mary inhaled sharply and then eased into a smile that melted years from her face. As soon as Jim began singing about the beauty of Mary in the morning, Beth understood her reaction. Jim shifted to look directly at his wife as he sang the loving serenade. Beth had heard the song before, but never had it touched her heart so deeply.

Jim sang about sunlight on golden hair, and a fine tremble rippled through Justin. His hand tightened, almost like an involuntary spasm, and Beth eased a little closer until their legs touched. When she dared risk looking at him, Justin watched her with sharp intensity that sucked the air from her lungs.

When did I fall so completely in love with you?

An immediate ache rocketed through her heart when Jim finished the song. She couldn't offer any applause to show her delight this time without pulling from Justin's grasp, and she didn't want to let go. As if sensing the need to alter the mood in the room, Jim picked up the pace and began singing about God's love being sent on the wings of a dove. Mary soon joined in, her glance occasionally drifting to Justin. Then she caught Beth watching her and smiled. The song was familiar and the chorus easy to remember. On the third pass, Beth joined in, winning a nod of approval from Justin's mom.

When Justin added his rich baritone to the singing, his tension eased. Beth began to clap with the rhythm. When that song was finished, Jim launched into another, and then another. Several songs later, he finished the song with a fancy set of chords and then set the base of the guitar on the floor and leaned the neck against the sofa.

"That was fun," murmured Beth.

"Nothin' like singing around the fire to lighten a mood." Jim pushed his arms over his head and stretched. "You should go out on the trail next branding season. We've been known to sing all night. The right songs settle the herd."

Silence coated the room in awkwardness. Justin cleared his throat and gave a weak chuckle. "Not likely to happen, Dad. Beth here's a tenderheart. She'd probably set the calves free to save them from the branding iron."

"Tenderheart, huh?" Jim tilted his head and subjected her to a long gaze. Then he shrugged. "Nothing wrong there... having a heart that's filled with kindness." He leaned back into the couch and sighed heavily.

Disappointment settled over Beth as the room fell quiet again. She could have listened to Jim sing and play all night.

But the lines around his mouth had deepened, and the shadows beneath his eyes had grown dark. Her regret turned to profound sorrow as she realized a few hours of singing hadn't taken away Jim McGee's illness... or the dreadful prognosis. And for all his talk of singing around the campfire during branding season, he'd never see another one.

She should leave them alone for some uninterrupted family time. Much as she wished differently, she wasn't part of this close-knit family. Beth peeled herself away from Justin's side — when had she moved so snugly against him?

Rolling her shoulders, she inhaled deeply. "I think I'd better turn in before I fall asleep right here."

Justin's piercing gaze told her quite clearly he wasn't buying her ruse. "Actually, I was wondering if you might like a little walk outside before you hit the hay."

Beth started to decline the invitation, but stopped. Maybe he was trying to give his parents time together. The thought of a moonlight walk with him shot tingles from her spine to her fingers and toes. So she angled her head and sent him a happy smile. "Okay."

* * *

They stepped onto the front porch and Beth shivered. The temperature must have dropped close to twenty degrees with nightfall. Justin backtracked into the foyer and grabbed his jacket from the coatrack. As he laid it over her shoulders, Beth snuggled into the soft suede with a sigh.

"What about you?"

"I'll be fine." Rather than risk her changing her mind about the walk, Justin would gladly risk hypothermia. But he was used to the sudden temperature dips, and for whatever reason seldom noticed the change. The way she gazed at him, all starry-eyed, the temperature could drop another twenty degrees, and he wouldn't feel it for the warmth his core was generating.

He laid an arm across her shoulders and tucked her close as he guided her off the porch into the night. She stumbled over a patch of uneven ground and laughed about it, but all the same clutched his arm a bit tighter.

"Sorry." He slowed his steps to a stroll and headed toward the paddocks. "It's a little rough out here since the storm."

Beth snuggled closer. "How is it you aren't tripping?"

"Cat's eyes, I guess." Justin shrugged. "It probably helps that I grew up here."

"It must have been wonderful. I can't imagine a better place to raise a family."

Stay and raise one with me. He caught his breath. Had he said that out loud? But she didn't respond, just kept ambling alongside him, and he eased the breath out again.

"Do you and your parents have sing-alongs like that often?"

"Was a time we might have done that every night." A smile tugged on his lips. Those days had passed a while ago. By the time he'd entered high school, sitting around the living room with his parents singing old songs hadn't been as appealing as dating Sylvia Sanders. "I hope Dad didn't overdo it tonight."

"He did look a little tired when he put down the guitar." Beth tilted her head back and studied him as they walked. "You know what, though? He seemed to draw energy from you and your mom."

Justin sniffed. "Maybe…" The weight of his impending loss was suddenly staggering and he missed a step.

Beth giggled and adjusted her hold on his arm. "I guess we'll have to hold each other up, huh?"

He chuckled.

"Justin…" She sighed. "Your dad was doing what he wanted to do. He gave you and your mom a gift tonight. One he very much needed to give. It made him happy to have that little bit of family time with you."

"Yeah…" He turned and pressed a quick kiss to the top of her head. "I know." And no doubt if his father passed overnight, the old man would figure he'd gone out on his own terms. It didn't make the circumstance any easier to face. "It's just if he overdoes it… tires himself out, it could make it happen—" At the first crack in his voice, he shut up, not trusting his composure to hold out.

They reached the first paddock and Beth stopped, sliding her hand along his arm until their fingers laced together. "I don't know which is worse. I mean my mom's death was so sudden... Sometimes it feels like a lot got left unsaid."

The sadness dulling her voice clawed at Justin's heart.

"But knowing something's gonna happen... that you're powerless to stop it." She lifted her shoulders and let them fall again. "Sometimes you must feel like you're just waiting for the end."

He nodded, unable to argue with her astute reasoning.

"Can you imagine?" she whispered, turning to face him. "Can you imagine what it must be like to know you're dying? Soon? So many things you realize you never did, dreams that never came true... things you wish you'd told the people you love..." A shudder wracked her. "I'd want to live as much as I could pack in." She tightened her hold on his hand. "Justin, don't bury your dad before he dies."

Annoyance sparked and spilled over in his response. "I'm not—"

She flinched away from him.

Instantly his irritation left him and he huffed out a breath. "Sorry. Sorry..." He pulled her close and buried his face in her neck, drawing in deep breaths filled with her scent. "My whole life my dad's been my hero. He was always strong, larger than life. I can't — I can't imagine—" He sighed. "This ranch... it's all him. When he's not—"

Beth slipped her arms around his waist and held on, surprising him with the strength she exuded. "Shh..." She leaned back and Justin braced himself for her to step away, but she only lifted one hand to cup his cheek. "You love him. You don't want to face life without him."

"Yep," he squeezed out and then shrugged. "That about sums it up."

"But, you know..." She moved her thumb back and forth just in front of his ear, the motion mesmerizing and oddly more comforting than arousing. "...people can die any time. Like my mom. I mean you — you could go riding, and..." She pulled in a shaky gulp of air. "Or I could—"

Justin locked his arms around Beth and clutched her to him, unwilling to let her finish the sentence.

She nodded, seeming to understand. "We... none of us know how long we'll live. So we need to live like it's our last day... every day." She tipped her head back, and then stood on her toes and gently pressed her lips to his. The tenderness in her touch unhinged him. "You still have him for now, Justin. You don't know for how long, but probably only a short time. Don't try to make him comfortable. Help him live. Help him to really live *his* life *his* way." She kissed him again. "It may shorten his life by minutes or days, but is it really living when someone's lying around waiting to die?"

Her words were a sucker punch to the gut that left him emotionally staggering. The thing was, he knew she was right. With her snugly against his side, he turned them in the direction of the house and began walking again.

By the time they reached the front porch, he'd regained his internal balance. She did that for him. Just being with her made him want to not waste even a second of their precious time together. By some kind of unspoken agreement, they both stopped just outside the front door. In silence they moved into each other's arms. The kiss started out with gentle caring, but quickly heated. With the slightest pressure of his lips, Beth parted hers, and he sampled her honey-sweet essence. Craving more, needing her with every part of him, Justin slipped a hand beneath the jacket she wore and gripped her along the ribcage, moving his hand upward until he cupped one soft breast. With a low groan, she bent backward, exposing her neck to his trailing lips.

The porch light flared and Beth jumped back, pulling from his embrace with eyes somehow wide and blinking at the same time. "What happened? What is that?" She stared at the yellow bulb as though just learning about electricity.

Justin chuckled. "That's my mom keeping her promise to your dad and looking out for your virtue."

"My virtue?" Beth turned her blinking gaze onto him. "My virtue was in danger?"

Justin offered a shrug and mentally relived the feel of her breast in his hand. "Getting there. Definitely getting there."

A slow grin spread across her face. "Fa-ar out..."

Laughter he could no longer contain erupted as he set his hand on the doorknob.

The sharp report of a rifle shattered the night's peace, bouncing off the house and reverberating in his chest.

Justin jerked. "What the hell—?"

That was close — from over by the outbuildings.

Another shot followed, that one eclipsed by Beth's startled cry.

The front door exploded inward, and they came face-to-face with Mary, a rifle in her hand. "That was close."

"Gus!" Justin snatched the Winchester from his mom's hands and gave Beth a shove toward the door. "Wait here."

"But I can—"

He raced across the porch and leaped off the side, instantly engulfed by the darkness. "No! Stay back!" he shouted over his shoulder, hoping she'd listen. It took him a moment for his eyes to adjust. Once they did, he picked up his pace until he was sprinting.

When he got to the stables, he kept to the shadows and slowed his steps, straining to hear something... anything that sounded off. Two cows huddled together in the center of the closest pen, heavy with calf, both waving their heads from side to side and making agitated groaning noises that masked any other sound.

Justin headed toward the farthest pens, squinting into the darkness as he skirted the fence. Where the devil was Gus?

A pale ghostly figure rose in front of him and Justin skidded to a stop, nearly colliding with the apparition.

"About time you got here, boy," said Gus, a growl in his voice. He leaned his rifle against the fence. His open white shirt billowed in the breeze, making him look more ghost than man.

A chill ran the length of Justin's spine and he shivered. "What's going on?"

"We got us a cat problem." Gus pointed at the ground between them.

Justin crouched, squinting through the darkness. Gus flicked his cigarette lighter and held it low. In the dim glow, the soft dirt next to the barn revealed the clear imprint of a cougar's foot. Justin held his hand over the track and splayed his fingers. Its span was bigger than his outstretched hand.

"Big sucker," he muttered, standing. "Think it's the same one?"

The same one. Had he really voiced that out loud? A chill climbed Justin's spine. *The same one* that had caused so much trouble a few years back...

Gus snapped the lighter closed, extinguishing the flame and casting them into darkness. "Looks like it. I hate to think there might be two the size of this monster."

Rocking back onto his heels, Justin rubbed the back of his neck. "What was she after, this close in? Are the new calves accounted for?"

"Dunno." Gus scratched his jaw. "Let me go get a light."

* * *

Beth sat on the edge of the sofa, waiting for Justin's return. Retiring to her bed was no longer an option. Not only was she wide awake, but obviously something was very wrong and she couldn't leave without knowing what had happened.

Mary paced between the fireplace and the window, every so often pulling aside the lacy curtain and peering into the darkness beyond, then dropping it and walking back to the fireplace. Jim stretched his feet out in the bed, shifted, uncrossed his legs then re-crossed them at the ankles.

Neither spoke.

"Was that..." Beth's voice sounded like a tree frog. She cleared her throat and tried again. "Was that a — gunshot — earlier?"

In unison, Justin's parents swung their gazes in her direction. Mary's lips were locked tight. A muscle worked in Jim's jaw as he inclined his head and studied Beth. After a minute or two, his expression softened. "It's probably just Gus chasing off a varmint."

Mary joined Beth on the couch and took her hand.

"We've had raccoons nosing around the stables before." But her gaze connected with her husband's and a glimmer of apprehension passed between them.

A chill tickled Beth's spine. How long had Justin been out there? An hour? Two? She glanced at the clock. Less than forty-five minutes had passed since Mary had hustled her inside.

The *thunk* of a door being closed drifted in from the kitchen, followed by a distant *thud* and then the whisper of soft footsteps on hardwood flooring. Beth stood as Justin strode through the archway into the living room. Worry had etched fine lines across his forehead. When his eyes met Beth's, he smiled and the lines smoothed. The shadows in his eyes lingered, though.

"That was just Gus running off a cat." He'd taken off his boots, but the bottoms of his jeans were smeared with drying mud. Unnoticing or uncaring of the little clods of dirt trailing behind him, he crossed the room and stopped in front of Beth, his eyes searching... but for what she couldn't have said.

She blinked, struggling to process his words. "But I thought... I mean, you and Gus said cats were okay... to catch the mice."

Justin pulled a hand down his face, but not before she caught the hint of a smile lifting the corners of his lips. When he dropped his hand the smile was gone. "Well, this is a somewhat larger cat, Dilly Gal, and she's not quite as obliging about earning her supper."

"I don't... I don't get it." Confusion clouded Beth's mind and she frowned. Understanding dawned suddenly. "Oh! You mean a wild animal... like a — like a bobcat?"

Justin stared at her in silence. Slowly, he drew a deep breath and shook his head. "Cougar. Big one."

"Oh, no," whispered his mom.

"Same one?" asked Jim, the lines at the corners of his mouth deepening.

Beth huffed out a frustrated breath, struggling to catch up with their inside conversation.

Justin nodded. "Followed the tracks to the edge of the stockyard. Big cat, missing half of her rear foot."

Mary gasped and covered her mouth. But Jim only squared his shoulders and nodded.

"But—" Breathing became impossible. Her lungs simply refused to work even though she was starved for air. Stories of cougars attacking children and pets danced across her mind's playground. "Mama and the babies?" she finally choked out.

"They're fine." Justin brushed a strand of hair behind Beth's ear. His fingers, cool from being outdoors, grazed her neck and sent a chill racing along her skin. "I checked 'em before I came in. Mama's kind of spooked, but she'll be okay."

"Mama?" Mary was frowning. "Babies?"

"Found some orphan pups at the old homestead." Justin shot Beth a wink and a grin. "They were too young to leave out there so we brought 'em home."

Mary gave her son a long hard look. "I see. And 'Mama'? We don't have any mother dogs. We don't have *any* dogs."

Justin's grin widened. "No, but one of the cats has a litter and she adopted them." He slid a glance at Beth. "So they're in the barn and not in the house."

Mary snorted. "Why would they be in the house?"

Heat rushed into Beth's face and she sought her feet with her eyes.

Jim burst into laughter and didn't stop, despite the hard glare Justin sent his way. "You're right, son. A tenderheart."

Beth puffed herself up. "I'm not a—"

Three gazes settled on her. Mary cocked one eyebrow upward.

Beth's bravado deflated. "Okay, maybe I am. But they're just babies, and they deserved a chance."

"They're teasing you, Dilly Gal." Justin slid an arm around her shoulders. "Dad here would have done the same thing. And *he'd* have brought Mama and the babies into the house."

Chapter Twenty

Bacon snapped and popped on the stove, attended by Mary McGee, who'd made no bones about reclaiming her kitchen. As a rule, Justin could take cooking or leave it, but something about having played house over the couple of days he and Beth had been alone left him feeling a bit out of sorts at having to give up the role of chief cook.

He added the fourth spoonful of sugar to the coffee his mother had set in front of him and stirred. The aromatic brown liquid formed a whirlpool that mimicked his mind and heart. Both swirled and churned like the coffee currently sloshing against the inside of his cup. Caught up in a maelstrom of uncertainty, his brain warned him he'd be foolish to take things any further with Beth. That path could only lead to a world of hurt. Yet she intrigued him... a mix of intelligence and insight balanced by tenderness and compassion, all twined together by an adventurous spirit to rival that of any Old West pioneer. And beautiful. His lips lifted at the memory of their physical encounters. Not a woman to be overlooked on any level. Besides, even if he could ignore the physical urges, his heart apparently had an agenda of its own.

The swirling slowed. Justin lifted the cup and took a sip. Bitterness tickled his tongue, quickly soothed by the sweetness of the sugar. As he swallowed his coffee, for the first time in his twenty-four years, he considered a life other than working the Cross MC.

"What are we gonna do about that cat?" His father's gravel-filled morning voice broke into Justin's musings.

Did his dad somehow know the direction of his thoughts? Peering over the rim of the cup, he met Jim's gaze from across the table. Clear gray eyes regarded him, the thinning charcoal eyebrows arched with interest. Didn't look like it.

The cup clinked into the saucer as Justin set it down and rubbed his chin. "I thought I'd explore some of the outbuildings this morning, make sure she hasn't set up a lair nearby. Then maybe take a hike up to the trailhead."

A ghost of a smile hovered around Jim's mouth. "Gonna take your lady?"

Justin's heart skipped a beat, and he tore his eyes away from his dad's glinting gaze. Yep, he'd known, after all. "She's not my lady," he muttered, picking up his coffee again and hiding his face behind taking a sip.

His father's smile stretched wider.

"I thought it best Gus and I head out alone." Justin drained his cup and dropped it onto the saucer with a clatter.

"Head out where?" asked Beth from the doorway.

Justin glanced up and forgot how to breathe. The dark jeans hugged her thighs like they'd grown on her. His eye tracked upward, drawn by the V-shaped hemline of a bright purple print shirt that mimicked an arrow pointing directly at... his breath whooshed back in and lingered... home base. Almost choking on his own tongue, he forced his gaze to move on.

The loose-fitting blouse should have taken the edge off the spikes of desire prickling along Justin's nerves. But he knew what was hidden beneath that roomy garment. He'd molded those curves against him, had felt the softness of her skin under his fingertips. The V-neck mirrored the hemline and pointed directly at the valley between her breasts. Her hair cascaded around her shoulders and kissed her slender neck. She lifted a hand and brushed a strand of gold from her face. The flared sleeve of her blouse slid across the curve of her breast and a surge of pure lust shot through Justin's veins.

How was a guy supposed to keep his *eyes* off... let alone his *hands?*

Jim cleared his throat and let out a long wolf whistle.

"Dad!" Heat blossomed in Justin's neck and sent fiery sparks to his cheeks. Beth hadn't had a chance to pick up on the McGee family's particularly friendly brand of humor. He stole a glance at her face, astounded to find her grinning at his father.

"My goodness, aren't you pretty first thing in the morning?" Mary pointed to the seat next to Justin, then turned back to the range where she loaded a plate with hotcakes and bacon.

Beth sank onto the chair and cast a longing glance at Justin's empty coffee cup. He jumped to his feet and almost stumbled across the floor to the counter, where he quickly poured her a fresh cup of steaming brew.

"Is it a special occasion?" asked Mary, setting the plate in front of Beth.

"No, not really." Beth gave a rueful shrug. "More like inappropriate packing for my trip." She pointed at her sandals. "I'm lucky I didn't end up with poison ivy on my feet."

Mary chuckled as she took her own seat.

Beth pinned Justin in her green stare. "Where are you heading out to this morning?"

He lifted a shoulder, striving for nonchalance. "Gotta find where the cat came in last night, see if it's a fluke, or—" He eased out a breath. "Or if she might have made a home here."

Beth smothered her hotcakes in maple syrup. Then she picked up her fork and used the edge to cut a neat bite from the stack. "So you seemed to recognize this — cougar, was it?" She turned the fork around, stabbed the bite, and popped it in her mouth. As she chewed, her green stare remained leveled in his direction.

He shrugged as he considered how much to tell her. He

didn't want to terrify her, but he didn't want her asking to come along on his scouting trip, either. "We've had a couple of run-ins with her. The first time was..." He rubbed his jaw, counting back the years. Finally he looked at his dad. "Five years ago?"

"Yup." Jim nodded, then swirled a forkful of hotcake through the plate of syrup. "That was probably her first year as a mother. She wasn't so much mean back then as ornery." He waved his fork in the air like some sort of exclamation point. "Protecting her cubs and feeding 'em was all she cared about." He shoveled the forkful of hotcake into his mouth.

"She came down off the mountains, through the high pastures, and made the mistake of crossing MacKay's land." Justin considered another cup of coffee, but Beth's proximity made him jittery enough. Instead, he pushed his cup away and warmed into telling the tale. "You don't mess with Brody's cows." Which was a joke, considering Brody was likely messing with Cross MC cows. Pushing the thought carefully to the back of his mind, he snickered. "Someone should have told that young mama cat. She and her three cubs feasted their way across his pastures. Near 'bout drove him nuts trying to catch her."

Beth cut another bite of hotcakes and stabbed it but made no move to pick it up. A frown pinched her forehead. "Are cougars always a problem? Is it just something to be expected?"

"Well, yes and no." Justin rocked his chair back on two legs. "Cougars prefer elk and mule deer, but something sent her off the mountain and down to ranching country. Another cat, maybe... arguing over territory." He dropped the front of the chair back to the floor. "Cattle are a sight easier to pick off."

Beth picked up her last piece of bacon and studied it in silence. The lines rising from the bridge of her nose deepened as her eyebrows drew together. "I get the feeling you're leaving something out," she said slowly, her tone more musing than accusing.

Justin mulled the story in his head, seeking a nicer way to tell the tenderhearted woman the uglier details.

"Brody set bear traps for the cat," said Jim.

So much for being indirect. Justin shot his father a pointed stare, but Jim only shook his head dismissively and took up the story.

"The cat got herself caught in one of the traps, her back leg. But the trap was set sloppy so it didn't catch her very high up — more on the foot than the leg." Jim pushed his empty plate forward. "And Brody... well, let's just say he's always been an impetuous sort. He didn't bother checking the trap when we came upon her. Just proceeded to shoot her cubs — one by one. He could have shot her first, but it was like he wanted her to see him killing off her kits. Ford and I tried to pull him off, but he was like a crazy man. Only he never got to the third one before that mama cat exploded free of the trap... leaving a piece of her foot behind."

Beth stared, her face pasty white. Then she shocked them all with her next words. "The poor cat."

Mary covered a snicker with her hand as she pushed away from the table and began gathering the empty dishes.

Justin shrugged. "That 'poor cat' mauled your brother-in-law pretty good. I shot a couple of times in the air but by the time I had a clear shot at *her*, she was already backing off." A shiver ran through him as the metallic smell of blood filtered up from the recesses of his mind. He swallowed hard, but pictures from that day flipped through his memory like some crazy whacked-out slide show, and his stomach threatened to flip along with them. It had been a blood-soaked nightmare. "I shoulda gone ahead and shot her."

Beth inhaled sharply and covered her mouth with one hand, her wide eyes centering on him. "What happened?"

Somehow Justin understood she wasn't asking why he hadn't shot the cat then. She wanted the rest of the story — the reason he knew in hindsight that he should have killed her. But he choked on the words.

"A young girl was found near Route 189, heading toward Jackson, about three years ago. Not too far up from Brody's ranch," Mary said quietly, sliding into her seat again. "Her car was parked nearby with a flat tire. She was..." With a heavy sigh, she reached out and slipped her hand into Jim's. "She was dead, and animals had been at her. They found cougar tracks leading from the body, big ones, and one of the back feet was missing all its toes and part of the pad."

"The same cat?" whispered Beth.

Jim cleared his throat. "That was my best guess. Given what we found in MacKay's trap after the mama cat ran off with her cub."

"*Some* people said she'd developed a taste for human blood when she mauled Brody," added Mary. She squeezed Jim's hand.

Justin clenched his jaw. *Don't let her ask the rest. Please.* He didn't want to rehash the grisly details or remember the sight and smell of the remains of someone who'd once been a beautiful girl, two years ahead of him at the local high school.

"It was Alice who said that, wasn't it?" Beth's voice held a resigned tone.

Justin let out the breath he'd been holding when she'd unwittingly moved the conversation in a safer direction. "Yeah, she made a lot of noise about the fact that the cat should have been killed when I had the chance." He shrugged. "She was right. And apparently it's not over yet." He caught Beth's wide-eyed gaze and held it while he said his next words. "And that's why you're staying here while Gus and I track this monster. I won't — *can't* have you out there with me."

She wanted to protest. Sparks flared in those green eyes, turning them closer to gold for a moment. She stared him down, and he held his breath until at last she sagged in her seat and gave him a curt nod.

* * *

Beth studied the mound of off-white dough on the cutting board in front of her and shook her head. With ragged edges and uneven lumps, it looked nothing at all like Mary's smooth round ball.

Mary punched hers in the center and formed it into a shallow bowl. Then she laid it onto her cutting board and picked up the wooden rolling pin with the red handles. She dipped her hand into the flour canister, brought up a loose handful of flour, and rubbed it up and down the roller.

"The trick is to keep your rolling pin well-floured as you work the pastry." She pushed the wooden cylinder into the dough and rolled it away from her, lifted it and repeated the process in a slightly different direction.

"Don't let her fool you," said Jim from across the room. He lounged against the doorjamb, watching them. "She has a secret ingredient… that's the real trick."

"Secret ingredient?" Beth eyed Justin's dad. He looked comfortable enough, but maybe leaning against a doorway masked some fatigue or weakness.

"Just a pinch of love," announced Mary in a sing-song voice.

When Beth turned back to the table, Justin's mom had rolled her piece of pastry completely flat and mostly round. "Wow, you did that fast." *And I missed it.*

Mary laughed. "Years of practice."

Jim shoved off the doorjamb and shuffled over to the back door. Moving the curtain aside, he pushed his nose against the glass and peered out. He reminded Beth of a little kid waiting for his father to come home, or maybe for a visit from Santa Claus.

"A watched pot never boils," remarked Mary, setting a pie plate upside down on her rolled-out pastry. She traced around the glass dish with a paring knife. "They'll be in when it's over."

Her words reminded Beth that Jim wasn't waiting for Santa Claus, but for his son, who was possibly in very real danger. A chill settled in the base of her spine.

"Why did they walk?" she asked. The pastry dough was cool and stiff under her fingers, and she worried at an edge that had dried to hardness. "Instead of riding horses, I mean."

Jim and Mary exchanged glances, and Beth sighed, feeling even more like an outsider.

"Please," she whispered. "I know there's a reason, and I promise not to freak out on you."

"It's easier to track the cat on foot than on horseback," Mary murmured. She flipped the pie plate over along with the pastry and began tucking the edges of the crust against the dish, keeping her eyes fixed on her task, though Beth suspected she could do it in her sleep.

Jim walked over to the table, his gait a little ungainly, and he winced when he sank into the chair. But his eyes when he lifted them to Beth's were clear and his voice was strong. "Horses might spook if they catch the cat's scent. Spooked horses and a big cat aren't a good combination. The horse can get hurt if the cat attacks. The rider trying to protect the horse can get... hurt."

Or killed, she added to herself. That was why Justin hadn't wanted her along. Because he'd feel compelled to protect her. "But won't the cougar... I mean, if it attacks and they're on foot, it'll have the advantage."

Mary stepped around the table and next to Beth. "Here, let's get your pie crust ready for the next dish. Has Justin told you his favorite pie is lemon meringue?"

Beth got it immediately. Some things just weren't mentioned out loud.

"I love lemon meringue," she said with a smile.

Chapter Twenty–One

The tracks disappeared into the patches of shale, but the cat was definitely heading for higher ground. Justin sighed. Looked like they'd be on the trail a while. Should have brought lunch.

Gus squinted up the cliff face. "Man, I hate walking through here."

Justin had to agree. Lots of openings along the path offered the agile cat the opportunity to climb. If she got above them, she could pounce before they even knew she was there. The space between his shoulder blades hadn't stopped burning since they'd entered the wash.

"There!" Gus pointed to the trail ahead of them.

But when Justin crouched down, the track was pointed in the direction from which they'd come. "This is old," he murmured, touching the edge of the footprint. It had been made when the ground was wet and once it dried, sharp ridges had formed. "Looks like she uses this trail a lot, though."

Gus drew in a deep breath and made a face. "Yeah, smells like it, too. She's marking territory."

"She wouldn't do that if she had cubs," murmured

Justin. "She'd be laying low, keeping them hidden." He stared at the muddy print, willing it to reveal something about its maker.

Had she left the trail to stalk her hunters? Was she waiting even now, ready to ambush them on their way back down the track? Justin stood again and adjusted his grip on the Winchester. He executed a slow pivot and scanned the brush along the sides of the trail, looking for signs a nearly two-hundred-pound creature had passed.

It was so subtle, he nearly missed it. If the wind hadn't rustled through the grass at that particular moment, he would have completely overlooked the thin trail of bare ground. Brushing his hands over the blades of tall grass, he parted it for a better look. There in the sandy earth lay a fresh cougar track. "Gotcha," he whispered.

He took a step into the grass, then stopped with a frown. The cat was heading back toward MacKay land. As much as he wanted to finish tracking her... to finish *her*... He sighed. The thought of following her onto Brody MacKay's land didn't appeal. It'd be one way of asking for trouble. Best if he called his neighbor, let him know the cat was back. Then he'd call Fish and Game.

He started to turn from the barely existent trail, but a bright bit of blue fluttered just inside a stand of scrub pine seedlings. He stepped toward it, moving cautiously.

"What're you doing?" asked Gus in a hushed voice.

"Something over here," said Justin, stepping gingerly along the trail, his focus on the fluttering bit of cloth.

The wind shifted and the scent of cat urine was overpowered by something far worse. For the second time in a handful of days, the putrid stink of cadaverine invaded Justin's nostrils. His stomach turned as much with dread as from the odor. Using the tip of the Winchester, he pushed aside one of the larger saplings.

He saw her instantly. Young, probably Beth's age, and same general build with pale blond hair. She lay on her back, staring blindly into the trees above.

"Oh, hell... damn it." Bile rose in Justin's throat. Her gut had been ripped open and fed upon. The cat had obviously been at her. But the cat hadn't stuffed the bright blue silk scarf into her mouth. And the cat hadn't made the bruises that circled her throat.

At the crack of a branch above him and to his right, Justin lifted his rifle, aiming in less than a heartbeat at the springing cat. He squeezed the trigger, scrambling backward at the same time. *Shit!* He'd had no time to swing the rifle straight and the shot went wide. He stumbled on the uneven ground and lost sight of the tawny animal in the spinning green and blue of pine trees and sky. A second shot rang out from behind him.

The cat dropped to the ground with a *thump*, then lay in a flaccid heap where seconds earlier Justin had been standing. One paw was stretched in his direction, less than a foot away, as though seeking to carry him with her to the world of the dead. Panting, lightheaded, he could only stare at the lifeless body with the bloom of blood marring her chest. Sightless amber eyes reflected back at him, already showing the dullness of death. If she'd completed the pounce, he would have been the one lying dead in the grass. Gus raced up from the trail and dropped to his knees next to Justin.

"Damn it, kid! Why'd you go off into the brush like that?"

"There's—" Justin fought against the bile that burned his throat, but his stomach gave a mighty heave. He turned his head and puked in the grass next to him. Eyes stinging, he wiped his mouth with the back of his hand. "There's a girl in there," he managed to croak.

Gus stiffened. "The cat got another girl?"

Justin shook his head, holding onto his wits by a mere thread. "No. No, this one was killed by something on two legs."

* * *

"That's the craziest thing I've ever seen," murmured Justin's father, crouching in front of Mama Kitty's nest and peering inside. With the bribe of a can of tuna pilfered from the pantry, Mama Kitty had finally allowed them to look at her unusual family. "We've had cows lose their calves and refuse to take on an orphan in its place — and that's the same species. Never seen a cat take on a litter of pups." Jim reached through the hole and picked one up, then rolled back and propped himself against the wall. Derby squirmed in his hand and then pushed his way up to lick him on the chin.

Beth giggled. "He likes you. Although I have to warn you, I think he likes everybody."

Jim chuckled, stroking the pup between the eyes. "Doesn't seem to have much problem being on three legs. Nice big belly on 'im." Shifting again, as though unable to get comfortable, Jim thrust the puppy into a stray finger of sunlight that poked through a vent high above. Then he angled his head and studied Derby, a frown pinching his forehead. "You say you two found him up at the old homestead?"

"Yeah," she said with a nod. "Justin said he thought their mother had been attacked by an animal." Her eyes widened as a frisson of understanding rushed her. "You don't think... I mean, would the cougar have..."

Jim's eyes flickered with awareness and he regarded her with a steady gaze. Assessing her, Beth realized, taking her measure, as though deciding — again — how much to tell her. Then he shook his head slowly. "No, a big cat like that one takes after a dog less than a third its size... it's not just gonna cause an injury."

Death would have been quick. The mother wouldn't have made it back to her puppies. Beth shuddered.

"You know, your sister and her husband have a couple of border collies. One of 'em has a blaze just like this one." He traced the jagged white line that split the black on Derby's head.

"Gus said the same thing." Beth reached out and scratched the puppy behind the ears. "But Justin said the mom was brown and white."

Jim's eyebrows shot skyward and he glanced back at the pup. "He did, huh? Guess that makes these someone else's dogs." He handed Derby off to Beth and swiveled to reach back into the hole in the wall.

That marked the second reference to Alice and Brody owning border collies. Had Justin lied about the color of the mother dog? Why would he do that? "Is it — is it unusual for a brown dog to have black puppies?" she asked, unable to resist the question burning in her mind.

Jim pulled his hand back without grabbing a puppy. "Not necessarily. The father could have had black markings."

But for all four puppies to look like their father? How likely was that? Equations of dominant and recessive traits filled her mind but she hadn't studied animal genetics. She had no idea what colors were dominant.

The small side door on the barn opened and Mary stepped through. "Pies are cooling. Got a nice hot apple pie and some vanilla ice cream."

Beth's stomach growled.

Jim pushed slowly to his feet then held his hand out for Beth. "That one's calling my name. Come on in and help me eat it."

With a happy smile tugging at her lips, Beth eased the puppy back through the hole in the wall and into the nest of straw and old rags.

As they stepped into the yard, brilliant midday sun flashed off the side of the barn, blinding Beth, and she raised a hand to shield her eyes. A movement and a spot of color in the distance caught her eye and she squinted. Pale cowboy hat, blue jeans, light-colored shirt. "Justin!" She grabbed Jim's arm and jumped up and down. "Justin's back!"

His parents exchanged a glance and both smiled.

* * *

Fatigue singed tiny holes in Justin's muscles as he trudged along the last hundred yards from the trailhead to the stable. He'd hated leaving Gus with the body, but it had seemed irreverent to leave the girl alone. With the cat eliminated, predator threat was essentially nil. She'd apparently had a wide territory and thoroughly marked it. Wolves were unlikely to drift so far off the mountains at this time of year. Nonetheless, Justin had alternated between a fast walk and an easy lope on his hike back to the ranch.

"Justin!" Beth's voice in the distance brought his head

up, and the weariness fell away, replaced by that prickle of alertness that took over whenever she was near.

She ran toward him, throwing up tiny clumps of sandy dirt in her wake. His lips pulled into a smile. At least she'd borrowed his mother's boots again. He kept walking, energized, eager to touch her, hold her... smell her. She was life. Maybe not a permanent part of *his* life. But his for a time.

While she's here.

He stopped walking and checked the safety on the Winchester, then leaned it against the white fence rail. From several feet away, she launched herself at him, and he caught her at the waist then pulled her against him as she twined her arms around his neck and pressed her lips against his.

Her touch was delicate, welcoming, but his emotions quickly took over with the need to reaffirm life and living. He loosened his hold on her waist just enough to allow her to slide downward along his body. When her feet met the ground, Justin ran his hands upward to cup her face, and then he drank deeply from her lips.

As her sweet taste washed over his tongue, he knew he'd never be sated. Touching her, being with her... it wasn't enough. It never would be.

He buried his face in her hair and inhaled the scent of flowers and sunshine that had become home to him. If she couldn't stay, then he'd have to go... would be compelled to follow her — to the ends of the earth, if necessary.

"Dilly..." he whispered. "I lo—"

She spoke quickly, breathless, her words tumbling over one another. "I was so worried about you. Did you find her? Did you find the cougar?"

Reality slugged him in the gut, and he stepped back. "Yeah, we found her. But I have to get to the house and call the sheriff." He grabbed his rifle and then took up her hand and laced their fingers together.

"Justin? What's wrong? What's happened?" Alarm sharpened her tone, and she grasped his arm with her free hand. "Where's Gus?"

"Gus is fine," he said quickly. "The cat's — it's dead." He started walking again. "I really don't want to go through the story more than once, Dilly. Please."

A gasp slipped from her lips, and she stepped next to him, her impetus somehow giving him strength to finish the long walk home. He held the back door open, and she entered in tense silence. As he followed her inside, he set the Winchester next to the door, bent and pushed off his muddy boots.

Mary looked up, her hand still on the knife embedded in a freshly baked lemon meringue pie. The welcoming smile on her face faded, replaced by concern, and she abandoned the pie with the knife still in it. "Jim!"

Justin opened the gun cabinet next to the door, picked up his rifle, and parked it in the appropriate slot. He'd take care of cleaning it later.

His dad appeared in the doorway, questions all over his face, and Justin sighed. He really didn't want to tell the story more times than he needed to.

"Gus is okay, but I need to call Sheriff Tenbaum," he said, a grim smile stretching his lips. "I'd appreciate it if you'd all listen in on the call."

His parents sat, their eyes meeting, exchanging unspoken worry with their stares. Beth hovered near him, as though somehow aware he needed her support, and he gripped her hand as he jammed the telephone receiver between his shoulder and ear and dialed the number for the sheriff.

"Sheriff's office," answered a pleasant female voice on the other end of the line.

What was her name? He knew her, could picture her face, but Justin drew a blank. So with a maddening quaver in his voice, instead of greeting her, he simply requested to be put through to the sheriff. Beth squeezed his hand three times, and a sense of calm blanketed him. When George Tenbaum came on the line, Justin spoke on autopilot, giving the bare facts without emotion.

"Does it look like the cat killed her?" asked Tenbaum.

Justin glanced around the room. His mother and father sat across from one another. Mary pushed her hand into Jim's. Beth started to tremble, her face a pasty white, and this time he squeezed her hand three times, the gesture somehow strengthening him all over again.

"No." He shook his head and chose his next words carefully. "No, that was some — something else."

"An accident, then?"

The picture of the brilliant blue scarf, spilling from the girl's mouth and fluttering in the wind, wove its way through Justin's memory. "No, not that either."

"Well, out with it, boy. What are you saying? Did someone kill the girl?"

"Yeah," said Justin softly, easing out a breath. "That's what it looks like."

"Aw, shit!" The sheriff added a few ripe curses and then asked for specific directions. He cursed again when Justin told him how far from the beaten path the body was.

When he hung up, Justin just stood still for a moment, not feeling anything but the need to breathe. So he gulped in air and blew it out, then concentrated on repeating the process.

His father stood and crossed to the kitchen sink, where he opened the cupboard to the left and withdrew a bottle of amber liquid and a juice glass. He poured two fingers' worth and pushed the glass into Justin's hand. When Justin only stared, Jim gave his hand a gentle push upward.

"You're numb... that's shock, boy. Drink this down, and then we'll saddle up a couple of horses and be ready for when the sheriff gets here."

Numb... Hell, yeah, he was. He'd stopped feeling when he'd lost his breakfast in the grass earlier. At another push from his dad, Justin put the glass to his lips and tipped his head back. The Kentucky bourbon seared its way over his palate and down. He closed his eyes, waiting for his stomach to kick it back up, but he remained steady.

A movement he caught in the corner of his eye drew his attention. Standing near the back door, Beth rocked back and forth, arms wrapped around her abdomen, eyes darting from him to the door, back to him, toward the hallway. Any second she'd bolt. When had he let go of her hand? The juice glass made a decisive *thunk* when Justin set it on the counter. She jumped at the sound, and he closed the distance between them, tugging her into his arms, resting his chin on top of her head.

"You look like you want to high-tail it back to Michigan." Part of him wished she would. At least there she'd be safe. Images of dark bruises around the dead girl's neck invaded his mind, but he squashed them.

"Did the — did the cougar kill the girl?"

Justin stared at the cream-colored linoleum floor and traced one of the lines between the squares with his toe as he tried to find words to put it delicately. In the end, he chickened out. "It — wasn't pretty. Kinda hard to say how she died."

Beth jerked and sucked in a hard breath. After a second or two, she released her breath and the tension eased from her stance. "Do you know who she is — was?" she whispered.

"No." Justin frowned, shaking his head. "No, I've never seen her before." In truth, he hadn't really taken much of a look at the body in the glade, but if he'd known her, surely he'd have recognized her. He'd recognized the cat's other victim immediately.

Except *this* girl hadn't been the cat's victim. He hugged Beth tighter.

"Let's go saddle up some horses, son." Jim stood with his hand on the doorknob. He'd pulled on his boots and held his plain gray Stetson in his hand.

"Dad..." Even on horseback, the ride up there wouldn't be an easy one. It was a bad idea for Jim to make the trip.

Beth squeezed his hand... hard. *Don't bury your dad before he dies,* she'd said.

Jim angled his head, eyebrows raised. "Yes?"

Stay here, stay safe. Don't overdo it. Don't leave us... Don't leave me. Justin swallowed his emotional response. "That'd be great." He turned to his mother. "Keep the doors locked, okay, Mom?"

Her hard stare warned him he'd explain himself later. But he'd never expected anything else.

* * *

Beth sank into the chair she'd occupied at breakfast. Why had Justin hedged about the girl? It hadn't been so much what he'd said, but his actions when he'd said it. Shuffling his foot along the floor. He'd done that before... when Gus had mentioned Alice and Brody having black-and-white dogs. He'd dragged his boot through the dirt and said the mother dog had been brown. And he'd taken a long time answering her question about the mother dog's death. Just like he hadn't really answered her questions about the girl. *Why?*

Mary stood for a long time, gazing through the window over the sink. Then she dropped the curtain and whirled about, offering Beth an encouraging smile. "You know life's full of surprises on a ranch, but for the most part, they're good surprises. It's not typical to have this kind of trouble."

"Justin lied," blurted Beth.

Mary jumped back as though Beth had physically slapped her. "Pardon?"

"Justin lied to me," Beth repeated slowly, still trying to process what it meant. "Two, maybe three times. He... he does this thing, delays his answer and shuffles his feet."

Mary pulled out a chair and sat, her full attention on Beth. "Why, yes, he does. So... what did he lie to you about?"

Beth swallowed. Why did she suddenly feel like she was in the third grade and tattling on her arch nemesis, Lori Wilkins?

"Beth?"

"About the dogs. He said the mother dog was brown-and-white when Gus mentioned Alice and Brody having cattle dogs. But he played in the dirt with his foot." Beth sighed. It sounded stupid now that she was saying it out loud.

"Please go on," urged Mary, not moving. "What made you think of that now?"

"Just now, when I asked how the girl he found had died... he played with the lines in the floor and told me he didn't know."

Mary pursed her lips. "Which means he does know. Or at least knows more than he's letting on. Why do you think he lied about the mother dog?"

Beth sucked on her bottom lip while she mulled it over.

"I guess, maybe he could have been suspicious of my relationship with Alice. I didn't know back then how people around here felt about her. So for all he knew I was out to cause trouble, I suppose."

The frown on Mary's face suggested she disagreed. "What do *you* think of your sister?"

"I think she's a bitch." Beth bit her tongue and drew in a calming breath. "I try every day not to hate my sister. But she doesn't make it easy. I kind of figured out she's hurt a lot of people around here."

Mary reached out and took Beth's hands. "And you? Has she hurt you?"

How had the conversation flipped from Justin's prevarication to Alice's malevolence? The thought wasn't even fully formed before Beth found herself nodding. "Sometimes I think the only thing Alice does well is hurt people."

"And if she found out the puppies were from her dog?"

"She'd want them," whispered Beth. "And she'd get rid of them. Especially Derby." *And if she knew I liked them... she'd make sure I knew what she'd done.*

Mary smiled and squeezed Beth's hands. "I don't know why my son lied about the girl, but I guarantee he'll tell his daddy the truth while they're riding up there. As for the dog, I have a suspicion he lied to make certain the puppies never went to Alice. Not because he didn't trust you, but because he didn't want you to bear the burden of the lie."

Beth could only stare at the candid woman in front of her. "You know him so well..."

Mary's smile gentled; the glisten of tear shone in her eyes. "He's my son... and so much like me, sometimes it scares me."

* * *

"I gotta figure out how to tell Mom and Beth about this before it hits the news." Weary and emotionally depleted, Justin turned Zeke onto the track that led to the ranch. It had been a rough couple of hours, waiting for the sheriff and his team, and then waiting for the okay to leave the scene — with the admonishment not to go anywhere.

Jim guffawed as he guided Gypsy to follow the same path. "The only thing you gotta figure out is how to explain to your mother why you lied."

Justin opened his mouth to protest that he hadn't lied. Not exactly. He'd just left out a bit of information. But the words sounded lame even before he said them, so he slumped in his saddle. "Yeah... I know."

"That gal of yours knows by now, too, I'll wager," Gus said with a snicker.

The crack of rifle fire interrupted the gentle teasing. Justin jerked taller in the saddle, and Zeke shied to the right, bumping into Gypsy. A second shot sounded. With a glance at the other two men, whose faces mirrored his alarm, Justin urged Zeke into a gallop.

They arrived in the stable yard just as another round was fired.

"Behind the house!" he shouted to Jim and Gus. Spurred by pure adrenaline, he jumped from the saddle and grabbed the Winchester from the holster.

On the run, he flipped off the safety and set the bolt on the rifle. He rounded the side of the house and skidded to a stop, just as Beth lifted a rifle and pointed it at the two tin cans resting on upended logs next to the patio. She squeezed the trigger. A chunk of wood from one of the stumps flew into the air, accompanied by the crack of splintering wood. The can on top of the log shivered but didn't even fall over. Beth opened the breech, and the spent shell casing flew up and to her right. She pushed the breech forward and rotated down, her movements a tad awkward, but manageable. She lifted the rifle again.

Wait! Was she closing her eyes?

She squeezed the round off and the bullet drove into the ground, raising a little cloud of dirt. Beth spat out a curse that singed the air, and Justin lowered his rifle, uncocking it and flipping on the safety. Adrenaline weakened his knees and threatened to explode his heart.

"Not bad. Gettin' closer." Mary handed Beth a couple of shells and pointed at the rifle. "Reload it like I showed you."

"What in heaven's name are you doing, woman?" bellowed Jim when he arrived at Justin's side.

Justin gave his dad a quick assessing glance. His face was a little flushed and his breathing a touch heavy, but other than that he seemed all right.

"Teaching Beth how to shoot," said Mary without looking up, her voice calm and resolute. She stepped back and motioned for her student to continue.

Mesmerized, Justin could only watch as Beth set the safety, opened the breech, and ejected the spent shell casing. One by one, she slid the cartridges into the chamber, pressing the last one with her thumb and then closing the bolt. She pulled in a deep breath and released the safety, then raised the rifle to rest against her cheek. When she shut one eye and squinted with the other, Justin cringed.

"She's aiming too low," murmured his dad.

"I don't think she's *aiming* at all," muttered Gus, taking a step backward.

Beth squeezed the trigger and again the bullet went into the ground, raising a puff of dust behind it.

"You're aiming too low," called Jim in a helpful tone.

She spared them a quick glance and raised the gun slightly. Have mercy, was she aiming for birds now?

"No, no, just a little lower." His dad chuckled. "No need to go eagle shootin'."

"Dad, I don't think you should encour—"

The explosive rifle shot split the silence. A chunk of cement flew upward, followed quickly by the ping of a ricochet, just as the projectile whizzed past Justin's head and smacked with a *kerplunk-splat* against the rear of the house. The window directly above the strike instantly developed a spider web crack, and the silver-dollar-sized chunk of cement landed with a *plop* and a soft rustle in the grass.

Beth had dropped the rifle and covered her eyes, and after a second she peeked between her fingers. "I'm sorry... I'm so sorry."

Gus pulled his hand down his face and shook his head. "Someone needs to get that gun away from her." His pointed gaze fell directly on Justin. "I got some stuff needs seeing to in the barn. I'll take care of the horses." He edged backward, then whirled around and took off at a lope.

"Coward," mumbled Justin, staring at the deep hole at the edge of the patio and the wide groove that radiated outward from it.

"You about finished with the lesson?" shouted Jim, crossing the expanse of grassy ground and joining the women.

"I told Mom to keep the doors locked," grumbled Justin as he followed his dad.

"The doors *are* locked." Mary dangled a key from her forefinger.

"I meant with you and Beth *inside*," snapped Justin.

"Well, maybe you should have told us a killer was running around," his mother bit back.

"Oh." Deflated, Justin blew out a breath. "You got that, huh?"

Jim shot him an *I-told-you-so* look, and Justin rolled his eyes.

Mary stalked up to Justin and poked a finger in his face. "Darn right, I got it. As soon as your gal here told me you'd lied when she asked how the girl on the mountain died, I called Mavis Morrow in the sheriff's office and asked what was up." She jammed her hands on her hips. "And do you know what she told me?"

"I can guess." Justin stood his ground. His mom would only follow him if he stepped back.

"She told me George got called out on a probable homicide. On *our* ranch. Is that true?"

His shoulders sagged with her decisive trouncing of his last line of defense, and he nodded. "Yep, that's about right."

Mary shook her head, clucking her tongue. "That poor child, whoever she was." She touched Justin on the arm. "Are you okay, son?"

Over Mary's shoulder he caught a glimpse of Beth, holding the Winchester against her cheek. His dad stood next to her showing her how to sight along the top. Then he raised the barrel with two fingers and pointed at something in the distance.

The warmth of family love swirled through Justin's

system. Smiling, he shifted his gaze to meet his mother's eyes. "I am now, Mom."

Chapter Twenty-Two

Finishing the dishes brought Beth a sense of accomplishment. At least that was something she could do to help carry her weight without needing her hand held. Jim had faded fast after dinner and retired to the living room. After catching Mary's longing glance at the doorway, Beth had shooed her to join him. "I promise if I can't figure out where to put a bowl or plate, I'll come find you." Then she'd turned on the radio and finished the dishes while she daydreamed of dancing in the kitchen with Justin.

Smiling, she drew the knife through the lemon meringue and then slipped the silver pie server beneath the slice she'd cut. Justin had gone straight into the study after dinner, and she'd left him alone. His day had been traumatic, and maybe he needed time to recover.

But not too much time, she decided, heading for the study with her lemony offering. The door was closed and she knocked softly.

After a second, Justin pulled it open. A smile spread across his face and lightened his eyes. "Hey, there!" He stepped back and she entered.

He'd cleaned up and changed before dinner and had looked nearly formal with his shirt buttoned to the collar. That shirt was undone to midway down his chest now, and he hadn't bothered with shoes.

"I brought you some dessert." She held up the plate.

Sparks of pure pleasure raced along her spine when he grinned and accepted the pie. He caught her hand in his and led her to an overstuffed chair. Beth's squeals of surprise turned into giggles of delight when he flopped onto the leather seat and pulled her down into his lap in one fluid motion.

Snuggled in his arms, Beth sighed and closed her eyes, allowing her hand to drift in aimless little circles over his chest.

It's like being home...

Justin scooped a forkful of pie and offered her the first bite, but she shook her head, watching as he slipped it into his mouth instead. His eyes lit up as he chewed. "Um-um-uum. Love lemon meringue."

He stabbed another piece and this time Beth accepted his offer. The tart-sweet combination melted in her mouth and she moaned. Alternating bites, they shared the pie until it was gone. Justin laid the empty plate on the table next to the chair and then tightened his arms around Beth's waist, bowed his head, and rested his forehead on hers.

Saturated with contentment, Beth could have lain against him forever and died happy. When had her dreams changed so drastically? The world outside Justin's life no longer held any appeal. Not even a glimmer of curiosity for exotic locations remained. What would he do if she told him she wanted to stay? Would he think she was being too forward? Presumptuous?

The desk across the room was littered with papers. Some appeared to be loosely stacked. Some were cross-stacked on other piles.

"What are you doing in here?" She cringed inwardly at her thoughtless outburst. Now, why had she asked that?

He tensed, but then released a deep sigh. "Trying to make the finances work."

Her heightened awareness of him picked up on the

stilted tightness in his voice. "Are — is the ranch in trouble?"

He huffed out another breath. "Not... in trouble, exactly. Not yet, anyway. But this isn't a good economy for any agricultural venture — even an established one." He shrugged and pushed a wayward strand of hair behind her ear. "We got behind on a couple of bills, and I'm looking at selling off some of our herd early to catch them up."

Beth frowned. It was more than just some of the herd. A lot more. And it was more than a couple of bills behind.

It isn't your business, so let him keep his pride intact.

She never had been good at listening to her own advice.

"Do you need a lot?"

"About a third of our cattle ought to bring us current. Then it'll be a matter of keeping our heads above water until we can build our reserves again." He ran the backs of his knuckles along her arm, down then back up again. "It's common — happens all the time. Kind of a 'robbing Peter to pay Paul' existence."

"A third of your herd?" she whispered. "That sounds bad."

He shrugged again. "It balances out. We'll need less feed when they come off the mountain if we sell them early."

"How much are you looking at to break even?"

Why couldn't she seem to drop it? She was grilling the man about his livelihood, like she had the right.

But he didn't appear to mind. "Mid five figures, to start."

Hope sparked. "Is that all? Justin, I can help with that!" She pushed away from his chest and turned her gaze on his face. "I can help so you don't have to sell *anything* early."

Mild interest flickered, but then he chuckled. "Oh, yeah?"

He thought she was joking! As if she'd joke about something so important to him. She balanced herself with one hand on his shoulder and squeezed. "Listen to me. I have a small trust fund. From my mom. It's just sitting there, doing nothing."

"A trust fund, huh?" His eyes twinkled with barely contained mirth. Obviously he still wasn't taking her seriously.

"Listen to me! I mean it." Urgency quickened her speech, and she gave his shoulder a little shake. "My grandfather set it up — my mom's father. I *have* what you need!"

The grin evaporated from Justin's face, and he completely stopped moving. He pushed her forward, but she tightened her grip on his shoulder, unwilling to break the connection.

"Just who was your mother?"

Warmth crept into her cheeks and she sighed, suddenly not so sure of herself. "Her name was Janice Byrd. Rushton after she married my dad."

His brows drew together. He obviously wasn't placing the name. She knew the moment he did, though. He broke from her grasp and leaped to his feet, only barely catching her before she landed on the floor.

"*Byrd?* The automotive family? Your mother was the Princess of Detroit?"

His incredulous words sucked the joy from her heart. Tracing the geometric patterns in the Navajo-inspired carpet with her eyes, she mumbled, "She wasn't a princess. The news media just called her that to be mean. She was pretty and sweet and kind. She was..." Beth lifted her arms and let them fall again. "She was my mom. And she didn't want all that attention."

Justin stared at her as if she'd just become a stranger. In a way, perhaps she had, since he was seeing her from a new perspective.

"You're an heiress...a damned—" He expelled an exasperated breath. "You're the daughter no one could ever get a picture of."

The burn of embarrassment lit her shortening fuse, and her words came out a little more shrill than she intended. "Were you *looking* for one?" She narrowed her eyes. "You seem to know a lot about my family."

"Your *family?* I don't know *anything* about your family beyond what's plastered in the news for the world to see." He shook his head. An indefinable emotion reflected in his eyes. "I thought I knew you... but apparently I was wrong."

What had she done? She should have kept her mouth

shut. *Please... don't let him hate me now.* Beth's heart lodged in her throat and pulsed there, threatening to toss up the pie she'd just eaten. How had things gone south so quickly? She tamped back her anger, knowing her revelation had been a shock. She hadn't meant to keep her identity from him. She'd simply never considered herself as anyone special.

She laid her hand on his arm. "Justin... please."

Justin stared at the hand. At least he didn't shake it off. His whole body trembled and a muscle worked in his jaw. "I don't understand. You can go anywhere you want." A harsh laugh passed his lips. "And get there in style. But you chose to study poison plants in Wyoming... in a hippie-reject micro-bus? Why?"

"Everything I told you about me being here is the truth." She pulled in deep breaths but still her head spun. "I'm a student studying plants. I only convinced my dad to let me travel alone by agreeing to meet up with Alice."

"And who's your dad? Some prince of the financial world?"

That wasn't fair, she wanted to scream at him. She hadn't done anything to deserve his derisive tone. But in a way, she understood. She'd shocked him, and he felt betrayed. So she answered evenly and without blinking. "He's a college mathematics professor."

Justin eased away from her touch, shaking his head. Fine lines of strain pinched the corners of his eyes. "I don't know you at all."

"I'm the same person I was ten minutes ago."

One side of his mouth curled into a mirthless half smile. "Ten minutes ago you were a student traveling across country with an old broken-down van. Not a, not a..." He waved his hand vaguely in her direction.

Rage welled again. He was like everyone else who couldn't see beyond her family's money. "Oh, so as long as you thought you'd rescued some dumb-ass little coed without any common sense, who was scraping her way through college, everything was just peachy, but the second you find out I'm not poor, your whole attitude changes?" Beth stomped her foot. "Maybe *I* don't know *you!*"

"Oh, you know me, all right," he said with a burr of annoyance in his voice. He spread his arms out. "This is me. It's *all* I am. What you see is what you get, baby."

"Well, maybe I don't—" At Justin's wince, Beth realized she'd been shrieking. She swallowed and forced a calmer tone. "Maybe I don't like what I see so much anymore."

He barked out a harsh laugh. "Like you ever really did? Was this all a game to you? A way to pass your time before you put on your crown as the Princess of Detroit?"

Tears welled, their sharp sting behind her eyelids begging for release. "I loved you," she whispered, backing up a step. She wheeled around and marched toward the door. Grasping the brass knob, she turned, unable to resist one parting shot. "I still love you, but if you think I'd ask to stay with you now, you're a complete jackass."

His strong hands encircled her waist from behind and he whirled her into his arms, pushing her against the door and closing it with a decisive click. Inches from her face, his eyes glittered deep blue in the lamplight.

"What did you say?"

Hatred of being manhandled warred with the thrill of his attention and stole her breath. "I-I s-said you're a jack—"

He captured her mouth with a hard fast kiss and she stopped caring whether or not she breathed. "Yeah, that part I got," he said against her lips. "What was that other thing?"

Beth clamped her mouth shut. She hadn't meant for those last words to come out. Especially now that she knew what he thought of her and her family.

* * *

Panic, bald and visceral, pulsed through him... writhing, electric. Paralyzing.

She loves me.

She's walking out the door!

Her words echoed through his head, elusive, the prize that remained just out of his reach. All because of his pride and obstinate stupidity.

He couldn't backpedal — he had nowhere to go. Could he

claim temporary insanity? *I'm sorry, but learning you're an heiress threw me for a loop?*

It had, but even in his addled state he recognized that wasn't nearly enough of an excuse.

Pinned against the study door, her body softened in his arms, and hope flared in his heart. He allowed his lips to explore every inch of her neck, her face, her mouth. He begged her to say it again.

She refused.

But she didn't push him away. He hadn't imagined it. The words might have slipped out, but they had been real. And he was a damn fool for becoming troubled at the revelation she had money.

Stop thinking!

"Why don't you tell me what you said?" He pressed closer to her.

"I already did. I said you're—"

He trailed kisses along her jaw until he reached her ear. "You said you love me," he murmured, rimming the shell of her ear with his tongue.

"Please..." she whispered, shuddering. But she twined her arms around his neck and sagged into his embrace.

He drew her soft earlobe between his lips and teased it with the tip of his tongue. "Please... what? Stop? Let you go? Send you away?" Justin brushed her hair back and followed the curve of her neck to the place where it met her shoulder, giving her a nip that made her jump and then soothing the spot with kisses. "I won't do any of that. I *was* a jackass, and I'm sorry."

She gave a half-hearted push against his chest. "I can't think when you're doing that."

"Then we're even... because I can't think whenever you're around." He pulled back and captured her gaze, bright with unshed tears. One sparkled on her eyelashes and then dripped onto her cheek. Leaning forward, he caught the salty moisture with the tip of his tongue and tightened his arms around her waist. "Don't go. Please."

She angled her head up and searched his eyes, not bothering to hide the vulnerability in hers. Visions pelted his memory. Bare feet with pink toenails peeking out from beneath a psychedelic van... Her hand holding his and pointing out the constellations... A shaky climb onto the back of a horse... Her nose pressed into the trumpet of a daffodil... nuzzling a puppy... A sheepish admission that she couldn't cook... Learning to shoot a rifle.

Justin found her hands — they were so cold. He laced their fingers together and stepped back, tugging her away from the door. "I'm sorry. It's not an excuse for being an ass, but you... surprised me." He chuckled, shaking his head. "*Really* surprised me. It doesn't matter who you are, or where you came from. Please... stay a little longer."

She didn't smile. He was used to her ready smile, and she just continued to regard him with those wide green eyes, as though waiting for her opportunity to run away screaming. Man, she was killing him. Parting would be bad enough, but to part on bad terms... He couldn't let her leave with harsh words and feelings between them.

"I'm sorry," she said quietly. She didn't pull away from him, but she aimed a pointed glance at their clasped hands. "I wish I'd never told you about my trust fund. I would give anything for you to think of me as Beth Rushton, crazy college student on an adventure again."

Not likely to happen. Justin released her, his movements slow, his fingertips lingering at hers. A physical distance of less than two feet lay between them. But an emotional distance miles wide and just as deep held him at bay. Agonizing emptiness crowded his heart.

He forced his misery back with a bold grin. "How about I keep thinking of you as Dilly?" *My Dilly... for now, at least.*

"I'd like that." Her smile reached into his heart and squeezed. "And I really can help you with—"

"No." When she jerked backward, Justin sighed and gentled his voice. "Things are changing for ranching, Dilly. The economy's going to hell, and regulations are strangling farms and ranches." He shrugged, trying for a show of nonchalance. "For the most part, I think the new regulations are an improvement. But some of them call for expensive changes. Prices are up for the consumer but somehow down for the growers. Sinking cash into a venture without changing the way things are…" He shook his head as the reality washed over him, as well. "It's a waste."

His most recent headache lay on top of the most pressing bills. The letter from Greenway Corporation. He'd read it with a sense of mixed hope and dread. Beth turned her head and followed his gaze. He should have picked the mess up and put it away when she'd knocked. Then things wouldn't have changed.

"Your mom said you were at college doing a double major in agriculture and business."

Justin chuckled and shook his head. Leave it to his mom to sing praises of his accomplishments, even when they weren't much to sing about. "Yep. Can't say I was entirely sad to put that behind me, though."

"I was a business major before I switched to environmental science," she said quietly, sending him a weak smile. "I know you won't take any financial assistance, and I won't insult you by offering again, but if you don't consider it prying, I think if we put our heads together, we might… I mean, they always say two heads are better than one." She pulled herself out of her slumped posture and shrugged then threw him a cheeky grin. "Whoever 'they' are."

The iron fist squeezing his heart eased some, and he answered her grin with his own. "You know, I've often wondered that same thing. Who the heck are 'they' and why should we listen to them?"

She nodded at the desk. "What do you say? I was top in my class."

"A financial wizard, huh?" He wasn't going to lay the Cross MC's financial problems in Beth's lap, but she'd tempered her offer rather than force the issue and opened the door on their friendship again. He wasn't going to rock the boat on that, either. He grimaced and shook his head. "It'll all still be there tomorrow." Laying an arm across her shoulders, he aimed them for the door.

Beth ducked and turned, stepping in front of him and halting his progress. "My grandpa always taught me to hit things head on as they're coming at you rather than waiting for them to get behind you and bite you in the butt." She pointed at his desk. "That *will* all be there tomorrow... but so will tomorrow's mail."

"Grandpa, eh?" That had to be Ralph M. Byrd, unofficial, but well-named, *King* of Detroit. Justin tilted his head and regarded her. She sure was a pretty thing when she was fired up. And apparently she was bent on saving him. He drew in a long breath and blew it out again. "You really want to do this, huh? It's that important to you?"

"Maybe." She grinned and walked across the floor toward the desk, confident, apparently sensing the victory he was about to hand her. "Maybe I just really like to win."

"Now *that* I don't doubt." He followed, pointing her toward the chair behind the desk while he pulled over the straight-backed upholstered model his mother had insisted made the study look more businesslike. The thing had probably never been used for more than his mother to read in while his dad wrote out bills and balanced books. He reached for the Greenway letter and began folding it.

"What's that?"

A sigh escaped as Justin stared at the correspondence. The paper was cool in his hand, the cool of a reptile about to strike. "It's... an option to consider. As a last resort." He folded the letter and shoved it back in its long white envelope, then slid it beneath the pile.

* * *

Beth jammed the top of the plastic ballpoint pen in her mouth and chewed the cap, mulling over the pink invoice in her hand. Absently, she reached for the goldenrod copy of a nearly identical bill.

"Did you change feed venders here?" She waved the pink copy. "This one's from Oslow and it's about ten percent cheaper than the local feed and tack..." She double-checked the name. "...Pickens."

"Pickens sometimes runs out of our blend, so we occasionally have to order from Oslow." He leaned over the desk and glanced at the pink copy then pointed to the date.

"Yeah, February, we got our order in late and Pickens was out."

Beth squinted at the sheets. "I understand you'd want to stay local just for the goodwill factor. But ten percent is a huge difference in price."

"Except Pickens doesn't charge for local delivery." Justin tapped the bottom row of the invoice. "And Oslow charges by the mile. It actually comes out a bit higher to use Oslow."

She pulled the pen from her mouth and laid it on the desk. Rubbing her burning eyes, she admitted defeat with a long sigh. Short of not feeding the horses or the people themselves not eating, the Cross MC really had no place it could cut corners. What had she expected... that she'd be a miracle worker, finding and plugging all their financial holes? Hard to do that when they had no financial holes.

When she dropped her hands from her face, Justin was watching her, his lips drawn up into an indulgently amused almost-smile. She gave him points for refraining from the obligatory *I-told-you-so* statement.

She lifted one shoulder. "You're good at this. I guess I just hoped I'd find something you missed."

Justin picked up a stack of papers and straightened it, then tapped the bottom edge on the desk before dropping it into a waiting manila file folder. "It was fun watching you work. I've never had a cuter accountant."

A giggle escaped, and the idea that she'd let him down dissipated. "Are you really going to sell off a third of your cattle?"

His mouth twisted into a wry grin. "Not tonight." He gathered the remaining bills and began stuffing them into folders. As he flipped the last folder open, his hand lingered over the letter he'd called a last resort.

"So what exactly is your last resort, anyway?"

Something that might have been fear flickered in his eyes. "Greenway Corporation is an outfit out of Cheyenne. Big fish that specializes in buying out the little fish, one acre at a time if it has to. They have the ability to wait out the little ranches until they're in trouble, then they swoop in with their solution."

"Which is?" she asked when he stopped talking.

Justin pursed his lips. "They offer to buy up land — a couple of parcels at a time. The trick is, they pay a small percentage of what it's worth, but they offer a quick purchase." His voice caught, and he flinched. Then, offering a little shrug, he continued. "And people sell because it's better to lose a tract or two than all the land that's been in the family for generations."

"You can't sell," whispered Beth, fighting the lump of emotion that had risen at the thought. "You told me yourself McGees have owned this land for over a century and a half."

"Might be the best solution — can't really run cattle if you don't have the land, and if you don't have the cattle, you don't need the land." He grimaced and rubbed his left temple. "So instead of selling off a third of our herd, we sell an eighth and a tract of land that we seldom use."

"Will that get you out of the hole?"

Justin heaved a sigh and dragged his hand over his jaw, seeming to struggle for the answer. At last he shook his head. "In the short run, yeah. But it won't last."

Leaning over her shoulder, he pulled open the center desk drawer and shoved the letter inside, then slid the drawer closed. His fresh woodsy scent reached out and caressed Beth's nose. It was soap from his shower, she knew, because she'd found the orange-gold bar in the soap dish when she'd bathed and spent a fair share of time sniffing it.

She slid her hand along his forearm before he withdrew, teasing the soft sun-kissed hairs. When her touch raised goose bumps, a thrill chased its way up from her fingertips and raced along her spine.

Justin rolled her chair backward and swiveled it around until she faced him. Then he sank to his knees in front of her, pushed his hands around her waist, and laid his head against her chest. Neither spoke as the rustle of cloth added a layer to the hush of late evening that cocooned the room.

He pulled in a long slow breath and held it, then released it in a fast whoosh that warmed her neck and started the butterflies in her stomach. He rolled his head back against her shoulder and locked onto her gaze with soft blue eyes. "I've never met anyone like you."

She finger-combed the errant curl off his forehead, stealing the opportunity to twine her fingers in his soft blond hair. "Ditto," she whispered.

Chapter Twenty–Three

Justin's long strides ate up the ground between stable and house. He followed the scent of another of his mom's killer breakfasts like a bird dog on the trail of a pheasant. Waking earlier than usual, he'd ducked out to check on the stock and get some other things out of the way. After he'd finished, it had been a toss-up whether he was more hungry or tired. Then the smell of fried eggs and ham had reached him halfway across the yard and hunger won.

A speck at the end of the driveway began to grow. After a last sniff in the direction of breakfast, Justin reluctantly halted his steps. If that was Alice, come back to cause trouble, she'd have a what-for from him before she ever made it to the house. The puff of dust grew, shrouding the vehicle in mystery. Spring had been dry enough that the rainstorm a couple of nights back had been swallowed up by the thirsty earth.

When the sheriff's car emerged from the cloud and pulled to a stop in front of the house, Justin's stomach clenched.

George Tenbaum pushed open the door of the black-and-white cruiser and grabbed hold of the frame, hauling his considerable bulk up and out. The tan uniform shirt stretched taut across his belly, the buttons straining for relief. The ruddy-faced man was probably close to Gus's age, but he didn't wear the years well.

"McGee." He nodded at Justin as he pulled a handkerchief from his back pocket and wiped his face. With an eye-roll and a giant sigh, he bent back into the car and retrieved his *Smokey the Bear* hat from the front seat and parked it on his head.

"Morning, Sheriff."

"I know you were wondering about that girl up in the hills."

The wind shifted, bringing with it the breakfast smell Justin had been chasing earlier. Tenbaum's gaze wandered toward the house, and he licked his lips.

"Yeah, I was." Justin pushed his hat back on his head. "Were you able to find out who she is?"

"Her name was..." The sheriff slid a black vinyl notebook from his breast pocket and flipped it open. "Earline Mortensen. She was a... waitress out of Jackson, worked in The Box Car Diner up there. Went missing about a week ago, after a fight with her boyfriend, Travis Carson." He looked at the notebook again and flipped another page. "White male, late twenties, described as five-ten or eleven, on the skinny side with black hair and long sideburns. May or may not have a handlebar mustache." Tenbaum flipped the book closed. "He's disappeared from his place in Jackson, so we're working on the presumption that he murdered Earline and then took off. He's probably long gone, but can't hurt to look out for strangers."

Earline Mortensen. Now he had a name for that battered face. A lone chill sprinted the length of Justin's spine and settled at the back of his neck. When he'd gotten a better look at the girl, he'd been struck that her coloring and stature had borne a tremendous resemblance to Beth. Of course, that was probably one of those weird coincidences. Things like that happened sometimes.

But the memory of coming across Beth alone and

vulnerable on the road, her van broken down... just wouldn't loosen its grasp.

Earline Mortensen had been missing a week. She hadn't been dead more than a couple of days when Justin had found her. His breathing hitched, and he concentrated on swallowing past the emotion lodged in his throat.

She's not Beth. Dilly Gal's here and safe.

"Thanks, George." Justin resettled his hat. The thought of any intrusion into the family breakfast he'd been visualizing left a bad taste in his mouth, but manners dictated that he offer. "Smells like my mom's cooking up quite a spread. You're welcome to come on in and join us."

Tenbaum smiled and patted his belly. "Sounds great, but I'll have to take a rain check. Got some reports to finish writing up." He opened the door of his cruiser and sat, removing his hat at the last minute.

Drawing his palm back and forth across his chin, Justin stared after the sheriff's car long after it vanished up the drive and the dust had settled. So that was it. A relationship that had likely gone bad. If Tenbaum was right and the boyfriend had left the area, that should be the end of the story. His neck prickled, and he slid his hand from his jaw to the back of his head and rubbed. Why did it feel like something was only just beginning?

"There you are," said Beth from behind him.

He swung around, a ready smile on his lips as he studied her from bottom to top. Her jeans, faded to nearly white and worn to mere threads in places, flared wide around her feet, but molded nicely to her hips. The breeze whipped around the side of the house and plastered the loose red shirt to her body, outlining every delicious curve and asset for his eager eyes. She shook her hair from her face, sending curls of sparkling gold raining over her shoulders. All his troubled thoughts fell away, save one.

What was he going to do about *her?*

"What are you doing out here?" she asked.

Justin shook his head to clear it. What *had* he been doing? *Right.* "The sheriff was here. They identified the girl."

"So fast?"

"She'd been reported missing from up Jackson way." He jerked one shoulder in a half shrug. "George seems to believe it's open and shut... she had a fight with her boyfriend before she went missing, and apparently he's disappeared, too."

Beth cocked her head and regarded him with one eye narrowed. "You don't. You don't think it's open and shut."

He pulled a hand down his face, not anxious to continue the conversation. "I'm not the law," he finally dodged.

Straightening her back, she planted her hands on her hips. "You don't have to be the law to get a hunch. So what's your hunch? What's eating at you?"

"It's not so much a hunch as a twitchy feeling in my gut." He grinned. "But that could be because I keep getting a whiff of breakfast, and I'm starving." He captured her shoulders and pulled her along with him as he walked toward the back door.

Beth's heavy sigh suggested she considered the discussion shelved rather than closed. That was fine for now... but he'd put off picking up that particular thread of conversation forever, if he could.

"So what's on the breakfast menu?" he asked as he held the back door open for her.

* * *

When the phone rang and Mary settled herself with a cup of coffee at the kitchen table to chat with the caller, Beth let herself out of the house. A charged heaviness clung on the chilly air. Was it going to storm again? She glanced up at the single puffy white cloud hanging in the clear blue sky. Well, not for the next few minutes, anyway.

She wandered in the direction of the barn. The bit of ham she'd saved from her breakfast wasn't much of an offering for Mama Kitty, but it didn't seem right, raiding the parlor without Justin's dad as her co-conspirator. Where had Justin and Jim gone, anyway? They'd taken off without a word in the direction of the stables not long after breakfast. Not that anyone owed her an explanation, but she couldn't help wondering if they'd gone off for a private conversation about Justin's twitchy gut. At least she hoped it was about his unsettled feeling over the murder and not because of their awkward conversation the night before.

As endearing as it was that Justin wanted to protect her from... whatever it was he felt the need to protect her from, Beth hated being treated like a child. Part of her reasoned that she was already privy to more things than were her business concerning the Cross MC.

But Justin's twitchy gut was about a dead young woman, not the financial woes of the ranch. Beth kicked at a rock and missed. Huffing out a fast breath, she stopped and took aim, drawing her foot back and then bringing it forward for a solid connection with the toe of her tennis shoe. Fueling the kick with her frustration, she watched with perverse pleasure as the rock went flying in a perfect arc and slammed against the cottonwood tree about ten feet away with a hard *thwack*.

"Feel any better for it?" asked Jim.

Beth spun around. Thank goodness he was alone. She was in a mood and not one she particularly wanted to share with Justin. She pushed her lips into a smile she could only hope was believable, unwilling to take out her bad temper on Jim, either. "I didn't see you."

He touched the brim of his hat. "That much was obvious. Did the rock do something to you? Or was it the tree? Did it say something inappropriate? Shake its leaves at you?"

A giggle gurgled out and suddenly she didn't have to fake the smile. "Kind of childish, huh?"

He gave a shrug. "Well, now, I'd say that depends on what the tree said that got you all het up." He started walking, heading them in the direction of the paddock where Abe and Zeke stood near the fence, along with a dark brown horse she didn't recognize.

"The *tree* didn't really say anything." She sighed, releasing her pent-up emotions with the breath. "In fact, the tree goes out of its way to *not* say anything."

"Hmm. Is that so..." Jim rubbed his jaw. "Maybe the tree doesn't have anything to say. Or maybe it has plenty to say but doesn't know how to say it."

Beth stopped at the paddock and turned to face him. "Mr. McGee?"

"Jim."

Warmth flooded her face and she smiled. "Jim?"

"Yeah?" He reached up to scratch the brown horse's nose.

"We're not really talking about a tree."

"Yeah... I know." He lifted his leg and propped one boot on the fence rail.

The brown leather was battered and scarred, covered in dust. It had seen a lot of use, and a pang of sadness tore through Beth's heart that it wouldn't see much more.

"You do?"

"I noticed a bit of tension between you and my son this morning. Wish I could tell you it doesn't mean anything. But fact is, I can tell he's wrestling with a problem..." He cocked his head to the left and narrowed his eyes. "Maybe more than one." He met Beth's eyes again. "Something's working at him, and he needs time to let it stew before the solution'll become clear to him."

A solution... but to which problem?

Jim went back to scratching the horse's nose, shifting his gaze over her shoulder into the distant field. "I met Mary on a buying trip over to Casper. Stock auction. She was there representing her family's spread down near Cheyenne."

Warmth hopped through Beth's system like a dozen furry bunnies cavorting in the sun as she pictured the two of them in younger days. "I'll bet it was love at first sight."

Jim barked out a laugh, and Zeke tossed his head with a soft whinny. "Oh, no. Not even close. I had my eye set on a particular bull. Good stock, great price." He sighed. "At first no one bid on 'im, so I figured I had it in the bag." He chuckled softly. "Then this little spitfire with caramel-colored hair glared at me with the clearest ocean-blue eyes I'd ever seen. Put her hands on her hips and started bidding me up. Every time I made a bid, she raised me. A couple of other ranchers made half-hearted bids, but they dropped out real quick. Then it was just the spitfire and me. Got to be kind of a game until the numbers got too high. I started noticing her increases were smaller and smaller with each bid, so I figured she was close to her limit. I was nowhere near mine."

Beth smiled. "So you got the bull?"

Jim scratched the bridge of his nose with his forefinger. "Well, I wanted that bull, that's for sure. But somewhere in all the bidding, I realized I wanted the spitfire more. And something just told me if I won that bull, I'd never win the gal."

A sense of wonder stole over Beth and she smiled. "You dropped out of the bidding?"

Jim pulled his lips into an answering smile and nodded. "Yes, ma'am. I let her win. Only thing was..." He set his hat farther back on his head and made a sour face. "It didn't turn out quite like I planned. She wasn't particularly happy about it... figured she didn't really win."

"Ah-ha! So she saw through you," said Beth with a laugh.

"Turns out my Mary don't like being handed things when she feels she hasn't earned them." He shrugged again. "She needs to find her own way."

Mary McGee did seem like the strong and independent type, Beth conceded. And yet... "Well, obviously she got over it."

"Yeah, oh, yeah. She got over it. But it took a fair bit of effort." He resettled his hat low over his eyes and gave the dark horse another scratch on the nose just before Abe nudged her out of the way. "And she made me work for it. I finally convinced her to go for coffee with me after I outbid her on a lot of eight heifers."

Beth's instincts told her the conversation was heading someplace specific, so she quelled her natural curiosity and simply listened.

"Justin's more like his mom than he is me." Jim chuckled softly as he shot an appreciative glance her way. "Leastways, in most things."

Beth chewed on the inside of her bottom lip. How much did Justin's dad know about the financial state of the ranch? If she confided what she'd done, the offer she'd made, would she be stressing Jim with the news that the ranch was in trouble?

She glanced up to find his gaze locked on her.

"There's one thing you in particular should never do, Miss Beth... and that's play poker."

"Yeah, I never got away with stuff as a kid, either." She leaned against the fence, not quite able to meet his eyes. "Justin admitted that he was struggling with some cash flow."

"He did, eh?" Jim leaned his elbows on the top fence rail. The brown horse ambled over again and nodded her head up and down several times until Jim extended his hand. "Come on, then, Gypsy." The horse pressed her head into his palm and he rubbed her between the eyes. "I know my boy, Beth. He can be mulish and he's got a fair bit of pride that sometimes gets in his way. It took a lot for him to do that."

"I know that. Now." She bit down on her lip again. "But last night... I made a mistake. I offered him money from my trust fund."

"Trust fund, huh?" He angled a look in her direction, his eyes crinkled at the corners as he laughed softly. "That didn't go over too well, I'd wager."

She clawed a hand through her hair, pushing it back from her face. "It was a disaster. I was so excited, thinking I could help, I didn't consider that I was walking all over his pride."

"I love my son as much as I love my wife." Jim shook his head. "But they both have stubborn streaks, and they have to work out their problems their way." He turned away from the fence and faced her. "Justin also has a tendency to push away the people he loves when he needs them the most. And I know that because that's what *I* do."

It was doubtful that Justin actually needed her. More like they just got on well. Really well.

"The boy's hurtin' and there's not a damn thing I can do about it," Jim continued, his voice going hoarse with emotion. "But whatever it was you said to him the night the cat came calling... it helped." A smile played over his face and he nodded. "Helped a lot. He changed, shook off some of his hurt. He'll try to push you away." Jim touched her on the shoulder. "I'm asking you to not let him do that. Don't let him push you out of his life."

Stunned, Beth's mouth fell open. She blinked, lost for an answer.

Jim dropped his hand. "I'm not asking you to saddle

yourself to my son or to ranching. But if you decide you want to be with him... fight for him. He's worth it." He smiled. "And so are you."

Though she drew breath and opened her mouth, no words formed. The thought of a parent — hers or anyone else's — holding such a candid conversation with her shut off her brain.

Jim nodded toward the mountains in the distance. "See those specks flying up there?"

If she squinted, she could just make out a pair of birds circling, so far away they were tiny as ants. "Are those... vultures?" Her stomach did a slow flip. Had someone or something else been killed up in the hills?

"Nope. Those are eagles." He shaded his eyes with one hand. "I'd say bald eagles."

She followed his lead and shaded her eyes, too. "You can tell from here?"

"That they're bald eagles and not goldens? Nah." Chuckling, Jim dropped his hand. "But I know bald eagles tend to range up that way... near the Green River. I see 'em up there a lot... soaring and gliding. I had a Shoshone friend once who told me eagles are considered *of* the earth but not *in* it... kind of spiritual overseers." He watched them for a few minutes in silence as he rubbed his fingertips along his jaw, obviously deep in thought.

In turn, Beth studied Jim. She supposed it wasn't exactly ironic that father and son would both have an appreciative affinity for flying objects. Had Jim ever taken Justin kite flying?

He sighed deeply and returned his focus to Beth. "You know as high as they are, they can still spot a trout flashing too close to the surface, just begging to be their next meal. They'll glide up in the sky for hours waiting for it... or they'll sit up in a tree perfectly still, makin' sure their shadow doesn't fall across the river. Soon as they see that sparkle of scales, they'll be on that trout like a lightning bolt."

"They just wait? They don't go hunting?"

Jim shrugged, more with his face than his shoulders. "That *is* hunting for them. Never seen an animal with so much patience as an eagle." He gazed into the distance again. "I reckon the view from up there likely makes just as good a reward for all that patience as the meal itself."

A breathy laugh escaped Beth's lips. "Heights kind of make me dizzy."

He swung his gaze back in her direction and winked. "Guess it's a good thing you have your feet on the ground, then. But whatever view you like best, patience earns the reward in the end."

She stared at the eagles. From so far away, they barely seemed to move. They appeared to have just been suspended against the sky.

"I think I'll go pester Mary about baking some oatmeal cookies." Jim pushed off the fence and tipped his hat at Beth. "Justin's in the cow barn pulling a calf."

Beth stared after the astute rancher as he ambled to the house. His gait was steady, if a little slow and tired. He opened the back door and paused, then tossed a casual wave in her direction. She raised her hand, but he was already stepping through the door. A chill tickled the base of Beth's spine.

Patience... not even close to her strong suit. If she listened to Jim McGee, though, waiting would bring about a reward. If only she knew what she was waiting for.

She turned her head and stared at the cow barn. *Pulling a calf?* What exactly was that?

* * *

Sweat beaded on Justin's forehead and streamed down, stinging his eyes. With one arm jammed up to his shoulder inside the laboring cow, and the other one holding her whipping tail, he had no means of wiping it away. "Come on, sweetheart, just push once more." As he felt her contraction build, he gritted his teeth against the squeeze that would make him want to chew his limb off. More sweat rolled into his eyes and he blinked, finally dipping his face to rub it along his bare shoulder.

Well, that had been a fairly ineffectual move considering

his shoulder was also coated in sweat and a film of barn dust. He listened for the sound of footsteps over the cow's labored breathing and occasional groans, but heard only the agitated buzzing of a few persistent flies.

Where had Gus gone to get the birthing chains? Laramie? His tenacious grasp on the one hoof he could reach began to slip, and he struggled to regain his hold. The problem was, every time the cow had a contraction, it seemed to be pushing the calf farther inside. He'd have to get the front feet together and worked lower so they could get the chains around them and assist the tired mother.

A soft gasp from behind warned him he wasn't alone. Well, whether or not Beth could handle gore no longer seemed to be an issue, since he had a good idea of exactly what he looked like, covered in the cow's birthing fluids and worse. So Beth would either run away or stay.

She pushed up next to him without him even being aware of her movements. Apparently she'd chosen *not* to run. Pleasure at the realization tickled him to his toes.

"What's going on?" she murmured.

"Calf's got its leg pushed backward — that's keeping it from coming out."

"How can I help?"

He twisted his head to meet her bright-eyed stare with a smile. She was incredible... and not freaked out at all.

"Oh, darlin', you're a sight for these sore eyes. I threw my shirt somewhere over there." He jerked his head back, attempting to point over his shoulder with his chin. "Can you get it and wipe the sweat off my face?"

She raised one brow and gazed in the direction of his gesture. "So not doing that," she said, wrinkling her nose. "It landed in something disgusting."

Another trickle of sweat made its way toward his left eye and he tossed his head, managing to spray some of it off. "Honey, at this point, I don't rightly care."

"Well, I care." Her eyes flashed with indignation. "It's filthy and I'm not touching it, let alone wiping your face with it. You ought to have some towels out here for that." Any minute he expected Beth to stomp her foot in the straw.

"Well, honey," he said, smiling around gritting teeth, "seein' as we don't, I need you to use my *shirt* — dirty or no."

She glanced around the stall, but Justin already knew she wouldn't find so much as an old rag. Shaking her head, she grabbed the hem of her red cotton shirt and ripped it up over her head. After she shook it out straight, she leaned close and dabbed his forehead and cheeks. Then she gently brushed it over his eyes.

Her musky floral scent clung to the soft material and filled his nostrils, teasing his senses and all but stopping his brain. When she pulled the cloth away, a tender smile hovered at the corners of her mouth.

"Okay?" she asked, eyeing his arm with dubious interest. "Is there something — else I can do?"

Justin tried to answer her, but his mouth had dried out at the sight of the rose pink bra with a quarter-sized cutout heart just below the right strap. At last he managed to free his tongue from the roof of his mouth. "Thanks," he choked out.

The jangle of stainless steel chains reached his awareness. "Got 'em," called out Gus as he rounded the corner into the box stall. "They were..." He flicked a glance over Beth's attire — or lack of it — then *almost* immediately focused his attention on the matter at hand.

Which was just as well, since Justin would easily classify his old friend seeing Beth in her underwear as sky high on his discomfort scale. He stole another glance at pink silk and lace just as the pregnant cow bore down again, and bone crunching agony seized his arm. He clamped his jaw and ground his teeth against the pain.

Beth's eyebrows shot heavenward, and she quickly looked down along her body. Great, she probably thought he didn't like the view. And, in point of fact, he did like it. Liked it a bit too much, given their current circumstances. It was early for swimming in the creek but boy, oh, boy, a guy could dream about taking a gal to a secluded spot for some recreation.

With a gush of fishy-smelling liquid, the cow pushed again.

"Ah-h-h." The moan started in his toes then tore through

him and out as the cow put a little extra effort into trying to rid herself of the calf. He turned the air blue with a streak of curses, but managed to push his right hand impossibly farther into the cow's business end. By stretching just a little more, the bruising pain finally rewarded him with delivery of two calf legs solidly into his grip. Oh, thank heaven, there was the nose brushing against the back of his hand. He'd managed to pull the bent leg forward enough to release the holdup. His grasp was high enough above the hooves that he was able to maintain his hold, and as the contraction eased, he tugged, keeping up a gentle pressure while taking half steps backward. Then Gus was there, securing the OB chains just above the fetlocks as Justin's arm came free with a wet *smuck*.

Gus took over the slow pulling. Justin flexed his fingers and shook out his hand, wincing at the tingling when the blood started flowing to his fingertips again.

"Where's the steam coming from?" asked Beth.

Gus chuckled and Beth glared at him.

Justin cleared the remnants of the amniotic sac from the calf's nose as he explained. "The inside of the cow, mostly. She's probably got a core temperature of a hundred and one or a hundred and two. So everything that's been inside her and coming out is like a spring rain on snow."

"His tongue is blue and it's just... hanging there." She clenched her balled-up shirt in both hands as she stared at the calf's nose. The cow bawled and gave another push, and the rest of the baby's head entered the world with a loud pop. The mother hollered again, her sides heaving. Only the headgear kept her from lying down in the bed of straw.

Justin swiped at his sweaty face with the inside of his relatively cleaner forearm. Beth was at his side in an instant, dabbing and rubbing with her shirt. Fine goose flesh decorated her exposed skin.

"You should get up to the house before you catch cold."

"No," she whispered, shaking her head. "I want to be here. This is... beautiful."

Before Justin could process his sudden deluge of emotions at her words, the bellowing cow gave a mighty heave, and her brown-and-white calf slid into the straw at her feet, along with fluids and afterbirth.

"It's a boy!" Gus announced as he pulled on the chain, quickly dragging the calf across the straw and safely away from his mother's feet.

The calf lay limp in the straw, his purplish tongue lolling sideways.

"Why isn't he moving?" Alarm sharpened Beth's voice. "Aren't they supposed to, like, stand up right away?"

Justin crouched next to the calf and ran his hand over his shoulders, giving him a little shake. "Come on, little man, time to greet the world."

The cow stomped her feet and took up a nearly continuous bellow.

"Stop yer caterwauling," grumbled Gus, moving to release her from the headgear.

"He's not breathing," whispered Beth, joining Justin in the straw. She touched the sticky fur and snatched her hand back, but then laid it on the calf again and began a brisk rubdown. "Come on, baby. You have to breathe."

Justin picked up a couple pieces of straw and jammed the ends into the calf's nostrils.

Beth jerked backward. "What are you—"

"Sometimes you gotta make 'em want to breathe."

The calf coughed and then opened his mouth wide and sucked in his first taste of air. Justin swept a finger through his mouth to clear the mucus.

"Oh, my," said Beth, sighing with a mixture of awe and relief as the calf immediately began struggling to his knees and then his feet.

Justin stood, grasping her hand and tugging. "Come on. You'll want to be out of his mama's way."

Beth shivered and snuggled herself tightly against Justin's bare torso.

"Whoa, hold on there!" He shied away. "I haven't exactly taken a shower in Ireland here."

"I don't care anymore." Her eyes looking up at him glistened with unshed tears. "You were so amazing."

"Amazing, huh?" He chuckled softly. Actually, Beth was the amazing one... the way she fit against him, the softness of her bare skin gliding over his. His body tightened with need.

She turned in his embrace and stood on her toes, brushing his lips with hers, back and forth until the grazing touch about drove him crazy. He slid his arms along her spine and pulled her closer. Primal need washed through his veins, and heat settled low in his belly. The world spiraled around them. The barn, the dirt, the cow... All spun into oblivion as awareness swirled into desire.

Beth pushed her hands upward in a long, slow caress over his chest. She paused to tickle his ear lobes and then locked her arms around his neck. With very little between them, heat rolled in like a summer storm. The fire in his blood neared explosive levels as Justin touched his tongue to her lips, seeking, finding, demanding more. And then her tongue stroked his, and she opened her mouth on a gentle sigh and let him in.

Gus coughed and Justin's awareness returned to the barn.

"You two want to go get a room somewhere?" Gus gestured to the cow that was licking her baby clean with her fat, pink tongue. "This here mama's just given birth... you think she wants to see that?"

Justin snickered. "I don't think she's watching anything." After a final glance to be certain the baby wasn't struggling, he stooped and snatched up his soiled shirt and gave Beth a gentle shove toward the barn door. "Come on. I might even let you have the shower first."

She twisted her head and looked him up and down, wrinkling her nose. "No, I think you can have it first. I'm good."

That was only because she couldn't see the straw clinging to her hair or the way her body glistened with a combination of his sweat and the cow's birthing fluids. In that moment, her beauty stunned his heart to a near stop.

"You might change your mind when you get a look in the mirror," he said, caressing her bare shoulder with his palm as they crossed the stockyard together.

Chapter Twenty-Four

As they neared the house, Beth edged from the shelter of Justin's arms, and the breeze licked icy fingers along her exposed skin. She shivered, but it wasn't the wind that chilled her. Mary McGee met them at the door, head tilted to the side, one eyebrow raised and her lips pursed.

Beth hugged her arms around her waist, though she wanted to cross them over her breasts. The bathing suit she'd worn on the family's last trip to Cancun had actually shown more than her bra currently revealed, but the knowledge that she was, in fact, standing before Justin's mom in an undergarment and not a bikini was beyond embarrassing. She should have put her shirt back on... even if it *was* covered with Justin's sweat.

"Got a nice looking bull calf out there." Justin motioned for Beth to precede him through the door. "His foot was turned back, but he looks okay and not too big. Might make good breeding stock."

"Good." Mary blocked his way into the house. "Beth, why don't you go on upstairs and have a nice soak, get cleaned up. You..." She pointed at Justin. "You need to take a walk out to the bunkhouse and get that mess off you."

"Come on, Mom. You know the water doesn't get very hot out there." He winked at Beth. "Besides, odds are better'n fair I'll score a back wash up here at the house."

"Think so, huh?" His mother shot Beth an assessing stare.

Heat invaded her face and Beth squirmed. "I didn't... didn't say... um..." *Stop talking!* She tried to smile but her mouth was stiff. "I... can just wash up after..."

Shaking her head, Mary heaved a sigh and spoke in a matter-of-fact tone. "Justin, give our guest the courtesy of a warm bath. As soon as she sees how much cow goo you got all over her, she's gonna want it."

Cow goo? Half afraid to look, Beth bowed her head and stole a glance. Her bra was only barely pink. Her skin was smeared with blood and streaked with dirt and the glistening gunk that had been all over the calf when it had slipped from its mother. Of their own accord, her arms moved away from her sticky body. She curled her lip. "Ew."

"Birthing a cow's messy business." Mary narrowed her focus on Beth's arms. "He didn't have you helping pull the calf, did he?"

"No, I mostly just watched," said Beth, unable to speak much above a whisper.

"My goodness! All that from *watching?*" Mary returned her focus to Justin and gave a long-suffering shake of her head.

He offered her a sheepish smile and a shrug. "Did I tell you we got a nice bull calf?"

"Don't know what I'm going to do with you." She smiled at Beth and pointed to the hallway. "Go." Then she quelled Justin's move to follow with a pointed glare. "Go on, hotshot. I'm thinking the cool shower in the bunkhouse is *exactly* what *you* need." She shooed him out the door muttering, "Back wash, indeed."

"Can't blame a guy for tryin'!" he called as the door closed in his face.

Mary turned from the door, a smile curving her lips upward. "Well, now that I got the hound dog off your scent for awhile, go make yourself pretty."

Beth scampered off, only too happy to be away from Mary's scrutiny.

In the bathroom, she wiped herself down before she climbed into the tub. No way was she going to sit in water with all that grime and yuck. The hot bath was pure heaven when she finally sank into it. Closing her eyes, she laid her head back against the lip of the tub and sighed. The corners of her mouth lifted. If Justin's parents hadn't been home, would he have asked for a back wash for real? A delicious little thrill rippled through her.

Watch it, girl! You've been having fun, but you're still leaving. And you'd better do it soon. Before you won't be able to.

Lifting one foot out of the water, Beth poked at the water faucet with her big toe. "I'm here today," she breathed into the steamy air.

She lazed in the bath, trying not to think of anything, to just feel the happiness of the moment. By the time she hauled herself out of the tub, her skin was just going pruny, and the water'd gone as cold as she imagined the shower Justin had suffered through on her account had been.

Make yourself pretty, Mary had instructed. A bottle of Rose Milk lotion sat on the counter. Beth pumped some into her palm and smoothed it over her body, delighting in the light scent that reminded her of the tea roses in her grandma's garden. She leaned forward and wiped some of the steam from the mirror. Her rash was no more than a faint pinkish darkening of skin in some places. It was healing much faster than she'd expected.

"Maybe I should be studying the cure instead of the poison plants," she told her reflection. As she drew on a soft, white lacy bra and hooked it in back, she stared at the grimy rose pink one lying on the counter.

Pinching it between her thumb and first finger, she briefly considered tossing it into the trash, but just couldn't bring herself to do it. With a shrug, she dropped it into the sink and turned on the faucet. Laundry detergent wouldn't have gone amiss at that point. But ever the innovator, she poured in a measure of lemon shampoo and swirled the water, smiling as a mountain of white bubbles began to build like a thundercloud. After she washed and rinsed the undergarment, she hung it over the shower curtain rod and turned her attention to dressing herself.

The white maxi skirt was soft muslin and a little sheer, but she solved that issue with a white silk half-slip. The material swished around her ankles like cool water. The skirt had a large splash of purple and orange embroidered flowers across the front. The diaphanous white peasant blouse she pulled over her head had smaller matching flowers embroidered along the neckline and hem. The addition of the hemp macramé belt with the long fringe that rested just on top of her hips completed the outfit, and Beth spun around in front of the mirror with a smile.

"Hopefully no cows'll go into labor tonight," she said to the empty room as she pulled the door open.

"I'll second that thought." Mary stepped up onto the landing. "Oh, my. I know I told you to go get pretty, but you've outdone yourself."

Beth's spirits took a slight dive. "Too much? Should I change?"

"Don't you dare! It's going to be nice, having another female in the house for a while." Mary gestured to her jeans and gray sweatshirt. "But you've certainly outshone me."

"Why don't you dress up, too?" asked Beth, the excitement of inspiration quickening her heartbeat.

Mary shook her head, her smile growing wistful. "I don't think so. It's been years since I've had a need to dress up. I don't really have anything."

"Don't have anything?" echoed Beth, struggling to imagine not being able to put on something lacy and feminine once in a while.

"Sad, isn't it?" Mary made a sour face that she offset with a chuckle.

Actually, Beth envied her just a little. She was obviously living exactly the life she wanted.

Chewing her lip, Beth studied Mary with a critical eye. "You know, you're taller than me, but a bit more slender. I have a really pretty eyelet wrap skirt that we can make fit you. And it's supposed to be a maxi-skirt so it might look like a midi on you. But if you have western boots, it'll look really cool." She angled a challenging glance at Justin's mom. "Or you can go barefoot."

The spark of interest that flickered in Mary's eyes told Beth she'd made the right call. "Come on." Tugging Mary's hand, she opened the door to the guest room and stepped inside. The red shirt she'd dropped off earlier sat on top of her suitcase and she pushed it aside, then popped open the bag and rummaged though the mass of clothing. The pale blue eyelet skirt had a couple of creases from being folded, but when Beth shook it out, the creases became nearly invisible.

Mary brushed her fingertips across the material. "Pretty."

Beth smiled. "And completely impractical, like the majority of things I brought on this trip. When I come for another visit, I'll know to pack jeans and sturdy shirts."

"Have you made any traveling plans yet?" Mary raised her head and locked Beth in a calm stare.

She faltered with her hand in her suitcase. What was Justin's mom asking? Did she want her to leave? "I... haven't really given it a lot of thought yet. I mean, I can leave any time once my van is repaired..."

"Please don't—" Mary bit her lip. "I'm sorry. I kind of thought you liked it here and I hoped—" She lifted her hands in a helpless gesture. "It's not fair of me to pressure you. Jim said I should stay out of it, but..." Her sigh was more wistful then sad. "I've never seen my son so happy."

The heavy pounding of Beth's heart echoed in her ears. Striving for casual, she closed her fingers around the shoulders of an off–the-shoulder white peasant blouse and lifted, giving it a little shake as she did. She laid it across the skirt and finally dared to meet Mary's eyes.

"I love it here." She smiled at the memory of Justin's touch, so recently at her waist, on her face, his hands tunneling through her hair, his mouth... "Very much."

"Do you think—" Mary bit her lip. "I'm sorry. I'm being pushy again."

"I do think..." Beth swallowed at the admission. The first

time she'd spoken it aloud, and she was telling it to Justin's mother. "I've never felt for anyone what I feel for your son. But..." She sighed, sought for the words that hung elusive, just out of her grasp. "I didn't expect to come out here and..." *Fall in love.* "...meet someone like him."

Mary's eyes lit with excitement. "But now that you have?"

She was so far from the aloof spitfire Jim had described, Beth had to temper the urge to laugh. Apparently time had sharpened her edge.

Except Mary was running out of time with Jim. The thought spun like a vortex in Beth's heart. Had Mary changed over the years, or had her husband's illness added a layer of desperation that her son not miss out on life?

Fiery heat bloomed in Beth's neck and rose to her face. "You know, I asked him to sleep with me," she blurted. "I-I-I mean, I... offered..."

"You did, huh?" Mary smiled. "And what happened?"

The heat built to a combustible level. "Nothing." She chuckled. "Literally. And then you came home the next day."

"And you think this means Justin's not attracted?"

"No, he is... and I am... but later — last night, actually, I offered to help with things — stuff around here. With money I have..."

"Oh..." Mary raised a hand to cover her mouth. "Oh, dear."

Beth nodded and concentrated on the pink chenille bedspread, unable to meet Mary's eyes. "Exactly. It was pushy of me. I should have just... left it."

When the room remained silent, Beth raised her eyes to find Mary with tears glistening in hers. "You care," she whispered. "You didn't do anything wrong. My son's just — well, Jim says he's exactly like me."

"Actually..." Beth hesitated, but then decided Jim hadn't asked for her confidence. "Jim told me the same thing."

Mary giggled. "You must think our son has the most meddlesome parents!"

"I think he has parents who love him." *At least as much as I do.* "Now, let's get you dressed. Where is Jim, anyway?"

"Oh, that's what I came to tell you. Walt delivered your van. Jim and Justin are outside going over it."

Beth cast a glance at the bedroom door. Should she go out there, too? She surely owed Walt payment for his work. She took a step away from the bed but faltered, unsure what to do.

"Don't bother," murmured Mary. "They've already decided they know more than you do, based on you being one of the fairer sex. And Jim's having such a good day... Let him and Justin take care of it."

Protests about paying her way and not being a burden half formed in Beth's mind, but they died when Mary drew her hand along the blue and green embroidered border on the peasant blouse, her eyes soft and her thoughts seeming far away.

Time enough for business and settling up. Tonight they'd dress to the nines and party. "Well, then!" Laughing, she draped the blouse across Mary's chest. "Let's show them just how pretty and appealing the fairer sex can be."

* * *

"You say your girl drove all the way from *Detroit* in this thing?" Jim kicked the back tire twice and shook his head.

"She's not my girl," mumbled Justin, fingering a bit of rust just above the rear wheel. *And she probably never will be.* Oh, he had no doubt she'd stay if he asked her to. She hadn't come out and said it, hadn't even hinted, but her willingness to help, the happy way she tackled every task...

The way her eyes lit when she looked at him and thought he didn't see.

She'd stay if he asked... and maybe end up regretting it. But even in her regret, she'd stick it out. Even if it was killing her inside to be tied down.

Jim cocked his head to one side and studied Justin like a bug under a microscope. "Got a lot going on in that head of yours. Anything you want to talk about?"

Justin pulled in a long breath and held it for a moment before blowing it out with a shake of his head. "Not really."

"Busy few days." Jim leaned back against the van, apparently not in a hurry to go anywhere. "Beth seems to like it here."

Oh, please, not the father and son conversation. Justin grunted and shifted his gaze to the lone cottonwood tree in the pasture across the driveway. About a dozen cows clustered beneath it, with a handful lying in the grass just outside the shade line. "Cows are layin' down. Think we're in for more rain?"

Jim scratched his boot in the dust. "The way the ground drank up that last storm, I'd say it'd be welcome if we get it." He pushed away from the van and stretched. "So what's really bothering you?"

"I keep thinking about that girl up in the hills."

Jim grunted. "Violent death and torn up by the cat. Not an easy thing to forget."

Justin swung around and met his father's eyes. "I keep thinking about the other girl... the one the cat got to before. What if the cat didn't kill her? What if—" He blew his frustration out in a sharp breath. "I found Beth broke down on the side of the road a week ago — 'bout the same time that girl went—" He choked on the words. "Anything or — any*one* could have come upon her same as I did."

"But it *was* you." Jim crouched and poked a finger into the tread of the rear tire. "Walt said these'd be good to get her home, but I dunno. Tread looks a mite thin to me." He glanced over his shoulder and caught Justin in his gaze. "What do you think?"

I think I want her to be *home. Home here.*

Justin bent his knees and joined his father's examination of the tire. The rubber looked old, but he didn't see any cracks from dry rot. He ran his fingertips over the outside edge of the tire and noted the wear. "She's been running 'em with low air pressure. They've probably got some wear left, but I *would* feel better if she was driving on new tires."

"That girl resembled Beth some," remarked his father, pushing himself upright. "Maybe that's got you spooked."

Justin stood as well. Used to his father's round-Robin's-barn conversation style, he'd known they'd circle back to the murdered girl. He lifted his hat and ran his fingers through his hair. "I considered that, but I didn't really associate it at first."

"I thought Tenbaum said the boyfriend did it."

"Maybe he did." Justin jammed his hat back on his head. "Maybe not. I didn't take much of a look, but it didn't feel like a passionate act to me. Not very personal or heat-of-the-moment. More cold and... I don't know... calculated, maybe."

"Might be a good time to pick up a couple of watchdogs. Gonna be awhile before those pups you picked up'll tell the difference between a threat and their next meal ticket." Jim rubbed his jaw. "Harry Sanders has a kennel full of coonhounds that go off like two-dollar alarms whenever someone drives into the yard. Maybe he's got a couple we can take on."

Justin's heart lurched in his chest then took up a mad beating against his lungs. "You're worried, too."

"Not worried, precisely." His father shrugged and drew in a long breath, the lines in his too-gaunt face deepening. "Caution generally never hurts, though." He turned toward the house and slapped Justin between the shoulder blades. "Let's go see what your mother has on for dinner. I'm kind of in the mood for stew."

"With homemade biscuits." Justin strode to the driver's side door of Beth's van and pulled it open, reaching inside for the two bright gold envelopes Walt had also dropped off.

"What you got there?"

"Pictures Beth left with AJ for developing the other day. Walt brought 'em out for her." Apparently at least two Orson's Folly residents had already embraced Beth as the next McGee bride.

He slammed the door with a bang and joined his father. They'd walked together across that yard at the end of the day ever since Justin had been able to walk. He remembered at one time he'd had to run to keep up with his dad, taking three steps to every one of Jim's. At some point, they'd started matching their strides, making the trek as equals.

Emotion tightened Justin's throat and his heart twisted

as he adjusted his pace to his father's slower one. A shiver teased the base of his spine as he glanced toward the hills, where the sun was just dipping to tickle the tips of the pines.

Chapter Twenty-Five

The savory aroma of beef stew tickled Justin's nose seconds before his ears picked up the slow gurgle of the thick liquid heating on the stove.

He glanced back at his dad. "How'd you do that? How did you know Mom would be making stew?"

Jim shrugged and hung his Stetson on the hook next to the door. "I might have mentioned I had a hankering for it this morning."

Breathing deeply, Justin filled his nostrils with the hearty, rich smell. "Huh. No biscuits, though."

"Not yet. But there will be. Nice and fresh."

The sound of Beth's giggles in the front foyer caught Justin's attention, and he hung up his own hat, jittery with eagerness to see her again. Then his mother's throaty laugh filtered in and he froze.

"Uh-oh. They're forming some kind of bond, Dad. You realize that can only lead to trouble."

Jim let out a long wolf whistle.

Justin spun around just as the pair of them walked, arms linked, into the kitchen. His jaw dropped as he took in his mother in her foreign getup. No more jeans and sweatshirts. The long, pale blue skirt fell almost to her ankles. Her *bare* ankles... on top of her bare feet. When was the last time he'd seen his mother in a skirt of any kind? The cotton blouse dipped off her shoulders, a lot more daring than anything he'd *ever* seen her wear. Obviously she and Beth had been playing dress-up from Beth's suitcases.

"Oh, hi," said Mary, slipping her arm from Beth's elbow.

Justin stole a glance at his dad.

Jim stared at Mary as though enthralled. His eyes had gone bright. A tender smile slid into place, and he walked forward, one slow step at a time. "Mary McGee, you steal my breath away," he murmured when he stopped in front of her. Then he crushed her into his embrace and buried his face in her neck.

Beth eased around the couple and entered the kitchen. Catching Justin's eye, she smiled, her cheeks flooding with the prettiest shade of pink. She'd given his parents a gift he'd never have thought of, and she probably didn't even realize how much it meant to him.

Beth stopped in front of him and lifted her hand to his cheek. "Hey there, cowboy." She stood on her toes and laid a soft kiss on his lips. "We're having a party tonight. Glad you could make it."

No other woman.

"AJ sent your pictures out with Walt," said Justin when he untied his tongue. Almost as an afterthought, he held up the packets.

"Cool!" Her eyes lit with excitement. "I can look at them while I watch you make biscuits. Your mom says you make the best."

Justin flashed his gaze over to his dad, who regarded him with one eyebrow raised, one lip pulled upward into a half-smile.

Score another one for his dad.

* * *

"Let's leave the dishes to soak," said Mary as Beth

gathered the empty bowls and plates and set them on the counter next to the sink. "They won't go anywhere overnight, and I'd like to enjoy what's left of the evening."

"Or I could finish up here." Maybe they'd like to spend some time together without an interloper.

"No, please join us. We're having a party. Remember?" Mary's sweet smile twinkled into her eyes as she caught Beth's hand and tugged toward the living room. "And bring your pictures. I'd love to look at them."

Beth grabbed the photo envelopes from the table. She'd barely had a glance at the first roll when Justin had decided she needed to learn how to make his favorite homemade biscuits. Not that she minded. He could teach her to cook anytime... all that hands-on demonstrating. She fanned herself with the envelopes as she crossed into the living room.

She spotted him instantly, bent over the long pecan wood hi-fi cabinet against the long inner wall. Justin adjusted a knob, and soon the breezy sound of Neil Sedaka singing about laughter and kisses in the rain spilled from the speakers, for a split second transporting Beth to the night of the storm.

"Can't have a party without music." Justin winked at her. Had he thought of their kiss and the sudden downpour as well? A grin spread over his face, and he snatched the pictures from her hand.

"Hey!" She reached for them, but he held the envelopes over her head.

"I want to see whatcha got." He sauntered to the sofa and dropped on the end opposite his dad, leaving Beth no choice but to follow.

"It's a lot of pictures of plants and things." She sat next to Justin, and when he threw an arm over her shoulders, she snuggled securely against him.

Mary folded herself gracefully beside Jim, one leg underneath her and one hand resting on his chest. He gave her shoulders a squeeze and pressed a kiss to the top of her head.

A twinge of envy tugged at Beth's heart, and she traced the edge of Justin's collar. Could she give up her dreams of traveling to be with Justin? Her breath caught in her throat.

She'd thought of nothing else but seeing the world since she'd known there *was* a world outside her front door. She knew Justin would never ask her to give up her plans. But if he did… would she?

Justin slid his thumb under the envelope's sticky flap and gently lifted it with a little tearing sound. Then he slid the inner pouch out and dropped the envelope onto his lap. "Lotsa layers to go through to get to these masterpieces."

Beth giggled away a pang of nervousness as he cupped the three-and-a-half by five-inch prints in his palm and stared in silence.

"Are they that bad?" she finally had to ask.

"No, they're…" He shook his head and slid the front picture to the rear of the stack. A muscle worked in his jaw. "I've lived here my whole life and never seen the land the way I'm seeing it in these pictures." He slid another picture to the back.

"I'd like to see them, too," suggested Jim.

"Give." Mary held out her hand and wiggled her fingers.

Justin peeled the pictures from the bottom of the stack and handed them over without looking, completely bypassing Beth in between them.

"Umm…" Should she say something?

Justin pushed another picture to the rear of the stack and then froze. He jerked his head around and met her gaze, his eyes flickering over her face, studying her as though he'd never seen her before.

Beth shrank inward. "What?"

"I almost didn't recognize myself," he murmured, slipping one of the photographs into her fingers. "I remember you taking this picture. When I startled you in the poison ivy patch."

Beth stared at the picture in her hand. It took a second for her addled brain to work, but when it did, the picture struck her in the heart. She could hardly believe she'd taken it… except she remembered the incident as well as Justin did.

The man and horse staring down into the lens were larger than life, probably because she'd been at the bottom of a small incline at the time. Sunlight fell across them in a dappled pattern, and he was leaning forward in the saddle, one arm resting across the horn. A ray of sunshine shot out of the trees from above and to the side, bathing his face in a yellow-white glow. His lips curved gently upward, one eyebrow raised in question.

Warmth swamped Beth and her heart squeezed her lungs. She blinked back the sting of tears behind her eyelids and traced a fingertip along Justin's cheek in the picture. "It's beautiful," she whispered, only just able to get the words out.

"May I?" asked Mary softly.

Beth handed the picture over, shifting her focus from the photo to Mary's face. A thrill raced through her the moment Justin's mom saw it and sighed.

"He's like an angel."

Jim bent his head and touched his temple to Mary's. Then his eyes sought and found Beth's. The most open and clear gray eyes she'd ever seen silently thanked her.

Three sharp piano cords cut loose on the radio, followed by an electronic synthesizer playing a driving melody. In spite of herself, Beth began to nod and tap her foot as Elton John began singing about stomping and shouting with Suzie. Justin grabbed her by the hand and stood, pulling her up with him. Without asking, he swung her into a jive.

The space was limited with the hospital bed in the room, but Justin adapted, managing a couple of tight spins right at the start. When he dipped her, Beth squealed in delight. The room became a blur of color as they whirled and kicked and stomped. Beth lost track of where they were, concentrating instead on Justin's warm hands holding hers. He spun her halfway again and pulled her backward into his arms, and they kicked outward three or four times, by some miracle not kicking each other. Then he spun her away and changed hands, so they reached across the space between them like half of an X, and they kicked outward in the opposite direction from each other.

She couldn't take her eyes from Justin's face. The corners of his eyes crinkled with tiny laugh lines radiating outward. A huge grin dominated the lower half of his face, and every time she shrieked in surprise, he threw his head back and chortled with glee, then spun her around again.

Dizzy, laughing hysterically, Beth fell into his arms on the final spin, and they dropped together onto the other end of the sofa. She gasped for her next breath while some man told his radio-assigned wife her coffee was good to the last drop.

"Where did you learn to dance like that?" asked Mary.

"I didn't know I could," Beth answered between quick pants for air. "I just followed Justin."

The low rumble of a guitar preceded Carly Simon singing about her vain lover, and Beth joined in under her breath.

"Louder," urged Jim.

Beth shook her head, already feeling the burn in her cheeks. "No. No, no. I don't sing in public."

"Well, you sang the other night," said Jim. "And darn good, too. Besides, we're not the public. We're family." He angled a look at Justin. "Come on, get her up there."

Mary giggled. "That's it. He's got it in his head for a full-blown sing-along."

Jim shrugged. "Why not? They're fun."

"Yeah, come on, Dilly Gal. Be a sport," chimed in Justin, giving her a little push toward the edge of the sofa.

"Okay, okay." Beth stood up and grabbed Mary's hand. "But you have to get up with me."

Mary shook her head. "Oh, I can't. I don't know this song."

"Don't care." Beth tugged. "You can wing it." She whirled around and pointed a finger at Justin. "But whatever song comes up next, *you* get to sing along."

"Yeah, yeah, we'll see if you get through this one."

It took a second to feel the rhythm, but when Carly sang about clouds and coffee, Beth picked up the lyrics. Mary didn't know the words, but she sure could dance. She swayed in a suggestive rhythm for a few notes, and then she began acting out bits and pieces of the song's story, taking on the role of the vain lover. As the last of the notes died out, soft electrical guitar music faded in, and Beth snickered as she recognized Helen Reddy.

Justin recognized it, too, and shook his head. "Ah, no. I'm not singing along to a woman."

"Oh, no, you don't! I got through Carly so you get to sing along with Helen. Besides, if Joan Baez can call herself Virgil, you can call yourself...ah, 'woman'." Beth pulled on his hand, but he wouldn't budge, so she tugged harder. "Up you go! We had a deal."

Jim laced his fingers behind his head and leaned back with a smug smile. "That was the deal, son. She's got you dead to rights."

"Enjoying yourself, aren't you, Dad?"

His father grinned. "Like you wouldn't believe."

Justin stood, but he pulled his father up with him. "The womenfolk got to do a duet, so let's show 'em how it's done."

Beth struggled to maintain a straight face, but it wasn't possible as Justin swayed in time to the music, singing in a falsetto about being able to face anything because he was *Woman*. Next to him, Jim smoothed a hand over his short, thinning hair, then gave it a pat. Justin claimed he had strength and invincibility, and Jim mimed putting on lipstick and then pursed his lips and made smacking sounds.

Beth and Mary clutched one another's arms, rocked by gales of laughter.

"'I Am Woman,'" said the announcer as the song faded. Then he chuckled. "Well, I'm not, but she is. That was Helen Reddy. Coming up — Elvis. Right after these messages from our sponsors."

"Oh, that's just great!" Justin raised his arms in a loose shrug, and then he flopped onto the couch next to Beth. "Now, Elvis I coulda done."

"Asking for a rematch?" asked Beth, snagging Justin by the hand.

A voice on the radio moaned and complained about eating too much.

"Ah, that'd be a solid no."

A gentle twanging guitar floated over the speakers and Jim listened for a minute then held out his hand to Mary. "May I have this dance?"

She hesitated and he winked.

"Let's show these kids a *real* dance."

Mary's lips stretched into an ear-to-ear smile, and she

rose in one long, flowing movement.

Elvis began a mellow croon about loving someone and not knowing how he'd lived before falling in love. Mary melted into Jim's open arms, and they swayed gently around the room, their steps sure and steady and perfectly in time with the music.

These two people loved each other the way Elvis was describing — completely and wholeheartedly. It was one of the most honest and beautiful emotions Beth had ever seen between two people. She turned to whisper to Justin and found him watching her instead of his parents, his eyes hooded and intense. Her heart slammed against her chest, and she blinked in surprise, but then his unfathomable expression was replaced by an easy smile. Had she imagined the pain in his eyes? It certainly was no longer present.

The song ended, and Jim stumbled just a little as he led Mary back to the sofa. It wasn't much and might have been just a misstep, except his eyes were heavy and dark with shadows. Beth stretched and pretended to yawn... and then discovered she wasn't pretending as a real yawn took over.

"I'm sorry," she murmured, covering her mouth. "It's been kind of a long day for me."

Mary caught her eye and Beth knew instantly she'd fooled no one. But Justin's mom smiled her thanks. Beth stood and stepped sideways to hug first Mary and then Jim.

He handed her the photographs they'd been looking at earlier with a smile. "Nice work, Miss Beth."

The picture of Justin on the horse was on top. Beth slid it off the pile and held it out to Jim. "Why don't you keep this? I have the negative so I can get a copy made."

Jim's mouth turned upward in a smile that warmed his eyes. "Thank you."

Impulsively, Beth bent forward and pressed a kiss to Jim's cheek. "Thank you for making such a wonderful son," she whispered. "I think you're right about the patience."

Mary glanced back and forth between them, questions burning in her eyes, but she only smiled.

Justin leaned over the sofa, giving his dad a hard hug and then kissing his mom. When he stood, he captured Beth's hand and walked her from the room. "You know, I suspect I'll never live down the 'angel' comment."

"Of course you will," Beth answered with a giggle. She squeezed his hand as they stepped onto the staircase. "In about ten, maybe twelve years."

"Cheeky, too!" Laughing, Justin pulled his hand from her grasp and swatted her lightly on the rear.

With a little squeak, Beth bounded up the steps two at a time. But when she reached the guest room door, Justin was right on her heels. He crowded her against the paneled wall, placing a hand on either side of her head. Leaning close, he stopped bare inches from her face, his eyes locked on hers, intense, but with gentleness that reached for her soul.

He really is an angel.

"Thank you for tonight," he whispered.

And then he kissed her, feathery and quick... the tickly kind of kiss she could experience every night for the rest of her life and know she was deeply... loved. Even though the word had never been spoken out loud.

Before she could respond, he pushed away from the wall and twisted the doorknob, pushing open the door to the guest room. "Goodnight, Dilly Gal."

* * *

Darkness shrouded the room as Beth blinked the sleep from her eyes and drew in a deep breath. What had awakened her? She never woke up before the sun. The glow-in-the-dark hands on the bedside clock pointed to a quarter after four. Maybe she'd heard Justin moving around, getting ready for the day. She rolled onto her side and pushed until she was sitting, oddly wide awake. Trying to find that last delicious dream would be a pointless workout.

She stepped onto the plush room-sized rug and squished her toes in the softness as she crossed the room in the dark. Maybe Justin could use a hand with his chores. Even the thought of participating in another calf pulling was kind of exciting in a life-affirming way.

When she eased open her door and stuck her head into

the hallway, a dim blush of light radiating from the living room graced the bottom few stairs. The gentle rise and fall of Mary's voice broke the quiet. Drawn to it, Beth crept down the stairs. Justin's parents were probably having a private conversation. She should just go back to bed, but instead she was heading to a life of eavesdropping.

The head of Jim's hospital bed was raised slightly, and Mary lay curled into his reclining form.

"I don't know if I ever told you how grateful I was you won that lot of heifers that day in Casper," she murmured, adjusting the button on Jim's pajama top. "We sure didn't need them. And I couldn't have paid for them if you'd dropped out." She sighed. "I was so filled with pride, and you came along and handed me that bull, dropping out of the bidding when I knew full well you could go higher."

Jim's eyes were closed. He looked like he was peacefully sleeping through Mary's one-sided conversation.

He was gone. Beth didn't know how she knew, but she did. A hole opened in her heart and she bit back a sob. Not fast enough, though.

Mary looked up. Tears glistened on her eyelashes and she offered a watery smile. "He said all he needed to say... and then he told me he was happy, that I made him happy and he loved me. And he drifted to sleep. Nice and peaceful." One eye at a time, she mopped the tears with her fingers and sniffed. "But I wasn't ready, you know. I still had things I wanted to say to him. It was stupid... I thought — if I never said them..."

Beth raised a hand to her mouth, hoping she could hold in the sobs that wanted out. "He knew... He knew the things you wanted to say. I don't know how I know this, but I'm certain... he knew." Her voice barely squeezed past the emotion clogging her throat. "Is there—" She coughed her morning hoarseness away and tried again. "What can I do?"

"I don't want to leave him," whispered Mary. "This is the last time I'll feel him next to me. I know he's gone, but maybe a little bit... isn't... yet... you know?"

Beth did know. "I'll get Justin." She waited a moment, until Mary laid her head back on Jim's chest, and then she trudged to the stairs. In the hallway, she found the light switch and flipped it up, instantly chasing every shadow to oblivion. She knew which door was Justin's, though she'd never actually been in his room. Her hand hovered over the doorknob, and she pulled in a fortifying breath. How could she tell him his father had passed? Knowing it was going to happen and finding out it had... two utterly different concepts.

The glow from the hallway reached a couple of fingers into his room. Enough to give her the impression of stark neatness. Books lined shelves along one wall. A long mirror hanging above the dresser on the far wall caught the hallway light and reflected it across the bed. Sprawled on his stomach, Justin had one hand pushed beneath his pillow, the other curled against his chest. His bare back gleamed in the diffuse illumination. He inhaled deeply and his lips curled upward.

"Did my Dilly Gal come to join me?" he murmured, his voice thick, difficult to understand. Then he turned his head and buried his face in the pillow.

"Justin," she whispered.

He lifted himself onto his elbows, his eyes wide open and shining in the reflected light. "Beth? You're really here. What's wrong?"

"I'm sorry, so sorry. It's..." *Why can't I just say it?*

He sat and then threw his feet over the edge of the bed, dragging the sheet around his waist as he stood. "Is it Dad?"

"He's... gone." Beth couldn't hold back the sobs any longer. Any words of comfort she might have offered became lost in her own mire of emotions.

Justin pulled her against him and wrapped his arms around her tight. His smooth skin was sleep-warm; his heart pounded beneath her cheek. "It's okay. It'll be okay," he whispered into her hair.

She drew back with a shaky nod. "Your mom's downstairs. She doesn't want to leave him alone."

He released her slowly, as though reluctant to break the connection. "I just need to get dressed."

Beth stared at him, not fully comprehending why he was telling her that. Then, as she took in his hand grasping the edges of the sheet around his waist, she got it. "Oh... right.

Sorry," she mumbled, heading for the door.

"Beth," he called softly.

She halted her steps, her hand wrapped around the doorknob. "Yes?"

"I'm real glad you're here."

* * *

Somehow he'd known when he hugged his dad goodnight that it would be the last time he'd see him alive. Justin shrugged into his shirt and buttoned it, but left it untucked. When he pulled open his door and stepped into the hallway, the aroma of coffee greeted him.

No other woman like his Beth.

He swallowed and took the stairs carefully, one at a time. Standing in the doorway, he listened to the sound of his own heart breaking in his mother's soft voice as she spoke to his father, telling him secrets and stories. She placed a tender kiss on Jim's lips, then rolled over and met Justin's gaze.

Slowly she stood, her knees seeming a little wobbly at first, but she caught the rail on the hospital bed and straightened her back. "Morning," she murmured.

As she stepped away from the bed, Justin's throat locked. Clutched in his dad's hand was the picture Beth had left with him the night before, wrinkled and worn, as though it was years old instead of hours.

"Your daddy wanted you to know how very proud of you he is. He didn't want to leave, you know? He'd have stayed here with us forever if the cancer—" She dabbed at her eyes with the hem of the blouse she still wore from the evening before. "He made me promise not to cry." A tear slipped over her lashes and rolled down. "This is the first promise I ever made to him that I've had to break."

"Mom." Justin's eyes burned with the effort of holding back his own tears. "He'd understand."

A movement in the doorway drew his attention. Beth hovered, her eyes wide, her lips parted slightly, as though she wanted to speak, but didn't know what to say. He motioned for her to come in.

"I didn't know what else to do," she whispered. "I did the dishes from last night and tidied the kitchen. Is there — can I do something else? Maybe call someone for you?"

Her face was pale, whiter than his mom's even, which was actually saying a lot. Justin straightened his spine, pulling both women into his arms. "I'll take care of everything," he murmured. The yoke of the Cross MC settled across his shoulders to the music of heartbroken sobs.

Chapter Twenty-Six

The New Life Christian Church wasn't large by any stretch. From the outside, the white wooden building had the look of a turn of the century one-room schoolhouse. Considering the modest two-story tower, in which hung an ancient-looking bell of tarnished silver, it might just have done duty as a school at one time. Beth gazed across the quickly filling gravel parking lot. Never would she have thought Orson's Folly had so many citizens, though she supposed some folks might be arriving from out of town.

The gravel was already covered by a sea of cars and pickups packed tightly together, but vehicles continued to pull in off the highway. Apparently Big Jim McGee's funeral was the destination of the day, almost as though the passing of the McGee patriarch called for a state funeral or a commemorative holiday. Even the construction on the bar across the street had stopped. A young man Justin had introduced her to as the pastor's son, Bobby, directed incoming cars and trucks to a grassy area just beyond the gravel.

How could so many people pack themselves into the compact country church? She glanced over her shoulder at the heavy wooden doors that had been propped open with wedges made of two-by-fours. She ought to go inside. Justin and his mom were in there. They hadn't asked to be alone, but Beth couldn't help feeling like she was intruding on some of their most personal moments. Three steps. Just three steps down off the concrete landing, and she could be in the parking lot and running away.

The powerful rumble of a slow-moving vehicle vibrated the ground beneath her feet, and she glanced up just as the shiny black pickup drove by. Beth's dark clothing was lost in the reflective surface, lending the appearance of her head floating in midair. At the wheel, Brody spared her barely a glance before returning his gaze forward. On the other side of him, though, Alice subjected Beth to a flinty stare.

Why are you two here? It had been apparent no love was lost between the families. Alice wasn't one to care about the opinions of others, either, so she hadn't shown up for the sake of propriety.

If he saw the frantically waving teenager who was directing traffic, Brody paid no heed and parked his ungainly truck in the shade of a cottonwood tree that towered over the church. His maneuver managed to trap an older red station wagon and Justin's pickup. Beth narrowed her eyes and shifted her stance, not quite blocking the door, ready to go toe-to-toe with her sister if need be.

In a tan shirtwaist dress decorated with black polka dots, Alice looked every bit the somber mourner. If the dress was a little tight and the arms a little sheer compared to the garments worn by other neighbors, well, that was typical Alice style. Without waiting for her husband to escort her, she glided with brisk steps across the parking lot, her black peep-toe heels crunching the gravel beneath her feet.

"What are you doing here, Alice?" Beth forced a smile.

Alice pulled her lip back in a silent sneer. "Good morning, Bethany. It's nice to see you, though I'm sorry for the occasion. We've come to offer our condolences to our *neighbor.*"

Implying I'm *the outsider here.* Bile burned the back of Beth's throat. She swallowed her revulsion and stepped aside. For Justin and his mom... and for Jim, she wouldn't allow

Alice to push her buttons. Not today.

"Good grief, Bethany, could you possibly dress more like a hippie?" Alice flicked a dismissive glance over Beth's brown peasant dress, sprinkled with tiny red flowers and edged with wide almond-colored lace. Then her gaze landed on the reddish-brown Western-style boots, and she rolled her eyes. "Oh. I see. You've gone all Annie Oakley on us."

Brody joined his wife on the steps of the church. His glittering eyes raked Beth's body, pausing at the squared-off neckline of her dress. She shivered and stifled the urge to cover herself with her arms. Only Brody could make her feel so dirty with one look.

A young couple climbed the steps, both of them wearing the same somber expression Beth had witnessed on every other person entering the church. The woman stared hard at Beth as they approached and then pressed a hand to the bulge beneath her cornflower blue dress. With a start, Beth realized the young woman was pregnant.

One more thing Jim would miss out on... being a granddaddy.

Sudden fierce longing flowed over her, longing to be a mom, to have children. Justin's children... a son.

So not the time, girl. Get yourself together.

With murmured apologies, the young couple brushed past Alice and Brody. Beth stepped aside, smiling at the couple, but they didn't stop to chat, and they kept their eyes forward as they walked through the door.

"I'm not going to let you do anything to ruin this day for the McGees," Beth warned, keeping her voice low.

Alice snickered. "I'd say your boyfriend's day is already pretty wrecked, since he'll be burying his dear old dad." Smoothing her already perfectly smooth blond chignon, Alice sidestepped and proceeded through the door. Brody dipped his head in a gesture Beth would have considered polite had any other man made it. But the way his eyes lingered in all the wrong places as he slanted a last appraising glance in her direction made her skin crawl.

She balled her hands into fists and counted to ten before she followed, praying she wouldn't have to sit anywhere near her sister.

Every pew was jam-packed, and the two outer aisles were lined with men of all ages standing shoulder to shoulder. The muted murmur of multiple conversations rose and fell, as though no one wanted to break the tranquility of the hushed atmosphere. Brody's red hair stuck out, making him easy to spot. He and Alice had chosen seats just off the center aisle about midway up. Good, the pew was full. No chance of being stuck sitting near her sister and brother-in-law.

Beth scanned the crowd in search of Justin but didn't see him. Mary stood alone next to Jim's casket at the front of the sanctuary. She adjusted his string tie and brushed her hand across the shoulder of his blue-checked Western shirt. The flared taupe skirt of the two-toned dress she wore swirled like silk draperies around her knees, and the button-up bodice lay cool and white against her suntanned skin. One of Beth's dresses, it had been a bit too large, but with a few strategic tucks and the addition of a wide brown belt, it fit like it had been made especially for Justin's mother.

And Beth knew just what Jim would say to her. *"Mary McGee, you steal my breath away."*

At the soft touch on her elbow, Beth turned and faced Justin, and found her own breath stolen... again. His dark Western-cut suit and white shirt were a far cry from the jeans and checked shirts she'd grown used to. She'd also grown used to the sparkle in his eyes when he teased her, but today those eyes carried the dullness of hurt and fine lines pinched the corners. His mouth wasn't stretched wide in his typical grin, and the slight upward tilt to his lips only accentuated his sadness. She wanted to wipe it all away, to hold him and soothe him and love him... to make his world right again, as impossible as that was. So hard to believe only three nights earlier they'd all been laughing and dancing in the living room.

Justin slid his hand along her bare arm and laced their fingers together. "How are you holding up?"

Her heart crowded her throat. That should have been her question to him. Smiling, she brushed his cheek with the back of her free hand. "I was just watching your mom. She looks so alone."

He nodded. "She asked for a moment. She's one of the toughest ladies I know, but I think she's getting close to her breaking point."

So are you, cowboy. Beth cupped his cheek and he leaned into the touch, closing his eyes with a soft sigh. *I wish this could all be over so your pain can begin to heal.*

But the only path to healing was to walk through the fiery agony of the loss.

The muted strains of a somber hymn on the organ signaled the beginning of the funeral.

Gus walked to the front of the sanctuary and gently clasped Mary by the hand, then steered her to the pew. With their fingers still twined together, Justin led Beth up the center aisle. He released her when they reached the first pew, standing to the side while she sat next to his mom, and then followed her down, taking the end seat.

A door at the side of the sanctuary opened and the pastor entered, rail-thin, with leathered skin and thick charcoal hair. His gray summer-weight suit gave him the look of a walking stick as he strode resolutely toward the pulpit. What was his name? Beth shuffled through her memory before she finally gave up and stole a fleeting glance at the metal plate affixed below the podium. Johnny Higgins. That was it. *Brother Johnny*, Justin had called him when he'd introduced them the day before.

The organ stilled, and the hush in the sanctuary was broken only by the shuffling of feet and a rustling of cloth. Across the aisle from Beth and the McGees, a heavy-set woman of middle years fanned herself with a funeral bulletin. Somewhere off to the side, a man coughed.

"Let us pray," intoned Brother Johnny. For such a slender man, his voice boomed out over the congregation. "May the words of my mouth, and the meditation of my heart, be acceptable in thy sight, O Lord, my strength and my redeemer. In the Name of Jesus Christ, who restores all life. Amen."

"Amen," called out a male voice from the rear of the sanctuary.

"The clock that measures each earthly life never pauses." Brother Johnny laid one elbow along the edge of the podium and leaned forward. "There are no power failures, no dying batteries. It keeps ticking until God determines that it should stop. As time marches relentlessly forward, with each tick of the clock we are swept along on life's second hand. Ecclesiastes tells us that everything has a season. There's a time to live and a time to die. We are all born, none of us with any say over the circumstances of our birth. But we can choose how we will live."

Mary's hand stole into Beth's. *Oh, dear! Justin should be sitting next to his mom. They need each other.*

Beth hadn't meant to sit between mother and son. Short of disrupting the service to rearrange the seating, though, nothing could be done at this point. So she squeezed.

Brother Johnny straightened his back and shuffled through the papers on the podium in front of him. "Sometimes on the road of life people get caught up in the dreams and illusions of the world, a world that values the accumulation of physical riches above the wealth of family and friendship." He paused and scanned the room from one side to the other, then brought his gaze back to settle on Justin, and finally focused on Mary with a gentle smile. "But there are other people, other individuals whom God has blessed, not with prosperity and power, but with insight. People who are given the precious gift of knowing that what really matters in the long run isn't the stuff we gather around us, but the relationships we develop in our lives. Some folks, like our brother James McGee, might at first glance appear to have been dealt a losing hand by God."

Sitting tall and rigid, Justin hadn't moved. His fingers had gone white where they clutched his knees. Beth eased her free hand over his. He jerked and gripped harder for just a heartbeat and then flipped his hand and laced their fingers together again.

Brother Johnny drew in a long, shaky breath. "But in fact, Jim was aware of the true richness of the life he'd been given. He knew the things that really count in life are the relationships we have with other people. When James was called home, he was forced to leave behind those people in his life he loved. But though he is gone from life with us, his beloved family and friends have fond memories of a man who ignored that ticking second hand in this frenzied world. James never failed to stop and spend some of those precious seconds visiting with someone else, to make that person feel valued and loved."

Beth sighed. The pastor might have been talking about her. Jim had to have been suffering great pain out by the barn, but he'd taken the time to talk to her about his son, to tell her about meeting his wife. He'd included Beth in his last moments with his family without blinking an eye.

"James McGee had a deep, abiding love for the land, too," said Brother Johnny. "He once told me that God had gifted him with a piece of land to look after, his own little Eden to enjoy even as he used it to benefit others. As we celebrate this man's life today, I invite all of you to stand and sing in his honor, 'For the Beauty of the Earth'."

Clothing rustled and a few people cleared their throats as those who were seated stood, and the organ began playing the first strains of the familiar hymn. Beth slid a glance at Mary as the singing started. Justin's mom mouthed the words silently, tears rolling over her cheeks and falling to her neck and chest. Justin's voice started low, with a little rasp to it.

Beth gave his hand a firm squeeze as she sang the second verse. "For the beauty of each hour… Of the day and of the night…"

Justin squeezed her hand back and his singing gained vigor. "…Hill and vale and tree and flow'r… Sun and moon and stars of light."

He held on, seeming to draw support, but he also gave back. His rich baritone rang out and washed over her, and from that she mustered the strength to finish with him. "Lord of all to Thee we raise… This our joyful hymn of praise."

The organ faded and the congregation sat. Brother Johnny nodded at Justin. "Jim's son, Justin, will read the scripture, from Ecclesiastes."

Standing, Justin released his grip on Beth's hand with a series of little jerks, almost as though he was being asked to relinquish his only lifeline. But he was steady as he strode to the podium. He laid his fingers on the open Bible and swallowed.

Then he just stared at the page. "I'm sorry," he said quietly when he looked out at the crowd. "Growing up, especially on a ranch, you get used to the cycle of life and... death. You know this sort of thing is always a possibility. That sooner or later you'll have to speak or read at someone's funeral. I just didn't expect it would happen this soon. Even after he got diagnosed with cancer, my dad didn't act sick. He just kind of... slowed down along the way until he stopped."

Beth blinked back tears. She couldn't fall apart now. She just couldn't.

Justin nodded at Jim's casket, with the guitar leaning against it, and waved his hand at the worn cowboy boots sitting next to the instrument. "Those boots..." His voice cracked and he cleared his throat. "When I was a little kid, I used to step into my daddy's boots and drag myself around the kitchen. They were too big, and half the time I stepped out of 'em, the other half the time I fell and landed on my tuckus."

A soft chuckle rippled through the room.

"The thing is... I might be bigger now, but those boots are still going to be pretty hard to fill." He turned his attention to the Bible and stared again. When he looked up, he sought Beth and smiled.

She smiled back, wishing she had the right to step up to the podium with him and offer the support to help him through his task.

"Please..." whispered Mary in her ear. "Let's all go up there."

Startled by the request, Beth jerked her head around to look at Justin's mom. Her eyes pleaded for understanding. Her other hand clutched Gus's arm.

Okay. Okay, you can do this, Beth. You belong here because this family wants you to be here. She nodded and stood, still holding onto Mary's hand.

A sharp indrawn breath from behind broke the hush. No need to wonder who *that* was. It had to be Alice. Then Justin smiled at her, one of those special smiles that never failed to embrace her heart. And nothing else mattered.

With Beth and Mary flanking him, and Gus next to Mary, Justin seemed to draw new strength. Standing straighter, he pulled in a deep breath. "The reading is from Ecclesiastes 3..." He frowned. "I don't know why I can't just read this," he muttered under his breath.

As Beth looked out over the sanctuary, it seemed to fade away, replaced by the image of Big Jim McGee staring toward the mountains, a faraway look in his eyes. *"...bald eagles... I see 'em up there a lot... soaring and gliding. I had a Shoshone friend once who told me eagles are considered of the earth but not in it... kind of spiritual overseers."*

With a small gasp, Beth understood. "It's the wrong passage," she murmured. She laid her hands on the Bible and flipped forward a good chunk of the pages until she found what she was looking for. Then she ran her finger down the page and tapped the specific verse that reminded her of James McGee.

Instantly Justin relaxed. His voice sure and firm, he began to speak. "The scripture is from Isaiah 40. 'Hast thou not known? Hast thou not heard, that the everlasting God, the Lord, the Creator of the ends of the earth, fainteth not, neither is weary? There is no searching of His understanding. He giveth power to the faint; and to them that have no might He increaseth strength. Even the youths shall faint and be weary, and the young men shall utterly fall. But they who wait upon the Lord shall renew their strength; they shall mount up with wings as eagles; they shall run, and not be weary; and they shall walk, and not faint.'"

The fire of renewal surged like a phoenix rising, pushing back Beth's shoulders, straightening her back, lifting her chin. Her stomach jumped and fluttered like hundreds of starlings as she took her seat back in the pew with Justin and Mary and Gus. She couldn't have named the closing hymn to save her life, and she didn't hear one word of the benediction. Beth only knew the service had ended because Justin and his mother stood, and when she glanced around the room, only a handful of people remained.

This is it. The last goodbye. Beth squeezed Justin's hand

and he stopped his slow shuffle toward the casket, slanting a questioning look in her direction.

"This should be for you and your mom," Beth murmured. They'd had precious little time together. "I'll be waiting for you."

Justin studied her face for several heartbeats. His eyes mirrored a mix of challenge, understanding, and gratitude, which Beth met without blinking. Then he breathed deeply and nodded once. "Thanks."

She walked along the dark blue carpet toward the rear of the sanctuary, carefully watching the placement of her feet. When she got to the door at the end of the aisle, she reached for the bar.

"Here, let me get that for you," said a smooth voice from next to her. At the same time, a blurry figure stepped forward and pushed the panic bar that opened the door.

Startled, she jumped sideways and nearly crashed into the doorjamb — likely would have if the man hadn't grasped her by the elbow and steered her across the threshold.

"Oops, careful now." The man was tall and probably somewhere in his thirties. Nimble and in good shape, judging from the way he sprang forward to keep Beth from a painful mishap.

"Sorry. I guess I wasn't paying attention. I'm Beth — Beth Rushton."

"Nice to meet you, Miz Rushton." He nodded as he slipped the hat he carried over his mop of curly dark hair. "My name's Will Douglas. Most people around here call me Doc."

Douglas... Doc. Why did that sound so familiar?

"How're those pups doing?"

Of course, Gus had referred to the vet as Doc Douglas. "Oh! You're *that* Doc Douglas."

He cracked a smile and the corners of his brown eyes creased. "You know of another?"

"Well, no, not really."

Beth stepped from the concrete landing and nearly ran into Alice. The spark of cold calculation in her otherwise dead green eyes sent a shiver to the bottom of Beth's stomach.

"Puppies?" Her top lip curled into a distasteful snarl.

"McGee has puppies? I didn't figure them for dog people."

The coldness in Beth's gut spread outward, and goose flesh rose on her arms. "I guess you had them figured wrong, then, didn't you?"

"What's the mother look like?" asked Alice. "I had a dog go missing not long back. Black and white border collie. She ran off when she was in season, so she might have had a litter."

Beth jammed her hands on her hips as irritation erased caution. "That was irresponsible, don't you think?"

Alice lifted a shoulder. "If the McGees have her, she's ours. We'll come by and pick her up this afternoon."

"They don't have your dog, Alice." Mary's words about Justin bearing the lie so Beth wouldn't need to rolled through her brain and she smiled. As it turned out, she didn't have to lie, and now Justin wouldn't have it on his conscience, either. A slow smile tugged at her lips as she pictured Mama Kitty. "The pups' mama is brown and black."

Doc coughed twice, drawing Alice's stony stare.

"Is something wrong with you?" she asked.

"No, ma'am." Doc shook his head and swallowed. "I just took in a bug with that last breath, is all."

"That's disgusting," she spat, and then spun on her spiky heel and crunched across the gravel to the pickup where Brody waited.

Beth gazed up at the lanky veterinarian. "I think you're my new hero," she murmured.

He shook his head, keeping his eyes on Alice and Brody as he spoke, a plastic smile gracing his lips. "Well, I'll tell ya. I'll do just about anything to keep those pups out of that one's hands."

* * *

"He looks like he's asleep," murmured Mary with a delicate sniff. "I can't believe he isn't going to wake up any minute. I really am going to miss him. Who'll sing to me?" Her voice broke. "Who'll tell me what I should cook for dinner?"

Justin laid an arm across his mom's shoulders. How

could he answer her when he had many of the same questions? Who would organize the branding? Who would he bounce new ideas off of?

Who'd tell him everything was going to work out the way it was supposed to in the end?

Mary stepped forward and picked up the guitar, then hugged it against her breast. Closing her eyes, she sighed. It was a heavy, desolate sound.

Her face was drawn and tired. Big Jim's battle with cancer hadn't been fought alone. Mary had hidden it well, but the fight had taken its toll from her, as well, and it showed now in the deep lines around her eyes, the pallor of her face, the sag of her shoulders.

"I will." The words tumbled from his lips with his need to reassure his mother that she might have lost her soul mate, but she wasn't alone. "I'll be around, Mom. Everything's gonna be okay. It always works out the way it's supposed to in the end."

Justin lifted the guitar from his mother's arms and slung it over his shoulder. Then he led her to the back of the church to wait for the pallbearers. The interment in their private cemetery on the ranch would be more intimate and personal. Only their closest friends would come along.

And Beth. Thank the good Lord for Beth. She was his anchor in this sea of chaos.

Brother Johnny and his son, Bobby, pushed open the double doors and propped them wide. Sunshine exploded into the sanctuary, its rays splashing across the aisle like a beacon. Six dark-suited pallbearers shuffled into the light, carrying the oak casket between them. Gus, at the right front... in an odd circling of fate, taking the same place Jim had when he'd walked Gus's father, Jack Hanson, along the very same aisle.

Sylvia Sanders' dad Harry walked on the left, followed by Wyatt Mitchell. One by one, names associated themselves to faces as Justin watched the men bearing his father on his final journey. Frank Greggs, Travis Ford... all of them Jim McGee's best friends, boys he'd played with as a child, now grown men and burying the first of them to die. Leather-faced Mike Morrow nodded a solemn greeting, first to Mary and then to Justin as they drew abreast.

The sun flashed on the glossy wood casket, engulfing it for a single heartbeat in blinding white light. Then it was through the door. The men stepped to the waiting silver and black hearse and slid Big Jim McGee on board.

Cameron Ford pushed the door shut with a thud that resonated across the crowded parking lot. The period at the end of James Joseph McGee's life.

Weakness crept into Justin's chin and threatened a wobble. Drawing in a long breath, he straightened his spine and locked his jaw. Beth stepped from the shade of the cottonwood that had stood like a welcoming sentry over the entrance to the church from Justin's earliest memories. Her eyes locked on his, and her lips curved into a tender smile as she strode with measured steps in his direction.

The urge to quaver left his chin instantly, and he no longer possessed the need to shore up his back. She said not a single word, just marched into his arms and hugged him hard around the waist.

"I never want to let you go," he whispered into her hair, and then held his breath. He hadn't intended to say that out loud.

"No one's asking you to, cowboy." Beth squeezed her arms tighter around his middle. "Not today, anyway." Then she stepped back and pulled Mary into the embrace.

"Thank you," said his mom, drawing away slowly. "It means the world, Beth, you being here… helping."

Beth's face went pink and she averted her eyes, offering a tiny shrug.

"Excuse me?" asked a hesitant voice from behind him.

He knew that voice. Justin swung around, smiling, to find his fifth grade science fair adversary. "Charlie Morrow!"

The stunning young woman standing before him laughed and shook her head. Sunshine sparked fiery blue off her cap of nearly black hair. "I may never forgive you for dubbing me with a boy's name." She gave him a quick hug. The bulge under her billowing pale blue dress pressed against him, and Justin drew back in shock.

"Charlie… are you expecting?"

She smiled and laid a hand across her abdomen. "Six months." She glanced around and motioned with her hand. "Henry, come over here. I want you to meet someone."

Tall and broad with nut-brown hair and a square jaw, the object of her attention detached himself from a conversation with a handful of men and ambled across the gravel. He nodded as he approached. "Hi, there. I'm Henry Haines."

Charlie smiled up at Justin. "And I'm now Charlotte Haines. But you can still call me Charlie. Henry, this is Justin McGee."

Recognition slid across the other man's face. "Ah... the fifth grade science fair..."

A blush spread across Charlie's face. "We don't need to get into that now."

Justin clasped Henry's outstretched hand. "Nice to meet the man who corralled this one." He scanned the group of people nearby, seeking Beth, and found her chatting with his mom and Doc. "Hey, Beth."

She glanced up and smiled, her eyes flicking over Charlie with the briefest flash of challenge that disappeared when her gaze settled on the couple's linked hands. "Hello."

"Beth, this is an old school friend of mine. Charlie — Charlotte Haines."

Her smile widened. "It's very nice to meet you."

The funeral coordinator appeared to Justin's right. "Whenever you're ready for the procession to the interment site," he murmured, his words slamming Justin back to the reason for the gathering.

"Okay. We're about ready." He returned his focus to Charlie. "Will you join us for a small wake out at the ranch?"

Charlie's instant smile warmed him through and through. "Of course. Wouldn't miss it." She glanced at Henry. "We just need to stop at our place. It's not much, but I made a dish."

Justin nodded, words eluding him. "Thanks," he finally choked out. Then, twining his fingers through Beth's, he led them across the parking lot toward his truck. His lip curled when he spotted MacKay's pickup blocking him in. "What the hell?"

Casting Justin a dark sneer, Brody started the engine and gunned it. The truck inched forward. In the passenger seat, Alice threw out a cheerless wave.

A cold sense of disquiet rippled along Justin's spine, stopping at his neck, where it clenched its icy fingers.

Beth squeezed his hand, drawing his focus. "So... Charlie..." She grinned up at him as he yanked open the truck door. "Dare I ask what happened in the fifth grade?"

Justin winced and rubbed at the lingering chill on the back of his neck. "Let's just say it wasn't one of my finer moments and leave it at that."

"That bad?"

He raised an eyebrow and slanted a glance at her but kept his lips firmly closed.

She giggled and the icy fingers released their grip.

Chapter Twenty–Seven

Sunlight peeked through a gap in the barn wall high overhead and pooled on the tack room's straw-littered dirt floor. Beth stepped inside with care, mindful of the tiny work room's scurrying occupants.

"Hello, furbabies." She dropped to a sit and crossed her legs, then plucked a bit of straw from the flared sleeve of her tan blouse and tossed it to the floor.

Four puppies and three kittens all romped together, bonded as siblings, while Mama Kitty sat on top of the wooden half-wall above her outlandish family. Her tail swished back and forth like a pendulum. Every once in a while she took pains to display a lack of concern by concentrating on washing one paw.

"You aren't fooling me, Mama." Beth chuckled. "I know you're watching."

Derby reared up off his front paws. The motion should have been awkward, but somehow he managed to balance on his good leg and the stub of his missing one, and only leaned a bit to the side. Then one of the kittens charged him. When it got to within a foot, he leaped up and pounced, landing on the feline sibling and rolling over, pulling the kitten with him between his front legs. The kitten kept up the roll, pushing its back legs against the puppy's fat belly and kicking.

They were already weaned. Gus had been feeding them puppy food soaked in water for the past few days. That meant they'd be ready for new homes unless Justin decided to keep them — which she doubted. Best to just accept it was time for the puppies to move on.

She sucked in a quick breath and blew it out. It was past time when she had to decide her next move. She picked up the calmest puppy, the one with the most black on her head and the black speckles on her white paws. Gently, she stroked the baby between her eyes.

"You know, little one, for as long as I can remember, I've wanted to see the world."

The puppy licked her fingers.

"And now..." Beth sighed. "I don't know what to do. Everything I had on my list that I wanted to see, everything I wanted to do... None of it seems important at all anymore."

Derby tore across the floor after his kitten sibling without so much as a wobble in his gait. Would anyone want the little guy? Maybe she should take him with her if she left.

Which of course would be the worst thing she could do — for her and the puppy. If she went back home to Michigan with a dog, traveling would become so much more complicated.

Maybe if she stayed on the ranch...

True, Justin had never told her he wanted her to stay. But he wasn't acting like he wanted her to leave, either. She'd given him space after Jim's death, but he hadn't wanted it. He'd gotten into the habit of seeking her out when she woke up in the morning. He spent every free minute with her... and maybe a few that weren't free.

"Not that I'm complaining, you understand," she said, scratching the puppy behind the ear. Tingles and chills rippled along her skin at just the memory of his touch... or the way his eyelids went heavy when he angled his head and leaned in for a long warm kiss. Better yet, the intense way his eyes turned to blue flames and held hers captive when he was about to strike with a passionate, mind-numbing, body-tingling kiss. She sighed. "We certainly have a delicious chemistry going on."

She stilled her hand. What if it was *only* chemistry? They got on well and had a powerful physical attraction between them. She loved him. She'd barely known him three weeks, but she knew her heart had involved itself from the moment he'd watched the stars and listened to her talk about her dreams.

But he'd never mentioned loving her.

Not even when she'd accidentally blurted out that *she* loved *him*.

Beth lifted the puppy and stared into her eyes. "What do you think? Am I way off base here? What should I do?"

"Talking to the pups, huh?" Gus stepped from the shadows. "Getting any answers?"

His usual plaid cotton Western shirt had been traded for a pale blue one, buttoned to the neck and finished with a black string tie. Bushy dark hair, just beginning to gray at the temples, had been tamed. The chronic five o'clock shadow had been replaced with a freshly shaved face and — Beth sniffed — cologne? The man did clean up nice.

She smiled. "No answers so far. Maybe they're too young."

"Maybe you're talkin' to the wrong species."

Cocking her head to the side, Beth raised one eyebrow. "Think I'll have better luck with a cow?"

Gus chuckled and propped his lean frame against the doorway. "I see why the kid likes you."

Oh, golly, this was painful. This had the potential to become junior high school *do-you-really-think-he-likes-me* stuff. Beth stifled a giggle along with the insane urge to ask Gus if he'd carry a note to Justin in study hall.

She used her toe to draw a line through the bits of golden straw while she considered how to change the subject. "Are you going somewhere special, Gus?"

Fiery crimson flooded his sun-leathered cheeks. "Aww, not really so special. There's a social at the rec center."

And a particular lady, if Beth wasn't missing her guess.

She smiled. "I hope you have a lovely time."

He opened his mouth as though to say something, but closed it and stepped from the tack room. In seconds, he poked his head back through the door. "Just please don't—" He puffed out his cheeks then slowly released the breath. "Don't hurt the kid, okay?"

"Oh, Gus..." Beth shook her head. "I'd never hurt him."

The foreman shook his head. "Not intentionally, no, you wouldn't. But he's going to be in a world of hurt when you leave. The longer you put it off..." He held his hands out, palms up, and lifted his shoulders. "Unless... you might not leave after all?"

Tears pricked like needles at the backs of her eyelids. "I don't know. We haven't talked about it," she said quietly.

"Talk about it. If he doesn't bring it up, maybe you should. And now, if you'll excuse me, I have a date with Miss Jenny Harris." He grinned. "She'll be the prettiest girl at the party tonight."

He settled a Stetson on his head — not the battered brown one he favored, but a pale gray with a crisp crease. Then he touched a fingertip to the brim, spun around on his heel, and ambled away.

Talk about it. So much easier said than done.

Beth had already stayed in Wyoming nearly two weeks longer than she'd planned. She couldn't hang around much longer without a definite idea of where things were going.

Derby pounced on a piece of straw, batting it back and forth between his front paws before he grabbed it with his teeth. Then he shook his head until he got the attention of one of his feline litter mates. The kitten leaped across the few feet between them, but Derby had already whirled around, and instead of reaching the bit of straw, the kitten landed on the puppy's back.

Beth stood. Was she really going to do it? Would she be able to ask Justin if she could stay? How could she make it clear she wasn't pushing for any sort of commitment if he wasn't ready to make one?

"Wish me luck, you guys." She gave Derby one last pat on the head. "And hope I don't get all tongue-tied and mess this up."

A burst of wind whistled down the aisle and whisked along the tack room floor, stirring up dust devils of limestone screenings and straw. Beth shivered in the sudden chilled air, just as the patch of sun poking through the crack in the barn wall winked out.

* * *

Justin stood on the southern end of the front porch, eyeballing the roiling clouds tumbling over the mountains to the west. So far they were billowing and white, tinged with gray at the edges, and none showed any sign of rotation. But the air had rapidly gone cold. A storm was definitely on the schedule for their near future.

"Looks like a bad one," said Mary from behind him.

His heart leaped against his chest wall and Justin whirled around. "I didn't hear you come out."

"That much was obvious." She stepped next to him and leaned forward to study his face. "You look like you've got a lot on your mind."

Justin blew out a breath, ending with a grimace. "Just trying to make sense of everything." Including a letter from the bank he'd just received, calling in a second mortgage he'd been unaware of.

Mary seemed to deflate in front of him. "You don't have to protect me. I saw the letter from Carver's Credit Union in the mail today. I can guess what it says."

"Dad told me he thought we could get away with just selling off a third of our stock." Justin shrugged. "I think I can make that work." If he also took Greenway up on their offer for a chunk of prime pasture at the edge of state land.

The wind picked up the ends of Mary's hair. Justin frowned. When had so much gray edged into her light brown hair? His mom was still a young woman, not even fifty.

She laid her hand on his forearm. "The ranch was your *father's* Eden. Holding onto it was *his* dream, Justin. It was mine *because* it was his." She squeezed. "We had it in our minds it would be your legacy... but it's not meant to be your millstone."

"Mom... it's not like that." Justin raised his eyes to study the yard. This was home. The only home he'd ever known. The thought of chipping away at it, parceling it out a bit at a time while trying to hold onto the rest, stirred an ache deep in his heart.

Or that ache might have come about because he knew Beth would be leaving soon.

"When is she planning to go home?"

Justin started. Had he spoken his thoughts out loud? Twisting his head to meet his mom's concerned gaze, he realized with a shock that he hadn't. He'd simply become that transparent. The wind began a low wail as a strong burst dislodged a handful of tender twigs from the cottonwood and flung them across the yard.

He closed his eyes to gather some internal control, but opened them before he answered. "She hasn't said, but I'm guessing soon."

"She won't stay?"

Why was she pushing so hard? "I haven't asked her to," he admitted, jerking one shoulder in a half shrug.

Mary dropped her hand and stepped back. "Why not?"

He shook his head slowly back and forth. "Got nothing here to offer her but hard times, Mom. At least for the next few years."

Anger flared in her eyes. "That's not true. You have a lot to offer her. You have your name... your daddy's name. You have *you*. You're a good man, Justin. You'll always care for her. And they won't be forever, those hard times. Things'll come back, you wait and see. You just need to tighten your belt and hold on a little bit."

"It doesn't matter." He gestured with his chin in the direction of the road. "Everything she wants is waiting out there. The world is waiting for her."

Mary lifted a hand to her mouth, regarding Justin through clear blue eyes. "Have you asked her what it is *she* wants?"

He nodded, the misery of his last few days wrestling with the problem gripping his heart and squeezing. "She's always been up front about her dreams and plans."

A gentle laugh escaped Mary's lips. "Plans change, my boy. I think you should talk to her."

He offered a noncommittal grunt. "I guess."

"Justin..." Mary turned from the approaching storm and scuffled toward the front of the porch. "Dorothy's opened a secondhand shop in Cheyenne."

"Aunt Dor?" The plump, round face of his mother's much older sister floated into his memory. "I thought she wasn't doing too well with her arthritis. That's why she couldn't make it for the funeral."

"Traveling is hard for her, but she loves dealing with the public, and if she owns the shop, she can set the hours she works." Mary spun around, excitement glittering in her eyes, the first sign of real happiness Justin had seen since the evening before his dad had died. "I want to run it with her."

"Wha..." Blinking with surprise, Justin took a half step back. "You do? But why?" He'd always assumed she'd want to stay on the ranch. His gaze strayed to the cemetery at the edge of the yard.

"He's not there... your father." Mary sighed. "Justin, his body is buried in that box but everything that was *him*... it's not there. He's everywhere and nowhere. He's always going to be with me. But here... in the bedroom we shared, at the table where we all ate our meals. It's too much for me. I'll always have the memories. I'll always love him. But everything here reminds me of him, and it hurts. I cry if I see his razor. I cry when I see his hat still on the peg by the back door."

"We can put all that away, Mom." Panic rooted in Justin's core. He hadn't wanted to rush her. He stepped close and laid a hand on Mary's shoulder as the rest of his world began to crumble. "You don't — you don't have to leave."

"I love it here, Justin. And if you tell me you need me to stay... to help you... well, you know I will. I love you." Tears brimmed and silently spilled over. "But I need some time. I need time to adjust, so I'm not looking for him whenever I enter a room, seeing him everywhere and realizing he's not there. My body just hasn't caught up to all that's happened. I keep expecting him to walk up behind me... and then he doesn't and it's like losing him all over again."

Her voice broke and with it Justin's heart. He'd been feeling many of the same things. He should have known she'd have felt them with even more intensity. Maybe it *was* time to let it all go. It had to beat the intense loss eating at his heart daily.

And when Beth left...

Mary closed her hand over his where it rested on her shoulder. "Talk to Beth before she goes away, Justin. Before it's too late. And—" She drew a deep breath. "If she doesn't want to stay, I think you should consider leaving. She's the best thing to ever happen to you."

He had to agree with her last statement, at least. A smile tugged his lips upward, but did little to lift his spirits. "I'll talk to her, Mom."

With a gentle sigh, her lips stretched into her familiar smile. "Good. She's in the barn with the puppies."

Justin planted a quick hard kiss on his mother's forehead before he strode to the end of the porch and jumped down. Wind whipped at his shirt, sudden sharp gusts pushing him sideways. The clouds overhead had darkened, slowed their fast boiling, and begun to build themselves into a wall, taking on the vague shape of a giant anvil.

Definitely a hell of a thunder-bumper brewing. But it was nothing compared to the tornadic forces already twisting apart his heart.

He slowed his steps, relishing the power of the incoming storm, drawing an odd kind of strength from the electrical charge in the air. His mom was right. He did need to talk to Beth. He had to release her — release them both — from the weird sort of limbo they found themselves in.

He loved her. More than his own life, he loved her.

That was why he had to let her go. Beth wanted to see the world. She deserved to follow her dream. Especially since it was apparent now that finances wouldn't keep her from doing that.

Well, neither would he.

A drop of rain splashed down, followed quickly by a second, then a third, then too many to count. Justin quickened his pace, but his shirt was drenched in seconds. As he reached the barn door, it slid open, and Beth stood blinking in the dim light. Recognition flared in her eyes, and she jumped out of his way as he slipped into the barn's shelter. Whirling about, he drew the door closed and secured it against the lashing rain.

"You're soaked."

The tinkle of her laughter mixed with the drumming of thick raindrops against the side of the barn and stirred the wildness in Justin's blood. She'd be gone soon. Gone and out of his life, because he'd not ask her to stay, and he couldn't go with her.

The frustrated thoughts burned a path to his belly, and the heat of longing pooled low. Every stolen moment could be his last with her. Each second should count — *needed* to count because memories of the moments would have to last him a lifetime.

Without a word, he snagged her hand as she moved to pass him, enjoying the little squeak that burst through her full pink lips. The lips he planned to thoroughly ravish and enjoy within the next few seconds. With a slow and steady tug, he held onto her green gaze as he reeled her in. After an eternity of seconds, she was flush against him.

Where she belongs, his heart whispered.

She didn't seem to care that she was instantly almost as wet as he. Justin aimed them for the first stall door and crowded her back against it.

Beth's eyes widened and her lips parted. He didn't wait for an invitation, just swooped in and claimed those soft, welcoming lips. She trembled as she molded herself against him and then wrapped her right leg around his left, pinning them calf to calf. Reckless, he plundered her mouth, her honey-sweet taste combining with her flowery musky scent and carrying him close to the brink.

Blue-white flashes poked through the cracks in the barn walls, quickly followed by the rolling crash of thunder. The storm was directly overhead.

Electricity surged between them and urgency took over. Denied too long, he had to feel more, was driven to experience more of her.

He nipped her lower lip and she gasped, tossing her head back with abandon and exposing her throat for his pleasure. Her cries of passion exploded inside his head as he trailed kisses downward to the sensitive little indentation at the base of her neck that never failed to fascinate him.

She softened and then sagged into his embrace, as though her legs no longer provided support. Lost in her, Justin fumbled with the catch on the stall door. It lifted with a *clank* and he pulled the door open. He walked them into the stall without turning her loose, and drew back just far enough to scan their surroundings. The stall was empty, as he'd known it would be, the straw bedding as fresh as when he'd pitched it only a few hours earlier. Justin sank to his knees and laid his forehead against her flat abdomen while he fought for control. The gauzy light brown cotton of her blouse whispered along his skin. He pushed the top up and settled his hands just below her ribs on both sides. Her skin warmed his already-heated palms.

Slowly she dragged her body along his as she lowered herself to her knees and joined him in the straw.

"Justin?" She whispered his name as a question, a plea to explain himself.

Please say you'll stay, he begged silently. *Tell me your dreams have changed, that you want to stay... that you want me.*

Because he knew she'd stay if he asked. She'd give up her dreams for him. So he couldn't ask.

* * *

On her knees in the prickly straw, face to face with the man she loved beyond measure, Beth searched Justin's eyes. What did this mean? Did he want to be with her? Did he want her to stay?

Rainwater dripped from the ends of his hair and trickled down his cheeks, but he didn't seem to notice. His eyes glittered with fiery intensity. A blind man couldn't mistake the desire reflected in them.

He seemed different, more desperate than he'd been

before. The thought that she drove him to such urgency was incredible… heady. But she wasn't convinced it was all her.

"Is something wrong?" she asked.

He regarded her with an even stare, though his breathing was still labored. "Not anymore," he murmured, leaning in close and nibbling at her bottom lip. "Guess I just missed you."

Beth's heartbeat quickened. There it was! Her opening.

"Speaking of missing me…" She reached up and snatched a bit of straw that clung to his collar, then dropped it to the floor. She frowned at his wet shirt. "You should get out of this."

Justin blinked. "I don't think I'm following you."

"Right… I guess you don't read minds." Giggling, she slipped the top button of his shirt through the hole then moved to the next one down. "Anyway, I've been staying here for a while now… and I've really loved it. But I'm kind of at a place where I have to decide what to do next… where to… go, or if I should…" *Stay.* Pride trapped the word in her throat and her hands stilled. She drew her hands back, leaving the fourth button fastened.

He'd gone still, staring at her with his mouth open as though he wanted to say something, but instead he only shook his head. "Beth…" he murmured.

Ask me to stay… please ask me to stay. Heart racing, she repeated the entreaty over and over in her head.

"I figured you'd be leaving soon," he said quietly. "Thank you… for staying longer and helping with everything."

"You know, I could…" She shrugged. Again, the word wouldn't squeeze its way out. What if he told her to go? *Ask me to stay…*

"Where do you think you'll go first? After you get home, I mean? I guess you're fairly eager to see your dad." Justin spoke quickly, apparently oblivious to her difficulty with words.

Or was he ignoring it? Avoiding embarrassment by pretending ignorance so he wouldn't have to ask her to leave? Her stomach contracted, and bile burned the back of her throat, leaving a bitter taste that lingered after she swallowed it back down.

I guess it was just chemistry after all — no promises asked, none given. Emptiness exploded in her heart, tearing it in two.

"I... Yes, I miss Daddy." Suddenly she missed him a lot. Missed his overprotective nature, his tendency to do too much for her. Tears welled.

"Hey, I didn't mean to make you cry." Justin wiped her tears with his thumbs, the tender act only ripping fresh wounds in her shredded heart. "You'll see him soon, right? You know, I was thinking... why not take a train, or I suppose you could fly. We could get you up to Jackson Hole."

Trains? Planes? What was he talking about? She had her little van. Beth shook her head, numb with hurt that she refused to let him see. It would only make him feel worse to know putting her off had hurt her feelings. "No... I, um... I have the van. The trip out here was nice. It'll be fun going home the same way. I was... I was thinking I'd leave tomorrow, actually."

Justin didn't look particularly pleased, but he nodded. Then he cocked his head to one side. "Hear that?"

"The rain's stopped."

He'd no sooner said the words than the early evening sun flashed through the cracks in the wood above them and brushed the inside of the dingy barn with slender fingers of golden light.

Beth sucked in a deep breath. She had to ask, though oddly saying the words out loud seemed to cement her plans. "The puppies... what will happen to them?"

"Doc's coming out first thing tomorrow. He called a vet in the next county and explained the situation. I figured with Alice sniffin' around it was only a matter of time before she tried to make trouble over 'em." He shot her a self-satisfied grin. "She can't make trouble over pups she can't find."

"And... Derby?" Beth bit her lip while she waited for his answer.

Justin angled his head and rubbed the back of his neck. "I understand he has the perfect home waiting for him. He'll have his own boy."

The vise around Beth's heart eased just a little. But she still didn't want to leave. She should have kept her mouth shut. Words half formed in her mind and she opened her mouth to speak.

He stood and held out a hand. "I'd best go see what damage the storm did."

"Would you — I mean, can I come along?"

Justin's brows shot skyward, followed by his easy grin. "Sure." He laid his arm along her shoulder as they left the stall.

How had she existed without that comforting gesture before she met him? And how could she expect to live without it when she left?

Chapter Twenty–Eight

Justin stared at the multicolored monstrosity that was about to carry Beth out of his life — likely forever. Irrational hatred of the vehicle rose. He stared hard at a chunk of granite, half-embedded in the ground near the front of the house. Maybe if she came out after saying her goodbyes to his mom and found the windshield busted out, she'd have to delay her exit.

Which of course was pointless, since he wanted her to leave. Well, maybe not wanted... needed was more like it. For her own sake, so she would be able to make something for herself, follow her dream without being tied to a faltering ranch. She thought she wanted to stay — he'd read it in her eyes. Just as he read the disappointment when he hadn't asked her not to leave. Once she was on the road, the romance of ranching would fade. She was a city gal, a tenderheart. A couple of weeks playing rancher wasn't the same as a day-to-day, year-after-year existence.

With a long shaky sigh, he suppressed the urge to chuck the rock at the van and turned instead to gaze across the Cross MC land. The rain had left the pastures lush and green, and even with the winds, only a few smaller branches had been ripped from the tree line. More important, they hadn't found any injured or dead cows.

A millstone, his mother had called the ranch. Maybe it was, but it was his burden to bear, and he'd make it or go belly up. But it didn't have to weigh Beth down. He refused to hook her to the yoke of generations when there was a whole world out there and a dream she'd had since she was a child.

The storm had been pushed out by a high pressure system, so the air was crisp and clear, but the breeze that tickled the hair along his neck was balmy. The weather would warm up fast, and summer promised to be hotter than usual. At the creak of the front door opening, Justin turned. Beth stepped onto the porch, a red duffel slung over her shoulder on a long white strap. She turned and gave his mom a hard hug, then walked across the porch and down the steps.

Justin met her halfway to the van and lifted the duffel bag from her shoulder, grunting when the weight of it wrenched his arm. "What's in here?"

"Camera and lenses."

At the van, he opened the passenger door and set the bag inside on the seat. His arms might have been made of lead, so heavy were they when he pushed the door closed. Justin didn't touch her as they rounded the van without speaking. The sluggish shuffle of their feet echoed off the front of the house.

This is it, then. Letting go sucked.

At the driver's side door, Beth flung her arms around his neck, pulling herself so tightly against him, they were almost one. She trembled as she pressed her mouth on his. With his heart pounding against his throat, Justin threaded his fingers through her hair and cupped the back of her head.

When he drew back, tears on her lashes glistened in the early morning sun. Then she spoke, the quiver in her voice pulling at Justin's heart. "Give all the puppies hugs goodbye for me, will you?"

"Yeah, I'll do that." *You can stop this insanity. Just ask her to stay.*

The blouse she'd bought on their trip to AJ's hadn't been tucked into the dark blue jeans, and it fluttered like a pale green flag in the wind. She'd more or less tamed her curls into a loose ponytail, but the breeze was already lifting wisps of gold to blow across her eyes. When she turned toward the sun, her eyes reflected bright green.

"I have something for you." She reached into her shirt pocket and slipped out a picture.

Justin's heart skidded to a momentary stop as he recognized the picture he'd snapped of her up at the old homestead. "Thank you," he murmured.

Beth touched his cheek. "Take care of yourself, cowboy."

Stay, his heart begged. "Goodbye, Beth," he said out loud, then bent to give her one last soft kiss, quick and easy-like. "Come back any time."

"I…" She drew a shaky breath. "I will."

He held up his hand, small finger extended. "Pinky promise?"

She caught her breath and stared. Finally she linked her baby finger with his. "Pinky promise."

They squeezed their fingers together and then slowly released one another. She nodded and took in a deep breath. With a final glance in his direction, she pulled open the door to her van and climbed in. After only a moment, the engine sputtered to life, and he stepped back, waving as the vehicle lurched forward.

The van disappeared into the distance and Justin dropped his hand, but the dust had long settled before he moved. The emptiness in his chest was sharp and heavy. He pressed his knuckles against his breastbone to ease the ache, well aware he'd just allowed the love of his life to drive away forever.

The mountain breeze fluttered the photograph, and he shifted his attention with a smile. She'd lifted her hands to frame her face and thrown her head back slightly and off to the side. The hat had slipped back, and the sun had turned her hair to spun gold. But her smile… her beautiful, easy, always-ready smile… That reached out to him, and even in the photo it was obvious she was what his grandfather would have called a "genuine person."

The wind ruffled the picture again, trying to steal it

away, and he tightened his grasp. He flipped it over to see if maybe she'd recorded the date, surprised to find not a date, but a single sentence written with black ink to form delicate letters. *I will always love you, and I'll always be your Dilly Gal.*

The hollow ache in his chest heated like a hot knife being put to a bleeding wound, and radiated from his chest outward until it consumed him. *Go after her!*

"Be happy, Dilly Gal," he murmured. "I'll always love you back."

* * *

Just at the outskirts of town, the red pickup passed with a blare of the horn, and Beth recognized Doc waving at her. She lifted her hand and forced a smile, grateful he wouldn't be able to see her furiously blinking back tears. Was he on the way to pick up the puppies?

Life would move forward in Orson's Folly... maybe a little slower than the rest of the world, but it would move on... and so would Justin. Even without her there to see it all... to be a part of it.

What would happen to Justin? Mary had told her she'd be joining her sister all the way across the state. Justin and Gus would be on their own. She sighed. Maybe not for too long, if Gus was serious about Miss Jenny Harris. Beth's heart stuttered at the thought of Justin eating alone in the big farm kitchen.

A white sign sporting the familiar giant red star appeared on her right. "So there you are," she murmured. Had it really been less than a month ago that she'd teased Justin about missing the only gas station in town because she'd blinked? It felt like half a lifetime.

She checked her gas gauge. It was only down by a quarter of a tank, but it would be prudent to top it off, so she pulled into the tiny blacktopped parking lot. Seconds later, she wished she'd skipped on past. The shiny black truck crookedly parked across the aisle between the two islands effectively blocked her from driving on through. Unless she stopped and backed up, she was trapped in the gas station parking lot. Briefly, she contemplated how hard it would be to back out of the place.

Don't be stupid. It's not like Alice or Brody can actually do anything to you. And if Alice is here, you can let her know you're on your way home.

Beth brought her van to a stop behind the giant pickup and judged her distance from the pump. If she was lucky, the hose would stretch. Sunlight flashed off the door of the small glass-fronted building as it was opened. The diminutive size of the wizened man who exited the building was more than made up for by his lively walk across the parking lot. His green cap with the star and T logo sat at such an extreme angle over bushy salt-and-pepper hair, it was a wonder it hadn't fallen off.

"Mornin', missy," he said with a grin that showed unevenly spaced and very yellow teeth. He spat a glob of tobacco into the trash can near the pump.

Well, that explains the teeth.

Stan, Sr. had been stitched in white letters over the pocket of his dark green button-up work shirt. Stan extended a hand that looked more like a grease-stained claw with tanned leather stretched across the bones. With a jerky motion she could only hope he didn't notice, she pushed her hand forward and clasped Stan's in a firm handshake.

"Shall I fill 'er up?"

Beth returned the smile, fighting the urge to check her teeth for leftover blueberry pieces from Mary's muffins earlier. "Yes, please. I have a long trip ahead of me."

With a quick nod, Stan stepped over to the pump and picked up the nozzle. It did make the stretch to her van, though barely. Stan's energetic movements as he washed and squeegeed her windows threatened to exhaust her just watching him. Beth shifted her attention to the gleaming black pickup, wondering where its owner was. She wandered over to the truck and ran her fingers over the slick surface of the side panel.

What on earth did Brody use the truck for? The back of Justin's truck had been filled with equipment he used around the ranch, a toolbox, rope, bits and pieces and all manner of things she hadn't recognized, but as Justin wasn't a pack rat, Beth had no doubt everything he carried had a use. Brody's truck was completely empty. She frowned as she studied the pristine truck bed, which wasn't marred by even the tiniest scratch and showed no trace of the smallest clump of soil.

"See anything you like?" Brody's surly voice came from behind.

Beth whirled to find him well within her bubble of personal space, and she took an involuntary step back. "Hey... hi, Brody. I was, um, actually looking for Alice. I wondered if she was here with you."

Malevolent eyes assessed her, scraping along nerves as he ran a squinty-eyed stare the length of her body and back. A grotesque, viperous grin stretched his mouth, and a bead of sweat broke out over his upper lip. "She ain't here." The coldness in his voice sent a chill to the base of her spine and weakened Beth's legs.

"Oh, well..." Beth backed up another step, scraping her knee against the rear bumper of the truck. "I'm heading back home today. Will you let her know?"

Brody rested an elbow on the edge of the quarter panel and leaned toward Beth. "That right? Leaving, huh?" He centered his gaze on her chest and ran his tongue along his upper lip. "Yeah... I'll tell her."

An unholy fire burned in his dark blue eyes, and Beth forced herself to look away from his face. Her gaze fell on a scrap of electric blue fabric caught in the hinge of the tailgate. It wasn't much more than a couple of threads fluttering in the wind, but it kept her from having to look at Brody. He must have seen her shift in focus. With a chuckle that made her stomach turn, he grasped the threads between his fingers and yanked them free, then released them into the stiff breeze.

They floated eastward, the way Beth would soon be heading.

"You're all set, miss." Stan seemed to just materialize at her elbow. He gestured toward the building. "If you'll step inside, I'll ring you up."

Brody touched a finger to his hat brim and spoke in a

voice smooth as silk. "I'll be seeing you again soon, Bethany."

Beth's heart slammed so hard against the inside of her chest, she was certain it must have left bruises on the outside. She breathed a sigh of relief when he pulled open his truck door and climbed in. The pickup engine growled to life, and the truck glided away with excruciating slowness. Beth released her pent-up breath when Brody made the turn onto the highway and headed east. Odd... he'd been pointed west when she pulled in so she'd assumed he was on his way home. But turning east... that sent him in the opposite direction from his ranch. No sooner had the thought crossed her mind than she rolled her eyes and shook her head. Not her business. He obviously had errands in town.

She followed Stan into the small modern building and paid for the gas. On impulse, she grabbed a Royal Crown from the cooler and a bag of hard candy from the rack next to the register.

After she made it back to the van, her hand trembled as it hovered over the ignition key. Finally, gritting her teeth, she grabbed the key and twisted. When the engine snorted to life as usual, she sighed. She had no reason to dawdle any longer, so she eased into first gear and drove across the parking lot, stopping at the highway. Her heart begged for a left turn, but she put on her signal and went right, east, toward... home. Except Michigan didn't feel like home anymore.

A white station wagon and a dark blue pickup stood in the parking lot of the athletic field where she and Justin had flown the kite. As she passed, a silver pickup pulled in and parked. Must be some sort of gathering.

Lying in the middle of the baseball diamond and watching their kite dancing in the sky had been fun. Too bad they'd never gotten around to more kite flying. Who would have thought it could be so relaxing? Did Justin do it often? Even alone?

"When you fly a kite, you look up, to the sky, the freedom. And you can be the anchor or you can be the wind. But me... I'm the kite! Tethered to reality yet floating on a dream."

The first tear fell less than a quarter of a mile later, and when the second one wouldn't be blinked away, Beth pulled to the side of the road. Leaning her head against the steering wheel, she gave in and let them fall.

"Why?" she asked the empty van. "Why didn't he ask me to stay?"

"Justin… has a tendency to push away the people he loves when he needs them the most."

Beth jolted upright and swiveled to stare at the passenger seat. But Jim wasn't really there. Still, his voice in her head had been so clear, he might have been sitting next to her.

Is that what Justin had done? Pushed her away so he could work out his problems his way? No, that couldn't be true. It wasn't like that between them. Sure, she'd made the offer to help financially, but once she understood his feelings on the subject, she'd let it go. And he *had* let her help out during his dad's funeral.

"…He'll try to push you away."

Her shoulder twitched where Jim had laid his fingertips that day by the barn. She held her breath and felt the ghost of his touch again.

"…Don't let him push you out of his life."

Justin had done *exactly* that. He'd pushed her away. He hadn't let her talk. He sometimes had a slow way of speaking, but he wasn't dense and stupid. He had to have known she was trying to say something, but he hadn't been his usual patient self, hadn't waited her out.

Why?

Because he needs you. Needs you and you won't be there.

Or was she just victimizing herself with wishful thinking?

The sharp rap on the glass next to her sent her heart leaping toward her throat and sent blood pounding into her ears. Beth jerked around, blinking as she tried to make sense of the man standing on the other side of the glass. Nut brown hair, kind eyes.

"Doc!" She rolled down her window with one hand and frantically wiped at her tears with the other, gulping in a few deep breaths. "You startled me."

"You all right? You didn't get very far." He leaned his

forearms on the van door.

How long had she been stopped there? "I... stopped to fill my gas tank. And then I came a little farther and..." She lifted a shoulder. "I decided to check my, um... map."

Doc raised an eyebrow but didn't call her out on the lie. "I see."

A change of subject was needed. Fast. "I saw you going in the other direction earlier. Did you pick up the puppies?"

"Yep. Got 'em in my truck if you want to see 'em one more time." He leaned even closer and studied her face.

He was probably getting quite the visual, too, with the way she'd been bawling. Beth wished she dared lean over and check herself in the rearview mirror. Then again, maybe she was better off not knowing. She smiled. "Thanks, but it's already hard leaving."

"Well, if you're okay, I'd better get going. Got a little ride ahead of me with the pups." He stepped away from the van and gave her a little salute before striding back to his pickup.

"But I'm not okay," she murmured, risking a glance into the mirror. A stranger with puffy red eyes, snotty nose, and blotchy, tear-streaked cheeks stared back. Beth shuddered.

And here I thought I couldn't feel any worse.

"Don't let him push you away," Jim's memory repeated.

She stared eastward. In that direction — a long ways in that direction — lay her roots, the place she'd come from. But that wasn't home any longer.

And her dreams... when had her dreams changed? When had she stopped caring whether she saw the world?

"The very first time he kissed me," she answered herself.

Checking the road and finding it empty of traffic, she spun the wheel into a one-eighty and gunned the engine. Vague impressions filtered into her brain as she whizzed past... buildings turning to fields... the blue and yellow sign advising she was traveling on a county road... a billboard with a giant brown beer bottle... grassy fields to scrub to open plain. Then the pine-covered mountains in the distance.

The wooden sign bearing *Cross MC* swung gently back and forth over the driveway, pushed by the breeze. The first time she'd driven beneath that sign, she had come home to her true dream. She just hadn't recognized it then.

She pulled to a stop near the front of the house, opened the door, and hopped to the ground. Twirling slowly, she took in the familiar surroundings.

A trio of brown-and-white cows ambled across the pasture in the direction of the muddy pond at the center. A couple more lay with legs curled beneath them in the shade of a small stand of trees. The house was silent and somehow felt deserted. Zeke and Abe stood in the paddock, swishing their tails over one another. The brown horse Justin's dad had called Gypsy stood at the rail staring into the distance. Had she been Jim's horse? She'd certainly seemed happy when he'd shown her affection. Beth hadn't really noticed her much in the days following Jim's funeral. But now Gypsy just looked... sad. A splash of dark blue in front of the cow barn turned out to be the ranch pickup, parked in its usual spot.

Maybe Justin was in one of the barns. Wherever he was, she'd find him. And when she found him? She'd tell him how she felt. What was the worst that could happen? He could laugh at her... pity her... send her on her way. It didn't matter. None of it mattered. She couldn't leave without — she frowned and huffed out a breath. What? Closure, she supposed. If she was right, if *Jim* had been right, Justin was pushing her away. If she was wrong... She shuddered. Best not to think of that or she'd lose her courage.

Fine limestone gravel crunched under her feet as she marched along the driveway, leaving the house behind. A gust of warm wind drove off the plain and whipped at her shirt. Brushing her hair out of her face, she glanced upward toward the mountains. Two eagles circled in an upward spiral. Beth paused her steps to watch them. One of the birds broke the circling and dove. The other followed barely an instant later, and then the sky was empty.

"So beautiful..." She'd been fooling herself to think she could leave.

A familiar low chuckle twined its way into Beth's awareness, followed by the rise and fall of Justin's voice, coming from around the barn's corner. Chills swept over Beth like the incoming tide, raising goose bumps on her arms, followed quickly by a flood of warmth that seized her lungs. He must be talking to Gus... or maybe his mom. Her lips tugged themselves upward. Would he be pissed at seeing her return?

Oh, she hoped not. Could she be right? Had the spark between them been something more?

She rounded the barn, opening her mouth to call out and announce herself, but stopped short when she saw he was alone and apparently talking to himself. She performed a hasty back-step, ducking from his line of sight. Then she peeked around the corner, wincing as she scraped her cheek along the rough barn wood.

"Now, come on out of there."

Justin hunkered down and peered beneath a giant piece of farm equipment. It looked like a red tractor sitting atop the open maw of a giant push lawn mower. Sunlight glinted off the lethal blades. What on earth was he talking to?

He moved his hand slowly and carefully, then pounced. A loud, high-pitched yelp split the air, and he pulled his hand back, hauling something black and white and squirming with it. When he stood, he cradled a puppy in his arms. *Derby!*

"Now, you aren't a blessed cat, so you'd best start acting like a dog, or you'll be eating mice for the rest of your life." He grinned and scratched the puppy between the ears.

"He kept Derby," whispered Beth.

Justin had been dead set against keeping any of the puppies, because they'd never used dogs on the ranch, he'd said, and an animal had to pay its way. But he'd also promised that Derby had a good home.

"...the perfect home waiting for him... his own boy."

"Own boy, huh?" she whispered. "You fraud. You're nothing but a big softie."

Justin set the pup down on the hard dirt and began walking. "Come on, little guy."

After a last, longing, puppy glance at the tractor-thing, Derby scrambled after his master. From the angle, it was impossible to tell the pup had only three legs, and he walked so smoothly, his gait didn't give it away.

"It's just you and me now, Derby." Justin checked his

wristwatch. "Beth's—" His voice broke and he cleared his throat. "She's probably halfway to the interstate by now."

She narrowed her gaze. If he was so broken up over her leaving, why hadn't he asked her to stay? She stepped around the corner and planted her hands on her hips.

"Actually, Beth's standing ten feet behind you."

Justin's head snapped up and he whirled around. Poor Derby tried to follow the movement and ended up falling over like a top that had lost its spin.

She huffed out a breath in exasperation. "Justin James McGee, you are either the stupidest or the stubbornest man I've ever met!"

His brows pulled together and his lips drew into a questioning O. "Wha-a-at are you doing here?"

"What am I doing? I'm standing here looking at a big fraud." *Looking at the only man I'll ever love.*

The lines across his forehead deepened and his eyes narrowed into wariness, but he remained silent.

"Say it." She folded her arms across her chest. "Say you don't want me here."

He shook his head slowly, once back and forth. "I thought you wanted to travel around the world... see places..."

Triumph slid over her like a comfortable blanket. "Now, why would I want to go to the other side of the planet when my whole world is standing right in front of me?"

It took him two strides to reach her and half a second to scoop her into his embrace. He angled his head and eased toward her but stopped a hair's breadth away from meeting her lips.

Yes! Kiss me!

"You have until the count of three, and then I'm never letting you go."

He didn't get to *one.*

"You big doof!" Beth wound her arms behind his neck and pulled him close, fusing her lips against his with a moan.

Raw need seared along her nerve endings. Desire heated her blood as Justin took control of the embrace. He slid his arms around her waist to the small of her back, then tightened his grasp and molded their bodies together.

Home. I'm home.

Agony, swift and razor-sharp, assaulted her left ankle. Beth broke the kiss. "Ow!" She pushed herself out of the embrace and stared downward.

Derby sat staring up at her. After a moment, he blinked his chocolate brown eyes twice.

"What kind of welcome home is that?" She bent and gave her ankle a brisk rub until the sting eased.

"Home, eh?" Justin sent her a sideways gaze, his blue eyes twinkling with silent laughter. "You plan to stick around for a while, then?"

Beth stood and laid her hands on his shoulders, meeting his eyes. "Home." She teased them both with a brush of her lips against his. "Just try and send me away again, and you'll see what a sticker I can be. I'll be a burr in your backside."

"You know what this means, don't you?"

"What?" She drew back again and held her breath.

"It means we'd best get married, since I don't plan to sleep in the bunkhouse any longer than I have to."

"What? Is that some kind of cowboy proposal?" Beth chortled. "You want to get married?"

A slow smile took over his face. "Dang, woman, I thought you'd never ask."

Flummoxed, she stared at him. "I didn't — you asked me — didn't you?" When he winked, she whacked him in the chest.

"Come on, let's go tell Mom. She'll be relieved not to have lost her chance at gaining a daughter." He slipped his arm around Beth's shoulders. A feeling of security exploded through her at the familiar gesture. "You know, I'm gonna want a pre-nup," he told her as they walked.

"What?" Beth twisted her head and looked up at him. "No way! We're in it together or not at all. And by the way, you're finishing school."

"No, that would be a deal breaker. I don't need a degree to run cattle."

"We'll table that one for now. But one thing you'll have to agree to." She reached over and patted his belly. "You're gonna lose a lot of weight if I do the cooking."

He hip checked her sideways. "Unless you take cooking lessons."

She full-out body checked him back. "Only if you give them." *Oh, yeah! With lots of hands-on action and stolen kisses.*

At their feet, Derby yapped and then clamped his teeth in the hem of Beth's blue jeans. Snarls and grunts accompanied several shakes of his head.

"And you're gonna have to control your dog, you know." She stooped and scratched the pup behind the ears.

Justin halted near the patio and turned her to look at him, his face reflecting deep concern. "You know it won't be easy. The ranch is hurtin'... hurtin' real bad."

Smiling, she lifted her hand and cupped his cheek. His early five o'clock shadow scratched against her palm. "I have an idea about that, too." She ran her hand downward along his arm and laced their fingers together. As they began walking to the house again, she cast him an upward glance. "Ever heard of a co-op? A cooperative business endeavor between several separate entities?" She squeezed his hand three times.

"Why do you do that?" he asked, lifting their linked hands. "What does it mean?"

She squeezed his hand. "I..." She squeezed again. "...love..." She squeezed one more time. "...you."

Chapter Twenty-Nine

Current time again

Justin shook his head as the ranch dissolved around him. Bright afternoon sun faded into pale green walls. The scent of the wildflowers on the warm breeze morphed into the antiseptic smells of the hospital, and he sighed.

"You saved the ranch with that idea," he told the smiling woman holding his hand. Too bad he hadn't been able to save her. Despair at the dark thought cascaded through him like a trail of falling dominos, and the pressure on his chest grew heavier.

Beth pulled his hand to her lips and kissed it. "Don't go there."

His voice, when he found it, surprised him with its steadiness. "You're going to go away again, aren't you?"

Holding onto his gaze, a flicker of sadness entered her eyes and she nodded.

"Take me with you, Dilly Gal." He glanced around at the stark hospital room. "Our boys are grown, got families of their own. They don't need me anymore, and I—" He swallowed hard, blinking back the stinging behind his eyelids. "I miss you. So much."

"I can't," she whispered. "I can't stay this time... and you can't go. Not yet."

Justin closed his eyes as searing pain grabbed his heart and clamped down.

She squeezed his hand three times and held on tight with the last one. "People still need you. Our boys... our grandchildren. Ricky. He's every bit ours, too, cowboy, and he's not finished needing you yet. And tell Melanie to separate those overgrown daffodils. She and Sean need some for their yard to welcome the spring." She cocked her head and winked at him. "Keep the sunshine going!"

Her face began to take on a glow, and Justin squinted. He tried in vain to lift his hand and wipe at his eyes as his vision became distorted and her image blurred.

"You still have things to say to people, Justin, and they still have things to say to you. But I'm only as far away as your heart... and I'll be waiting for you when you're ready. Pinky promise." She linked her pinky with his.

"Wait..." he begged, pushing against the unbearable sadness. He wasn't ready for her to leave. Not yet. "You have to tell me. Why? Why did you come now? Why not before? When I had my first heart attack?"

She tightened her baby finger around his. "You never needed my blessing before. You weren't made to be lonely, my love." Then she stood and bent over him. Her lips still tasted of honey, and she still smelled of flowers. The soft brush of her kiss was quick, tender.

Forever.

The kind of kiss that only came with a deep, abiding love.

The nice, safe wall he'd had in place to shore up his heart since her death cracked. Then in a silent explosion of brilliant white light, she vanished. The beep-beep of the machine invaded his brain, and he shook his head, trying to clear the jumbled thoughts.

The room dimmed around him as blackness reached out to comfort him once again.

* * *

The acrid-sweet scent of daffodils teased his nostrils. A whiny *beep-beep-beep* filled his ears. Justin lay on his right side and partially upright on the hardest, lumpiest surface he'd ever had the misfortune to suffer. He shifted and his neck cramped. Wherever he was, he'd been there a while. With a soft moan, he moved his shoulders against the stiffness that had settled in. Damn, getting old sucked eggs. He rolled his shoulders, and a crackling, crunching noise under his right ear briefly overpowered the steady beeping. What *was* that, anyway? Sounded like the back-up warning on the ranch's front-end loader. Only not quite.

With extra effort, he managed to push his eyes open. Green walls faded into view. Diffuse light flowed through a tall window, framed by gaudy orange-and-green striped drapes. Yellow daffodils in a blue pot nodded their heads at him, moved by the gentle breeze of an overhead vent.

"Beth," he whispered. No, that's right... she wasn't there... she had to go. The pain of losing her swamped him all over again, and he closed his eyes, squeezing back tears.

"Dad?" Ryan's deep voice came from the chair next to the bed.

Justin swept his gaze in that direction and met his eldest son's bright green eyes. Beth's eyes. "The calves?" he croaked.

Ryan's grin flashed and he shook his head. "Two girls, a tad small, but healthy."

"Good." He rolled onto his back. "And the mother?"

"Not a bit worse for the wear and taking care of 'em both like a pro."

"I had a heart attack." Justin laid his hands on the unforgiving mattress beneath him and pushed upward.

"Yeah, you did." Ryan sprang to his feet and helped Justin sit. "Scared the crap outa me and Sean, but the doc says you'll be okay."

"Sorry," grunted Justin with a grimace. "Didn't do much for me, either." He pointed to the daffodils. "Your wife bring those in?"

"Sandy? No, she hasn't been in yet. No one's been in here but me and Sean so far." Ryan shot a quick glance at the flowers, then paused and stared as if only just noticing them. "Huh. No card."

Warmth edged into Justin's heart. So it hadn't been a dream... it had been a gift. He smiled at the dancing yellow blossoms.

"Are you up for some visitors?" Ryan adjusted the pillow behind Justin's shoulders. "The whole family and about half the town's here."

Justin managed to wheeze out a laugh. "Everyone came running, eh?"

"Yeah, but only family are allowed to see you."

Something that sounded like a tray of china crashed on the other side of the door.

"Let me tell you a thing or two about family," a raucous, but unmistakably feminine, voice rang out. "That man and I have been 'family' since we were in the fifth grade together."

Muffled footsteps approached the door and seconds later it was pushed open. A short cap of salt-and-pepper hair framed the welcome face of Charlie Morrow Haines as she stepped into the room. She must have come from work, since she still had on her red-and-white checked Western shirt with *Valentine's* scrawled over the breast pocket in blue.

Puffing out a breath, she stopped at the foot of the bed and crossed her arms over her chest. "Old man, what are you doing pulling calves at your age?"

Conscious of his vulnerability in the thin hospital gown, Justin brought the bed covers up to his chin. Charlie could be damn scary when she was in one of her moods. Uncaring that he'd just been thinking along the same lines, he blustered at her reference to his age. "Who are you calling old? I'm twenty-eight days younger than you are."

"Hrmph." She fussed at the blanket, straightening a wrinkle at the foot of the bed. "You're memory's going. I'm five years younger than *you.*"

"You want to explain how that works? We were the same age in the fifth grade."

Ryan snickered and sauntered to the door. "I'll, ahh...

just... let you two catch up while I go tell the rest of the family you're awake, Dad." He slipped through the door, pulling it closed behind him with a soft click.

"You have one hell of a man in that boy," murmured Charlie.

Pride surged as it always did when he considered any of his sons. "Yep. Beth would be real proud how her kids grew up."

Charlie angled her head and shot him a considering stare. "You were dead, you know. Your heart stopped cold after you got that last calf out. Ryan performed CPR on you for over a half hour before the air ambulance got there. He refused to give up."

A mix of sadness, consternation, and gratitude filled the dead space in Justin's heart. As much as he missed Beth and had wanted to go with her, now that he was awake, he wasn't really quite ready to leave his kids and grandkids.

Seeming uncomfortable with the lack of conversation between them, Charlie nodded at the bedside stand. "Who brought you the daffodils?"

Justin turned his gaze onto the cheery flowers. Sunlight streaked through the window and caressed them. For the briefest of moments, Beth's face framed in glowing gold curls smiled up at him. Her soft, tender laugh raised the hairs on his arms. Then the light was gone, and the flowers went back to nodding in the breeze of the vent.

"I had a visit from... an old friend." He returned his attention to Charlie, taking in her large blue eyes and the pallor of her face. She reminded him of a mare he'd once owned that spooked at the rustle of prairie grass. A smile slipped over his face. He'd best keep that comparison to himself. "I think I want to plant them by the patio at home."

A tinkling laugh burst from her lips, and the pinched look around her eyes disappeared. "Don't you have enough of those things?"

"Naw." He glanced at the pot of flowers and then back at Charlie, a smile tugging at the corners of his mouth. "You can never have too many daffodils... happy flowers, aren't they?"

Charlie chewed her bottom lip as she studied the yellow

blooms. After a long pause, filled by a lot of those *beep-beeps* from the heart monitor, she finally nodded and laid a wide smile on him. "Yeah... Yeah, they do look happy."

About the Author

Kay Springsteen cannot remember a time when she wasn't telling stories... beginning with her earliest memory from about age 3, when, rather than accept punishment for changing her father's alarm clock and making him late for work, she placed the blame squarely on the pink fuzzy shoulders of her faithful companion, Flopsy, a 10-inch tall stuffed rabbit with satin ears and black thread whiskers. Over the years, her tales have become more creative and a bit less self-serving. The mother of four adult children, she often draws on her own life experiences as well as the experiences of her kids and their spouses for her writing. The kids all know the only way to keep their own lives from being spotlighted is to give up a sibling's sad or funny story. Everything's fair game with Mom. And that all makes for lots of fun in her widely scattered but somehow close-knit family. Find Kay on Facebook and at her blog:

http://kayspringsteen.wordpress.com/

Did you read the first book in the series?

Lifeline Echoes

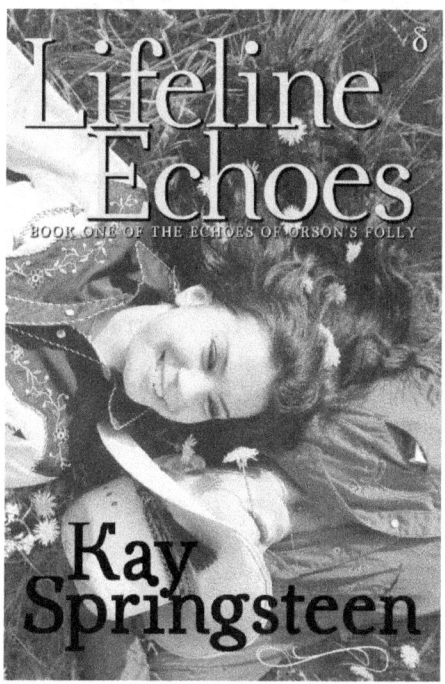

Prologue

There is no natural phenomenon which is held by all mankind in greater dread than earthquakes. Our ideas of permanence, solidity and strength are based upon the condition of the earth, as we daily see it; so that when the firm ground shakes under us, there naturally comes over the mind a feeling of abject helplessness. ~New York Times, April 9, 1872

Seven years earlier...
   Splat.
   "Son of a—"
Sandy glared down at her double chocolate iced mocha.

Pale brown slush slid off the toe of one white shoe to form a sticky puddle on the blacktop.

A quick glance at her watch told her she'd have to hurry or she'd be late for her shift as a dispatcher for Los Angeles City Emergency Services. She kicked the melting mush from her shoe and stepped around the puddle of yuck and raced across the parking lot to the low brick building. Behind her, traffic on the packed freeway growled and honked.

Good morning, Los Angeles.

Sandy yanked on the heavy glass door and stepped into the coolness of the air conditioned building with a sigh.

"Morning, Alley Cat!" greeted Rose from behind the reception desk. "Lunch at Del Rio's today?"

"Hi, Rose. Yeah, lunch sounds great. Gotta run. I'm late." With a wave, Sandy hurried past the desk and into the ladies' restroom. She set her oversized purse on the counter and grabbed several paper towels. Crouching, she dabbed at the mush, noting with dismay that it had worked into the seams of her athletic shoes.

"Gross," she muttered. She'd be lucky if it didn't stink like sour milk at the end of her shift. After she mopped off the worst of it, she pushed to her feet and staggered sideways. Her hand hit the cool marble wall of the first stall as she fought to steady herself.

"What the hell?"

A low primeval rumble surrounded her, invaded her midsection and radiated up into her heart and throat. Sandy stumbled to the left then the right. The fluorescent light overhead became a flickering strobe.

Earthquake!

The word registered in the recesses of her mind, and spurred her toward the door. She had to get out of the enclosed space before the ceiling collapsed and buried her.

Sudden blackness swallowed her as the lights lost the battle to stay on. The grumble grew to a roar and then a scream. She lurched to the right, pushed off the wall, and careened through the bathroom door. The scream grew louder before she realized it came from her own mouth. The floor beneath her rolled and writhed as her cries were echoed by a half-dozen coworkers at their workstations. Shelves toppled, notebooks tumbled to the floor.

The roar dwindled to a dull grating, the heaving slowed and finally halted. Sandy lay on her side, her back jammed against the wall. Her insides still quivered and shook like jelly, the remnants of the quake continuing in her viscera. Chills washed over her as she sat up and took stock of the dispatch room. Her coworkers moved slowly, sitting and looking around, dazed expressions gracing their faces.

"Holy cow," murmured Rose, pushing to her feet and doing a three-sixty. "That felt like an eight or a nine."

Fluorescent lights overhead sputtered then half of them winked on. That would be the backup generator, running nonessentials at half power.

More operators pushed to their feet, their faces all wearing uniform dazed expressions. Jabbering filled the air as a dozen people seemed to find their voices at the same time. The cacophony crescendoed. Any second her head would explode. She closed her eyes and attempted to sort out what was being said.

"...my kids..."

"I think my arm's broken..."

"Maybe we should get..."

"Comm's down!" called out Albert Torres, IT wizard and technical problem solving guru. "Switching to backup."

Phones began ringing. Frowning, Sandy oriented herself and located her desk. Someone had to answer the calls. And there would be calls.

She located her station and placed the headset over her ear, then punched the button. "Emergency services—"

A shrill scream came over the line and assaulted her ear. Forcing herself to speak calm words of reassurance as she wrestled open her desk drawer and pulled out an empty notebook and a black pen, Sandy managed to discern that the caller was an elderly woman who was merely disoriented and frightened.

The phone lines began to flash as more calls came in. Around her, more dispatchers followed Sandy's lead and began answering.

"Backup comms are on line," announced Albert, emerging from the computer room.

The first report of a fire came ninety seconds after Sandy started answering calls. The gas line alongside the Convention Center had burst and somehow ignited. Hell had erupted in Central Los Angeles.

Sandy couldn't stop the tremors running along the inner fault lines of her own neural pathways. *I'm a professional. People are depending on me.* She studied the older system that had just been replaced by a two million dollar upgrade, only months earlier, and re-familiarized herself with the buttons and switches. Then, in a voice that only barely trembled, she dispatched Fire Station Number 9 to the L.A. Convention Center.

The first shift after Sandy's vacation was off to a very rocky start. Before that shift was over, she would learn two important things. First, she was getting the hell out of L.A. Second, it was possible to fall in love with someone, sight unseen, in twenty-three hours and fifty-seven minutes.

Chapter One

Present day

Sunny and warm, the perfect day for mourning lost love. Maybe this would be the year she'd finally be ready to move on. Even as the thought teased her, Sandy suspected it might take another cataclysmic event to let go of the man she'd given her heart to in less than a day.

Summer was a handful of days off, but the mountain air was clean and brisk, nothing like the heavy smog of L.A., where she'd first met *him*. She had no memories of the man in this place except for the ones he'd painted into her mind while they'd talked. Yet Wyoming was where she felt his presence.

Her red roan colt pranced beneath her, needing to run off his teenage-intensity energy. Dry dirt kicked up by Domingo muffled the sound of his hoof-falls to dull scuffling *plunks*, which he punctuated with occasional impatient snorts.

As they traveled, the dusty ground became more firmed and flattened. Gray rocky outcroppings thrust upward amid a tan landscape dotted by the washed-out green of desert grasses. More of the same lay between them and the scrub pines along the swell of foothills in the distance.

Sandy pointed Domingo toward those hills, finally allowing the exuberant colt to set his own pace. He catapulted them across the plain, brawny muscles alternately flexing and contracting beneath her, racing at a full gallop. The denim jacket she hadn't bothered to fasten caught the wind and billowed behind her. Chilly air worked icy fingers along the exposed skin of her neck, bringing with it a wonderful ache.

They topped a gentle rise and a sea of yellow and purple wildflowers surprised her, God's own casually sown garden. The sky overhead was deep blue and cloudless. With the prairie behind her and the snow-covered peaks ahead, Sandy pulled Domingo up inside a cathedral of Ponderosa pines, closed her eyes, and inhaled the pungent scent. It was exactly as he had described it, which made it the perfect place to remember him.

Seven years had passed, yet her pain was an exquisite, fresh wound, probably owing to the fact that she revisited the memory once a year on the anniversary of that horrific day. In the hills of Wyoming that he had loved and missed so much, in the place he had brought her to with just his words, Sandy picked the scab off the wound she never quite allowed to heal.

* * *

The job was all that mattered now. Sandy made herself disregard the toppled shelves and scattered books. She blocked out all thoughts about the likely state of her own home. As she listened to the chatter on the official channels, she kept meticulous handwritten notes regarding the status of each unit checking in.

"Battalion 9-Alpha, this is Engine Squad 9-Bravo, do you copy?" The connection was filled with static and the voice was muffled, hard to hear.

Sandy waited for the response of the battalion chief on scene. None came.

The callout was repeated, the voice sounding a bit more urgent. "This is L.A. Engine Squad 9-Bravo, dispatched to the Convention Center—" Again static broke the transmission.

Following protocol, after the second unanswered call, Sandy intervened. "Copy you, ES-9-Bravo. This is central dispatch. Your transmission is breaking up."

She checked her watch and jotted the time in her notes: 0724 hours.

The response was drowned out by a loud burst of static in the earpiece.

"9-Bravo, be advised you are breaking up," she repeated.

More harsh squawks of static burst from the receiver. Sandy winced. If that kept up, her head might explode — or at least an eardrum. Then, amid the static, she clearly heard the code every dispatcher dreaded. "9-Bravo is 10-60, this location. Code three, code three, code three... trapped..."

The code for firefighter down!

Static filled the airwaves again as Sandy punched buttons on her console, frantically trying to boost the signal.

"Dispatch, are you there?" The voice was screaming. "Central! This is 9-Bravo in need of assist. The building's

coming down around us!"

Afraid to switch over to relay, with the risk of losing contact altogether, she motioned to Ellen, the dispatcher sitting next to her. Quickly, Sandy wrote on her notepad in bold black ink: UNIT IN TROUBLE.

At the next desk, Ellen nodded and switched channels to contact the Battalion 9 squad leader over the comm.

"9-Bravo, this is Central Dispatch," Sandy acknowledged. Stomach-wrenching fear threatened to leak into her voice, so she bit the inside of her cheek. Dread shot out little tentacles of hopelessness to curl around her lungs, squeezing the breath out of her. "I'm reading you, sending help your way. What's your location?"

"Civic Center parking garage — A level. The building's coming apart! We need extraction." The voice was still urgent but the panic had faded.

She had to get her own terror under control and keep it that way, Sandy reminded herself, or she couldn't help anyone.

"Copy you, 9-Bravo. Who am I speaking with?"

"Mick-" More static, then, "Mic-key."

Sandy scribbled everything she could make out into her handwritten notes. "Mickey, you're breaking up badly. How many do you number? How long have you been trapped?"

"Two confirmed, dispatch, possibly three. I can feel my partner. He's not moving. I heard someone else moaning down here earlier. I don't know how long it's been. I think I've been unconscious — I'm pinned — can't move. It's dark — can't see a thing."

Sandy passed off the information to Ellen so her coworker could convey it to the battalion chief. The sarcastic part of Sandy's mind registered the irony of having crossed into the twenty-first century and being reduced to the mockery of a child's game of telephone.

With a pointed shake of her head, Ellen caught Sandy's eye and handed her a message from the battalion chief. As she read, Sandy's heart fluttered in her chest before moving upward to stick in her throat. Her free hand rose of its own volition and covered her mouth, as if to prevent her from saying the words she was reading.

The Convention Center had collapsed with several men inside. Some of them were buried under four floors of rubble, while above them the fire from the gas main explosion burned fully involved and uncontained. Rescue efforts would be delayed and prospects for extraction were grim. A chaplain was en route.

God help them all! How could she tell the man on the other end of the comm that he wasn't going to be rescued? What could she say to someone when her words were likely to be the last he'd ever hear?

* * *

Ryan kicked in the clutch and rammed the gearshift into second to take yet another turn on the series of switchbacks through the mountains. The 1967 Corvette Sting Ray had been a mess when he'd bought her, but she'd been his mess. And a bargain at the price he'd wangled. It had taken almost every one of his days off over the past two years, but he had fully restored her from the engine up. The work had been a welcome distraction from other aspects of his life.

Currently, on his first long trip in her, he was enjoying the way she held fast to the road, caressing the pavement around the twists and turns through the mountains the way a woman caressed a lover.

The throaty growl of the engine wasn't quite drowned out by the whoosh of the wind over his face. It was early in the year to drive with the top down in the mountains, but Ryan didn't care. The bracing cold reminded him he was alive.

It had been too long, the guilty whisper nagged. He should never have let his life get so far out of hand. It shouldn't have taken an emergency letter from his baby brother for him to come home and make things right with the old man.

Tires squealed just a bit when he took the downward curve a little sharply. He was in the foothills now, only a few miles to go. He'd be able to open his baby up on the two-lane once the last hill was at his back. Soon the sun would drift down into the shadowy embrace of the mountains behind him, leaving him the stars for company. Damn, he'd missed the mountains of home.

Halfway through what he recognized as the last switchback, Ryan downshifted again and punched the gas. His mind registered the apparition blocking the road in front of him a bare second before reaction set in. He stood on the brake, sending the car into a slow sideways skid and stalling the engine.

"Holy hell!"

Darts of adrenaline screamed through his veins, sending his heart into a staccato rhythm as he stared at the horse and rider in the road.

Washed in the golden blush from the setting sun, the horse reared, angrily striking out at the air between them with menacing hooves, nearly unseating his rider. With a toss of his head, the startled horse reared again, baring his teeth and screaming defiance.

The red roan colt had excellent lines, but he was clearly too much for his rider. Though the horse responded to her steady touch, it was obvious any sense of control she had was an illusion. Ryan shoved the car door open and jumped to his feet, ready to pick up the pieces when the rider was thrown. But when she swung her gaze in his direction, fury blazed in eyes the color of chicory blossoms. Her face mirrored the horse's defiance.

Sparks of awareness replaced astonishment, and a grin pulled Ryan's lips upward as he lifted a hand in greeting.

"Jackass!" The rider shoved at the wild mass of dark hair falling across her face. The motion distracted her, giving her mount the opening to misbehave.

With a clatter of edgy hooves on asphalt, the big colt danced and circled, threatened to rear again, but she recovered quickly and held him down. Then she tugged on the reins, steering the agitated horse away from the road, and sidestepping him down the steep, gravel-covered incline. Upon reaching solid footing, the colt wheeled sharply around. The rider cast a scathing look over her shoulder as the horse erupted into a reckless gallop across the prairie.

Pain shot through Ryan's neck, and he realized he'd been

clenching his jaw. Absently, he rubbed the back of one hand along his chin, but he kept his eyes on the horse and rider until they were no more than a speck in the distance.

"Well," he said to the early evening sky. "I've just been schooled."

He wasn't sure if he was going to shake things up with his return or get himself shaken up. But he sure as hell planned to find out who lived behind those haunting chicory blue eyes.

Shaking his head, he started to lower himself into the car when he froze. Why was it sitting at such an odd angle? He strode around to the passenger side and groaned at the sight of the front tire, rolled right off the rim from his sideways skid.

* * *

By the time she had encountered the stranger in the fast car, Sandy's earlier upbeat mood had degraded, thanks to the dull heartache she'd given herself from lancing her old wound. Ordinarily she would have laughed off the incident and introduced herself once she'd realized no one was hurt. But the moron had just sat in his car staring in disapproval, apparently waiting for her to move out of his all-important way.

Wherever the aggravating stranger was going, she sincerely hoped he didn't so much as make a pit stop in Orson's Folly. She was pretty sure another meeting of that sort would result in her doing more than yelling at him. Pictures of strangling the shit-eating grin off his face popped into her mind.

Her heart raced with the need to dispel her jitters, and Sandy let the colt have his head again. Domingo calmed them both by doing what he loved most, streaking at breakneck pace over the plains of western Wyoming.

By the time they slowed to a walk alongside the fence leading to the stable yard, her ire at the stranger on the road had mellowed to a mildly bad memory. Whoever he was, it was likely he'd already hit Orson's Folly and driven on through. The sun rested in the cradle between the peaks of two mountains, sending lingering shafts of red to cast long shadows against the blue and white buildings. Sandy closed her eyes, bracing against the little pinprick of pain, and allowed herself to remember the reason she'd first come to Wyoming.

* * *

"You hang on, do you hear me?" she ordered. "I won't go anywhere until they have you, I swear. But you have to stay with me. Promise!"

"Okay... promise." His words were slurred, his voice weary.

Sandy struggled to think of something to talk about — to keep him speaking and alert. "Do I hear an accent, Mick?"

His laugh was slow and soft. "Yep, I'm afraid so. I can't seem to get the Wyoming out of my voice."

That worked! "Tell me about Wyoming."

He sighed. "There's nothing like a wild gallop across the plains on a fast horse. If you can be up on that horse at daybreak, you feel like you're flying up to meet the day. And to be in the Red Desert at sundown's even better. If you time it right, just a split second before the sun's gone, you feel like you're inside all that red and orange glow. Then in your next breath you're standing in pitch black. When you look up, the stars are already popping out. So many stars they blend together. And there's always shooting stars for making wishes." He laughed softly. "I guess I sound a little pathetic."

"No." She wished she could touch him with more than her voice. "More like a homesick cowboy."

He was quiet for a time, then, "I guess maybe I am, Angel. I am homesick."

His quiet admission brought tears to Sandy's eyes, and she prayed he'd see those sunrises and sunsets and stars again. "So you lived in the desert plains?"

"I had the best of both worlds," he answered, his words filled with pride. "Our ranch is in the middle of a finger of desert that's nestled between two legs of mountains and forest."

"Why did you leave?"

"That's a story for another time," he said. *"I'll tell you when we're on our first date."*

"Are you asking me out?"

"Oh, we'll go out." His voice gave her visions of an easy cowboy grin. *"I was just making the plans."*

Her lips twitched at his audacity.

* * *

Cooled and brushed, Domingo nickered a soft goodbye as Sandy left the comfort of the stable and walked into the cold night air.

Stars twinkled into view overhead, millions of glistening pinpoint lights fusing into a lacy curtain of soft illumination against the darkness. A trail of shimmery light tracked across the sky.

For the first time in seven years, her automatic wish wasn't for something impossible. "I want to feel alive again."

Emotionally and physically exhausted, she tore her eyes from the stars with a heavy sigh and climbed into the rusty Chevy pickup. It was older than she was by several years, so she counted her blessings it still ran. Driving past the main homestead, Sandy tossed a wave to Justin McGee, sitting on the wide front porch of the ranch house puffing on his nightly cigar. With a smile and a nod, the old rancher politely touched a forefinger to the brim of his battered tan Stetson.

Just as Sandy reached the cedar fenceposts marking the entrance to the ranch, a pair of headlights swung in from the main road. So, the McGee men were about to receive a caller. Maybe Sean had finally convinced Melanie Mitchell to drop by after her shift at the bar.

The two sets of headlights collided, the bright beams briefly joining forces and splitting the darkness. Then the moment was gone, leaving Sandy with a vague impression of something low and fast before she was engulfed by the cloud of dust chasing behind.

Nope. She coughed against the sting in her throat. Definitely not Mel, who tended to drive her ancient economy car with the caution of a grandmother. Tough break for Sean.

* * *

Ryan braked in front of the old ranch house and killed the engine. He popped open the door but took some deep breaths before climbing out of the car.

Though the land slumbered beneath a blanket of darkness, the nighttime couldn't mask his memories. He knew just beyond the edge of the light lay open spaces, fields of green and gold dotted by brown-and-white cattle and rolls of cut hay, all in the protective embrace of the Rocky Mountains to the west.

Closing his eyes, Ryan inhaled deeply, intoxicating himself on the aromatic blend of cow manure, freshly mown hay, and mountain wildflowers that hung in the air. The sweet, somewhat earthy scent of home.

Overhead, a shooting star blazed a fiery arc through the myriad visible stars. Ryan thought of a time, so long ago, when he and Sean had lain next to their mother on a sleeping bag, watching the stars overhead. Every time she saw a shooting star, she had urged them to make a wish.

The memory faded as suddenly as it had come. What the heck was he doing, coming back to Wyoming?

"Not much call for such a fancy machine on a ranch," admonished a gravelly voice from the porch's shadows. "But you always did love speed, didn't you, boy?"

Ryan stiffened as Justin took a step forward into the light cast by the moon.

"Hello, Dad." Ryan kept his response respectful and reserved. Leave it to his father to act like this was just another homecoming after a night in town. "You look good."

Justin chuckled. "Still spreading it thick, I see." But fondness had crept into his voice. "What I look is old." He nodded in the direction of the huge barns that had been standing since before Ryan was born. "Your brother's out there locking up... if you want to go find him, let him know you're here."

The statement startled Ryan. "Since when do McGee

barns need locking?"

The old man leaned against the porch railing and examined the tip of his cigar.

Ryan waited. It was maddening, but no amount of pushing would get his father to talk before he was ready.

Finally Justin shrugged, fixed Ryan with a pointed stare. "A boy goes away for sixteen years, he's bound to see some changes when he comes back a man."

Same old shit with you, isn't, Dad? But Ryan held his tongue and acknowledged the well-deserved punch straight to the heart with a nod and a wry smile. Then he turned and strode toward the barns.

Strong floodlights, mounted at the corners of each building, lit the yard. Sean was clearly visible as he slid the barn door closed and set the lock. He walked toward the stable, a black-and-white dog at his heels.

Ryan stood just outside the light's edge watching his brother, looking for a trace of the kid he'd left behind.

The skinny boy's frame had become lean and muscular. Glow-in-the-dark blond hair had toned down some, but Ryan noticed it still had a tendency to curl at the ends even though his brother kept it cut short. Sean had been thirteen when Ryan had left. He'd grown into a man.

When Sean emerged from the stable, he ordered the dog to stay inside. Then with a flexing of his muscles, he slid the door closed. Ryan raised an eyebrow. His little brother had developed some broad shoulders and strong arms. While setting the latch, Sean's hands stilled. He eased around, his body tense, ready for anything. It had always been uncanny, the way the kid had been so acutely aware of his surroundings; it still was.

Ryan stepped into the light. Green eyes identical to his own met and held his gaze. Ryan marshaled his expression and waited, unmoving.

Sean's tension visibly drained. His smile started slowly, in his eyes first, then spreading to his mouth, where it bloomed into a full grin.

"Ry!" In two long-legged strides, Sean was in front of him. "Oh, man, it's good to see you!"

In a move too sudden for Ryan to dodge, Sean folded him into a bear hug and lifted him off his feet, his carefree laughter driving out the last vestiges of Ryan's uncertainty.

Welcome home, Ryan McGee.

Also from Dingbat Publishing

AMANDA MOORE OR LESS

If Jason does have the itch, Amanda is after the tramp who's scratching it.

Scratching
the
Seven-Month
Itch

J.L. SALTER δ

Chapter 1

Friday, May 22, 2009

Amanda Moore knew from the *Maneater* ringtone which friend was calling: the older, bossy, impetuous one. "Hello?"

"Not sure how to tell you this, but... he's cheating." It came out so easily that Christine Powers must have practiced. A rather startling announcement, considering she didn't even say hello.

"Okay, *who's* cheating?"

Christine's tense silence provided the answer.

"Jason? No way!"

"I wouldn't have said anything, but the evidence is overwhelming."

"That's insane! Jason?" Amanda's voice quavered. "Who the heck with?"

"Not certain... yet."

"Exactly how reliable is this evidence if you don't even know who she is?"

"Overwhelming." Christine always sounded certain.

"Well, spit it out! And quick. My *perfect* sister Kaye will be here any minute!"

"Oh. Maybe we should wait 'til you're not in such a rush."

"Yeah, well, thanks a bunch for getting me all riled up when I don't have time to talk." Amanda scanned her duplex as she struggled to process two domestic emergencies on top of a new crisis at work. "Look, I know Jason's not playing around. But this is very important — Kaye canNOT know ANYthing about this!"

"Mum's the word." Christine probably thought Mum was a deodorant. "Call me later and I'll give you the rest of my intel. Bye."

Amanda flicked her phone shut without reply. Her honey brown hair framed an attractive face which barely avoided being beautiful. Her bright blue eyes could make someone melt or cause them a chill, depending on the person and circumstances. Right now they were icy. Christine, Kaye... and Jason were all ganging up on her.

She checked the kitchen clock — about two minutes until Hurricane Kaye's arrival. Though distinctly skeptical of this sudden accusation, Amanda worried anyway. She knew Jason Stewart better than she'd known any other man, but significant gaps remained. In fact, maybe they didn't really know each other all that well. After getting comfortable within their relationship, Amanda had stopped trying so hard to "learn" him. And probably vice versa.

But even if Jason were taking her for granted, it didn't mean he was playing around. "Jason wouldn't cheat on me. Why would he?" *But if he IS boffing someone else, he's a dead man.* Amanda examined her short, unpainted fingernails.

*Might need something else to claw that slut's eyeballs...
whoever she is.*

Outside the apartment, a car door slammed — her elder
sister was literally seconds away. Amanda sucked in a quick
breath. *Remember, keep a hard shell so Kaye won't find any
weak spot to probe. And not a word about this Jason mess,
because she will immediately tell Mom and Dad that I've lost
another one.*

Amanda glanced down at her work heels and smoothed
her skirt. Her only ace in the sibling race — she had even
prettier legs than perfect Kaye.

The doorbell rang. *She's ba-aacckk!*

Amanda's hand trembled slightly when she turned the
knob. "Hi, Kaye!" There wasn't time to invite her inside
because Kaye Moore-Smith was already lunging forward.
They hugged awkwardly, with noticeable space between them.
No bags? "I didn't have time to move much since you called
yesterday, but there's still room to sleep and that single bed is
pretty comfortable." Amanda pointed down the short hallway.
It had been about two years since she'd seen Kaye and they
didn't talk much on the phone, either. "Come have a look."

When Kaye had toured shortly after Amanda moved in,
she'd acted like nobody could survive in less than 2,000 square
feet. Now Kaye assessed everything as though she wore white
gloves. With higher grades, fuller bosom, better hair (dyed
blonde, of course), Kaye had always seemed the favorite
daughter. Growing up, she'd been bossy and rather cold... and
eight years older. She'd married right after college, moved to
an upscale Indianapolis neighborhood, and quickly produced a
child... a big plus. With her looks and ability to role play, Kaye
could sell anything; currently she represented high-end office
equipment. But their parents ignored the facts: Kaye was
separated with a pending divorce and her thirteen-year-old
daughter was a witchy brat.

And Kaye was finally developing a belly! Amanda hid
her glee.

When Kaye peeked into the cluttered guestroom, which
Amanda used as an ad hoc storage depot, she wrinkled her
nose and delivered a short speech (which sounded rehearsed)

about needing space to spread out, so she would find suitable lodgings in Nashville, about 25 miles west. She'd be in the area for most of four days, Kaye had said, so perhaps her company was covering the hotel costs.

"You hear anything much from Mom and Dad?" In their predictable e-mail-and-Facebook sibling conversations, this was Kaye's opening move.

Amanda sighed. "Mom forwards nearly every e-mail she gets, especially the ones telling you to send it to ten people in the next minute so you'll have good luck."

Kaye nodded without replying. Evidently she received the same.

"But she rarely sends anything about herself."

"And Dad?" Kaye asked.

"He still won't use a computer." Amanda smiled, rather tentatively.

"Well, he doesn't use phones much either, as I recall. Unless Mom slaps it to his ear."

They laughed together — the first time in many years. Amanda thawed a bit. Perhaps this visit would be different; maybe they could be more than estranged sisters. Probably not friends, but it would be nice to share something more than coolish civility.

Funny, how Kaye always seemed to be looking for something better. *Must have been tough on her soon-to-be-ex-husband.*

"So, how are things with your, uh… legal proceedings?" Amanda didn't know if her sister wanted to discuss this.

"The divorce? Oh, it's dragging out, but the lawyers prefer it that way. Tom and I had mostly agreed on all the big issues, but they keep finding wrinkles that supposedly have to be documented up the ying-yang." Kaye frowned. "More fees for them, of course." Without warning, she blurted out, "He cheated on me." Then she clamped her lips shut and looked away.

Amanda felt her jaw dropping. That was the first divorce detail Kaye had volunteered. "Oh, Kaye, I'm sorry…"

"Son of a gun was diddling somebody at work." Kaye's eyes reddened. "You want to know how I found out?"

Amanda *did* want to know... intensely. But — unlike celebrity breakups — with her perfect sister being the topic, it felt like prying. "No, you don't have to..."

"She left her nasty panties in Tom's glove compartment!"

They'd used his expensive BMW? *Shocking.* Her sibling was on the verge of tears and normally such pain would give Amanda a tiny bit of pleasure. But she just felt compassion, possibly for the first time since she'd been ten and Kaye had finally left for college eighteen years ago. "Your daughter... how's she adjusting?"

Kaye held her hand vertically. *Don't go there.* She and her witchy daughter had been at odds since Chelsea was nine, almost four years ago. Obviously the trip to Nashville was also an excuse for a beleaguered mom to just get away. Kaye shook her head. "I should leave. My reservation..."

Since she'd never intended to stay, why hadn't Kaye said so last night when she'd called? Nearly two hours of cleaning and straightening... Amanda shrugged. *Same old disapproving, resentful, competitive Kaye.* Maybe that was normal between sisters. *But it shouldn't be.*

By the time Kaye had used the bathroom and emerged with her nose wrinkled, only about twenty minutes had elapsed since her arrival. It was their longest visit in Amanda couldn't remember how long.

Amanda watched her depart. Kaye's home metropolis was much larger and finer — better stores, more culture, and supposedly fewer hicks. But Amanda would rather live with hicks than pretentious snobs. Besides, small town friendliness — underrated by most big city dwellers — was dependable and comforting.

"So Kaye is too refined to stay here overnight." *Fine.* Kaye's presence would have complicated the newly-launched crisis management effort... in case Jason the creep *was* playing around. Amanda inhaled deeply and put on her game face — she had a dinner date with Jason the cheater.

* * *

Thanks for reading! Dingbat Publishing strives to bring you quality entertainment that doesn't take itself too seriously. I mean honestly, with a name like that, our books have to be good or we're going to be laughed at. Or maybe both.

If you enjoyed this book, the best thing you can do is buy a million more copies and give them to all your friends... erm, leave a review on the readers' website of your preference. All authors love feedback and we take reviews from readers like you seriously.

Oh, and c'mon over to our website:
www.DingbatPublishing.Weebly.com

Who knows what other books you'll find there?

Cheers,

Gunnar Grey,
publisher, author, and Chief Dingbat

δ
Dingbat Publishing